AFTER ME

A NOVEL BY

DEBORAH COONTS

Book published by Deborah Coonts

Book Formatting by Austin Brown,
CheapEbookFormatting.com

Cover Design by damonza.com

ISBN-13: 978-1-944831-81-3

OTHER BOOKS BY DEBORAH COONTS

THE LUCKY SERIES

"Evanovich....with a dose of CSI"
—*Publisher's Weekly* on *Wanna Get Lucky?* A Double
RITA(tm) finalist and NYT Notable crime Novel

WANNA GET LUCKY?
(Book 1)

LUCKY STIFF
(Book 2)

SO DAMN LUCKY
(Book 3)

LUCKY BASTARD
(Book 4)

LUCKY CATCH
(Book 5)

LUCKY BREAK
(Book 6)

LUCKY THE HARD WAY
(Book 7)

LUCKY NOVELLAS

LUCKY IN LOVE

LUCKY BANG

LUCKY NOW AND THEN
(PARTS 1 AND 2)

LUCKY FLASH

CHAPTER ONE

The body dumped in my bathtub was a warning; that much I got. Dropped by a pro and left where I couldn't miss him. Not a speck of blood on the tile floor. No careless footprint. No thumb whorl on a chrome fixture. A slip of paper stuck out of the guy's breast pocket, in case I'd missed the larger message. I used a pair of tweezers to ease the note loose and laid it on the counter.

I know what you did.

The shiver of a memory, a whispered sin—a moment of a life left behind. How had they found me? My trail had been rubbed clean behind me.

The dead man, eyes bulging, open and sightless, skin the white of old snow, begged to differ.

Questions bolted through my brain, brief illuminations that flared only to deepen the returning darkness. Who? Why? Why now? What *had* I done? All good questions, but I had no answers.

It was hell to lose one's memory and not lose one's mind.

I'm known as Kate Sawyer. Some days that name rolled off my tongue with a comfortable familiarity, as if it really was my own. Other days it sounded like a random stab in the phone book.

Surprised by my practiced efficiency, I finished checking out the man in my tub. Five foot eleven, probably 190. Gray hair. Brown eyes. Fifty or a hard-worn forty. One stab wound under his ribs and a gash downward to his belly. No murder weapon. I made a quick inventory of the knives in my kitchen—all accounted for. According to the items listed in my phone, the only other one I owned was a serrated hunting knife hidden under my mattress, but the killer hadn't used it. The perforation in the dead guy's chest was too narrow, the edges clean.

I didn't do this.

He wore a white shirt with a tattered collar, yellow stains circling under the arms, a red stain over his chest. Brown slacks with a suit jacket that didn't quite match. No tags in any of it. No jewelry, no watch, two extra holes punched crudely in his belt which gathered tucks of cloth at his waist, old shoes with mismatched laces, and an uneven wear pattern on the soles.

Not much to go on. I used my iPhone to snap a few photos from different angles.

A 9mm SIG Sauer nestled in his shoulder holster. With a finger through the trigger guard I lifted it, then cradled it in a towel. A sniff of the barrel. Hadn't been fired recently. After protecting the note in a plastic bag, I secured both it and the gun with my getaway stash, under the false bottom of the lowest dresser drawer in my bedroom. The notes in my phone reminded me of its location. I took a few minutes wondering if I'd missed anything then called 911 from my cell.

Back at the tub, I sat on my haunches, hands on my thighs, the weight of a forgotten past on my shoulders. My eyes roamed over the body searching for clues to something I didn't remember.

Who are you? I silently implored.

The corpse remained mute, his eyes unseeing.

What horrible thing have I done that drove someone to take your life and put you here? I stifled an urge to reach out, touch his cheek, push back a lock of hair that had fallen onto his forehead. He was beyond comforting. So was I. Cold seeped through me, and I started to shake, the man's death stealing me by inches.

The sound of sirens echoing from the streets below drove me to my feet. I don't like sirens. I don't like cops.

I don't remember why.

I brushed down my clothes, wiped my eyes, and took a deep breath, but calm wouldn't come. Each morning I awakened to a new reality—disjointed memories, lost connections, the past distant, the present fleeting. And now this.

The sirens multiplied. Despite the size and newfound sophistication of Portland, Oregon, murder still drew attention. With wailing sirens and flashing lights, two squad cars rounded the corner off Burnside, skidding as they slowed, then arrowed into the drive below, disappearing under the *porte-cochère*. People on the sidewalk didn't even pause to look—except one, an old homeless guy playing a tenor sax on the corner. He was always there, always watching. I'd dubbed him the Watchman. I bought him meals; he played my favorite song. The closest thing I had to family. He didn't know that, and I doubted he'd care. I wondered if he knew the sirens were for me. As if he could feel my eyes on him, he looked up, staring at my corner apartment. Unnerved, I stepped back.

Even though I expected it, I jumped at the pounding on the door. Pulling air deep into my lungs, releasing it slowly, I calmed myself. Like a shark trailing blood, a good cop could follow one bead of sweat to a life sentence. I knew that in my bones. Doing my best to shake it off, to adopt an innocence I wasn't sure I could claim, I straightened my back, tilted my chin, and stalked to the door, my legs stiff, the ache in my knee making me limp.

I wasn't very good at games. *"Not anymore," whispered the past.*

A solid slab of hardwood, the door had no window, not even a peephole. Again the banging, this time more insistent. "Portland P.D., Ms. Sawyer. Open the door." A male voice, low, demanding.

I was prepared for the man in front of me. Tall and broad, slouched, salt-and-pepper hair topping a face creased by things nobody should have to see. A normal cop. But the hurt in his eyes, that was unexpected. They were blue.

He took me in with a glance.

"Detective Hudson, ma'am." He flashed his badge, then pocketed it.

Turning my back, I kept my arms crossed across my chest and expected him to follow me. "This way." At the bathroom, I stepped aside. With a look, he told his men who had followed him in to stay back. As he brushed by me, I smelled rain.

Squatting by the tub, the detective pulled a pen from his pocket and gently lifted the dead man's coat, exposing the empty shoulder holster. "You touch him?"

Not trusting my knees, I anchored myself to the doorjamb. "To check his pulse, that's all."

"You know him?"

I shook my head and hugged myself tighter.

"Did he have a gun?"

"Not that I saw."

This time the detective angled a look my direction. "You sure?"

I nodded.

He leveled his gaze. Unblinking, I met it.

"Security downstairs is pretty tight. Any idea how he got in here?"

"Ask them."

"I'm asking you." His voice had turned hard. He still eyed me, hiding his thoughts behind a flat expression. "You didn't let him in?"

I shook my head as I worked to control my anger. This was my *home,* my safe place. How dare they take that from me? All these people sucked up the air, leaving me gasping. I wished they would leave, take the corpse in the tub, and I could pretend it hadn't happened. Of course, for me, by tomorrow the memory might have faded like a photo losing itself to the sun. Or it might be seared into my fragile memory with the heat and terror of a cattle brand. The doctors could never predict.

I felt the other officers who had come with the detective

gathering behind me, crowding me. A trickle of nervous sweat snaked down my side.

He had to question me; I knew that. I also was pretty sure I hadn't let the guy in. I didn't know him—although a dim bell chimed somewhere in the dark recesses of my brain. "I didn't let him in. And I didn't kill him." At five feet and a hundred pounds, I would've had a tough time wrestling the guy into the tub, and I doubted he'd just lie there while I released his soul to a higher plane.

After a glance that took in all of me, the detective appeared to reach the same conclusion. He gave one of his officers behind me a tilt of his head. The young man turned on his heels. I heard the door open and close. Blue Eyes fixed me with a stare. "You live alone?"

I nodded.

"Anybody else have a key?"

"No. I've lived here a couple of years, I think." I frowned as I struggled to work back in time. Did anybody else have a key? I couldn't remember. "Changed the locks when I moved in; I remember that." I clamped my mouth shut. Only give them the info they asked for—I remembered that, too.

If he thought my memory issues odd, he didn't let on. "You been here all night?"

My pulse sounded in my ears. My vision tightened to a pinprick. Then I remembered to breathe. "No, I don't think so."

"You don't think so?" The soft blue turned darker. He glanced at my wrists, exposed as my sleeves retreated. I knew what I looked like. People had commented before, hurtful things. I tried to hide but his eyes took in every detail: the bones jutting against almost translucent skin, the meticulous lettering, block letters, black semi-permanent ink...a way to remember.

Self-conscious, I knew people didn't understand, and what they didn't understand they feared. So they judged. I knew that, too, and I didn't care. At least that's what I told myself. Still, I tugged my sleeves down. I ran a hand through my hair, short, curly, with a mind of its own. My hair used to be long and straight before they shaved my head at the hospital. With the other hand I pulled out my phone and tried to hide my shaking as I scrolled through today's schedule. "I was taking a class tonight. It started at six. I was here at home until then."

His impatience, on a slow simmer, now boiled over. "Why do you keep doing that, looking at your phone? Is this some game to you? Someone told you what to tell us, and you're reading it from a script in there?"

"And how's that working?" My anger spiked. I never knew when it would, or how to control it. One of the downsides. "Before you assume I'm stupid, you might want to make sure."

A tic worked in his cheek, but he backed down a bit. "I'm assuming the guy wasn't in your tub when you left."

I gave him a hard look.

"Right. I'll take that as a no. Since you're being so cooperative and all. So, your class ran from six until now? It's almost midnight. Why don't you see what your phone says about that?"

I thrust my phone toward him. "Everything I know is in here. Without my phone, I can't remember what I had for breakfast, when I got up, who I talked to—hell, I can't even remember who I am." My anger kept me rolling, telling him things I didn't want to admit even to myself. "Most days I can't remember to log all that in the damned thing, so I'm totally at sea. Some days are better than others. Pressure makes it worse. You can ask at the hospital. I'm sure my doctor's name and number are in here." I was starting to hyperventilate. My vision swam.

The sudden softening of his voice surprised me. "Are you okay?"

Tears welled and I swiped at them with the back of my hand, then fisted it back in my pocket. I hated weakness, especially my own. "Sure, fine. I come home to a dead guy in my tub twice, maybe three times a week." I couldn't control the shaking anymore. Rounding my shoulders, pressing my elbows to my sides, both hands balled tight, one around my phone, drawing peace, I prayed I could hold it together.

"Sucks, that." A hint of warmth. "I can see where that

would throw you off."

I didn't want his pity; I just wanted to be me again. Adept at this game, he switched gears to throw me off. *That's what I would've done.* I scowled at the thought. I tried to focus on the cop. I'd forgotten his name. "What did you ask me?"

"I asked if you were okay." His voice had lost its edge.

"I think we've established the answer to that. What else?" My elbows pressed to my sides held me together as I tried to focus.

"Were you at the art school all evening, until you called us?"

I lifted my phone. "May I?" He nodded, so I scrolled through my last entries. "The class ended at nine. I must've stayed late to work on a new piece." I fought the urge to chew on a fingernail. I'd bitten them all to the quick already. I stuffed my phone in my pocket. My hand followed, fisting around the device. The phone held everything I knew about myself, but the most important bits I transcribed to my skin with a black Sharpie. As time passed and the messages faded, I wrote over them, preserving my history. I liked to think the faded words had found their way inside where they would lead me back to the me I once was.

"Anyone stay late with you?" He turned back to the dead man, checking his pockets.

"Not that I remember. They gave me a key to the place. I stay late a lot. Sleep isn't my thing."

He looked like he understood. "Where?"

I pulled the phone back out. "The art school. It's a few blocks down."

"You like art?"

"It's cathartic." I stole a glance over his shoulder at the dead guy. "I'm thinking right-handed killer, tallish, strong, a single thrust to the heart." Like bats escaping a cave, the words rushed out, riding the cool breeze of a knowledge so deep it had held on when everything else had left.

"How do you know that?" His words were sharp, the edge of a shovel digging, probing for something solid. But his eyes stayed kind.

"I...I don't know." *You know; you've done this before.* I shook my head. Drowning in a sea of confusion, afraid of the voice in my head, afraid of him, my thoughts like feathers riding the wind, I fought to stay present, but my eyesight telescoped, the world faded as if rushing away from me.

In one move, the detective rose and caught me as my legs crumpled. "I've gotcha." He maneuvered me out of the bathroom to the couch in the great room. "Sit." He waited for a moment. "You good?"

I nodded, pulling into myself. The first human contact I'd had in I don't know how long. I rubbed my arm where his skin had touched mine.

"Want some water?"

I nodded. My eyes followed him around the counter as he searched for a glass and some ice. His eyes absorbing, judging, weighing, as they roamed over my things: the phalanx of pill bottles arranged by time and day on the counter, the white leather furniture, the original prints, the metal sculptures, the total lack of anything personal. For the second time tonight I felt violated.

"Here." Ice clinked when he thrust a mug of water at me and managed a smile—he looked out of practice. "I couldn't find any glasses." The logo on the mug read "Keep Portland Weird."

"You know we stole this slogan from Austin." I drank, grateful for something to do, an excuse to avoid his eyes.

"How can you remember that and not who might have dropped a stiff in your tub?"

"I keep asking myself the same thing. The doctors have an explanation. This is what the doctors told me." I pulled up my canned explanation in my phone and read it. "Early-onset Alzheimer's. I'm in an experimental study at the hospital, one of two in the country, cutting-edge stuff I don't begin to understand. It's like the disease has cut chunks out of my head, so I remember some things and not others, with no logical explanation, really. The folks at the hospital can confirm—they can tell you more than I can." I stopped reading when I got to the part about voices in my head. Hallucinations, they called them. Another gift of the genetic form of the disease. But somehow, as scary as they were, I sensed the lost me in them. "The treatments are working. Memories are coming back. But they're disjointed. And the current stuff still disappears. Like the old lady mumbling to herself on the street. She can remember every kid in her grade school class but can't remember what she had for breakfast." Except I didn't even have that much. I shook the phone in front of him, demanding his attention. "It's all in here. The numbers to call, the people to talk to. Check it out."

I handed him the phone. *Don't do that. Secrets. No cops.*

While he rooted through my life, I stuck my hands in my pockets and ignored myself.

"You don't call very many people."

"I don't remember very many people." I contemplated my slide into the oblivion that now substituted for a life. Huge chunks were missing; some had been reduced to feelings but without any visuals like an overexposed movie reel—the sounds, perhaps a smell, but no picture.

He rubbed his chin, his stubble making a sound that jogged something. I reached for it. *Sandpaper.*

"When was the last time you ate?" he asked. His concern seemed genuine, but I wasn't an expert.

"Eat?" I couldn't remember. My phone wasn't any help. Neither was my stomach.

He gestured toward the kitchen. "May I?"

"Sure."

He opened the fridge, a few of the cabinets. "Make a note to go to the grocery store."

Had he asked, I could've told him he wouldn't find any food. "I used to buy groceries, but then forget I had them until the neighbors complained about the smell."

"Your smell affected, too?"

"No, just associations. I used to be a whole lot worse than I am now; at least that's what they tell me and that's what I want to believe."

"That why you write on yourself? To remember?"

"Yeah."

"You have experience with murder?" Circling back. Smart cop.

Yes. More than you can imagine. I shook the voice away. "Not that I recall."

He looked beyond me, the window pulling his gaze as if there was something compelling outside, something other than brick walls and a flat night sky. "I'm at a loss here." His eyes flicked back to mine. "A dead guy shows up in your bathtub, and you haven't even a hint as to why?"

Guilt tugged at something deep inside. "There must be a reason the killer chose this guy and put him here, in my home. But I'll be damned if I know who or why."

A lingering hint of mistrust shifted to sympathy in his eyes before they drifted from mine.

Sympathy, the last way station on the pity path. I hated pity, but I was used to it. Alzheimer's in someone my age—I'd not yet reached forty, according to the information in my phone—was more than most folks could process.

The detective paced around the room, stopping in front of each piece of art. "You do these?" Interest flared.

"Yeah." When I'd first moved to Portland, I'd painted. Canvases that were happy and bright, soothing in a way I couldn't remember my life ever having been. I stopped for a while. I couldn't remember why. Recently, I'd broken out the paints again, bought some new tubes of oil and a few of acrylic, but the images that flowed through my brushes scared me. "Right now, I'm mostly working on the sculptures. Turns out I have a talent with the TIG welder."

An eyebrow arched in surprise. "That what you take at the art school?"

I chewed on my lip. "Maybe." I breathed deep, focusing on each breath, and stole a glance at my phone. "Yes."

He paused a moment in front of each figure, all similar—large and black, hooded, with head bowed in supplication, hands fisted at its sides. "I like your work. Not very hopeful, though, are they?"

Before I could answer, the young officer the detective had sent away stepped through my front door. After nodding once to the detective, he moved to the side to wait with the others still guarding my door.

"Did you see the crime scene guys down there?" the detective asked him.

"Right behind me."

The detective's attention landed back on me, all business again. "Is there anyone I can call who might be able to shed some light on any of this, besides the medical guys?" He lowered his voice to a deeper level of serious. "You *can* appreciate the fact that this has personal written all over it."

"I may not remember everything, or even most things," I said, "but I still remember how to be afraid." I didn't tell him that when you started losing the past, fear became your grounding in the present. He looked like he understood.

"What has me worried is how the killer or killers and the victim got in here. There're no signs of forced entry. Was your door locked?"

"I don't know. I try to remember to throw the bolt when I leave. I have a note there to remind me, but even that is no guarantee. That's why I live in a secure building."

We shared a moment of irony.

Keeping his eyes on me, he called over his shoulder. "Peterson?"

The officer he'd sent downstairs stepped forward. "Sir?"

The detective's attention shifted to the young officer. "Any info from the security cameras?"

"Tape from tonight is missing."

"Of course it is. I'm assuming the guard didn't see anything."

"No, sir."

The detective looked put out but didn't seem surprised. "Okay. We need to talk to all the security personnel; see if they've noticed anything irregular."

"Time frame?"

"Start with the last twenty-four hours. See what you get, and we'll go from there."

The young officer motioned for another to follow him as he headed toward the door.

The room seemed a bit more my own after they'd left. My mug was empty; yet, my mouth was still dry. I startled when my phone chirped.

The detective's head swiveled in my direction; his eyes bore holes.

I rose, and, turning my back to the room, moved to stand in front of the window. I bowed my head and cupped a hand around the phone as I lowered my voice. Still, my words crackled with anger. "Dan, what the fuck? You said I'd be safe." I looked at the reflection in the window of the activity behind me. The cop was watching. I couldn't read his expression. I didn't care. "You promised."

Deputy U.S. Marshal Dan Strader was my lifeline. He and my phone were the two things holding me together. Now his voice came over the line, warm, reassuring. There was something about his voice that always made me feel protected, safe...that called me back.

"Don't worry," he said. "And I know what I said. I'm on it. I'll find the leak." His voice held concern and anger all rolled into tired. Crisp with dulled edges, he hadn't been asleep. I knew his nuances. "Kate, it has to be that damned brain study."

Squeezing the phone, I vibrated with an anger laced with fear and shock, but it was the anger that threatened to consume me. "So, this is *my* fault?"

"Breathe, Sawyer. I can't help if I don't know what's happened. What's going down?"

The simple question stymied me. You'd think anger would bridge the faulty synapses in my head, but I couldn't be so lucky.

"Are you okay?" I could picture him rubbing his eyes, the skin bunching between them in a perpetual frown.

Shutting my eyes, I focused on breathing—in, out, in, out. "The police are here." In, out, in out...

Dan's voice switched gears, dropping into a low growl. "Why didn't you call me first?"

"I don't know." I momentarily lost my footing. "Was I supposed to?"

"Let me talk to them."

I extended the phone to the detective. "He wants to talk to you."

The cop raised an eyebrow but took the phone as he joined me at the window. His face was hard to read. "This is Detective Hudson with the Portland Police Department. Who are you?"

Hudson, that was his name. I repeated the name over and over then, losing faith, I snagged a Sharpie—I had them stashed all over. In tiny letters I wrote his name on my forearm, blowing on the ink until it had lost its wet sheen.

As he listened, his eyes kept flicking to me, then away—little darts of interest, curiosity, disbelief. "There's been a murder," he explained to Dan. Then his expression lost any hint of nice. "I see." He didn't sound happy. "You want us to—" He listened a bit longer. "I'm in the middle of questioning—" His eyes flashed to mine. They were no longer light blue but dark and angry. "Got it."

He handed the phone back to me and directed his words at his officers, but his eyes never left me. "Tell the ME to process the scene, bag the body, and get it out of here. He needs to hold it for the Feds. Guess we don't own our own dead anymore. When the crime scene guys are done, so are we."

Turning my back, I lowered my voice and lit into Dan. "Now you gotta go pissing off the cops."

"Don't tell them anything. Can you do that?"

"Why not?"

"Kate, just do what I ask. It's important."

I terminated the call, a shudder rolling through me.

What could be going down that I couldn't trust the cops?

An earlier question floated through my mind. *Who was I?*

And another.

What have I done?

CHAPTER TWO

The cops had taken hours, people filling my space, pushing me back into the corner as they worked. Dan called back, catching me pacing in front of the windows. "Are you okay?"

"Of course. Just another day on *Fantasy Island*."

"Kate."

"Sorry. I've been better. At least I'm pretty sure I have."

"Are the cops gone?"

"It took them long enough. Why did you send them away?"

"Jesus Christ, Katie! I told you no cops."

It was hard enough to try to keep my story straight, my life moving forward. And now I had to remember who played on which team? "Aren't cops the good guys?"

He muttered an epithet. "Yes, some of them. But you're in the Witness Protection Program. Remember?"

"Yeah." I wasn't lying, not exactly. I could remember the big picture, but the details were gone.

"You need to keep your head down, stick to the script. Calling the cops about a dead guy in your tub is hardly lying low."

Anger sizzled through me as I squeezed the phone, my anchor in a life out of focus. "So, leave him there until you can get here? Dan, seriously?" I tried to picture him, but the slate was blank.

"You have a point." His voice had softened, dampening my anger. "I worry about you. We've been through a lot. You know I've put myself out there for you, the stem cell thing and all, and I'm worried something is going to happen."

He cared about me. I knew that, felt it even if I forgot and had to be reminded. And I relied on him for so much. He knew my past, helped me remember. "Something is going to happen regardless."

"I know." He sounded resigned.

Standing in front of the windows, I stared at the reflection of me looking back. Even I didn't look like the me I remembered. The latticework of scars on my body bore testament to hardships I couldn't remember, ones that I'm sure had changed me. So disconcerting, losing oneself—like being lost in the fog, no landmarks, nothing familiar, no map back to me. "Who was I, Dan?" I whispered.

He drew in a sigh, a parent reading a child's favorite story for the hundredth time. "You were deep cover, so I don't know all of the facts. You were highly placed in a criminal organization. You'd been working your way up for a long while. Apparently, you'd managed to work your way into the inner circle."

"I was a cop?" I remembered that, vaguely, in bits and pieces, snatches of time like a patchwork quilt.

"A really good one."

A few things slotted into place. Like how I'd managed to deduce so much from the body. "Is that why you didn't want to bring the local police into this?"

"Partially. When it comes to you, the brotherhood can't be trusted. You don't remember, but you had nothing to lose. You...pushed it. A lotta guys got rolled. You damn near died."

"Who should I be afraid of?" I asked.

"A guy named Khoury, remember him?" Dan spat the name.

"No."

"A money launderer. He converted the take for a bunch of criminal organizations. He took their money and sold them diamonds in return. You took him down." Hope turned Dan's voice up at the end as if he willed me to remember more.

I didn't. "What does he want with me? If it was revenge he was after, wouldn't he have just killed me? Why put the guy in my tub? I don't have a clue who he is, but Khoury must think I know."

"Khoury has a bit of a problem."

"One I can solve, since my memory is so good and all." Curiously, sarcasm was something I remembered. I kept staring at my reflection in the window, trying to picture the old me, the undercover cop. "What did I do, Dan? Tell me."

"The last bust, Khoury's takedown. Twenty million in street ice went missing."

"Street ice?"

"Unmarked diamonds. Worse, they'd already been paid for."

"What did I have to do with that?"

"He thinks you took them." Dan sighed, exhaling a bad memory. "And since he's still looking...hell, he's tortured and killed practically everyone who could've touched that ice...we are assuming he hasn't found the diamonds. Now he's closing in on you."

Everything inside of me turned to ice. Dan had promised they wouldn't find me. He'd lied. "How do you know?"

"It's my job to know."

I cocked my head and stared at the woman staring back at me, a thin reflection captured by the glass of the window. Could I have stolen the diamonds? "I can't believe I would've done that."

"Not now. But back then you were different. You had nothing to lose. You didn't have much use for rules. Of course, no one knew what was going on in that head of yours, about the Alzheimer's. Hell, everyone thought you were just getting burnt-out or in too deep."

"Everyone?"

"There were notes in your file to that effect. Your superiors were starting to notice your erratic behavior, but you were a huge asset and the takedown was close. It's all in your file. Dr. Faricy told me the disease must've been burning through your brain, affecting your judgment, your impulse control, among other things."

I couldn't argue since I didn't remember that version of me. "Did you know me then?"

"By reputation. Like I said, it's all in your files. And then there's your brother. None of this bad shit happened before we let him in on the fact you were alive and needed some stem cells. Siblings apparently can be very good matches, lower the rejection issues and all. And that's how it turned out for you. You have the genetic thing that caused all of this. He doesn't."

"My brother?" My voice came out in a whisper. My soul remembered what my brain could not.

"Yeah. Hank."

The name flickered through me. That name I knew. A chill. *Careful.* "How does he factor into the diamonds?"

"He was there, Katie. Part of the team that screwed up the takedown. Man, it was a nightmare." He swallowed hard, like bolting whisky. "The political fallout alone was catastrophic."

"So, you really think I took the diamonds?" For some odd reason, I wasn't offended. It was as if we were talking about someone else. I felt no connection to the person Dan says I was. But there was something about diamonds that tickled a memory.

Dan's sigh rolled through the line. "What I think isn't important. What Khoury thinks, now that's a different matter."

"You really think my brother sold me out?"

"Hank? We couldn't prove it, but the timing's awful coincidental."

My brother. The whisper of a distant connection. My family. My life. I'd given up so much. I couldn't remember whether it had been worth it or not. I put Dan on speaker and frantically scrolled through the notes on my phone. Surely I would've entered something about my brother. Nothing. I wondered why? "You really think he'd hurt me?" I whispered, afraid if I spoke too loudly someone would hear and tell me what I most feared. I typed madly into the phone: Hank=brother=bad. Reading the words left a hollow place in my heart.

Dan's tone made it clear he didn't want to talk about this anymore. "I said it made sense. I don't know exactly how it all went down, just what I read in the files. I wasn't there, nor was I involved. But I just want you to be aware that Hank could be working his own angle on this."

"But he gave me his stem cells. You said that, right?"

"Yes. He's your brother, and we haven't proven anything, but think about it. He could have an ulterior motive."

"Like?"

"To help you remember where the diamonds are. Twenty million untraceable could set you up pretty good."

"No doubt." I didn't have any argue left. I quit staring at my reflection—that version of me wasn't telling me anything I needed to know. Plopping on the couch, I barricaded myself with pillows in the crook of the arm.

"Dr. Faricy told me the treatments are working," Dan said, his voice brightening.

I had a solid kernel of hope in my chest, which I tried to ignore. "Yes, but my memories are disjointed. They don't make much sense. Some of them don't even seem familiar, which is alarming."

"It'll all gel; don't worry. But if you're getting a bit careless, we've got serious troubles. Pay attention. This is life and death, Kate."

With a dead guy in my tub, I didn't need convincing or reminding.

"I know the leak wasn't on my end," Dan continued. "Hell, there's something like three people on the planet who know who you were and where you are—yet somehow, they found you."

"You said something about the hospital? The treatments? The docs couldn't be behind this. And they wouldn't talk."

"No, we kept the hospital staff involved to a minimum, and their knowledge of you is strictly from the new script we gave you. You must've slipped up, Kate. I don't know how else it could've happened."

The anger I'd managed to tamp down to an ember flared anew. "I find a dead guy in my tub and you think it's *my* fault? What the fuck is the matter with you?"

"I've gone to great lengths to keep you safe. Create a new life, one without links to your old fuckups."

"Well, you fucking failed." I resented the reference to fuckups but since I couldn't remember, it was hard to argue.

"Look, Kate, I'm on this. Don't worry."

I find a dead body in my bathtub, and he says not to worry. They guy needed a laugh track.

"I convinced the cops to keep an eye out until I get there."

"What's the point? *They*, whoever *they* are, already know where I live."

"Well, it'll probably cut down on the number of dead guys you find in your bathtub." He anticipated my anger and didn't give me an opening. "Kate, with your background, hell, you've got a neon target on your back. Let me protect you. It's what I get paid the big bucks for."

"If you're trying to make me feel good, you suck at it."

"I'm just trying to keep you alive."

"You suck at that, too." Overstating, but probably not by much, which had me worried. I didn't tell him about the dead guy's gun I'd stashed in my dresser. I was pretty sure I wasn't supposed to have it. Something about people with mental issues and firearms made folks twitchy, including the U.S. Marshals Service. I got it, but their rules, not mine.

"Too bad you haven't forgotten how to be an ass." He sighed, and I could feel his weariness. "Sorry. Uncalled for."

I burrowed deeper into the couch, pressing the pillows close as I reached for a smile. "No, I deserved that."

"Apology accepted." Like I said, Dan knew me pretty well. "If they contact you, play along, but let me know, okay?"

"If I find another stiff you'll be the first to know." I almost wished they'd try again. Maybe then I could *do* something. That's what kept me so pissed off, the not doing.

"Kate, this is serious."

"Damn serious. The dead guy messed up my tub. Now I'm going to have to take a shower. And you know how I hate showers."

"You're a real pain in the ass."

"Maybe that's why I'm still alive." *Hank. A face mocking, taunting. Blond just like me.* I bolted out of my fortified position. "Of all things, you'd think betrayal would've left a scar I couldn't forget." Propelled by the hint of a bitter memory, I paced the apartment, rechecking all the hiding places the cops had checked before. I was alone.

"You were in bad shape. Died twice on the table. They had a hell of a time saving your leg. How many surgeries? How much general anesthesia? Then the Alzheimer's thing, which the doctors think might have been precipitated by all the other stuff. And now, Jesus, they're injecting stuff into your brain. It's a wonder..." he trailed off.

I could almost see his face flush with embarrassment.

"What?" I said. "That I'm allowed out by myself without a keeper?" A potted plant in front of the front door told me I'd already checked it and secured the deadbolt. It was the only way in or out of my apartment—totally against code. The building manager had left me so many notes to that affect, I left them stuck where he'd put them. I didn't care. An occasional C-note ensured he didn't either.

"Hell, you got me, what would you need another keeper for? I've got your back."

We both knew that wasn't quite the kind of keeper I was referring to, but it gave him an out. I let him take it. "Dan, what if they come back?" Feeling violated, powerless, and pissed, I half-hoped they would.

"If they'd wanted you dead, you would be." Anger honed his voice to an edge. "God damn it, I should've seen this coming. It's my job to protect you, and normally I'm damn good at it. I'll find the person who squealed, Katie, I promise you."

Dan sounded pretty sure about that. I didn't share his conviction. To the diamond guy, I could be a mouse to a cat, something to play with before eating. Once the door was opened, all the Furies of Hell would rush through.

"I'll head your way in a bit," Dan said. "I'm in D.C. Lay low until I get there."

After tucking my phone back in my pocket, I retrieved the dead guy's gun from my dresser. A chambered round, a full magazine, it felt like an old friend in my hand. My eyes roamed around the large room, reestablishing my bearings, taking back my home.

Once the ME had taken the body and wrapped up, the cops had left as quickly as they'd come, leaving fingerprint dust, a few shreds of tape that had secured the plastic runners over the wood of the hallway, and unanswered questions on both sides. I could tell that questions without resolutions bothered the detective. He had been a detective, right? I checked my forearm. Yes. Detective Hudson. His name printed with a few keywords to help me remember. Bathtub. Note. Professional killer.

By morning I might not remember the police. But I had a feeling the dead guy would stay with me. Which was why I hoped my memory of whatever fuckup that had sent me to Dan would emerge sooner rather than later as I went through my treatments. The two had to be related.

Short-term memories faded the quickest, but the traumatic ones tended to linger. Tonight that cut both ways. I'd like to forget. But if I was going to avoid ending up like the guy in my tub, I needed some answers. Answers would be hard to come by if I couldn't remember the questions. I grabbed my phone, launched the verbal note-taking app, and started talking into the mic. Remembering the details was like trying to catch butterflies—I'd reach for one, close my hand, only to find it empty, the butterfly winging out of reach.

Pulling up the sleeve of my sweater, I chose a spot on my forearm where the black lettering had faded. Pulling the cap from the Sharpie with my teeth, I meticulously wrote next to "Hudson, detective" the phone numbers from his card, surprised he included his cell. Crime was a twenty-four-hour business; I remembered that, too. Then I chewed on my lip, concentrating, capturing the lightning bugs of memories before the light went out. Next to Hudson's info I blocked in: "Khoury, diamonds, thinks I took them. Hank, trouble." I blew on the ink to make sure it dried before recapping the pen and tossing it on the counter.

Once again, I took my position in front of the windows as I dictated and tried to remember. The Alzheimer's hadn't robbed me of language or geography, at least. Below me, the Willamette River arced to the south, holding downtown in its embrace as it curved away. On a clear day, I could see the stunted, ragged remnants of Mount St. Helens, made all the more forlorn by the hulking mass of Mount Rainier behind. Today had started out pretty and bright, the mountains showing off a new powdering of snow, the city preening in the sunshine. Or had that been yesterday?

Or did I really remember that at all?

As I watched, clouds gathered, blocking out the moonlight. This view, these mountains, the rivers, looked like Heaven, or at least how I thought Heaven should look.

What a fool to think I'd left the darkness behind.

I felt edgy and apprehensive. My leg ached. The scar from the latest surgery, the fifth maybe, still looked puckered and angry red. It throbbed, sometimes worse than the other scars. Now it pounded like a mother. Opening the tin on the coffee table, I flaked off a paper, filled it with the good stuff, rolled it, then licked it closed. A flick of the lighter and I inhaled deeply. The best medicinal-grade black gold on the market. When I was a kid, weed would get you busted; now they wrote you a scrip for it. Life wasn't all bad.

My memory exhausted, bone-tired, I sat on the couch, encasing myself in bright pillows and a cashmere throw, a meager fortification, but comforting. Another pull, then I flicked the ashes into a nearby ashtray. As I held the smoke in my lungs, the calm returned, the pain dulled.

I know what you did.

I should've left the note for the police. But the note and the gun were the only threads I could pull that might open a hole to the past.

I sucked in another lungful of smoke, holding it before letting it trickle through my lips, surrendering to the calm.

The killer surely chose the messenger for a purpose. I had the tickle of a memory as I scanned the photos of the dead guy. The clothes, the smell—both said he lived on the streets. But his hair had been neatly cut, his face clean-shaven, his fingernails trimmed and buffed. A fleeting caress of familiarity—I knew him, but from where?

I thumbed backward through the photos in my phone. I knew he wouldn't be there as anything but a corpse—the photos only went back so far—but I had to look, to keep jogging my balky synapses.

My doctors had told me to make a memory book. Just in case, they'd said. I loved that.

Just in case what? In case I stopped remembering where I lived, what my name was, what I liked and what I didn't, what I ate and what I didn't, the people I loved, the people I didn't?

And what exactly was I supposed to memorialize in my memory book? I had a new identity, a whole new history and background. No new friends who knew the real me, the me that Dan had told me to erase. Convenient, when you think about it. Life was doing that for me. But the more they wanted me to forget, the harder I clung to hints of who I used to be.

Who would I be when I ceased to be me? Former cop, painter, sculptress, collector of dead bodies. Lost, with no tether of a memory. No life behind, and none in front.

I felt under the couch; my fingers found the cool brush of wood. Reverently, like a priest holding a sainted relic, I cradled the worn wooden keepsake box. When I lifted the lid, strains of music, a tinny music box rendition of *But Not for Me*, began to play. No matter the time or place or the state of my memory, that tune propelled me back into the past, to a time when blood was thicker than water, when good was easy to recognize, bad was everything else, and the good guys always won.

I sifted through the items in the box: one golden jack from a game long lost, a plastic soldier I'd rescued from my brother intent on blowing it up with a Black Cat; a gold ring, worn almost smooth, the shadow of a family crest from a time when folks like my grandfather took pride in such things; a medal Hank—yes! Now I had his name—had won in a track meet. My fingers searched, finally finding the tattered and bent corner of an old photo. This was my heart—I could feel it warm me, a flooding emotion that I couldn't attach to anything.

I flipped the photo over. In a bold, elegant cursive, someone had written "Hank and Kate, 1995." My brother and me, arms around each other, matching grins—a moment in time captured by someone who had cared. That thought alone kept me sane. Someone had cared.

My brother and me. Ten months between us, we'd been of the same soul. At least I thought we had. Thinking about Hank, I brushed my finger across his image. "What happened, Hank? When did you stop loving me?"

I just couldn't accept that he'd sold me out. Maybe I didn't want to. Maybe I couldn't handle it. Either way, I wouldn't let myself believe it.

Memories, the warp and weft of the fabric of our lives. Who knew they could be so fleeting, so fragile? I tucked my box out of sight. Dan would be apoplectic if he knew I'd kept these things, these ties with the me I used to be, the version of me someone wanted dead. But if I didn't have me, I might as well be dead, so I didn't see the big deal.

I know what you did.

Funny, my past had never struck me as important until I'd started losing it.

Now it was the key to staying alive.

CHAPTER THREE

The alley is dark. Someone has picked off the lights. This part of town calls to the darkness. I hold my semi-automatic clutched in both hands, my arms extended, breath coming in short gasps. I squint into the darkness. Moonlight outlines the walls on either side, bricks under a layer of filth, a fire escape accordioned above. Nothing moves, as if the world was frozen in ice, the air so clear, so cold, it crackled.

"Show yourself."

A can moves in the breeze. I flinch toward the noise. "I know you're there." Something heavy in the large pocket of my jacket swung with me, a pendulum.

He'd chased me through the shadows into the alley. I know this alley. No way out. If he wants me, he'll have to come get me.

Quiet. Working to control my breathing. Listening. Waiting.

"Kate, where are you?" A familiar voice, my lifeline to safety, through the small receiver in my ear. Worried. "Kate, answer me."

I can't. Not now. Not with him near.

Not with what I'd done.

The hint of a familiar scent. Pine. The rasp of rough fabric. A quick breath. Behind me. I whirl. Too late.

Pain explodes in my head. My left leg buckles. My gun clatters into the shadows as I stagger and go down.

I awakened with a start, bolting upright on the sofa. My head throbbed. Blinking against the light burning on the table, breathing hard. Where was I? I scanned the room. My place. Still alone.

A pounding on the door.

Lost to the nightmares, the world on tilt, I struggled to pull pieces together out of the darkness.

"Kate!" someone shouted. Dan. "Goddamn it! Open the door!"

"Just a minute." Still fuzzy, I worked the locks.

He burst into the room, grabbing me in a hug. "Jesus, when you didn't answer the door or your phone..."

I squeezed him back. Truth of it was, I liked seeing him. He'd put my life back together, nursed the broken me. If memories were the glue that held the pieces of me together, then I was starting to re-form, take shape. And I had Dan to thank for that. He helped me remember.

Dan stepped back. With his hands on my shoulders, he took a good long look. "Well, you don't look like a person who sees dead people."

"Only when someone drops one under my nose."

He nodded toward the kitchen. "Got any coffee?"

"It's Portland," I said as if that was an answer. Trouble was, I was pretty sure I couldn't survive without coffee so I must have some. But I wasn't sure. "I'll see what I can find."

Whippet thin, Dan knifed with a nervous energy into the great room and around the counter separating the kitchen. His clothes were rumpled, his tie a noose around an open collar. Although I was unsure, it seemed his hair had grayed and thinned since I'd last seen him, which was...I didn't remember when. Wrinkles bracketed tired eyes startling in their faded green. I noticed his socks didn't match—both were black, but one had a pattern, the other didn't.

Taking a stool at the counter, he crossed his arms in front of himself, leaning on them as he followed my movements in the kitchen. I found the Keurig cup and followed the picture I'd drawn for myself, placing the cup in the holder, closing it, then hitting the button. Always on, the machine gurgled to life.

"The mug." Dan motioned to the coffee machine.

Just as the dark stream started, I thrust the mug underneath, angry at myself for forgetting.

"I do that sometimes, too. Easy to do." Dan gave me a sympathetic shrug. The guy looked like death—sunken cheeks, dark hollows under his eyes, his smile weaker than the one I thought I remembered.

"I wasn't expecting you until later." I shoved the coffee in front of him.

"It is later." Dan wrapped both hands around the mug. He sat there watching me as though I might vanish. "I had a plane waiting. Got to go to New York next."

"Convenient, since Portland's on the way and all."

"Needed to nail down some things here. I'm not used to having my people burned. The DOJ gets a bit twitchy."

"Doesn't feel so good on this end either." My stomach growled. I had a serious case of the munchies.

"We need to move you. I can't keep guys on you all the time, and they know where you live, obviously, so you need a new place."

"I figured that's what you'd say. I've thought it through. The answer is no."

"What do you mean, no?" Dan's tone had the hard edge of someone not used to being defied. "Look, we can't protect you here. You need a new identity, a new place."

I pulled a bag of Doritos out of the pantry. "Want some?"

"Good to see you're taking such good care of yourself." Dan didn't smile. "Katie, this is serious. Your cover's been blown. I can't take care of you without moving you."

"Stop saying that." I grabbed a handful of chips and started in as I took the stool next to him. The nightmare still vibrated through me. I tried to hang onto it. There was something there, something I needed to know. But the memories faded like the roll of thunder into the darkness.

His face hardened. He sniffed. "You still smoking?"

"Helps with the pain."

That chiseled more fissures into the granite planes of his face. "Katie, if I'm to protect you, I need to move you to a safer location."

"I get it, but I can't. I mean, I don't want to die, Dan. I don't. Certainly not at the far end of a gun. But short-term memories are the worst. I remember this place, how to get here, the people who work here, who look after me. It's my home. You cannot take it away from me. Not when I'm really starting to get better. I'm remembering, Dan. Really remembering."

After a long stare, Dan relented with a shrug, but the set of his jaw told me the discussion was far from over. "Why don't you tell me what you know?"

I put my phone between us on the counter and pressed play. He stared straight ahead, his eyes unfocused and his expression intense as he listened. As the recording finished, Dan stepped to the bar and made himself a drink—three fingers of single malt, one ice cube. He threw the drink back then went for round two.

"If you're looking for a cheap drunk, I'd appreciate it if you'd use the cheap stuff."

Dan, his back to me, shrugged one shoulder with a tilt of his head. "Cheap stuff gives me a headache."

He looked like he'd been running on adrenaline and Scotch for far too long.

"You look like shit, by the way," I said, then regretted it.

"Feel like it, too."

"Hell of a business, this." I studied Dan's weary face and felt a surge of gratitude. Maybe he wasn't much of a family. But he was what I had. At least he'd been there for me after...after whatever it was that happened. "I know how I got here—well, bits and pieces and stuff you've filled in—but how'd you end up in the Marshals Service?"

Dan, maybe catching my need, relaxed. "I was a kid when my mom married a cop. Eventually, we all went into my stepdad's business. My stepbrother stayed local. I went Fed. Not a popular choice in my house." He fixed me with a bloodshot stare. "You going to tell me where you've been stepping outside the lines?" He returned to the stool next to mine. Staring straight ahead, he caught my eyes in our reflections in the mirrored backsplash behind the sink. A water spot on the mirror looked like a tear on my cheek.

I pushed my phone over to him. "It's all in the calendar thing. See for yourself. I go to the hospital, the art school, and home. I don't make friends or invite confidences."

He ignored the phone, my words lying between us as he stared into his glass. "I know where you've been. I'll figure it out. But if you stay here, it's like shooting fish in a barrel."

"Like you said, they don't want me dead, not yet anyway. Apparently, they just want information. Like I could remember." I didn't laugh.

"They don't know that. So, if you won't move, then keep the deadbolts thrown, security downstairs on alert." His head bowed, he turned and gave me an odd glance. "You remember why you're under my protection?"

Given the dead guy in my tub, I thought "protection" was overstating, but I let it slide. "Just what you told me." There was something in the way his eyes looked at me but didn't seem to focus, as if they were seeing something else. I glanced at the block lettering on my forearm.

I know what you did.

"So, if we busted Khoury, what's he doing out to chase after me?"

"They lost him. Someone busted him out on his way to the courthouse. Killed one of the guards." Dan eyed the bottom of his empty glass. "The FBI is all over it. If he's findable, they'll find him."

"They can start with the dead guy in my bathtub." For some odd reason, I felt some of the logic blocks in my head fall into place like tumblers in a lock. Of course, going back over it all as Dan listened to my recording helped. But that was the real heartbreak of this disease: one day you couldn't remember your name, the next you had a clear vision into the past, only to lose it again the next. Although welcomed, these moments of clarity amplified the returning loss.

Dan stared straight ahead as if the mirror held more than the pair of us. "From the beginning, word on the street was one of the cops took them, stashed them somewhere, and never made it back to collect their stash."

I know what you did.

"And everybody thinks I was that cop."

"Not everybody, but the scenario fits. Why wouldn't the thief go back to collect?"

"Unless they had no idea they'd done it." Fear pooled in my stomach and seeped into my legs. Back when I had nothing to lose, I didn't remember knowing fear. But the docs had given me hope. Hope to crawl out from under a genetic life sentence. Hope that I could have a normal life, whatever that meant. A hope I cherished.

A hope that made me weak.

———

Standing in front of my wall of windows, I squinted against the sun, which had chosen to make a rare appearance. Most of my fellow Portlanders would be outside absorbing the rays. Preferring the usual drizzle and fog, I didn't share their enthusiasm.

After Dan left, I'd spent the rest of the night dictating into my phone, going over and over all I could remember, turning each thought like a squirrel with a nut. Notes in my phone, the most important stenciled on my arm. As the sun milk-washed the sky, I went over it all one more time.

Now, blowing on my fifth mug of coffee, I scanned the sidewalks below. The Watchman had yet to claim the street corner; he was late. Not like him. I worried something might have happened. The streets were rough; he was old. It dawned on me I had no way to find out if he was alive and well or not. That struck me as sad. Paths cross, but lives don't touch.

Nothing else on the street seemed odd. People scurried

past, heads down. A few raised their faces to the sun in smiling supplication. Dan's guys were down there somewhere. I didn't spot them, not that I expected to.

My phone buzzed in my pocket, and I glanced at the screen. I had to leave now if I wanted to make my treatment time. Dan had told me to sit tight. I'd been vacillating most of the morning. He wanted to take me to the treatment himself. When work had allowed, he'd been at quite a few. But he said he had an important meeting somewhere back East he couldn't miss. I couldn't remember where. He'd wanted me to reschedule. I said I would, but I lied. The doctors were making such progress. The memories were brighter now, still out of reach, but there. So close.

Carefully I washed the mug then set it to dry. One last look, decision made, I grabbed my jacket and strode toward the door. I hadn't made it this far by keeping my head down. Fear, an unwelcomed companion, nipped at my heels, a rabid cur demanding attention.

I shoved it down, knowing it wouldn't stay. Fear had no place in keeping me alive.

I picked up the first tail as I pulled out of the garage and turned right into the heart of downtown. A black sedan. Stopping for the light at the corner, my bike, a BMW F 800 GS, thrummed beneath me, its raw power vibrating through my hands and up my arms. My route, remembered by the GPS on my phone in my pocket, an irritating female voice in my ear telling me where to go, I tugged up the zipper of my jacket and shivered. My breath, a white mist in the sharp air, hung like fog. Despite the sun, the air was damp, holding a chill that seeped in through every seam. On green, I rolled, keeping a sedate pace until the second guy in a green sedan pulled in front of me from the right, angling across my path. I'd hoped they were cops keeping tabs on me, but that last move convinced me otherwise.

Fishtailing, I accelerated down the street on my left. And my GPS route went dark. Tires screeched behind me. I leaned forward and opened the throttle. Blinking against the assault of air rushing past, I wished I'd bought a helmet, but I hadn't wanted to waste the money. Brain buckets were only useful when you had a brain to protect. A little middle finger gesture to Fate.

Two more turns and I accelerated up the Morrison Bridge, braked as I crested the middle, then dropped down the off-ramp on the far side of the Willamette. A quick glance behind as I braked and put my left foot out. The first car was closing.

I popped over the curb, cutting into the area under the flyover. Grass flew as I accelerated over the triangular median and through the cement dividers of the construction project onto an open dirt roadbed awaiting its mantle of rebar and cement. Brakes squealed behind me. A thump, then acceleration, as the car tried to follow. It came to a halt at the barriers, its tires slipping in the sand.

I'd lost the second sedan—the green one.

Standing on the pegs, I timed my reentry into traffic, weaving and jogging. Dirt kicked up to my right. They were shooting. And they must have a silencer. A bullet hissed into the tire of a car approaching from the right. The driver slammed on his brakes as he fought for control. Wide-eyed, he missed me by inches. Seeing my opening, I twisted hard on the throttle. A burst of speed, I moved between the two lines of traffic, wedging in with the flow in the right lane, putting a line of cars and growing distance between me and the shooter.

Keeping pace with the traffic, I worked to steady my nerves and slow my breathing. The GPS and its female mouthpiece recalculated a new route. All my normal landmarks—the ones engraved on my memory through countless repetitions—were gone. I focused on the voice in my ear, letting her words quiet the panic.

I missed the second guy waiting as I exited the bridge, back in downtown on the south side of the river. I sensed him and reacted just before he bumped my back tire.

Stupid!

Dan was right. They didn't want me dead. But they sure wanted something.

A motorcycle has a distinct advantage over cars, and I used it. Weaving in and out of traffic, working my way forward splitting the lanes, I used the largest vehicles to block my position and movements from those chasing me. After I'd left them a good way back, I turned, then turned again, before they had a chance to see me. After that, I slowed and pulled over, pausing to let the GPS reroute me from my current spot. Following the red line, I wove a careful, watchful path toward the east side of downtown. Instead of winding up the hill, I eased into the parking lot at the base of the aerial tram that would take me to the top of Pill Hill to the hospital.

In another life, I probably would've found a way to separate and engage one of the jerks following me, make him talk, but that was a former rendition of me. Today, I had no gun, no guts, and an appointment I couldn't miss, not unless I wanted to end up like the Scarecrow before he met Dorothy, wishing he had a brain.

The tram left from a small glass-encased building near the south bank of the Willamette in a new development. I'd forgotten what the developers had named it, but I did remember that it was a place for people like me, with failing memories and perhaps failing health. A place for those needing to be close to medical care, with shops and restaurants and a four-minute tram ride to the hospital—or so the sign said. Convenient, but a bit fatalistic for my tastes.

The parking lot was almost full. Instead of parking with the motorcycles, I eased in beside a smaller car, then worked the bike in front of it. Unless they were really looking, nobody would spot it. Keeping my head down and my eyes scanning, I trotted for the tram, taking the stairs as quick as a balky knee would allow. The doors were just closing as I jumped through and stepped to the middle of the car. Anyone below would have a hard time seeing me. Clutching a pole to steady myself, I closed my eyes and took a deep breath. My heart beat a steady rhythm. I felt only a light sheen of sweat, a nervousness.

No, an exhilaration.

I liked being the prey.

"Anything new I need to know about?" Dr. Logan Faricy, the geneticist in charge of my treatment cycles at the hospital, asked as he readied the necessary equipment. The guard, as he always did, had escorted me through the maze of hospital corridors that still all looked the same. "You have a healthy pink in your cheeks today. Looks good on you."

Getting shot at could do that. I didn't say that, of course, but it would've been fun to see his reaction. Logan only saw a glimmer of the person I used to be. I wondered what he would think if he knew the truth. Better yet, what would *I* think if I knew the truth?

I studiously avoided looking at all the tubes and wires and needles. I'd taken a peek once and regretted it. It still seemed impossible they could inject things into my brain and I wouldn't feel it. But I didn't spend a lot of time thinking about it. If I did, my stress level would be so high I'd probably stroke out, which would defeat the purpose. So I looked at Logan instead. According to my own notes, I'd been in and out of more hospitals than I could count or remember, and I'd come to realize that doctors were like puppies. The young ones were all uncoordinated enthusiasm as they barked and snapped, establishing the alpha and the pecking order. As they aged, they lost that youthful abandon and gained a quiet loyalty that engendered both trust and irritation. Logan had reached that stage. I didn't know his age, but I guessed it to be somewhere close to mine. With his hair always in need of a trim, his beard the same, and those dark, doe eyes, he did sort of have that loyal companion look to him. And, like the blind with a seeing eye dog, I trusted him with the very essence of me. I had to.

I knew that because I'd written that down in my notes, too.

"What?" One eyebrow raised in question, one side of his mouth ticked up.

"I was thinking doctors resemble canines."

That earned a full-wattage smile. "You've discovered their darkest truth."

"Their?"

"Oh, I'm addressed as a doctor, but I'm the Ph.D. kind, not the medical kind."

Considering what he was about to do to me, I tried to ignore any perceived distinction in competency. "Fits. And it doesn't disqualify you."

"Is that the kind of thinking I'm trying to save?"

"Hey, what I think about wasn't a question on the entrance exam."

His smile wilted, like a collar losing its starch, but his eyes remained kind. "Seriously, what *do* you think about?"

Did he really want to know? I thought about that for a moment, unsure how much I should share. At some point, I had to answer *some* questions. "I think about death a lot, probably way more than is healthy."

"Natural, given the circumstances. I can't really help you there."

"I thought you were trying to improve my thoughts."

"Quantity. You're in charge of the quality. Well, you and Dr. Matthews."

Dr. Matthews, was the psychiatrist assigned to my case. Not long on formality, I called her Stella. She officed in the medical arts building adjacent to the hospital. "I think that's a good thing." I always found it amusing how Logan and I bantered to diffuse the tension. It worked, but it still seemed somehow inappropriate. "So how is it you know where to inject that stuff?"

I'm sure I asked that question every single time. Maybe Logan had been chosen as much for his patience as his skill.

"DNI scan—a fancy PET scan that can detect where the amyloid plaques and tau tangles are forming. And where there is some white matter degradation that can be an indication of the Alzheimer's at work in those sections of your brain. Your latest scan is looking really good. Want to see it?"

"No. Just tell me about it." But I really wasn't sure I wanted to know. I doubted I'd remember. Bad news would be as fleeting as good. What I wanted, what I so desperately hoped to regain, was me and the functionality that goes with a memory that stretches longer than a minute or two.

"When you entered the program, you were pretty far along:

what we classify as a moderate level of the disease. Most telling was that you had lost some long-term memories, some facts about yourself. Your ability to think logically, your word choices and some spatial abilities were impacted. The treatment has restored your verbal acuity for the most part, and your recognition of your surroundings and your ability to get to and from home and the art school, and other places nearby, is good and improving. I have verbal results from the testing lab. Based on the results from your recent testing, you are improving in many areas, especially lexical and navigational parts." He raised an eyebrow, looking for my confirmation.

I nodded. "I'm still having trouble with details in long-term memories, and, of course, the short-term is pretty unreliable."

"Yes, the transference from short-term to long-term is still impacted. We're hoping to encourage the neuron migration to those areas of the brain. But, as you know, memory is a very complex mechanism, and we are only beginning to understand the inner workings. You are a very large piece of that."

"A lab rat. I wish I could say I'm delighted." I pretended to be put out; he knew I meant the opposite. "I don't struggle for words as much anymore, that's true. And getting around town is more second nature rather than following a computer voice from the GPS. And, although your testing didn't really address this, memories are coming back. I'm getting bits and pieces. Disjointed and random, but more are coming through. Sometimes it seems they're triggered by the oddest things: a bit of a song, a smell, a sound."

"What about place?"

"Everything in Portland is new, so I couldn't say."

"It might work as a trigger, too. We know so little about how the brain works and how memories are stored. But there are different pathways, different locations, redundant systems in a way, so all that makes sense."

"Will they all come back? All my memories?" Logan and his colleagues had probably answered the question before, but the disease had robbed me of it. Now it took all the courage I had to keep my voice calm, my hope disguised.

He looked at me, kindness softening his features as he gave me a slight shrug. He didn't have any answers, and pounding him with questions wouldn't alter that, but I couldn't help myself. "They're all still there, it's accessing them that has become impacted. We're working to reverse that."

"What about my logical thinking? I'm finding it a bit easier to string thoughts together to reach a conclusion."

"Improvement in contextual processing is a great sign."

"I just wish I knew."

"Give it time, Kate. We've made huge progress."

"It's just..."

He squeezed my hand. "I understand."

No, you don't understand. You couldn't possibly understand. It's as if whole pieces of me have been erased. I wrestled with an urge to blurt out everything that had happened in the hope that somehow the synapses would fire and all the facts that were caught in those tangles in my brain would tumble out. I needed to remember whom I'd crossed, and who'd crossed me. And who wanted information about some diamonds I wasn't sure I remembered, and then presumably wanted me dead once they got them.

Dangerous information. A picture of the dead guy in my bathtub flashed through my head. Wow! I remembered that. In stunning visual detail. Things *were* sticking. Now if I could just figure out why and how to control that, and how to build a cohesive wall out of the separate blocks.

The last thing I wanted was for Logan to be the next dead guy in my tub.

The thought stopped me. Was the first dead guy someone close to me?

And what if he wasn't the first one? I pushed that aside. He was the first. And he had to be someone close to me. Otherwise, there'd be no message, not a personal one anyway. I needed to work on that. I pulled out my phone and let my thumbs fly.

"What are you doing?"

"Taking notes." The lie came smoothly. "So I'll remember. Go on."

"The neurons are proliferating and migrating to the affected areas in your brain. We seem to be at a tipping point, if you will. I believe you will start seeing more rapid effects of the treatment, and your short-term memory ought to start improving. That's where we're focusing."

Hope again. Demon and necessity. "I've got a lot riding on it."

"You and me both." Logan sounded serious. What he failed to appreciate was that while he might have a career setback if this thing didn't work, I'd be dead.

"You've done this before, right?" I probably had asked that question before, too.

"In rats."

"Not a huge leap across the evolutionary abyss."

"It'll work." A pained look crossed his face. "You'll be you again."

After what Dan had said, I wasn't sure that was a good thing. But what is it they say—the past is the only thing in life you can't change? I could deal with it if I could remember it. "Were you part of the team that harvested the stem cells?"

"No, that's not really a big deal. Your brother is in New York, so we had a team from NYU do it. But I grew them and then regressed them to the kind of stem cells that we could turn into neurons. That's my special kind of magic."

"What do you know about my brother?"

"Not much. He was a good match genetically and histologically; that's all I cared about. Why?"

"Curious, that's all. I have a few bits and pieces from long ago, but not much more than that. Do you think any of the medical team in New York told my brother where I was?"

"Not a chance. The New York team wasn't given any information other than what we needed. The Marshals Service delivered the harvest." He paused, angling his head to get a look at me. "Did you hear from him?"

"No. It's just...well, curiosity. I'm sure you can appreciate my difficulty. You're helping me remember a history I'm supposed to forget. Thinking about family, being kids, it helps me connect my history to my reality."

"I hadn't thought of it that way—you need to remember before you can forget. It must be hard. Most of my patients don't have realities as complicated as yours."

"A good thing. Do you have family?"

"Four older sisters."

"Tell me about them."

He launched into family stories, probably more to distract and appease me, but it was easy to see the love he had for his sisters. I really liked him for caring—about me, about them. It shocked me to realize I liked him...for everything. One of the many downsides to being cut off from myself was being cut off from others.

I hung on his every word, each a tether to the big messiness of life. He fitted me with a cloth helmet much like the aviator caps the early pilots had worn. The fabric was embossed with a grid on which he'd marked very specific locations. Of course, he really didn't need it anymore to guide him, not since they'd inserted the electrodes and left tiny wire nodules on my scalp. Not only did these mark injection points, but they also allowed Logan to electrically stimulate the cells in my brain with light. Somehow this helped him see where the injected cells migrated and whether they'd turned into neurons, presumably to fix the faulty synapses due to the Alzheimer's.

As he worked on attaching wires, he moved close. He smelled of the woods, and something musky and masculine. I liked it. Even though I didn't recall the last man I'd been with or what it had been like, my body remembered.

Connection, the most elemental part of a human heart.

The disease had robbed me of that as well. Would I ever get that back? Would I ever know myself well enough to love someone and allow them to love me? Would I remember how to do that? Feelings without memories were like roses grown without natural sunlight and soil, pretty but lacking the scent that entices and delights.

I focused on Logan's voice, the cadence, the warmth infusing his words. Listening to his history created a larger hole in mine. "Is it true that when you lose one sense, the others become heightened?"

He kept working. "What sense have you lost?"

"Common sense?"

That got a laugh. "Are you sure you had any to begin with? From the stories Dan tells..."

"Dan. He's going to be pissed I'm here."

"Why?"

I realized too late I'd spoken a bit freely—harder to control since the disease had taken hold. Could Dan be right? Could I have let something slip and not realized it? Suddenly my faith in myself and the world around me diminished. No one was above suspicion, not even me. "Oh, I had a bit of a mess at the apartment. He wanted me to stay there while he fixed it up." It wasn't a total lie.

Logan let me off the hook. "Tell me about the memories that are returning."

Back on solid emotional turf, I relaxed. "Bits and pieces, like I said. Disjointed. Foreign. I can't make sense of them or put them in any meaningful context, but they are there. Some are diffuse as if I'm looking through a filter. The foreground is sharp, but the background is all fuzzy. Then others are completely clear, detailed. And I'm getting a little short-term stuff, like remembering I ate lunch, although what I had can sometimes still be a mystery."

"Might be a good thing depending on where you ate."

I grinned. "True."

Logan looked smug in a way.

"What?"

"You got my joke. You couldn't do that when you enrolled in the program. Your ability to make those connections, those distinctions, wasn't there."

That damn hope flared brighter. The treatments *were* working.

"Anything else?" He leaned back, giving me a serious look.

It was one of his best looks. "Can you describe what you're getting?"

"When they hit, it's like looking through a pair of binoculars. First, the image is out of focus, but each turn of the knob—each treatment—brings more clarity. Although some of the memories remain cloudy. And I'm detached from them. Almost as if they weren't my own."

"To be expected, I should think. It's hard to recognize something if the context is missing. But all this is terrific news." He moved to hug me, but stopped, leaving an awkward distance between us.

So I hugged him, my arms snaking through the wires like reaching through the bars of a cell. His nearness, the warmth of him, brought my aloneness into bold relief. My need for human touch, for kindness, for genuine feeling surprised me. Searching inside, I couldn't find a hint that I'd needed this kind of connection before. Had that distant, walled-off person been the me I used to be? If so, did I want to reinhabit that skin or grow a new one? I held onto him, perhaps inappropriately, but the nearness of him shifted things inside. Finally, I released him. "Don't get too excited. Some of the stuff is scary as hell."

"Dan said your background was tough, hard. Maybe you saw some bad things."

And maybe did some bad things. "The memories, even though distant and unfocused, are there. That's a good thing, right?"

"A very good thing. And your cognition and the verbal fluency I mentioned earlier seem to support your assertions." He stepped back, his handiwork completed. "Anything else?"

I shook my head as the tiny flame of hope in my chest burned bigger, brighter.

"Do you remember this treatment is the first at the next level? We're going to amp up the intensity a bit. You've tolerated everything so far really well, so I'm not worried. Nor should you be alarmed."

"When is my next one?"

"Not for a couple of weeks. You need time to stabilize and for us to assess how things are progressing, how you're tolerating the higher doses."

"Will I notice anything different?"

I could tell he wanted to reassure me, to lie if he had to. Instead, he shrugged and said, "I don't really know."

CHAPTER FOUR

Dusk deepened, muting the day, as I pushed through the glass doors. The cool mist that had ridden in on the light breeze earlier thickened in the cooling night. I loved the night, the fog. I felt hidden, invisible. The real world fell away, and life was as it used to be. I felt the familiar buzz that accompanied my treatments. For a bit afterward, it always felt as if my brain had been zapped and was sizzling as dormant synapses fired anew. Unfortunately, that shift into overdrive didn't last long, but I wallowed in it while it was there. And most of the time, even after the electrical energy in my brain normalized, more pathways than before remained open.

So I hadn't lied to Logan—things were starting to stick. Like being a cop, living so deep undercover I couldn't touch the real me. I remembered faces, a few names, the Academy. Good times. Until they weren't.

Hope burned even as I felt an overwhelming loss. Not for my memories this time. But for family. Pausing in the pool of light cast by a sidewalk lamp, I hiked up my sleeve and read, searching for the word, the name.

Hank.

Had he really chosen money over me? Was his gift of stem cells really just about the diamonds? I didn't want to believe it. The truth wasn't always comfortable or welcome; I knew that and could accept that. But this? It didn't feel right.

Hints of juniper and cedar perfumed the air. The downtown lights below winked as they sputtered to life, strings of red and green lights looped between buildings in anticipation of the impending holidays. The festive spirit left me hollow.

My hand closed around the small key in my pocket. A motorcycle key. A tag attached to it noted the license number. On the back I'd scrawled where I'd left it. The tram parking lot at the bottom of the hill. And the words "bathtub" and "hunters." Stella and Logan had insisted I get into the habit of making notes. Reading my words, a thrill went through me. I remembered writing these words. More, I remembered why I'd written them. I'd abandoned my bike because someone was hunting me. Bits and pieces of the day tumbled in my head like rocks in a swollen mountain stream. The dead man. The cops. Dan. I took a seat on a bench at the head of the path leading down the hill and took time to listen to my latest recording. When that was done, I perused my notes. Remembering relit the fear.

In a game of cat and mouse, I was the mouse and I had no idea who the cat was, or what they even looked like. I checked the photo of the dead guy in my tub. They'd look like him—like they were trying to fit in but didn't.

The long path to the road across I-5 and back into town snaked down the hill at my feet. Not really that long, easily walkable, but the pools of shadow between the lights bothered me. So many places for dark things to hide.

But the guys who had chased me would be looking for me on my bike.

I decided to ditch my bike where I'd parked it. I'd come back for it later. With my heart pounding, my senses on alert, I headed toward town on foot. I wandered on the edge of the lighted pathways, keeping to the shadows, always looking and listening for anything out of place that meant something wasn't right, that someone followed. But no one did. As I hit the Gibbs Street Bridge, I relaxed a little bit. No one seemed to be paying any attention to me.

Once back in town, I used the crowds lining the streets for

cover. Most of the people walked with purpose, eager for home or friends, perhaps even a lover at the end of the workday.

As each shop door opened, dispelling chattering customers laden with packages, a bit of holiday music trickled out with them, stirring a memory. *Cinnamon and spice perfuming the air, with a little smoke mixed in. Bing Crosby's smooth tones. White Christmas. Another time; same song. A woman, still lithe with youth, stirring a pot on the stove. Two children at the table, very young, crayons clutched in fat fists. The details of the kitchen blur in the background. Whose house? I can't tell. My heart swells with love...and fear. I clutch a hand to my chest. Yes, fear.*

Who were they? My mother, my brother and myself? But, I was almost sure, my mother had dark hair, not blonde like the lady at the stove. I closed my eyes. I could smell the sauce simmering in the pot. Something Italian with oregano and basil, a hint of garlic. My mother, caught by her own demons, never cooked and hated Italian food. I suddenly knew this as if two synapses touched, closing the connection.

Captured by the memory, relaxing into the crowd, I startled at a bump from behind.

"Sorry." A male voice. Strong hands grasped my shoulders.

Without thinking, I grabbed one hand in both of mine, shrugging from under his grasp as I whirled, peeling his hand back and over. I bent his arm until his knees buckled. Pain cut short his cry.

The flash of fear in his eyes stopped me. Horrified, I let go of his hand and backed away as shocked by my response as he was. "I'm so sorry."

He knelt for a moment massaging his hand, working his elbow.

"Are you okay?" I eyed him, ready to move in again if I had to. My breath coming in ragged gasps, blood fueled by adrenaline pounded in my ears.

He pushed to his feet. Working his shoulder and elbow, he backed away. "I'm fine. Learned a lesson for sure. Merry Christmas."

"Merry Christmas," I said to his back as he hurried away.

Why had I done that? How did I know how to protect myself like that? I ran a hand through my hair and tried to pull myself together. A memory. That's what had happened. I'd lost myself in a memory. I'd been afraid of something. Then the man had grabbed me.

The memory was gone. But the emotion lingered. Love. A trace of cinnamon. Fear.

Determined not to be surprised again, not to lose myself to the memories searing through my brain, a cauterizing caution, I stepped into a doorway. Pressing against the glass storefront, I gathered myself. *You knew how to do this. To stay safe. To see them before they saw you.* Searching deep inside for that knowledge, that instinct born of a life undercover, I stepped back into the flow of humanity.

My head on a swivel, my eyes searching, I spotted the first guy leaning against a post across from the Apple store. Dressed in jeans, trail shoes, plaid flannel shirt, and a down vest, he had the Portland uniform down. The hard look on his face though, that set him apart. His thin lips pulled into a tight line as his eyes probed the crowd. When he scanned my way, I tucked into a doorway. Looking through the corner of the display window fronting the street, I watched him. He pulled a pack from his breast pocket and shook out a smoke.

There wouldn't be just one.

I watched the sea of people flowing past, cataloguing behaviors, glancing quickly at the reflection in the glass in front of me, watching my back. Wouldn't be good to let someone sneak up behind me.

The guy across the street, sitting in front of a Chinese takeout shoveling noodles into his mouth with a pair of chopsticks, caught my attention. I watched him longer, but I wasn't sure.

The man on my corner with the sax, the Watchman I'd dubbed him, ambled into view behind me, his duster blowing in the breeze, a scowl on his face as he hunkered against the chill.

I didn't turn as he stepped in behind me.

"They're looking for you." He smelled of soap and the

woods and a hint of greasy fries and cold hamburgers. A serious look replaced his normal kind smile. His eyes were hard. He looked hungry.

"How do you know?"

"They were hanging around outside your place. I guess somebody told them you weren't coming home. I followed them. They led me here. And here you are."

"How many?" My attention turned back to the crowd.

"Four. That one." The Watchman nodded toward the man leaning on the pole. "One more on Yamhill one block down at the corner—he followed you here. Don't know where he picked you up. Figured you'd be on your bike."

He followed me? How did I not know? How did I not see him? "Where are the other two?"

"One is watching the river road."

"Let me guess. The last one is at my place."

"Across the street on my corner. From there he can see the front entrance and the entrance to the garage."

"I know they didn't follow me to the hospital. How'd they pick me up again?"

"You're sure you weren't followed?"

"Absolutely," I said with more conviction than I felt, given a brain that often misfired and attention that was often railroaded. Then my shoulders fell, burned by the reality that someone had indeed been tailing me and I hadn't picked him up.

The Watchman, his breath a thin trail of white in the cool, moist air, watched the guy through narrowed eyes. "You got a phone?"

I tugged the device from the front pocket of my jeans. My lifeline. No, my life. "Yeah."

"iPhone, nice. It has an internal GPS. If somebody's got the right app, they can pick up the signal, track anybody."

"That easy?" I was horrified.

"Anybody can do it. Hell, the cops even have this device that can trick your cell phone into giving up its number, its location, all kinds of stuff. Wouldn't be surprised if some of those things are floating around in the private sector. Stuff has a way of getting out. Nobody's got secrets anymore."

If only he knew. "How do I turn it off?"

"Technically, they say you can turn off the GPS by turning off something called Location Services. But everything I've read says the GPS still radiates your position."

"How do you know all this?"

"I've been around. Amazing what you learn."

I didn't know what to make of that, so I parked the thought, hoping I'd remember it later. I'd felt in the crosshairs since the dead guy showed up. Nice to know my paranoia wasn't overblown. "Any way to really turn it off?"

"The phone doesn't ping the system when it's powered down. But the minute you give it juice, they'll be waiting. Best to let it go."

"What?" My brain ground to a halt. The world around me disappeared. "Give up my phone?" I could hardly say the words.

"You can get another. The GPS tracking is tied to your phone number, though, so you'll need a new one."

"I can't." Fear scattered my thoughts like a cue ball at the break. Everything I needed to remember was in that phone. I stared at the small device cradled in my hand. *I* was in there. Where I lived, where I worked, my schedule, my thoughts, my needs, my goals, the details, the semblance of a life...of me.

The Watchman nudged me. He angled his head toward the man leaning against the light pole. "See."

As if on cue, the guy glanced at his phone. As he pocketed it, he turned and looked straight at us. Before I could react, the Watchman grabbed my phone and set it on the window ledge. "Let's get them chasing someone else for a bit." He grabbed my elbow and pulled me with him. "Come."

My legs refused to cooperate as I staggered like the Tin Man, fear binding my joints as surely as rust. "I can't leave my phone." I reached back for it.

"You must." Despite the years etched into his face, the Watchman was surprisingly strong. He pulled me away. He lifted his chin in the direction of the man following us. "Now is not the time. We are at a disadvantage."

Light pierced the confused cry in my head. "I don't want to get somebody else killed."

The Watchman eased me around the corner of the building and down the alley. "Okay." He stepped around me and grabbed my phone. "I don't think they want you dead. It looks more like they want you."

"I wish people would quit telling me that." I stopped, jerking my hand from his. I remembered someone saying that before! Things *were* sticking.

As we strode away, he flicked the phone into a sewer drain in the curb.

I stifled a scream as I felt myself falling into darkness with the phone.

"Come," he demanded, bringing me back from the edge.

After rounding the next corner, heading south now, the Watchman pressed me back against the building with an arm across my chest. Sneaking his head out, he peered around the corner, then pulled back. "The other guy I fingered is gone. It didn't take long for them to see you were on the move." The Watchman smiled. Perfect teeth. Mean eyes.

"I wish I could see their faces when they think we disappeared down that sewer."

"After all you've seen and been though, I'd expect a bit of anger." The words escaped before regret shut him down. I saw it in the downturn of his eyes.

"How do you know what I've been through?" Something cold and sinister licked the back of my neck. "Who are you?"

"You don't remember?" Grabbing my hand, he pulled me with him as he took off again back down Fourth Street, then right on Taylor.

I worked my hand loose as I struggled to keep pace with his long stride. I stopped. A car horn blared. I ignored it as I held my ground in the middle of Fifth Street at the end of the block. "Remember? Remember what?"

From the safety of the far side of the street, he looked at

me. He didn't try to convince me to come with him. He didn't cajole or plead. No, he said the only thing I couldn't resist. "Kate, I've known you a long time."

My breath came fast. I raked the hair out of my eyes. I tried to focus. The horns multiplied. "What?"

"New York." His eyes flicked toward the traffic. "This isn't the place." He extended a hand. "Come with me. I mean you no harm. I'm trying to help."

The guy in the lead car rolled down his window and leaned out. "Lady, I don't know what he did or didn't do, but give the poor sucker a chance and get out of my way. I got my own woman who's gonna be pissed if I'm late."

The Watchman stood ramrod straight and watched me with those silent, knowing eyes. He wore an old duster that fell below his knees, making him look like a character out of an old movie. His hair military-short, his strong jaw, he looked trustworthy. And he'd never hurt me before. If he'd wanted something from me, he'd had plenty of time to show himself. Months in the making, our relationship had been cordial, caring, if not warm. I'd not detected even a whiff of ulterior motive. Now, I wasn't sure, distrusting of everyone, even myself...especially myself. He glanced over my shoulder then motioned with a slight come-here movement of his left hand. "Come. I can tell you what I know. How I know you." He leveled a stare. "I can help you find what you're looking for."

"And what would that be?"

"You."

Despite every warning bell on the planet going off in my head, I couldn't resist. Not that. Not the chance of some of the holes being filled in. Yet, I wavered. *Be smart.* I sensed the noose closing. Darting out of traffic, I joined the Watchman.

He pulled me tighter against the building, then slowed our pace, letting the holiday throng shelter us a bit. "Remember, they're watching. Four of them. Two of us."

We inched our way west, taking the less traveled streets. "Where are we going?"

"First, Pioneer Square—Portland's living room." He gave a wry smile, just a hint of tick-up at the corner of his mouth.

Scanning, his eyes moving, probing the crowd, he didn't look at me. "We need to find you a few clothes so you can blend in."

My worn jeans, torn on one knee, flannel plaid shirt faded from love, and the scuffed Merrells cushioning my feet squarely branded me as a local. "Fit in?"

"Different crowds have different uniforms."

At the next corner, he stopped. Easing his head around the corner, he muttered, "Shit." He pulled back and pressed up against the wall.

"What?"

"The guy at your place is walking this direction. He has a friend with him. They act like they know where they're going."

"What?" I tried to put the pieces together but I couldn't. "How?"

He bent around me, looking over my head back the way we had come. "Damn. The other two."

I whirled. I could see them in the gaps, working their way toward us like salmon swimming upstream.

"We need to split up," the Watchman whispered. He grabbed my shoulders, his eyes locking on mine. "Pioneer Square. Remember that, Katie. Meet me there."

My heart thudded. I could feel the cold of sweat as it dotted my upper lip. "Pioneer Square."

My vision tunneled.

"Breathe," he said, his voice calm. "We can do this. Hurry now. Pioneer Square."

"How did they know?"

"It doesn't matter. Go."

The billow of his duster as he whirled around the corner, then he was gone. Lost, no phone, my mind racing, my heart in my throat, I spied the opening of an alley to my right. I darted down it and ran as if the hounds of hell were chasing me. Which, in all likelihood, they were. I repeated "Pioneer Square" over and over under my breath as I ran. The alley intersected another. Without slowing, I took a right. The lights of the street at the end taunted me. I so wanted out of the darkness where bad things hid.

The night closed around me. The smells. Garbage. Pizza.

Another alley. A different place. The same fear. Something horrible hiding in the shadows. Someone. Yes! Fear wrapping around my heart and squeezing. I can't breathe. My knee. Pain.

I ran from the memories, from the reality, and from the place where the two overlapped.

Lungs screaming. Leg throbbing.

Pioneer Square. Pioneer Square.

At the end of the alley, I burst into the light.

Rounding the corner to my left, I dodged and darted through the crowd, a human pinball. Shouts behind me.

Pioneer Square. Pioneer Square.

Steps running, closing. I couldn't breathe.

The crowd parting. I stumbled. A hand reached out. Grabbing my arm. Jerking me around. My hand fisted, I didn't resist. Instead, I moved with him, using his momentum. As I swung, I saw his surprise.

Hank? No, someone else.

Then another face. A feeling of recognition.

Fear. Pain.

I drove my fist into the soft flesh of his throat. His hands went for the spot. A roundhouse kick to the side of his knee buckled it. He fell hard.

The crowd that had gathered parted when I turned. Once through, I ran.

Pioneer Square. Pioneer Square.

Flashes of a chase. Another time. A different place. Different faces...but one.

Hank.

Demons nipping at my heels. Gotta get away.

A tornado of thoughts, memories, fears, tore at me as it caught me in its swirl.

When the whirlwind settled, calm drifting into the edges of my consciousness, I looked around. I was alone, hidden against the cold metal of a dumpster. The place was unfamiliar.

How I had gotten here, lost?

The sleeves of my fleece and coat were hiked up exposing my arm. I'd written in large, shaky letters, "Pioneer Square." The Sharpie lay on the ground where I had dropped it. Tucking it away, I eased around the side of the dumpster.

I patted my pockets, searching for my phone.

It was gone.

Bolting to my feet, I checked each pocket again, sure I'd missed it. How could it be gone? It was *me*, for Chrissake! But it was gone...and so was I.

Except for the hastily scribbled words on my forearm.

Pioneer Square. It sounded like a place. Yes. A place I knew.

I brushed myself off and started walking. Hunched against the cold, hands jammed in my pockets, I hurried to the street. At the corner, I took a look at the clouds. The brightest concentration of light reflecting off the scudding layer would lead me to the center of the city—a good place to start. My limbs were stiff with the realization that my worst fear had been realized—I was completely lost in every way.

I'd come a mile, maybe more, before the crowds thickened. People streamed around me. With no idea as to how to get where I needed to go, I walked more slowly, ceding the outside of the sidewalk to those who strode with purpose.

Holiday music taunted me with its cheer, with a familiarity, a comfort I didn't feel but felt I should. Strains of a memory.

A shout stopped me. "There!"

My feet grew roots as a man rushed toward me. Did I know him? Squeezing my eyes shut, I searched for the answer. None came. When I looked up, he was in front of me, grabbing me roughly by the arm. "You're coming with me."

His voice was tight, hoarse. He limped.

That voice. The face. Familiar.

His slap caught me by surprise. I staggered. Stars whirled.

"You bitch." His voice carried hate and hurt.

I knew it. Fear, the hit of adrenaline. The stars vanished,

my head clearing.

"Hey!" Two men emerged from the crowd. "Don't hit her."

I didn't know them. I cowered back but the man who had hit me held my arm, his fingers cutting, biting...hurting. He pulled a gun.

The men from the crowd skidded to a stop, and raised their hands. "Whoa," one of them said. "Why don't you put that down? We can talk about this."

The man with the gun smiled a tight smile, but his eyes remained dead.

Grabbing one fist in the palm of the other hand, I bent my elbow. Using all the leverage I had, I turned, driving my elbow up into his stomach, forcing his arm higher.

The gun fired.

The shot went high, missing the men and the crowd. The two men moved forward.

One kicked the man who had hit me in his crotch, dropping him to his knees, then he kicked the gun from his hand. It skidded across the pavement and disappeared into the crowd.

With a foot to the gunman's back, the second man pressed him down. He glanced at me. "Are you okay?"

I nodded as the first man helped me to my feet. "Pioneer Square?"

"Two blocks that way." He pointed across the street.

I turned and ran.

At the entrance to Pioneer Square, I stopped. Okay, so I was there. Now what? Keeping to the shadows I moved through the park. Huddled in corners, people slept. What was I supposed to do here? I jumped at a movement to my right. A dog slinked out of a bush. Seeing me, he ran. I don't know how much time passed as I wandered, lost; then a voice hissed out of the darkness. "Kate."

I froze.

"Katie, it's me. I didn't think you'd come. I've been sick with worry."

The tall figure of a man shrouded in a long coat that

brushed his feet stepped in front of me. I stepped back. "Do I know you?"

"Yes. And I know you." He moved toward the light at the edge of the park. "Come. You will see."

I followed him; I really didn't see any other choice. At the light he turned and waited, not making a move toward me.

"You told me you know me. Who are you? How do you know me?"

"Later."

"No. Now." I pulled to a stop. Panic scratched under the surface. Already, without my phone, my grasp gone, I felt myself floating away. "I need some answers, and I need them now. Everybody seems to want a piece of me. And you're awful insistent I come with you. Why?"

His lips thinned with effort as he summoned patience. "I met you in New York. You helped me."

Breathing deep, I willed my thoughts to quiet. "New York?" I pulled back. New York is where it went bad. I was pretty sure of that.

"You were a cop." He moved in close and put my hand on his face. "Look. See. You know. You remember."

I tried to calm myself, focus...go back. *The street. Cars. People. Another cop laughing. A man.* Looking back in time was like trying to make out details as daylight faded. "You were lost."

"In a way, yes. You helped me find my way back. You didn't have to." Kindness and concern softened his face and took the darkness out of his eyes.

The person he said I was helped me deal with the person I had become.

"We need to go," the Watchman whispered. "They are looking."

We stepped back into the square at the corner of Yamhill and SW Sixth Street. The night's darkness deepened as we moved away from the streetlights. Figures, huddled in mounds under the cover of blankets, cardboard, newspapers, or whatever they could find to fend off the winter's chill and hold in what body warmth they could—which would have a lot to do with what they had found to eat that day. The Watchman stepped over figures, greeting each with a hushed word or a squeeze of a shoulder. Periodically, he would pause to question someone further. Items changed hands. Occasionally, he would drop to even more hushed tones and nod in my direction. Most didn't bother to look. Barter for food and shelter, the necessaries. No need to feign interest when there was none.

I crossed my arms, ducked my head, and hid in the shadows. Without my phone, I worried I was disappearing. My thoughts turned inward. I couldn't even reach Dan. What had I done?

But I remembered Dan. And the guy in the tub. And a cop, a detective...like I had been.

"Don't think that way." The Watchman materialized at my elbow.

"What way?"

"Once you let it in, doubt has a way of eating away at you, killing you from the inside." Separating the garments, he shook them out. "Not the cleanest, and they may have bugs, but it's the best I could do." He proffered a knit hat and a stained down vest. "Give me your jacket."

Reluctantly, I shed my new Columbia with the bright green collar. "It keeps the wind out, too." I didn't watch. I knew he would give it to one of the mounds under a tree. "Not an even trade," I groused when he returned.

"We had the more immediate need."

I pulled the hat low to hide my blonde curls and shade my face. I tried not to think about lice. The vest was a bit easier, but it smelled of old grease, rotten food, and a broken life.

"You'll be fine." The Watchman grabbed a handful of dirt from one of the seasonal flower installations in the square and scrubbed my face with it. "No one will see you now."

Two beams of light poked and slashed through the darkness.

"Flashlights," the Watchman whispered, his hand on my arm. "Did you tell anybody you'd be here?"

The lights paused, illuminating faces. Gruff voices barking questions. Moving closer.

"I don't know." I forced myself to stay still, to not turn and run. I had a vague feeling I'd asked someone how to get here, but I wasn't sure. "Why?"

"Cops. They're looking for someone."

"Me?" I let him lead me further into the darkness.

"Not going to stay to find out."

We kept to the shadows. Leaving the park, we were exposed for a moment before we ducked into the swarm of people. As I followed him through town, the river of people parted to go around us. Not one person made eye contact. No one saw. The Watchman was right—dress the part, hide in plain sight. I'd done this before. I felt the whispers coming back to me. I'd learned how to handle the streets. But how? Where?

CHAPTER FIVE

Once we'd left the Christmas crush behind, I spoke in a whisper, perhaps in reverence to the ghosts I felt lingering near. "I don't give a rat's ass about me, but I sure as hell have a bone to pick with the lowlifes working hard to get my attention. Where are we going?"

The streets turned narrower, darker. Old buildings pressed close like wolves circling their prey. The air felt colder here. Boards warped with time and inattention covered most of the storefronts. Metal latticework covered those not boarded up. Graffiti spoke to those who knew the code and served as a warning to those who didn't.

The bulbs in the corner light had been shattered—probably a gunshot. The cold fingers of a slight wind brushed the back of my neck and skittered trash in the alleyways. Somewhere a dumpster lid banged. An animal scuffled in the darkness. I reached for the gun I didn't have. No gun, no phone, and short on wits.

"In here." He stopped at the opening into the hull of an abandoned warehouse not too far from my apartment building. Urban revitalization had yet to reach this far into the old warehouse district. He pushed aside a thick plastic covering and ushered me inside.

A few steps in, I paused. The light was dim, the air heavy with a fog of acrid smoke that made my eyes water. Fire pots glowed, bright spots of warmth across the room, disappearing into the far reaches of the cavernous room like lights smothered in a fog. Billowing columns of smoke arose from the ones I could see, collecting into a rolling cloud on the ceiling, fingers of smoke probing each crevice looking for a way out. People huddled in small groups around the fires. Some were cooking. I thought I smelled hot dogs. My stomach growled.

The Watchman moved from group to group. A whispered word, a package of food—scraps from a restaurant folded in nice white paper—a piece of clothing, a book, he had something for most of them. They greeted him warmly. Some gave me a wary glance, but most nodded or tilted their chin in greeting.

"What is this place?" I asked when he returned to where I waited.

"Home."

He motioned me closer as he greeted a woman with a child in her lap, kneeling next to them. "This is Angelicka." The woman, dark, angry, most likely younger than she looked, eyed me warily. An old blue blanket, the kind furniture movers often used, wrapped her shoulders, but still she shivered. A bruise bloomed under her left eye. She flinched away as the Watchman reached out. He caught her chin, arresting her gaze. Her dark eyes turned wild, like a cornered animal, submitting but afraid.

"Who did this?"

She jerked her chin free. The child didn't stir. "I couldn't get warm. I went inside for a moment. Just a tiny bit."

"I see." The Watchman's eyes turned hard, a tic worked in his cheek. "I can—"

She grabbed his hand in one of hers. "No," she pleaded. "You mustn't. It would be worse."

"There are people who will help you."

"I have no papers. They will send me back." She gave him a piercing stare. There was madness there, or maybe unadulterated terror, which I'd learned were pretty much the same thing. "That would be worse."

He glanced at me, catching me off guard. "There are people who will help, even without papers, right?" There was something lurking in his words, a subtext lost to me.

I shrugged. "Sure." The word sounded as noncommittal as it was.

The Watchman ruffled the child's hair. It didn't stir. "Who is this fella?"

From the curls, I would've guessed a girl. The woman tightened her hold on the child, bringing him to her chest. "He is my way out."

The Watchman pulled a sack from the folds of his coat. "Here's some food. Looks like you both could use it." He touched the child's face, the brush of his fingers lingering before he pushed himself to his feet.

At the far end of the room, we climbed a circular steel staircase that was missing a few supports. It shuddered, recoiling with our weight, but safely deposited us in a small room on the fourth floor. At the top of the building, the ceilings here were higher with skylights. The Watchman ratcheted a couple of them open with a long pole, bent into a handle at the end, releasing the gauze of smoke that had filtered up from below.

Once able to breathe again, I took stock. The fact that I found myself with a slightly familiar face, in totally foreign surroundings, helped ease my mind only a little. The sight of his saxophone leaning in the corner made me relax a little. Anyone who could play like the Watchman couldn't be all bad—I just had to watch out for the part that was. "Who was that? I don't remember her name."

"Angelicka."

"Right." I wiped my sweaty palms on my jeans. I didn't even try to remember. With no phone to dictate into and panic scattering my composure, remembering was an impossibility. I patted my pockets until I found my Sharpie. "What's her story?"

"She is one of the many who pay to be smuggled into the country. Once here, they have no family, no place to go, and, worse, no papers. They end up doing what they can to survive.

Most don't make it."

"Was that her child?"

"No. He was stolen from somewhere. Not close by. The thugs who run the ring make sure of that." His voice turned hard. "The take is more for a woman with a child."

"Stolen?" My voice turned hard. The Watchman didn't answer. What could he say, really? "The take?"

"Panhandling. It's like pimping but without the sex. Less money but less exposure and fewer consequences for the guys who run the ring."

"Beggars don't get arrested; usually just run off," I said, my thoughts hanging up on something in my past. How did I know this? "The kid." I fisted a hand in the fabric of his coat. It was thick with grime. "Shouldn't we do something?"

"Yes. But not yet."

I started to argue. He put a hand up, quieting me. "The time is not right."

"But that child. Something was wrong."

"Yes, the child complicates things. We can't wait long."

"Why didn't he move? He didn't move, did he?" Even now the memory was escaping like the smoke through the skylights.

"Drugs."

"Shit." My blood boiled. At his warning glance, I lowered my voice. "How can you sit here and not do anything?"

"We will. When we can do something good. You must trust me." He unfolded my fingers from his coat. "The child will be okay for a bit, as long as we keep tabs on him."

Like a spur to a horse, the prick of anger prodded me. Anger born of frustration, the unknown, a feeling of powerlessness, long smoldering, was quick to light. "Trust you." Misplaced trust had bitten me once before—I felt the sting. How did I know that? I turned inward, searching, and found nothing more than a feeling, a sense of dread. "How do you know me? I want details."

The Watchman didn't answer as he set to lighting a fire in a small hibachi which he'd vented through a side window. "Hungry?" he asked as he blew gently on the coals. The glow from the coals painted his features an otherworldly hue. The side pipe whisked away any smoke. Clever, really, which created more questions.

Chilled, I moved closer to the fire. Crouching down, I warmed my hands as I met the Watchman's eyes. "Tell me."

"What do you remember?"

"No details, only feelings, really. Trying to see into the past is like looking down the highway in the fog. Outlines. Movement. Something familiar. Perhaps that's why I stopped to listen to you in the first place. I have a problem with my memory."

"I know."

"How do you know that?"

"I watch you, follow you."

"Why?" I eased back, putting a little distance and the hot fire between us.

"To keep you safe."

"Why?"

"Return the favor. I figure I owe you." He rooted in a cooler chained to a support column within reach and brought out a pack of hot dogs.

"How'd you find me?"

"Like I said, nobody has any secrets anymore." He popped open a blade he'd pulled from his pocket and meticulously cut a slit in the package. "If I can find you, I figured when they started looking, they'd find you, too."

"But the—"

"Marshals Service?" The Watchman gave a derisive snort. "You're not a high priority for them now. And, being Feds, they drop you once you've served your purpose."

"I don't believe you." There was a story lurking there in between his words, one that perhaps jaded his perspective.

"Free country." The Watchman carefully laid three hot dogs on the grate over the whitening coals. "One or two?"

"Two, please."

He put one more hot dog next to the others. The aroma

and the sizzle had me salivating.

"You have a unique medical situation. How many experimental programs like the one you're enrolled in are there, do you think?"

"I have no idea."

"Two." He let that sink in while he stuck each dog with the point of his blade, then rolled them a half-turn. "Here and Stanford. They know what you look like, how old you are. Someone your age with your condition...it's damn rare."

"Thank God." Pulling my knees to my chest, I circled them with my arms. They'd found me. Now what? I let my mind drift. Memories flashed by like space debris at warp speed—a flash too quick for recognition or even full awareness.

Sam.

"Sam." The name burst from me, unbidden. "Your name is Sam."

A sadness crinkled the skin around his eyes. "Yeah. Sam."

Excitement thrummed in my chest, scattering my focus. Could I remember? Willing myself to calm, I closed my eyes and relinquished myself, traveling on snippets of history. Broken and disjointed, my thoughts wandered down dark alleys only to find a dead end. "You were on the street. Don't know where." I opened my eyes, seeing him in a new light.

"New York."

I reached for my phone. It wasn't there. Panic. Where was it?

"We'll get you a new phone."

"My phone is *gone*?"

"Don't worry. You're safe here."

Curiously, I did feel safe, which beat the demons back. I knew this place, or one like it. I carefully blocked in small letters "Sam" and "New York" on my forearm, then pocketed my Sharpie. "I need my meds."

"Going home wouldn't be in your best interest right now."

"It's not in my best interest to miss my meds."

"I know. Tomorrow." Understanding softened the hard set to his jaw. "We'll think of something. Do you remember the men who are after you?"

I sat, crossing my legs, keeping my hands to the coals. The warmth felt good, but it didn't reach the cold I felt deep inside. "Bits and pieces. They are after me?"

"Seems like."

"What do they want?"

"I can't really say." He busied himself with the coals. "They're pretty damned persistent, though."

My stomach grumbled as the tube steaks sizzled.

He broke open a package of buns, tucking four of them open-face down onto the edges of the grate.

"You'll have to watch those. The fire is hot." I pulled my Sharpie from my pocket and looked for a clean patch of skin.

"What do you write on there?"

The Watchman's flat stare chipped at me, a knife on stone. "Stuff I want to remember."

My sarcasm shut down pursuing that line of questioning. "Tell me about what you remember about our first meeting."

"I was on the street. Forced down a path by..." He paused for a moment. The memory made him grimace. "I'd lost my home, my identity, and my sanity. You helped me find them all."

"Why?"

He shrugged. "Because. At least that's what you told me when I asked you the same question." He smiled at the memory. "All piss and vinegar you were back then, fancy detective you were."

"I'd like to think I was that person."

With his thumb, he separated two paper plates from the stack, arranging them on the ground in front of him. He had an old-world air about him, a quiet dignity. "You're not as bad as you fear."

"Maybe not. I hope not."

"Everybody has meanness in them when they need it. It's the ones who use it when it's not needed that are the problem."

"One vignette of my past is as indicative of the real me as

one brushstroke is of the Mona Lisa."

"How can you remember the Mona Lisa and not the particulars of your past?" He motioned for me to take a plate.

I inhaled half of a hot dog before I answered. "I asked the same thing. I'm not sure I understand the explanation, but only certain parts of my brain are affected at this point. And the distinction has something to do with how one learns and how one stores experiences. Slightly different mechanisms and different locations in the brain." I stuffed the remainder of the hot dog in my mouth and chewed. "How long were you on your corner last night?"

"Most of the night. Why?"

"When did you get there?"

He took a deep breath. "I went to Voodoo Donuts around five. Sometimes they give me some of the leftovers from earlier in the day. Yesterday I scored two maple-bacon bars. It was a good day."

"So you set up on the corner just before dark?"

"It was getting pretty dark by the time I got going. You going to tell me why you're interested?"

"I think you know."

His eyes darted away. His head ticked to the side. "I know the cops were there for you."

"Not for me, exactly." I waited until he looked at me. "There was a guy. Dead. In my bathtub."

His eyes widened. Blood pulsed in a vein that had popped out on his forehead.

"You know anything about that?" My stomach rebelled as I eyed the remaining hot dog. I needed to eat, but my body wanted no part of it. I set the plate down.

"Don't you want the other one?" The Watchman popped the end of his last hot dog in his mouth and chewed with relish.

"In a bit."

"Wait too long and the rats will give you a run for it."

"They can try."

"Who was the guy in your tub?" The Watchman removed the grate with a bent wire hanger then stirred the coals.

"I was hoping you could help with that."

"I didn't see anything that would make me take notice. Cars coming and going. Nothing unusual. With their lights on, it was hard to see much when they turned into the garage other than an outline."

"The dead guy's photo was in my phone." Another thing I'd lost today.

"Can you remember?"

I told him what I knew, not having any idea whether it was complete or just what was left.

"Could've been one of the hired muscle that comes around. Fancy boys who dress down to walk among us here. They don't know squat. Strangers stand out. Even though these folks have precious little, it's all they got and they aim to keep it."

"Do you know who the tough guys are?"

"They're tied to some higher-ups who've been running game downtown."

"Running game?"

"Money. The girls, like that one with the kid that's got you so hot and bothered, belong to them. The guys come to rough them up a little, keep them scared. And they want their cut of the take."

"Is that the endgame?" Every now and then I could string together a couple of links in the logic chain.

He shook his head and gave me a wry smile, like somehow he knew I'd ask. "No. The streets are dangerous as well as lucrative. Most folks down here flying signs have organized somewhat. Groups of folks have gotten together to stake out and manage a corner or a street block. They even have assigned shifts. Sometimes they make so much they pool some funds and rent a flophouse. They all live there, share the expenses, and panhandling is how they make their roll."

"But that's not what the tough guys are about."

"No. Those guys are just the money collectors."

"For whom?"

"Big shots who're into most everything. Drugs, whores at the high-class hotels, you name it. Those are the guys I want."

"Why?"

He held me with those eyes. There was pain there, buried deep, but it was there. "They're former customers of the guy who's looking for you."

Tilting my head, I read the notes on my arm. "Khoury?"

The Watchman's eyes went dark and hard. "Yeah."

"I need to know what your angle is, what side you're going to fall on when things turn rough." I glanced at the hotdog on my plate, not wanting it, but knowing I should eat it. "What's your beef with Khoury?"

"You." A tic worked in his cheek.

"Me?"

"They messed you up, and, like I said, I owe you." He closed one eye and tilted his head as he looked at me. "I gotta ask you this, so don't go gettin' all puffed up on me, okay?"

"Fire away."

"You tied in with the pretty boys? That why they've got business with you?"

His question didn't surprise me. Seemed valid since we were coming clean and all. "Not that I remember. And if I did them wrong somehow, I'm thinking it'd have been me bleeding out in the tub."

He pursed his lips. "You don't seem to work. How'd you pay for those fancy digs and that bike? That's gotta take some green."

"A friend bought it for me." I wasn't sure that was the truth, but I did know Dan had a hand in my relocation.

The Watchman flashed his perfect teeth in a broad smile. "Someday you'll have to tell me how to work that game."

I rubbed my leg and picked up my hot dog which had gotten cold. "First, you have to darn near die."

CHAPTER SIX

I hated sleep, resisted its torment. The dreams, the demons drifted in when I slumbered. Time removed from the present left me unmoored when I awakened.

Despite my warring against it, a fitful sleep had captured me. Disjointed memories, associations made by an injured mind.

"Kate! Kate! Where are you? Are you okay?"

"Let me help you."

A noise prodded me, a nudge in my side. I tensed, the voice lingered, echoing in the present. Who had that been? Someone I trusted. I felt that lingering, too. Someone I relied on. Then it was gone.

My eyes flew open, scanning for something I recognized, something to ground me in the here and now.

I didn't know this place. Panic squeezed my chest. My breath reduced to short gasps. Where was I? I didn't dare move, call attention.

I waited for the sound to repeat. The night hung soft and silent around me. Had I imagined it?

The outline of a man.

The Watchman.

Panic let go of me, and the memories trickled in. Vague, faded, but there.

The fire in the hibachi cold, the embers had lost their glow. Enough light to see by filtered through the high windows, frosted with dirt and neglect—the city lights reflecting off the low clouds. Cold seeped in through gaps in the boards, around the metal frames of the windows, making my nose run as I huddled in my blanket on the bare floor. An itch bloomed on my right shin, another on my stomach. What I'd give for a hot bath.

In the dim light, the Watchman sat cross-legged, his back propped against a metal support. He twisted the cap off of a small bottle then shook the contents into his open palm. Lowering his head closer, he closed one eye, squinting as he poked a finger at the contents of his cupped hand. He counted, then recounted, and then counted again before folding his hand and funneling the contents back into the bottle. Shaking his head, he stuffed it into an inside pocket. He leaned his head back. From his posture I could tell sleep wasn't a common ally.

But what was in that bottle? If he was juiced up, we both had a problem. "What you got there?" I tried to keep my voice casual, nonjudgmental.

He clamped his lips tight and darted a glance my way.

"You can tell me. I've been straight with you."

He licked his lips and rocked back and forth. "These keep the crazy away."

"Man, I need some of those. We all got crazy. What's your kind?"

"Schizophrenia. At least that's what the shrink at the VA says. Without my meds, bad shit happens."

When he looked at me, I could see the haunt in him. "Well, we won't let you go off them, then."

"I'm getting low. The VA, well, you know the problems. I've been waiting for an appointment for weeks. But since I got no address, no phone, I might as well be invisible."

Just another vet who'd fallen through the cracks. Politicians and bureaucrats. The whole lot ought to be boiled in oil.

"A kid who bunked here some scored these for me, but I

haven't seen him in weeks. I'm worried about him, but you can't save them all." He tried for cavalier, but his voice stumbled on the pain.

"I know some folks up on the Hill. Maybe there's something I can do. How long until you run out?"

"You've got time. Thanks."

I relaxed back. Tired of running. Tired of thinking. And more than tired of worrying, I longed for peace. "Can you play me that song?"

He reached for his sax. "*But Not for Me*? That the one you want?"

"That's the one I like, right?"

He nodded. "Pretty sad song."

"Makes me feel better."

"Like somebody else traveled your pain." A knowing smile lifted his lips, then was gone. "That's what art does, connects us, fills in all the empty places. Before there were words, we had music." He settled back, cradling his sax. "I played at this club back in the day, The Easy on One-Twenty-Fifth in Harlem. A guy named Louie runs the place. We go way back. He knows more about me than my own mother. A sweet time." He shook his head at the memories, but didn't say any more.

Life was funny that way: riding high for a while, but it never lasts.

He played softly, caressing the notes. Music, the language of the heart; the key to a locked soul. This song in particular opened me wide. Don't know exactly why. Just did.

The melody massaged my tired shoulders, rubbing away the hurt, the pain...the dread. This time, in my war against sleep, I won. After he finished the song, he put away his sax, then cocooned himself in blankets.

Leaning back against a pole, I watched him drift and twitch and utter an occasional unintelligible word. Demons dogged him as well.

Keeping my eyes open, I summoned the voice from my dream. "*Where are you, Kate? Kate, talk to me!*"

He spoke to me more and more now. I tried to place the

voice, the man, but no face would come. Instead, only the disembodied voice shouting, desperate to know where I was. Maybe he was giving voice to my own fears, to my own desperate need. In many ways, I was lost. And I so desperately wanted to find all of me.

The room seemed colder, the darkness deeper than I remembered when movement downstairs caught my attention, dispelling the voice, the memory, pulling me into the present. I raised my head, cocking it to catch the sound.

"Don't move." The Watchman whispered. He remained affixed to the pole. "They usually don't come up here. The staircase stops them."

I lay back. My muscles coiled, ready, I waited and I listened. Shouts. A child cried out. Metal clattering. Men's voices, angry, mean. A woman's wail, choked in pain. It took everything I had not to fly down that staircase and launch myself into... What? Unarmed. Ill-prepared. I'd be just another casualty. That idea didn't bother me nearly as much as just lying here not lifting a finger. "I can't do this."

"You will make it worse."

Salve for a battered conscience, but not enough to deaden the need.

Cries reverberated, caught in my soul. I jumped when someone shook the staircase. The old metal rattled and groaned.

"Ain't nobody up there." A voice from below.

"You sure?" Another voice, deeper, meaner.

"Look at this thing." He rattled the metal again. "It wouldn't hold me, much less you."

"The girl is small."

My breath caught. *The girl.* A foot scraped on the rough metal. The spirals of metal groaned as they absorbed his weight. Another step. The beam of a flashlight probed the darkness through the opening in the floor. The Watchman hadn't moved. Only his eyes darted, the whites catching the light. We waited. My heart rate slowed. I closed my eyes, listening, waiting. Ready.

The metal shrieked. A pop. The whole structure sagged further. "Shit." A string of hastily muttered expletives. A thud. Free of weight, the staircase recoiled like a spring, clamoring in complaint like a wraith shaking its chains.

I let my breath out slowly. Eyes closed, I tried to imagine the movement as I listened.

Shuffling. The men moved away. Voices stilled as their footfalls retreated until I lost them in the noise of folks shifting, getting back to where they'd been. A few angry mutters. A lone child's cry. I waited until silence returned before sitting up. "They were looking for me."

"Could be. Or any other girl. But best you watch your back." The Watchman's voice was measured; I could tell he didn't believe it was another girl they'd been looking for. He shrugged out from under the blanket wrapping his shoulders. With one hand, he folded the blade of his spring-loaded pig-sticker back into the handle.

Chased by the voices calling from the past, I needed to move. "I got to get some stuff from my place." My head pounded, the pain a sharp stick behind my left eye.

"They'll be watching."

"Got any better ideas?" I rolled up my blanket and put it next to his by the pole. The chance for sleep had evaporated in the heat of unspent adrenaline. We squatted by the hibachi, staring at the dead coals.

He raked the coals with the bent wire hanger. "A fire would be nice. Let's get comfortable and we can think of a—"

He fell silent at a scraping sound from downstairs. Hurried voices hard to make out. More grumbling. Shuffling. The smell of smoke. Stronger than before. The voices rising. People yelling. Running. A feather of thin gray smoke filtered through the hole. I jumped to my feet, scanning the area as the smoke thickened. "You had to ask for a fire. Any other way out of here?" *Stupid, you're always supposed to look for a way out— or be prepared to defend your position.*

The Watchman grabbed his sax, leaving everything else. "No. Fire escape is rusted closed. Other stairs fell down weeks ago."

Quickly, I grabbed our bedrolls and blankets, then dove for the stair hole, peering into the darkness below. I didn't see the lick of flame; I just saw smoke. "I'll go first." I thrust the sleeping stuff at him. "Here, take this."

The Watchman took the blankets, already rolled tight. The bare metal, now warm to the touch. The fire was near.

"Hurry." I curled my legs around the outside of the staircase curve, then slid into the smoke, my feet reaching for the floor, my hands tight on the metal arresting my fall. Bent knees absorbed my landing, and I rolled out of the way. The Watchman tossed my bedroll after me, then disappeared. I bit off my shout when his face reappeared. He tossed down his blankets then slipped down behind me, the metal groaning with his haste. He'd slung his sax across his back, a leather strap crossing his chest. I grabbed a couple of the blankets. Shaking them out, I slung one around his shoulders then did the same for myself. Not much protection, but better than nothing. I let him take the lead. Clutching the blanket wrapped around him with one hand, I held mine closed at my chest, and tried to keep pace—not slowing him down, but not running him over either as we groped through the darkness. Everyone had cleared out. We stumbled down another staircase. The second floor. The fire must've started here. Wood groaned as flames licked. A sap pocket heated and exploded, the pop like gunfire. The fire raged as it consumed time-cured wood, sucking in oxygen until there was precious little left to breathe.

I pulled the fabric of my shirt up over my mouth and nose, breathing only through my mouth and only when I had to. The smoke was thick, our time short. Wood crackled around us until I worried the heavy beams above would come crashing down. But they held. Metal shrieked, writhing with heat. The fire roared in its greed. Bent low, keeping close to the floor where the freshest air would be, we'd covered perhaps two-thirds of the distance to the far wall and the stairs to the street when I heard a whimper.

Instinctively, I let go of the Watchman, turning toward the sound. The air thickened, a slag of smoke and embers. "Who's there?"

Silence. Then a muffled cry. Slightly to my left. I pivoted. The heat tore at me...the fire a living breathing beast gnashing in hunger. I pulled the blanket tighter. Smoke filtered through the thin fabric covering my nose and mouth, but it was all I had. Short breaths. Hold the air until I couldn't anymore. Another quick breath. Squinting against the smoke. My skin felt like it bubbled in the heat, the blood underneath boiling. My foot hit something soft and it moaned. I dropped to a knee.

"Hurry." The Watchman shouted. He'd waited.

Damn. Blind, feeling with my hands, I found him, the boy with the curls. "Angelicka?" I shouted above the roar. Surely the woman would be close. She wouldn't have left the child. Clutching the small body to my chest, I felt around a bit more. Nothing. Out of breath. Out of options. The fire licked at me, testing, tasting. I pulled the blanket until it covered the child. "*Get out now!*" a voice echoed in my head. I heard the shout as if it was real. I staggered once then tripped. Fell to a knee. My lungs cried. My vision blurred. I dropped to both knees and crawled, searching for air, one hand pressing the child to me, the other holding my weight. My knees catching splinters from the time-gouged wooden planks of the floor. I'd lost track of time, of my orientation, of everything as my world funneled down into this moment. Reach, slide, reach, slide. Nothing else existed. Each reach shorter, each slide weaker. My world imploded—pain, heat, lungs screaming for air, a brain struggling against the instinct to breathe. My vision telescoped. My elbow weakened. I faltered. *Just a little bit more.* The voice inside prodded but it too grew weaker.

A shout. "Kate! Keep going!" Hands reached out of the blackness. Pulling, tugging. Taking the weight of the child. I half fell down the stairs. A hint of cool mist hit my face. I gulped clean, fresh air. I rolled onto my back. Strong hands pulled me into the tangle of trucks angling in with their sirens blaring. I hadn't even noticed the sirens.

"We'll be safe among the firefighters." The Watchman, his eyes stark in a face blackened with soot, cradled the child against his chest. "The boy needs help. So do you. Breathing smoke is shit for your lungs."

Spasms of coughs choked my reply.

Men and women leapt to action. I watched one shoulder the hose which unspooled from the truck as he ran for the hydrant at the corner. An ambulance parked behind. Doors opened in the back, ready to take the wounded.

With one hand fisted in my vest, the Watchman pulled me toward it, but he was weakening. "They might be watching. Stay out of sight."

"Take the boy," I wheezed. "I'll be okay. I just need a moment, some air." He checked the area around us, squinting into the deepest darkness. Then he pressed his knife into my hand, closing my fingers around it. I didn't watch him go. Instead, I lay back, sucking as much air into my lungs as I could without hacking one up. I stared at the sky, mesmerized by the flames also fighting for air. At first, they leapt at the glass windows that constrained them—frantic as the oxygen within dwindled. With a boom, the heat shattered the glass, letting loose giant orange fingers that roared in their greed, feeding on the limitless sky. Smoke billowed as shards of glass rained down, glinting orange and gold.

Finally, I rolled to my knees. Spasms hit my lungs and I coughed and gagged. Firefighters stepped around me, intent on saving those still caught by the fire and keeping the blaze from consuming more. One firefighter paused, placing a hand on my shoulder. "You okay?"

I looked into blue eyes, an earnest face and nodded, my voice lost to a coughing spasm.

Another set of eyes. Faded. Green? Hazel maybe. Looking down at me. Mean. Angry. Sirens sounded in the distance. The pop of gunfire.

A scream.

Mine.

A hand on my shoulder. I refocused. Kind eyes. Dark and serious.

"Thought I lost you, there." He squatted next to me. "You got a full load of smoke. Let me help you."

"No. The fire."

His eyes, serious now, flicked to the fire.

"Did everyone make it out?"

He shook his head. "Smoke. It gets them every time."

"Go." I choked back another spasm. "Save them."

He motioned toward the ambulances. "Get some help." Then he disappeared.

More sirens. Soft. Growing louder.

Doubled over, I pushed myself to my feet. I left the blanket. It smoldered where embers had landed on my back, burning through the fabric in places. Glancing behind me, I saw the Watchman spotlighted in the angled light shining from the open rear of the ambulance. Head erect, hands in his pockets, he watched as an EMT worked on the child. The boy's arms flailed. I thought I heard an angry cry, but perhaps I imagined it. The Watchman's head dropped to his chest, his lips moved.

As I drifted into the shadows, I wondered which god the damned would offer thanks to.

* * *

Hiding had become second nature. Fitting in until I disappeared, a skill set honed through hard years. A life I'd lived. Another me I used to be. I remembered.

So many personalities. So many lives.

Which was the real me?

Was she still there? Did it matter?

This was my life now.

The knife felt good in my hand, lying across the crease of my palm blade-side out, my thumb light on the switch. I felt energized, happy in a way. This was the kind of game I liked: straightforward, win or die—it was up to me. So much of the last few months had been reactive—to a disease, to doctors, to overprotective Dan. For the first time in as long as I could remember, I felt alive, like I fully fleshed out the skin I lived in...like I could *do* something about my life, not have it done to me.

My place wasn't far—I remembered that. I traveled these streets every day. The comfort of familiarity wrapped around me. I could do this.

A new building, glass and metal, my home clung to the edge of the new gentrification of the old warehouse district, right in the middle of the Pearl. New restaurants and shops tucked in industrial loft-like settings attracted a younger crowd. Tonight was no exception, but most of them, heads up, voices excited, rushed to get a closer look at the fire that painted the low clouds orange and red. I kept my eyes roving, scanning for someone still. Most people on a busy downtown street are moving. Still stands out. A predator. Watching. Waiting.

A man pushed himself off the wall as I approached, his face hidden in a hoodie. His shoulders hunched, one hand in his pocket, the other fisted by his side. I tensed as the distance between us dwindled. I couldn't see his face. I popped the knife, holding it loosely at my side. It unfolded in my hand with an audible click.

"Hey, man. Any change?" The words were raspy, his voice roughened by a lifetime of unfiltered smokes.

"I'm tapped out. Sorry."

He angled his head up to get a better look at me. Apparently, my appearance gave credence to my words. He melted back against the wall, enveloped by the shadows. I kept glancing back until I had rounded the corner, then folded the blade back into the handle, and tucked the knife into my front pocket.

Instead of approaching my building directly, I took the street one block south. Keeping my building in sight, I cut through an alley and scaled a fence behind the property. It took me three tries to hit the security camera with a rock. I just needed to angle it slightly—enough for me to squeeze in next to the side door. With the knife, I made short work of jimmying the lock. I tucked my hair into my knit cap. Then hunching my shoulders and keeping my head down, I strode across the parking garage to the stairs. Once in the stairwell, I used the railing to help haul myself up the stairs. My place would have to be on the top floor. I wheezed and coughed my way up, pausing between floors to fight for air. The smoke still lingered, leaving roughened tissue.

I tried the handle on my front door. Unlocked. I couldn't remember if I'd locked it or not. I eased inside and stopped, listening.

Home.

But it didn't feel like home anymore. Funny how a dead guy could do that. Take away a sense of security and a home became just another box. Grabbing the flashlight I kept on the small table by the door, I left the lights off as I moved quietly. The steady beating of my heart pumping mingled with sounds of sirens and the low hum of distant traffic. Diffuse light from outside, orange as it reflected off the low clouds, outlined the furniture and painted the walls, giving me enough light to see that I was alone.

Even though drawn to the windows, I stayed back. The Watchman had said the men would be looking for me, keeping guard at my place. I had to assume he was right.

Periodically, I paused to read my scribbled notes that peppered the walls, reminding me of where I put things. Away from the windows, I used the flashlight to follow my own clues in the eternal mystery of my present existence.

I gave myself a couple of minutes, max. The last note led me where I wanted—the false bottom in the lowest drawer of my dresser opened easily. I grabbed the gun, tucked it in the pocket of my vest, and zipped it closed. The note, which I'd protected in a plastic bag, I secured in an inside zippered pocket. Quickly, I stashed the credit cards in a different name, a driver's license to match, and enough cash to keep me clear for a while—remnants of a former life. *Always have an escape plan.*

I grabbed a daypack for my meds. Couldn't get too far without them. Rejection issues were the worst, Logan had said. The meds helped, but the trick was keeping the dose exactly right. Like a tightrope walker teetering over the darkness, I had to keep perfect balance. Too much one way and my body would reject the stem cells. Too much the other way, with my immune system too suppressed, cancer could take root. As if losing my mind wasn't enough to worry about.

One last thing. I reached under the couch for my memory box and gently tucked it in the daypack with my meds.

I let myself out of the building the way I had come in, careful to lock the side door to the garage, not wanting to raise an alarm when the rent-a-cop made his rounds. I didn't bother with resetting the camera. The guys weren't that good, and Dan would eventually check the tapes. I knew him; I knew what he would do. And he'd see I was okay. Maybe then he'd back off. This fight was mine alone. I had to know: *What had I done? Why did my brother hate me enough to want me dead?*

The night was cold. Perhaps, with only thin memories to warm me, I felt the chill more now. The low clouds had drifted to earth, capturing the city in white. Visibility wasn't more than a half-block. A good cover. For me and for them, whoever they were. With no destination in mind, I headed toward the center of town. My adrenaline long gone, my body cried for rest and for food. Rest would come later, when the night finally settled into its slumber. Right now, I needed food. There was a twenty-four-hour place not too far. I'd forgotten the name. Striding down Burnside, I stopped as I caught my reflection in a storefront when I passed under a streetlamp. My face soot-covered, my eyes wide, watchful...alive. My clothes filthy. The diner wouldn't turn me away. I'd been in this neighborhood before...with Stella, I thought. Yeah. With Stella.

The Roxy's neon sign blinked a pale pink. A tight, single-wide retail space, long and narrow, the diner had a counter on the right, fronted by a few red leatherette-topped stools, with a mixture of soda fountains, coffee machines, and other diner necessities along the wall behind. A pass-through from the kitchen opened at the far end. A row of cheap tables and chairs lined the left side, challenging anyone to wedge between them. Jesus hung on a large cross on the back wall next to a poster of Marilyn Monroe, a large red stop sign, and an analog clock that ticked the days away. The vibe was diner meets soda-shop eclectic with food to match.

The place was pretty empty. Nobody seemed like they had

meanness on their mind—Roxy's wasn't that kind of place. In fact, nobody even looked up when I walked in. At this time of the morning, everybody was nursing his or her own set of hurts. I took a stool at the counter. The one bleary-eyed waiter let me enjoy my three avocado bacon grilled cheese sandwiches and large vanilla shake. The shake was medicinal. It had been a million years since I'd had one. I couldn't imagine why.

"Kate?"

My back straightened. I'd checked the place out. I hadn't missed anyone.

"Kate?" The voice closer now.

Relief washed away the fear. Stella. Big and broad, with a personality and attitude to match, Stella was the closest thing to a friend I had. She was also my shrink. And as such, she knew more about me, about my past, than I did.

"It's you, right?" She brushed back a cascade of dark, tight ringlets from her face as she ducked to look more closely, her mocha skin flawless as usual. Her shawl and scarf clashed appropriately, giving her the gypsy look she cultivated. A black gypsy. I'd told her that was a stretch. She'd just smiled and told me a tall tale about a distant cousin who was Romani. "Kate. What's going on?"

Stella and I met at the beginning when I'd landed in Portland, bent and broken, lost and alone. Now we met each week. She'd told me her story until I no longer forgot.

I could learn, apparently. Just not very quickly.

"Where'd you come from?" I backed off my stool. "I'd hug you but..."

"Bathroom. The Women's was busted so I commandeered the Men's." She pushed my excuses aside and wrapped me in a bear hug. "This here's one of our safe places. You remembered."

Tears sprang to my eyes, infuriating me. But Stella was the one person on the planet with whom I could let my guard down, and just be me. No secrets. No walls. No lies. She knew the deep-down dirty as far as the official version went. And she was fine with it.

She held me strong and tight as if she knew what I felt and could give me strength with a hug. "Let's take a booth in the back. Nobody can hear, and you can tell me all about it."

Wanting to make a note to check the bathrooms before I assumed the place was safe, I reached for my phone. It wasn't there. A moment of panic. I tried to remember. "Tell you about what?" I patted my pockets. Something had happened. I couldn't remember what, exactly. I hiked up my sleeve and read the few notes I'd scratched there—a reality forgotten, that always shocked the hell out of me.

"Lose something?"

Defeated, I looked at her. "Me."

"So you gonna tell me, or are we going to stand here for the rest of the night, or what's left of it?"

"Tell you about what?"

She gave me a look, taking in the length of me. "About all of that."

I followed her gaze. "Oh."

"Yeah. Oh."

I carried a new vanilla shake for me, a chocolate float for Stella, and my daypack over my shoulder as we tucked into the shadows in the back. I sat where I could see the door. I couldn't remember why I was dressed the way I was. The streets had been in my past. Thoughts jumbled and tumbled, riding on the fear of the forgotten. What had happened to me? I worried the zipper of my fleece up and down.

"Would you quit?"

"Sorry." I leaned forward and lowered my voice. "Stell, I'm scared. I don't know what's happened. These clothes. I'm dirty and I stink."

"It's okay, honey. We'll figure it out. You know stress and panic make everything worse—you can't remember very well. Can you try to take a deep breath, relax? You're with me. I got you."

Just the sound of her voice, her presence real and tangible in front of me, helped me calm. "Okay." I breathed deep—an exercise I thought maybe Stella had taught me.

"I'm crazy so I have an excuse for being on the streets this time of night. But what are you doing out here?"

"Girl, I could ask you the same," she huffed, trying to put me off.

"We've established I'm not too sure."

She slugged a good third of her float and groaned out loud. "God, this is like an orgasm in a glass."

"I'll have to try that next time. You look unhappy. Why?"

Her smile faded as quickly as it had come. "It's Kelvin. That man will be the death of me. His place isn't far. He wanted me to stay. I wanted to go home. He didn't take it well, so I started walking."

"By yourself?" Anger flared. The ass! I knew what kind of meanness lurked at this time of the morning. While formidable, Stella was too nice to be their match.

"He had his delicates to protect, his ego being the largest by far." She waved the thought of Kelvin away. "So, let's talk about you." She placed both palms flat on the table, pushing herself backward as she gave me a sideways look. "What is going on? You shouldn't be out here all alone."

"I can't really tell you. I've got bits and pieces. Something happened to my phone. I'm dressed in these clothes." My panic started to burn a hole through me again.

"Have you talked with Dan?"

I felt my face crumple into a frown as I tried to remember.

"Honey, it's okay." She patted my arm as if that would make me feel better.

I thought for a moment. Something tugged at me. "There's something about a middleman. Somebody who had ties with a bunch of syndicates." I hiked up my sleeve and read. "And something about missing diamonds. They think I took them." I read the name twice, then looked up. "A man named Khoury."

After avoiding them for most of this conversation, she met my eyes. "What do you remember?"

"Right now? Only things I'm told and only if I write them down." I showed her the rows of neat letters on my forearm. Well, all of it was neat except for the last bit I'd written in a panic. Pioneer Square. The Watchman. I hoped he was okay. "Damn." I patted my pockets and felt lost.

"What?"

I shook off her question. I read what I'd written one more time. "Yeah, somebody thinks I stole the diamonds."

Stella nodded, looking uncomfortable, Judas applying the kiss. "I never thought you did."

"Why not?"

"In the beginning. You don't remember, but you said a lot of stuff. With your injuries and your Alzheimer's unchecked, you lacked the filters normal folks have. If you were guilty, you would've said so."

"Translation. You didn't believe I stole them because you didn't want to."

She collapsed under my logic.

"Where'd the diamonds come from?" I glanced at my forearm again. "This Khoury guy, tell me more about him."

"A money launderer. And a real badass."

I tried not to look surprised.

"As you might expect, your file was a little short on specifics, it being a criminal matter and all. You were supposed to testify against him, this Mirko Khoury guy. He had some connection to the diamond trade in Western Africa. Bad business. Blood diamonds and all of that. They flow through India and the Middle East and end up on the fat fingers of all us comfy folks."

"And he's still out there."

"Far as I know."

"Diamonds—the perfect currency for criminal operations. Their transport unregulated. The perfect currency for a criminal operation." The door in my head opened, and I told her about the guy in the bathtub, being chased, the Watchman, the fire.

"So the missing twenty million already was bought and paid for?" Stella asked.

"Yeah. I'd hate to have to tell any of those guys their untraceable diamonds just vanished."

Stella sat back, the look on her face one of disbelief. "Honey, do realize what you just did?"

"What?"

"You remembered all of that. The treatments..."

"They're working." I felt a half-smile lift the corner of my mouth. Did I dare let the hope take root?

Stella reached across the table and grabbed my hand. "You're playing in the big leagues. You're remembering, but it seems to come and go." She gave me a piercing look. "Where's your phone?"

I touched my pocket even though I knew it was empty. The realization still rocked me. The pain of the loss was as real as if I'd lost a limb. I could stagger, but my progress would be slow. "Gone." I pulled out my Sharpie and bolded Khoury's name.

Stella ignored my tiny impermanent tattoo. She'd been in favor of it in the beginning. I wasn't sure what she'd say if she got a good look at my body now.

"What do you mean, gone? I told you to tether that phone to your badass self."

"There's a good reason I didn't. Something the Watchman told me. Something about being able to be tracked through my phone. He threw it away." The memory of that moment still took my breath.

"We need to get you another," she said.

"But all my notes and photos—all my memories—are lost."

"No." Stella threw back the rest of her float like it was a martini and motioned to the man behind the counter to bring another. "We synced it to the Cloud, remember? For exactly this possibility."

"That's a good thing?" *God damn it! Why couldn't I remember?*

"All we gotta do is sync the new phone, and it'll be just like your old one—I've got all your passwords and account info. Everything will be there."

Relief flooded through me. A lifeline back to my old self. "Can you order me one?" I didn't want to go to the Apple store—my account was under one name, my ID and credit cards under another. I wasn't going anywhere as me anymore. Or at least as the most recent me—the me everybody seemed to want a piece of.

"Sure."

"Have it delivered to your office, but don't turn it on. I'm not going home for a bit. Something about finding dead guys in my tub has sort of put me off." I gave her a weak smile. "If it's okay, I'll pick up the phone and pay you for it when I come see you next. When is that, by the way?"

"Sure." She punched at her phone. "Tuesday. Nine a.m."

"And today is?"

"Sunday. Well, along toward Monday morning now. They're going to kick us out soon. This place may be open twenty-four hours, but it's closed on Monday."

Okay. Monday. Today was Monday. A good start, remember that...*Just beginning.* I used all kinds of associations to try to plant things in my memory—sometimes they worked. So many things to remember and no phone...and a limited amount of unadulterated skin. I felt myself starting to hyperventilate. Stella reached into her bag and pulled out a small notebook and pen. She pushed them across the table. "You can't go writin' everything on yourself. I need notes sometimes, too, if that makes you feel better."

It did. "My brother's name is Hank, right?"

If Stella was surprised, she didn't act it. "Good for you. Yes, Hank. Hank Hansford. He's in New York, or was, according to your file. The info on him in there was pretty recent though. The doctors..." Her face creased into a frown. "He's a cop just like you."

My surprise must've registered.

Stella nodded. "NYPD."

"Is that my name? Hansford?"

She nodded. "Kate is your real name, the one your momma gave you, if you're wondering. When they put folks into Witness Protection, they like to keep the first names. Makes them easier to remember. Fewer chances of screwing up."

I scrawled my notes then stuffed the pad in my pocket next

to the gun. "Anything else you can tell me?"

"If it were me, I'd start with your brother. But don't trust him. Terrible thing to have to say about somebody's kin. But I love you." She nodded once as if that was explanation enough, which it was. She picked up a spoon and started in on her second float.

"Why? Why can't I trust him, Stella?"

"Nobody was chasing you or stashing dead men in your bathroom until we had to bring him into the loop."

"Good enough."

"I don't like you back on the streets." Her tone had turned all motherly. "You haven't been on the streets since you were first kicked up to detective. It's been awhile. A lot has happened."

"Like riding a bike." I focused on my shake, now a molten mess.

"But you were full-throttle then, had all your wits. Now the streets are no place for you. You'll stay with me." It wasn't a question.

"No." I held her eyes with my own. "I'll not bring my kind of trouble into your home."

"I know how you are," she said. "I can't make you do the smart thing. Well, actually I can; I could call Dan. He'd have my ass if he knew I was letting you wander by yourself, what with the men after you and all."

"WITSEC is voluntary. I've done my piece. Not that I don't appreciate your concern." The not knowing, the weight of possibilities threatened to bury me. "Stell, I have to know what I did. Who I was. Why the men are after me. I *have* to."

"Oh, baby, I know you do. But what if you don't like what you find?"

CHAPTER SEVEN

Even though I wasn't the sentimental type, I'd lingered over my goodbye with Stella. She was hurting; that much was obvious. She hadn't wanted me to, but I'd walked with her, the two of us weaving our way in the dark, arms looped, me listening, Stella doing the talking for a change. The connection had been medicinal, which surprised me, and the goodbye harder than I remembered, which didn't. She was the only accessible link to my past. Somewhere in the years gone by was the key to my survival. I didn't know where. Not yet, anyway. Dan was the only other person with my complete WITSEC file. I fought the urge to call him—Stella had his number. He'd always been there, but he would just argue with me, and right now I didn't need another voice in my head. I'd have my phone soon. I'd call him then. He deserved it. Pressing myself against the building across the street from Stella's, I waited until I saw a light flick on, her familiar face pressed to the window as she gave me a wave. Had I told her I'd wait? I didn't know, but she'd looked anyway. Somehow, that made me feel good, as if I was the kind of person who would wait, and not the kind I feared I might be.

With my hands stuffed in my pockets, one curled around the grip of my gun, the other holding the knife, I kept my head down but my eyes moving. I'd read the notes on my arm. *Pioneer Square.* Surely there would be a corner I could hide in there.

Safety in numbers. The thought sizzles through my brain. *Kids. Someone lecturing them. Stay together. They look up...at me. I stop. Blinking, holding the memory. A boy and a girl. Blonde, blue-eyed. Young. Maybe four and three? I don't know them. And yet, I do.*

A guy stepped around me, jolting me back. *Pay attention.*

Two blocks and I eased into the relative comfort of darkness and a quiet crowd huddled in sleep. I chose a spot near the top of the steps, with a wall to protect me on two sides, and pressed into a corner. The shadows were deep here. If I stayed still, I wouldn't draw attention. From here I could watch the movement, people stirring, folding blankets, walking among those who slumbered on.

I waited. Shivers spasmed through my body—the vest and my light sweater poor protection against the coldest part of the night. When I'd gone home, I hadn't remembered to get anything warmer, not that I had much. In fact, I couldn't remember what I had. Seasons came and went, fading into each other. The days drifted by. Sometimes I had to check my phone to see what day it was, what month. My days had no structure, no link to the changing of the seasons.

But cold. That was a visceral reminder that time was not.

Working to control my body and contain the pain as the cold robbed my flesh of its warmth, I scanned the area in front of me.

Fog still hung low, tiny crystals of ice that sparkled with the first glow of morning. A woman shuffled by, then stopped, peering into the darkness at me. "You're the fancy rich bitch who had the slick jacket the other day. The pretty warm one with the green collar. Look at you now—Miss Fancy Pants shivering in the cold like the rest of us." Her eyes held a gleam of hate. "Excepting Benny, he's the one who's got your fine coat. The man gived it to him for all he done." She gave a cackle that raised the hair on the back of my neck. I'd had a jacket, a warm jacket? With a green collar? I tried to remember, but the memory was gone.

The new day brightened, the fog slowly lifting, when I saw the new owner of my jacket. Benny. I'd written the name on my forearm. Actually, I caught sight of a jacket and its lime green collar poking out from under a mound of blankets, and figured it was mine. And I wanted it back.

Huddled, his knees tucked, his chin lowered, Benny still slept. Numb with cold, fighting sleep, I really needed that jacket. I knelt beside him, careful to keep some distance, stay out of his space. Folks on the street guarded their space with the ferocity of junkyard dogs. Leaning over, I jostled his shoulder, then retreated. He didn't move. I jostled harder. "Hey, wake up!" Still nothing. "I want my jacket back." My teeth were chattering and this guy was out cold. That would've struck me as funny if I wasn't so damned miserable. "Hey!" I pushed harder. "I can pay."

A female voice growled, "Leave him the hell alone. Man needs his sleep. He won't take kindly to your pushing on him. So go away. And shut up while you're at it. I need my beauty rest, you know." She challenged me to smile at that last bit.

I didn't. Something in me snapped. I was cold, tired, hungry again, and running for my life from people I couldn't remember. Anger flared and I pulled out my gun, leveling the sight on her. "Shut the fuck up."

Big Eyes watched me, but she kept her yap shut while I prodded the guy again, this time so hard he rolled over onto his back. His eyes, open and sightless, stared up into the foggy darkness. His lip was split, his eyes blackened. A cut across one cheek had oozed a bit, the blood now crusted. I felt for a pulse, even though his skin was already cold. I pulled open the jacket. It took me a minute but I found it, a slit, just enough for a narrow knife blade. Another stab wound under the ribs, then the rip down his belly. This time the guy hadn't bled. *Fuck.* I sat back on my heels. "What the fuck did they want with you?" I whispered, willing his silenced voice to answer. He still had his stuff: my nice jacket, a bedroll, things that had value on the streets. Then it hit me.

They hadn't wanted *him.*

They'd seen my jacket with the reflective piping and lime green collar. Pretty distinctive. And expensive. But nobody had taken it. No, they'd left it because that wasn't what they were looking for.

They had been looking for *me*.

"Well, look no further, assholes." Tired of running; tired of being chased by men I didn't know because of a past I couldn't remember, I stripped the jacket off the guy. The green collar felt like pasting on a target. Scared the hell out of me. Could I see them coming? Could I stay alive? As I rolled up the man's sleeping gear and tucked it under an arm, I realized I didn't much care.

If I couldn't remember my past, I had no future.

If I couldn't find the answers, I couldn't solve the problem.

Before I left, I crouched down and brushed his cheek with my fingers, then closed his eyes. "I'm so sorry."

The lady who'd been baiting me started mewling, her eyes wide with fear. "You stuck him. You gonna do me, too?"

I couldn't tell whether she feared I might or hoped I would. "Don't be stupid," I hissed. Ducking into an alley around the corner, I transferred my possessions to the coat pockets, then ditched the vest next to a dumpster. Somebody would find it soon.

Then I turned and slipped into the fog.

Curled into a storefront down by the river, I waited for the daylight to chase away any hint of darkness as I made notes in my journal. I couldn't face the demon that drifted in with sleep, not today, not now.

What a difference a jacket and a bedroll made. I felt bad about taking the guy's stuff, but if I hadn't, somebody else would've. Things didn't go to waste on the streets.

Despite my fear, sleep found me. When I awoke, the sun was higher, the gauze of fog now lifting. After tucking my journal in my pack and rolling the bedroll up, I stood, testing the aches and pains. My body rejoiced at the movement as I strolled through town. My knee hurt, but less so as I kept moving, watching, looking for the guys who'd chased me. I'd gotten a pretty good look at two of them. I blended in with the thickening foot traffic as everyone headed to work. The clock on the top of the courthouse said nine o'clock.

I'd asked a bum last night where I could get warm and find some information. The library, he'd said—I'd made a note. He'd even given me the address. As he'd talked, some of the skills of surviving on the streets filtered back—I'd remembered.

The Central Library probably wouldn't be open this early. Coffee sounded good. I bought a large cup off a food truck two blocks down. The steaming brew barely warmed my semi-frozen insides. My stomach growled so I went back for a bagel.

With forty-five minutes to kill, I tried to think about what I might need if I was going to keep moving around, living on the streets. A pair of gloves would be nice. Hurried, my focus fractured by random thoughts forming...staying. Memories? This sort of fogged state was normal after my treatments—Dr. Faricy had reminded me. But this one seemed stronger, more distracting...more hopeful.

As hope lifted me, the prick of reality brought me back—I hadn't been able to remember to grab warmer gear when I dashed through my place. The gun, the note, and some money, those things I'd gotten. Glad I had, but still.

I pulled out the key in my pocket and read the note. I'd left my bike in the hospital tram parking lot. The note didn't say anything about any gloves I might have left in one of the hard cases. But recent events had me jumpy and I didn't want to go near my bike right now.

Prodded by nervous energy and a disquiet, I kept moving. And kept watching. Counting the blocks, squaring turns, I marked them in my journal. Without my phone, I didn't trust myself to stay oriented, especially with the bolts of memory flashing.

After making the turn on the west side of downtown, I found myself in front of the Columbia Employee store. Shivering, hunched against the cold, I cupped my hands around my eyes and peered through the glass. Gloves, parkas, and scarves, goaded me to push through the door. Keeping contact to a minimum was one of the keys to handling the street; I remembered that. But I didn't think the guys looking for me would be hanging in the Columbia store.

A bored clerk gave me the once-over, not even trying to hide her look of distaste mixed with compassion. "Hey, you got any gloves? I can pay."

She reached into a bin under the counter and pushed them across the counter to me. "Take these."

I pulled out a crumpled bill. "Will ten bucks cover it?"

"Forget it." She pulled out a wool cap and a scarf. "Here. Keep warm. It might snow later."

I ducked my head in thanks. "Merry Christmas." Once outside, grateful for the added warmth, I pulled out my pad and made a note. Her nametag had read "Carey."

With the new hat pulled down to just above my eyes, I ditched the old one the Watchman had scored for me...it probably was infested with something awful. Just the thought had me scratching. I wrapped the thick scarf, covering the bottom half of my face. With both in place, I was unrecognizable. Except for the green collar on my jacket. *Come and get me, assholes.*

Life on the streets was a disconnected existence in the middle of a sea of humanity. Libraries provided a haven from the cold, a cup of hot coffee, often a warm smile, and, almost as important, the Internet.

The warmth hit me as I pushed through the doors into the marble interior. I pulled my cap off my head and unwound the scarf, sticking both in my jacket pockets. Running my fingers through the curls, I tried to rake them into some order, some acceptable appearance.

Apparently I succeeded. The girl at the desk didn't recoil; in fact, she helped me negotiate the computer connection and explained Google, which I was grateful for. Then she moved away and left me to figure out the rest out. My brother's name was Hank. I checked my notes on my arm, which earned some curious glances. I was glad everything I needed didn't require me to look at my leg, too. Just my arm and in the notebook Stella had given me. Hansford.

Amazing all the stuff you can find about somebody on

Google—perhaps I knew this before. Scanning the screen, I felt the pang of familiarity. I scanned the various files, making notes about his work history. Couldn't find anything personal, though. No family information or pictures. Maybe cops kept those sorts of things close. What I found were random facts I should've known; they felt familiar. I didn't remember, not consciously anyway, but I felt the memories. Closer now.

His official photo stopped me dead. Even if I hadn't squirreled away a photo of the two of us, I would've recognized him. The heart remembers even when the brain forgets. He was with the NYPD, just as Stella had said. Didn't look like he still was though. And she hadn't said there'd been an IA investigation. Nothing ever proven, but I could imagine how that had affected his working environment. Trusting your life to people who no longer trusted you. Somehow, I knew what that was like.

Sucked when those things went down. Memories tucked in around me. I could remember—bits and pieces, mostly the bad things. I wondered why the good was so hard to hold onto. As a cop, I must have brushed up against the wrong side every day. Some of that taint could rub off. Living with another set of values could change your own. Had that happened to Hank? To me? I reached out and touched his face on the screen, willing a connection, some answers, but there were none.

"Somebody you know?" A man pulled out the chair next to me, jarring me back. Young, studiously scruffy, he wore cords and a parka, and an open smile.

Not one of them.

My blonde curls often attracted his type; I didn't know why. When he caught the whiff of homelessness clinging to me, something shifted in his face.

As if living on the street was my fault.

"You need help?" A lick of his lips, his eyes darting from mine. He didn't really want me to say yes.

With a shake of my head, I brushed him off. When he found what he was looking for, he left, and I relaxed with space around me.

On a lark, I decided to Google myself—well, my old self.

Kate Hansford. I checked the spelling against Hank's name to be certain. Kate Hansford. The name carried a warm familiarity—each block letter scribed in my notebook, on my skin, another step on the path back. Once sure I'd transcribed the letters correctly, I hit the search button and began scanning the list of Hansfords in New York.

But I wasn't among them.

I widened my search.

Still no me.

I was gone. I'd been erased.

I tried several more times, different spellings, formal variations of Kate. Nothing. Not one mention of the me I used to be.

As if I'd never existed.

As if I was already dead.

I logged out. Even as I'd worked, I'd kept a close eye on everyone who came near, who milled about in the corners, who even threw a glance my way. No one caught my attention. I pocketed my notes and hurried out—the cute guy was gone. The pang of hollowness inside surprised me.

Lives cross, but don't touch. A brief connection that left a deeper awareness of its lack. A safe world—a hollow life.

Once on the street I gulped the fresh air. I was gone. How could I be gone?

One thought kept pinging in my head.

I needed help.

The Central Precinct of the Portland Police Bureau was on Second Street in the heart of downtown. The detective who had worked the call the other night had given me his numbers, which I'd carefully transcribed on my forearm. I still remembered that; a pyrrhic victory, but a victory nonetheless. His office number matched the main number of the Central Precinct.

The building was gray, forbidding in its austerity, as if

challenging anyone to step inside.

The innocuous smells of old coffee, sweat, and pine-scented cleaner hit me like a drunk in full rage. I lingered near the door, leaning against the wall, fighting demons that lurked in the dark recesses in my brain. The smell reminded me of something, something bad. Something about cops. Pain. Shivering, I rubbed my arms and tried to calm the fear, the fear twisting my gut told me to run.

Snippets of my history, voices, a few random faces glaring at me. I felt alone. Exiled. *What had I done?*

I forced myself up the stairs to the front desk, fighting my limp. The officer behind the glass gave me the once-over. "Can I help you?"

What had started out as a good idea quickly faded in the harsh light of his flat stare. Dan had said something about the cops. I couldn't remember exactly what, but whatever it was, he'd left me with a bad feeling. And the sterile surroundings, the harsh institutional air didn't help. The officer gave me a look reserved for those to be pitied or scorned, depending on the capacity of your heart. That made me angry. Pity was an emotion people used to convince themselves they were compassionate. Two different things in my book. "My name is Kate Sawyer. I called in a murder the other night—a dead guy in my bathtub. I'd like to talk to the detective working the case."

"A dead guy? In your bathtub?"

I remained anchored to the wall but stood my ground, even though doubt gnawed away at me. "Yes. The detective in charge." I checked my forearm. "Detective Hudson. I want to talk to him."

"What about?"

"That's between me and him." I raised my voice. "I can see you don't believe me. Look it up. Kate Sawyer." I felt the silk rope of my self-control slip, loosen, the fingers of anger working the knot.

"And you live where?"

That stopped me. "Close." I patted my pocket for my phone. It wasn't there. "I can tell you how to get there. But I can't remember the address."

"Look. You're upset. I understand. But I can't help you if you can't give me your address."

"My name—surely my name is in there?"

"Okay." His hands poised over the keyboard, he looked at me. "What was it again?"

I stopped, Dan's voice ringing in my ear. "Your name can't hit the system, Kate. You can't trust the cops." Warm, reassuring. He'd saved me before; he had my back.

"I can't tell you."

"You gotta give me something." His look told me what he was really feeling. His words confirmed it. "Can I give you the contact info of someone who can help? At least get a hot meal in you, clean you up, and talk a bit?"

"I'm not crazy, I'm not high, and I need to speak to the detective. Now." I stuffed my hands in my pockets. One hand touched the cold metal of the gun. Seeking control, my hand closed around the grip, a finger poised on the trigger guard. My muscles tensed. My anger sparked. My voice held the edge of a threat.

"Lady, crazy comes through those doors every day." He held up his hands.

"I. Am. Not. Crazy." My hand tightened on the grip on the gun.

A head peeked through the door from the back. "You got a problem out here, Officer?"

The officer filled the second guy in. He listened, then motioned to me. "Yeah, Beck's been bending my ear about that."

"Her name isn't in the system."

"Nope. And it won't be." He waved me forward. "Come. Detective Hudson is who you're looking for. He's at his desk, but I warn you, he's in a foul mood." He motioned me through a metal detector.

A metal detector. I hadn't anticipated that. A gun and a knife. Strolling into the police station. Man, I'd just proven that officer's theory about crazy. I backed down and eased toward the door. "No. I don't want to come back there. Police stations aren't my thing. Please tell Detective…What was his name?"

"Hudson."

"Right. Please tell Detective Hudson to meet me across the street." I glanced over my shoulder out the window. "The coffee shop on the corner. It's about the dead guy."

"I can try, but no guarantees." Then he disappeared.

With rush hour over, only two people stood at the counter when I pushed inside, grateful to be out of the cold. I joined them, bought two large coffees, then picked a table in the back, away from the windows. I sat facing the door. Only one other person occupied a table—a scruffy-faced kid on a Mac near the door. I reviewed my notes, rereading them until I thought some might stick for longer than a minute. I left the notebook Stella had given me open on the table.

The detective kept me cooling my heels. I was on my second cup of joe and his was cold when he pushed through the door. His face hard, his shoulders hunched, he pulled out the chair across from me, his back to the door. "I'm working your case in name only. The Feds are holding my leash."

"I need your help."

His eyes took in all of me. I couldn't tell what he was thinking. He motioned to the gal behind the counter, who rushed over with a new cup of coffee. "You got five minutes."

I gave it to him in three.

Blowing on his coffee, he leaned back. From his expression, it was hard to tell if he was interested or not, but at least he hadn't left. "Chief's orders. Everything is supposed to flow through your buddy, the deputy marshal. He's got a tight lid on you and I'd like to know why."

"Dan didn't fill you in?"

"I got the impression he doesn't hold us brothers in blue in high regard. Or maybe it's just me and my winning personality." He didn't smile.

"He's probably thinking you're a potential leak."

"And you're not?" The look on his face told me he thought I might have been the one to bring all this down on myself.

"Who's going to believe anything I say?" I challenged him. He hadn't struck me as stupid. He could figure it out. "You don't look like the type to go talking."

"That why you're asking me to put my badge on the line?"

I hadn't thought of that. My courage leaked away. "I don't want that. I can't ask you to do that."

His face softened. "It's okay; I'm going a bit hard on you. I live with my badge on the line. Don't you have someone else who can help?"

"You're the only one who I'm pretty sure had nothing to do with what went down, what got me put in with the Feds in the first place."

"You're pretty sure?" He seemed to find that amusing. His smile, if that's what it was, was nothing more than an easing of his features, a softening of his glare. He rubbed his two-day stubble as he thought.

"On the streets, I became a skeptic," I said, playing all my cards. "Once a cop, always a cop."

He took a tentative sip of his coffee as he eyed me over the lip of the mug. "I didn't know. Where?"

I checked my notes. I couldn't write as fast as Stella talked, but I'd gotten most of it. "Undercover. New York."

"A detective, too." His posture eased a bit. Pieces of my story falling together for him, I guessed. And that whole Brotherhood of the Blue thing counted for a whole lot to those who served. I wasn't above playing that card.

I leaned forward. "Look, I'm flying blind here. I don't know who I was, who I took down, what I did. Makes it awful hard to fight back."

"What makes you think you did something?"

"My memory may have as many holes in it as a roadside sign in Arkansas, but don't play me for stupid. Innocent people don't end up with dead guys in their bathtub. I know I did something. I'm trying to find out whether it was a crime or I just stepped on the wrong toes. I don't need to know much about who I was, but that? That I need to know."

"Can you live with what you find?"

"I can't live without it. Please, I've got nobody else."

"What about Deputy Marshal Strader? Dan, I believe you called him." He eyed me over the top of his cup, the steam frosting his steely stare.

"Dan's gone way out on a limb to make sure I'm getting treatment and all of that. He set me up here because of the options for my...issues. And I love him for it. As a friend. He cares. He's saved me in more ways than I remember. And he'll keep doing that. So he will tie my hands."

The detective stared up at the mirror in the corner behind me. I'd noticed it when I came in. I let him think.

His eyes shifted back to mine. "What do you need from me?"

"For starters, do you have an ID on the dead guy?"

The corner of his lips ticked up. The smile didn't reach his eyes. "We're still running him. Funny thing. The M.E. told me the guy had sliced his fingers. One vertical cut in each finger. Old cuts; heavy scars."

I knew that trick, or at least I thought I'd heard of it before.

The detective didn't need prompting to fill in the gaps. "Two-bit hoods do it to slow the computerized fingerprint analysis down."

"And?"

"That sort of stuff pisses me off. Enough to go through some old-school channels. The guy's name is Nesto, Johnny Nesto. Been busted a couple of times in New York. Strictly small stuff. The guys back there thought he was tied in with some big players, but they never could tie him up."

Unsure of how he fit, I made notes, hoping more pieces would eventually let me see the whole puzzle.

"There was another odd thing about the guy."

I reread what I'd written before I looked up. "About Nesto?"

Beck nodded. "ME told me he had a scar down his abdomen, thick like he'd been cut open numerous times, but the M.E. couldn't find any scars on any organs." He eyed me, gauging my reaction.

I had none.

"My guess is he was a mule."

"Mule?" I didn't follow.

"Transporting contraband internally."

I flinched at the thought, my hand finding my own belly. "Like what?"

"Could be a number of things: drugs, money, things that won't trigger metal detectors."

I flipped back a few pages in my notes to the conversation I had with Stella. "What about diamonds?"

"That'd work."

"Did the name Khoury show up in any of your research? A diamond merchant in Manhattan."

His pupils dilated. *Bullseye.* "What do you know about him?"

"Apparently, a whole lot. So Dan tells me, I was deep undercover, had infiltrated the organization pretty high."

"How high?"

I reached back, but the memories were elusive. "I remember handling diamonds, large plastic bags of them and some loose stones, I think. I must've known the players, the scheme; otherwise, why would Dan go to all the trouble to keep me alive?"

"And to help restore your memory."

"I was supposed to testify against Khoury." Hope flared in his eyes, but I doused it when I held up my hand. Then I summarized from my notes—some that I'd gleaned from Stella, some from the computer at the library. "Diamonds are used to launder money and finance terrorism. They are personal property, not subject to confiscation, easily transportable across borders with no requirement to report their value. Once the diamonds are in another country, or here, it doesn't matter, they are broken down into small lots and sold to jewelry stores, that sort of thing. Most enforcement agencies aren't trained or don't have the budget to chase these guys. But men like Khoury, they are the bankers of the illegal trades. Khoury had a big pipeline of diamonds out of Western Africa, a whole herd of human mules. He facilitated the movement and the laundering of hundreds of millions of dollars a year. His cut was twenty percent...if he liked you. More if he didn't. It took me years to infiltrate, gain his trust. And then everything went to hell and I ended up here."

"Did you testify?"

"I don't think so."

He jotted notes in a notebook, then stuffed it back in his pocket. "You've remembered a lot."

"Things are coming back. The trick is holding onto them."

"From what I can see, you're running out of real estate."

Self-consciously, I tugged on my sleeves, trying to cover the letters that marched down my wrist.

He put his hand on mine. "I'm kidding. You're doing great. Does anybody else have any more information?"

"I'd love to see what's in my WITSEC file."

"Somehow, I don't see the Feds playing nice."

"There's someone else. Another file. Because of the medical issues, they keep a full file locally."

"Who has it?"

My voice turned hard. "Don't put her name down anywhere. I don't know exactly who's chasing me, and until I do, I have to assume they could be anybody, with access to everything."

"Agreed."

"If anything happens..."

"If it does, it won't be because of me."

I took my time. Could I trust him? My hand shook a little as I lifted my coffee mug to my lips. Everyone seemed to have an angle, some skin in my game. But not the detective.

Finally, I said, "My shrink, Stella Matthews. She's more than a professional handling my case; she's a good friend. One of the few I have. You can imagine how hard it must be to have friends when you can't share anything real or personal. When you don't even *know* anything real or personal."

Clearly not a man who coddled anyone, he shrugged that

comment away. Another hastily scribbled note. "Your file was restricted. I expected that. You do know Khoury got away?"

I chased that memory, then confirmed it against what Stella had said. "Do you know what happened?"

"It made the papers. Khoury was being transported from the Metropolitan Correctional Center in Manhattan to a court appearance. It was one of those operations you only see in the movies. Precisely timed. No gunfire. Boom, they hit, and Khoury was gone. The NYPD followed them through the City, but they had an elaborate plan, changing cars, driving into warehouses to avoid cameras. It was a work of art."

"Proving once again that money can buy you anything." The guys were organized, clever, and dangerous. Terrific. "Any hint of Khoury since then?"

"The Feds aren't the most sharing, especially when they're the ones with the black eye. Apparently, Khoury was busted out a little over a year ago, then vanished. Last month the Feds started hearing whispers of him getting back in the game, wanting his stolen diamonds, and dead bodies started showing up."

"Bodies?"

"Like Nesto, your uninvited bather." Beck sipped at his coffee, then grimaced. "I hate cold coffee. Look, this isn't making me feel good. Khoury is systematically taking out every person in his organization who could've turned on him. One by one."

"And the trail is leading to me."

Beck nodded, looking not at all happy.

So, he'd run me. And chased all the threads he could find. Of course he had. "Is it normal for someone to have erased all mention of me, the old me, on the Internet?"

"I wouldn't think so. The old you is common knowledge. Why?"

"Somebody took the time to scrub my digital profile."

"I know. I ran your name."

"So you know I have a brother?" I inched up my sleeve and angled my head to read. "Hank."

"The New York cop?"

I eased my notebook around so I could read what I'd written. The detective waited while I scanned. I turned it back around so he could see.

"IA investigation?" He looked up at me. "Any idea what that was about?"

"No." I pointed to the date. "I was gone by then. Everyone says he had something to do with the diamonds missing and with the Khoury bust going bad."

He pursed his lips, then bent his head over his notes, making what looked to be a list. Arrows circling, joining thoughts and actions to be taken, notes like I used to make. His brow creased in concentration, his tongue in the corner of his mouth, he looked like a kid slaving over homework.

"I've got something else I need your help with."

He finished his notes before looking at me. "Somehow I figured that."

I took out the plastic-covered piece of paper I'd removed from the dead guy's pocket from my daypack, then laid it on the table. Using my forefinger I pushed it toward the detective. I didn't meet his eyes. I knew what he'd think, how he'd feel— didn't blame him at all. "I took this from the dead guy's pocket." I didn't tell him about the gun. The serial number had been filed off, so there was nothing he needed it for, and a whole lot of use I had for it.

The detective didn't move or speak. I hazarded a glance.

"You took evidence from my crime scene."

"The Feds' crime scene."

"Still."

"If I hadn't, you wouldn't have anything to go on."

"Not sure I want it." He masked his interest.

As a detective, he had to be interested. I pressed my advantage, slight as it was. "What'd you expect me to do? I'm no good to the Feds anymore. Khoury is...somewhere. My memory is...compromised. Can you imagine what a good defense lawyer would do to my testimony? So, despite Dan's best intentions, with limited resources and more pressing witnesses to protect, they'll bury this and leave me exposed. It's how that world works. You know that."

"Yeah, but maybe you should let them—"

I cut him off. "Do what? Find the guys that are after me? They won't do it. Oh, Dan will try, but he's limited by resources and his higher-ups. If it's really Khoury working his way back in, then maybe the FBI might be interested, but not the Marshals Service. That's not their thing—they protect witnesses like me, but only if the witness has value. What good is a witness who doesn't remember?" I could see my words were making a dent in his resolve. "I'm a cop. I'm in trouble. Maybe I don't remember a bunch of details, but I've still got the heart of a beat cop, the nerves of an undercover detective. I can't sit on my thumbs while the Feds dick around with this." Emotions welled from some deep, primal place. A tear trickled out of my eye and ran down my cheek. I swiped at it with the back of my hand. "I've lost so much. My brother. My chosen life." I gave a short laugh. "Maybe even myself with this fucking disease. I've got to *do* something. I can't sit and let them take it all away." My eyes sought his. "Can you understand that?"

He stared at me long enough that my heart skipped a beat, and I thought he was going to shut me down. Then he dropped his eyes and focused on the note. "There's two stains. One looks like new blood. Most likely Nesto's." He held the note to the light as he shook open a pair of cheaters. Resting them on the end of his nose, he tilted his head back to look through them. "That other stain could be anything."

"Could be blood, too. Like maybe this is a message in a message."

"Interesting theory. The lab will test it, of course. I'll try to put a rush on it. One of the techs owes me. If it's blood, they'll run it. Who knows, we might get lucky." He didn't sound convinced as he squinted through his glasses.

"You know, they have stronger magnification in those things."

"But then I'd have to admit I needed it." The joke brightened his eyes. They had gold flecks in the blue. "I know what you did," he read from the note. "Interesting choice of words. A veiled threat, perhaps. But what response was the writer looking for?"

"Maybe they were just rubbing it in."

He rewarded me with a flash of dimples. "Or maybe they want to force your hand. Make you do something."

"Maybe. But what?"

"Depends on what you did."

"And we've come full circle."

Detective Hudson glared at the note as if trying to intimidate it into giving up its secrets. "Maybe they're trying to scare you."

"No maybe about it. But they don't know me very well. This sort of shit just pisses me off."

Finally, a full smile bloomed across his face. Yes, dimples. I so didn't want to like him. I didn't want to need him, either. At this moment, both seemed unavoidable, and I didn't know what to do with that.

"God help me, but I like you, Kate Hansford Sawyer. But, if I'm going to help you, no more holding out on me."

I nodded, knowing it was a lie.

Hank.

The detective had given me a card with all his numbers; his cell he'd added with a scribble. Told me to call him Beck.

He hadn't patronized me by asking where I was going to stay or whether I'd be all right. I liked him. That was a bad thing. Feelings had no place in a life like mine. Feelings could get you killed. Worse, feelings could get him killed.

I'd agreed to give him twenty-four hours, then we'd meet again at the same place. Before I left, I pulled my Sharpie from my backpack and hiked up the sleeve of my jacket. Exposing my forearm, I compared the numbers on the card to the ones on my skin. They matched. I added the name "Beck", after "Detective Hudson." He was there. On my skin. Leeching inside. A memory to stay. I also noted our next meeting.

With nothing to do while I waited for the detective to work his magic, I staked out my building for a while to see if the guys chasing me showed. They didn't.

With hunger gnawing, the short day dropping toward dusk, and a bite of cold riding in on the afternoon wind, I decided finding a place to bunk would be a good plan. I trailed several street folks who led me to a bunch of the homeless congregated under the Morrison Street Bridge—it looked like a regular gathering place. Another night on the streets wasn't appealing at all. I thought about a hotel room. But I had to watch my spending. Besides, a woman alone who looked like me would stand out—a clerk could be convinced to give me up. I'd be safer in the anonymity of the street. But, on the street, folks didn't readily admit a stranger. Oh, they might share their food, a smoke or two, but they wouldn't sleep next to somebody they didn't know.

Already several clusters of people had gathered under the bridge seeking shelter from the drizzle that had turned into a steady light rain. December in Portland, consistent in its damp gloom. I claimed a spot near the edge of the group.

"I don't know you." An older woman, her cap pulled low, a dirty skirt over leggings, her feet tucked into hiking boots, a parka so soiled its color was unidentifiable, gave me a harsh look.

"And I don't know you." I handed her one of the bags of hamburgers I'd bought on the walk over.

Her eyes lit when she looked inside, and I thought I was in. But then when she looked back at me, she narrowed her eyes as she looked me over. "Sheila said some gal killed Benny last night. Took his coat. One with a green collar. Like the one you got on."

I sort of remembered taking the coat back. The woman in front of me seemed certain, so I went with it. "I took his coat. He didn't need it anymore—he was already dead. I didn't kill him."

"She said you have a piece. We don't allow none of that down here."

I squatted and spread out my bedroll and blankets. "Seems to me the one with the piece makes the rules."

The others behind her grumbled. Hard to tell what they were saying, but I caught the drift. Couldn't fault them for being wary.

"She's okay," a strong voice behind me said. The Watchman. Why did his face stick so clearly when others faded? There was a memory there, something bad, or it wouldn't be so clear, so immediate.

What was it? What did he know?

The others backed down. I glanced up at him looming over me. He smelled of smoke. Smoke. I gasped as a memory caught me in its net, holding me, trapping me. The men looking for me. The fire. I cringed as it released me. "The kid okay?" I managed to stutter.

The Watchman eyed me. "Fine. Turned him over to the cops. A friend told me they got a hit. Reported missing a week ago."

I wished I could read the thoughts I sensed there behind a veil. "Where from?"

"New York."

"New York sure is cropping up a lot lately. You think the Universe is sending me a sign?"

"If you believe in that kind of thing."

"Gotta believe in something." Faith had abandoned me years ago, or so I'd thought. Yet, I'd seen some strange stuff—coincidence, intuition. No real explanation, which was what faith was about anyway. So, maybe I still had some, but I wasn't sure what I believed anymore. "What do you know about the child abduction thing?"

"May I?" He motioned to the spot next to mine.

"Be my guest."

As he spread out his bedroll and settled in, he motioned for the others to move away, out of earshot. "I've been working my way into the local organization I told you about, gathering information. I'm not far in. Those things take time."

"Don't I know it? Were you a cop? You're sounding a lot

like one."

"On the fringes a long time ago."

"You worked for them?"

"In a way. Cops need eyes and ears on the streets."

"Why don't you give the info to the cops, let them handle it?"

"They'd just fuck it up." He gave me an eye. "They fuck up a lot of things. Do some bad shit."

Did he know? Did he know what I had done? Or was I just paranoid? Secrets were like that. Tell a little lie to cover them up, and they grew and grew until you couldn't remember what was real anymore. Of course, no one expected me to remember, which played to my hand...if I could keep all of it straight. "What is it about you and me? Why do I remember you? What do you know?"

"Not much. Just a kind deed you did. I have no idea why I've stuck." He jutted his chin toward my leg. "How's the knee?" Something flitted across his face, something angry and sad.

"How do you know about my knee?"

"I've seen you limping and rubbing it. I can tell it hurts you. I'm sorry."

Something in the way he said I'm sorry...

He cradled his sax across his lap. "Going back for the kid like you did? Really stupid."

"I've done stupider." Unable to shake the feeling he knew more than he was telling, I watched him, looking for a sign, but I didn't see one. Regardless, I couldn't shake the feeling.

"Doubtful." He squatted down on his roll and motioned to the space he'd claimed next to mine. "Do you mind?"

"Hanging with me won't do much for your longevity."

He gave me that toothy grin. "I've done stupider."

"Doubtful." I settled myself, tucking my legs under the layers of warmth, then I leaned back against the concrete abutment. His presence helped me relax a bit. "Play for me?"

He rolled his eyes toward Heaven as he chewed on his lip. Then he nodded, a self-satisfied smile playing as he wet his lips. "This one's perfect. It's called *One Step Beyond*." He settled himself cross-legged on his bedroll.

He knew something, something bad. But his choice didn't sound like a rebuke. So maybe it wasn't me he knew something about. But he didn't want to say right now, and I figured I didn't have enough sway to make him. I'd learned to live with the not knowing, with the waiting. I could do it a bit longer, but I'd keep my guard up.

As I let the music wrap around me, it dawned on me he could've meant it as a warning.

CHAPTER EIGHT

I hurried through the commuters, dodging the well-dressed and the well-heeled who didn't see me or pretended not to. Winter drizzle added to the cold and misery, but everyone ignored it. The smell of coffee from the food trucks hoping to catch the hungry, hungover, or tired permeated the air, calling to me. My lack of sleep settled like a weighted vest across my shoulders, slowing me down. I wasn't sure which was worse, the demons or the dead weight of fatigue.

With tired and hungry making it two out of three, I was in serious need of a caffeine hit and something warm with lots of cheese, eggs, and bacon, but I couldn't stop. The lines were long, and I was in a hurry. Stella had said my appointment was at nine a.m. I'd written it down. As I stepped onto the tram, the clock scolded me. Five minutes late and a four-minute tram ride, then a few minutes to get to her office in the maze of buildings at the top of the hill.

Out of breath, I was surprised to find Stella's office door locked. Not like her to be a no-show. The shade drawn over the window to the side of the door set me on edge. Stella never lowered the blinds. Something about wanting people to feel welcome, comfortable...I couldn't remember exactly. I'd walked into bad shit before. The same feeling niggled at me now. The rational part of me admitted she had no way to reach me. Something could've come up and I'd have no way of knowing.

The primal part of me knew that wasn't the case.

After glancing up and down the hall, I made short work of the lock with the Watchman's knife. How I knew how to do that, I didn't know...not exactly. But, like my ability to protect myself, it was more of the flesh of the me I'd lost.

The smell hit me first. I recoiled. I knew that smell. The metallic tang of fresh blood. *"No!"* I silently screamed.

The outer office was empty, undisturbed, an open box from the Apple store on her desk. My phone still rested in the top tray in the box. I eased the hall door shut behind me, holding the latch so it wouldn't click, as I listened. Rustling sounds from the inner office, hurried but quiet. The inner office door was cracked. I repocketed my knife and grabbed the gun, holding it in front of me, as I eased the door open enough to get a look.

One man sat at the desk methodically working through the drawers. A nose bent to one side, small eyes, dark hair slick with oil, he looked familiar. Another stood behind him, fingering through the filing cabinet, his back to me. This guy I didn't know. Dressed in a suit shiny with age, greasy hair, thin like hard times. They both smacked of being from somewhere else, somewhere where one was either a predator or the prey.

Stella had put up a fight. Overturned chairs littered the room. Papers from open files scattered across the floor. The lamp usually in the corner lay in the middle of the small room, its shade smashed, its bulb broken. Light streamed through the windows. Stella's feet protruded from behind the desk. She'd worn her red heels. They didn't move. A splash of dark red, slick in the light, painted the corner of the desk. My temper flared. *How dare someone hurt her?* I tamped it down. Anger would earn me a spot alongside Stella, which wasn't part of my plan.

I couldn't see the rest of the office without opening the door wider and running the risk of alerting the two assholes.

So nice of the dead guy to have left me a gun. I chambered a round, leaving the gun cocked and ready.

"When's the girl supposed to be here?" A deep voice that

stopped me cold.

"Nine o'clock. She's late." The guy I recognized had an accent. I'd heard it before.

They were waiting for me. I was Stella's nine o'clock.

Fuck it all. This *was* about me.

I tucked the gun away. It wasn't a good idea anyway—the offices were tight, the walls thin, the risk of hitting an innocent in an adjoining office too great.

Besides, this was personal.

I left the knife in my pocket—they had the advantage of size, strength, and number. That was the first thing I needed to change. A stone obelisk glinted at me from the table in the corner of the vestibule to my left. I hefted it in my right hand, testing its weight. Light enough I could swing it, heavy enough to crush bone. It would work just fine.

This time when I hit the door, I'd taken a running start. As I leapt, the guy behind the desk looked up. "What the—" Stone connected with skull—a meaty thunk, then a soul-warming soft crunch. The light in his eyes blinked out as he slid to the floor.

The second guy whirled toward me. Lying across the desk, trying to pull the heavy weight of the obelisk back to reload, I rolled on my back. A second too slow. He landed on top of me. My breath left me in a whoosh.

He smelled of smoke.

Then I knew, tumbling into the memory, propelled by a smell. The warehouse. Looking for me. Rattling the stairs. The fire.

My hand too weak, my hold too tenuous, I couldn't stop him as he wrestled the stone from my grasp. I let it go. He relaxed, an easy smile drifting across a pockmarked face as his hands tightened around my throat. My eyes held his as he squeezed. I could see the moment when his attention shifted to worry. I could almost hear him asking himself why I didn't beg, why I wasn't afraid. As his fingers dug into my flesh, I smiled. My hand snaked out. I grabbed Stella's pearl-handled letter opener and in one motioned buried it to the hilt in the guy's chest. Surprise, then a fleeting hint of hate, colored his eyes before they went blank. I knew that look; I'd seen it before, up close. The moment when the balance of life shifts and death is no longer a possibility but a certainty.

The warm flow of blood oozed across my hand, still clutching the letter opener. Air burbled out of the hole in the guy's chest with a sucking sound. Surprise stretched his features. Empty and unseeing, his eyes rolled. I shoved him off of me, careful he didn't land on Stella.

I dropped to my knees next to her; one knee found the floor, the other, the guy's chest. As death inched through him, he clutched weakly at my leg. I ignored him. His arms fell. Air stopped burbling.

"Stella?" My fingers sought the pulse point in the hollow of her neck. She didn't move. I concentrated, fighting adrenaline.

A thready pulse jumped under my fingers. She was alive.

My eyes never leaving her, I grabbed the looped cord hanging off the desk pulling the phone to me. I gave the pertinent information to the 911 dispatcher.

"Where are you again?"

"Hell, I'm in the goddamn hospital. The office annex. Tell them to get a move on. Now!"

I brushed her hair back from her forehead. "They're coming, Stell. Hang on." A deep cut across her cheek gaped open. Blood oozed from the pink tissue underneath. Burns on her face. Small puckered circles. Cigarette burns. One eye swollen almost shut. The other swollen all the way, blood starting to pool underneath it. Blood matting her hair. I felt for the wound, the bone soft under my touch. One arm was twisted unnaturally behind her. Rolling her slightly, I eased her weight off of it. Cradling the arm, I eased it back around, laying it across her stomach. *Shit.* Revenge latched onto me like a rabid dog. One guy was dead. The other? I felt like finishing the job.

Stella moaned, stopping me.

Leaning down, I brushed her cheek. "Stell?"

From behind me, a hand grasped my shoulder. *Fuck, there were more of them.* In one movement, I pulled the letter opener out of the guy's chest and cocked my elbow. Thrusting upward with my legs, I threw the guy off of my back. Turning, using momentum, I threw him across the desk, my body on top of his. He landed hard on his back, his breath rushing out. With a forearm across his windpipe, the letter opener at his cheek, its tip drawing a drop of blood, I held him there, my weight crushing his windpipe. He didn't fight.

A rasp, barely audible. "Kate." His eyes bulged as mine focused.

Dan.

I scrambled off him. "What the fuck are you doing here?"

Released from my weight, he lay there, massaging his throat, pulling air through the damage. Rolling, he propped himself on one elbow, dabbing at the blood with a handkerchief. His eyes raked down me. "What the hell are you doing here?"

"I have an appointment."

He glanced around as he worked to straighten his tie, tightening it with a wince. "I've tried to get in touch with you a million times—you're not answering your phone. When you didn't answer the voicemails I left, I called the front desk at your place. They told me they hadn't seen you for a couple of days. I thought something was going down. Got here as fast as I could. Glad I did."

"A wee bit late if you planned on riding to my rescue. Which I don't need, by the way." I dropped back down to Stella, grabbing her hand, stroking it. "Stell, the cavalry is on the way. You'll be okay."

Eyes closed, she rolled her head then winced. She licked her lips and mumbled something unintelligible.

"Relax. Don't talk. Right now we need to get you fixed up. Everything else will wait." I reached up and grabbed Dan's handkerchief. Gently, I raised Stella's head and covered her wound, afraid to press too hard. The threads pulled the blood, painting a crosshatched pattern in the thin cloth as her life leaked away. "Hang on, Stell. I've lost too much already; I can't lose you. I couldn't live with that."

Stella opened her eyes, seeking mine. She fisted a hand in my jacket. "Hank. Hank's men," she said, her voice a hoarse whisper.

Her words carried the jolt of a cattle prod, but I didn't move. *Oh, please, not my brother. He didn't do this. He couldn't do this.* "You sure?" I asked, praying she was wrong. Cradling her, I gently lowered her head. I felt her nod. "How do you know?"

Her eyes fluttered open and for a moment she was there. I saw her fear, her sadness. Then her eyes rolled back and she drifted away.

"Stella!" My fingers sought her wrist. I held my breath. A rhythm, faint and erratic. "Where are the paramedics?"

Dan jostled my shoulder. "You've got to go. The police can't find you here."

"Why the fuck not?"

"If you get pulled into an investigation, they'll figure out who you are."

"Who am I, Dan? I mean, really?"

"Important. But not here. You have to go. What good are you going to be to Stella if you get burned?"

"I've already been burned."

"Not if you weren't here." He played the trump card knowing he'd won. "I'll stay. It's my crime scene now anyway. And we've got the perpetrators." He thrust my new phone into my hand, closing my fingers around it as he bent down seeking my gaze. "Take this. Go. I'll make sure she's taken care of."

Unable to take my eyes off of Stella, I resisted. This was my fault.

"I can't have you here where the police can try to strong-arm you and I end up in a pissing match. That's not the way, Kate." He urged me toward the door. "Go. My guys are down the hall. They'll keep you safe. I'll be along when I can."

Dan's insistence, his appeal to common sense, and his hint he would give me more of my story had me backing toward the door. With one last look, and a reassuring nod from Dan, I turned to go.

On high alert, listening for sounds from the hallway, I eased into the outer office. Panic scattered my thoughts, and my world fuzzed around the edges. *No. Not now. Think, Kate. Think.* Stella's end table drew my attention. A filing cabinet concealed as a nice piece of wooden furniture—normally Stella kept it secure, her keys hidden. Not today. Today her keys were on the top, by the ashtray, the door a half-inch ajar. With the knuckle of my index finger, I opened the door wider so I could see it. Unlocked. With a haste born of self-preservation and a desperate need to know, I fingered through the files in all three drawers. Although I knew Stella was a stickler for keeping her files secure, I looked in all the places Stella might have kept a file. Nothing.

My file was gone.

Stella never took them out, at least not that I knew of. They weren't current files, but more background stuff, stuff she needed once but didn't need each week.

My file was my history.

I scanned her desk. Not there either. She'd scribbled on a notepad. I looked closer. My name. Some other words. I recognized them but couldn't place them. I tore off the top half of the pad and stuck the sheets in my shirt next to my heart.

***

I'd forgotten how good it felt to be clean, but nothing, not even a long scalding shower, could drive out the deep cold of dread balled inside me. Stella, if not dead yet, was damn near. Dan's men had stashed me at the Marriott, paid cash, and told me to stay put. Although they'd wanted to take my things, I hadn't let them. They weren't Dan—when I pushed, they hadn't pushed back.

Adopting the persona of Stella's sister, I made a quick call to the hospital. No word yet. Still in surgery. When she came out of it, no doubt she'd be surprised she had a sister. But in all the ways that mattered, I *was* her sister. I loved her like a sister; I depended on her like a sister. Blood didn't make family; heart did. Stella was family.

I would die for her. Worse, I would kill for her.

I shrugged into my jacket. The gun weighed heavy in one pocket, the knife in another.

The itch of dirty old clothing, stiff with dried blood kept me focused as I sat cross-legged on the bed and stared at my new phone. Powered down it looked like any other phone. I knew not to turn it on—I'd written that in big, bold letters in my notebook. But, God, I wanted to. When I did, would I find all of me in there? Was that what they were counting on? That I wouldn't be able to resist and I'd ping the system, drawing them in? I breathed deeply several times, closed my eyes and worked to calm my thoughts. Perhaps, knowing I would show up eventually, they left it for me to find. A random play, but in the game of life, it was impossible to tell which of the seeds planted would grow. And what would the cops do?

The cops! I glanced at the clock, then thumbed through my notes. I had to meet my detective shortly. Dan would be here soon, and he'd keep my shackles on tight. Putting me in the same room with the cops was clearly not on his agenda. I understood and appreciated his position. I couldn't have my name hit any of the systems, not with Khoury still out there and him thinking I knew enough to put him away. I had to figure out what it was that I knew.

Whoever they were, they were desperate. They'd upped the ante, pushing me harder, pulling the noose tighter. Attacking Stella had either been a brilliant move on their part or an incredibly stupid one—time would tell which, I guessed.

If I could get out of here, I could figure a way to use their desperation against them. Despite Dan's escort, I had made sure I wasn't followed, so now was the time to make a run for it. For this brief moment without Dan here, the cage door stood open.

I stuffed everything I had into a plastic laundry bag and tried not to look at the bed. Clean sheets of soft cotton and a plush mattress, a siren's song of rest and comfort. But not for me, not until I'd avenged Stella and solved the riddle of me.

With the laundry bag slung over my shoulder, I stuck my head out the door. The hallway was empty. I took the stairs to the basement and let myself out.

The cold made my leg ache, and I favored it more than usual as I hurried, head down, eyes sweeping back and forth, watching. Sleeping on the ground had made everything else ache. Life on the street was anything but comfortable. I used the pain, harnessing it to keep alert, stay focused. When I hit the corner of Second and Madison, I double-checked my notes. The Coffee Note, that was the right place. Hiding myself, I watched from across the street. After five minutes, I felt comfortable enough to step into the open. Hands jammed in my pockets, skullcap pulled low, I hurried across the street.

Beck was waiting, watching the door when I stepped through. I eased in across from him—he'd left the seat facing the door for me. I accepted the coffee he pushed toward me with a nod. "Thanks."

He nodded to my laundry bag with "Marriott" in bold red lettering. "You've acquired a few things since I saw you last."

I stuffed the bag in my backpack. "Needed a shower."

He gave me a long look, his eyes narrowing. "Nice coat."

I cupped my hands around the warm cup. "Keeps me warm."

"Where'd you get it?"

I took my time as I pulled my notebook out of my pack and scanned my notes. When I looked up, I faced his flat stare. "Most recently off a dead guy in Pioneer Square."

His eyes widened slightly. He wasn't expecting the truth.

I put a finger through the cut in the fabric over my heart. "The same guys who killed the guy in my tub, or the same MO at least. However, this guy in the park was dead before they stabbed him. No blood. You know what killed him?"

"A witness said a woman matching your description killed him."

"And ruin a perfectly good coat? Why would I do that?" I couldn't remember all the details, only bits and pieces—a woman, angry, missing teeth, a sense of fear...not hers, my own.

"That his blood on you?" The detective nodded toward a brown stain splotched across my middle.

I pulled my jacket closed. "No."

"You going to tell me about it?"

"Nothing to tell."

He glared at me for a moment. "So the guy in the park. That woman..."

"Your witness." I didn't try to hide my sarcasm.

"Still, she was right there. Said you shoved the guy, were pretty insistent. You could've stuck him."

"I could've, but I didn't. Why would I?"

"Want to tell me why you have a gun?"

"That should be obvious."

"You're not making this easy."

"He was already dead." I focused my energy on remembering—I knew this. "Even if you don't believe me, if you want to believe I stuck him, you could arrest me for what? Mutilating a corpse? Ask the M.E.; he'll back me up."

Beck turned to look out the side window, taking in the river of humanity flowing by.

I didn't know whether he was really interested or simply wanted to avoid looking at me. I waited. I tried to imagine what he was working through as a cop, and what he felt as a man. "Already talked to the M.E. The guy died of a heart attack."

"Any idea who he was?"

"Didn't get a hit on his prints. It'll take a while to sift through missing persons. Maybe we'll get lucky."

"Maybe he's just a guy down on his luck who happened to be wearing my jacket, a very distinctive jacket."

Beck paused, focused. "Wrong guy, wrong place?" This time it was Beck's turn for sarcasm. "He's got the same scar on his abdomen as the dead guy in your bathtub. You want to tell me that's a coincidence?"

"I don't believe in coincidence."

"At least we agree on something. How'd he end up with your jacket?"

I looked for the details in my notebook—they weren't there. "I don't know. They were looking for me."

"We've established that. Who?"

"Somebody." I wiped a hand across my eyes. Flashlights. The park. Feeling pursued. The bum. My jacket. The Watchman.

"Somebody'd beaten him pretty badly." I extended my hands, palms down, fingers splayed. Not a bruise on them. "Wasn't me."

"Witness said you'd been hanging with a tall guy, short gray hair, wearing a long coat. Was he the one who gave your jacket to the John Doe?"

The Watchman.

Images, disjointed but clear. "Yes. Yes. He said I needed a new disguise." Guilt tugged at me. "Is that why the guy got killed? I never would have wanted that."

"He died of a heart attack."

"Still, they beat him. Trying to get answers."

"You don't know that."

"Tell me I'm wrong." I challenged him.

Beck stared into his coffee cup, then glanced at the line at the register. "I might as well start mainlining this stuff, be a lot easier. Never had this problem until you showed up."

"Bullshit."

Beck stepped to the counter and motioned for the pot of coffee, then poured himself a new cup. Not the kind of guy to wait in line.

I took a quick glance through my notes. The bad stuff had a way of sticking. The details, the unimportant stuff, disappeared like smoke in the wind. And, somehow, I knew the answer was in the details.

When he returned, a tic worked in his cheek, but his eyes were the color of a summer sky. "Kate, I'm on your side. I really want to help. How well do you know this tall guy? What's his name?"

I sifted through the memories, the ones that had stuck anyway. "I don't know. At least I don't think I know. I call him the Watchman."

Dan had warned me against confidences, against the police—I'd read that, too, in my notes. The question was whether that was important or a detail? I felt so alone. And lonely. Hell, I didn't even have myself to keep me company anymore.

"You're sure he's your friend?"

The Watchman was the only friend I had still functioning. I tired not to think about Stella. An uneasiness churned my stomach. The Watchman had known me before.

I turned my notebook around so Beck could see it. "Look, there was this kid. Last I saw the Watchman, he was watching the EMTs work on the kid—a boy, blonde hair, around two. I think the woman I saw him with died in the fire, or left him or something. It's a bit confused. Maybe you could check that and the time of death of the beaten guy. Maybe get my friend an alibi?"

"He *is* your friend, then?"

"He understands crazy."

"You're not crazy. You have a medical thing."

"So does he." I couldn't remember what, but I remembered the connection.

"Point taken. I'll check it out, see what I can find to get him off the list. You sure you don't have a name for your mystery guardian of the homeless?"

I looked for a hint of irony in his voice, his face, but I couldn't find one. "No name. He's one of them. He plays the sax on the corner across from my building. Hits Voodoo up for their day-olds. I buy him real food. He plays for me. We've become friends of a sort, I guess. When I got pushed out of my home onto the streets, he let me bunk at his place."

"The place that burned." Beck leaned forward, capturing me with his intensity. "You do realize you are the only common denominator in all of this. If you want to stay alive, you're going to need my help. You can't hide forever."

"Hiding presumes I know who my enemies are."

"And you've got the deputy marshal, Strader, right?"

Even though he shaped that as a question, he knew the answer. "I took the dead guy's stuff, okay. That's it. I wanted my jacket back—I was cold. I was ready to pay, but he had as much use for my money as he did my jacket. If that's a crime, arrest me. At least I'll have a dry place to sleep and three squares."

"Let that go. I got it." Turning inward, Beck shrugged slightly.

I knew what he was thinking, but two people had already been killed on my account. My well of human kindness was bone dry.

"You got a knife?" he asked.

I pulled the Watchman's knife out of my pocket and laid it on the table between us. He popped the blade. Pulling a paper from his inside pocket, he shook it open. Tilting his head, he read his notes. He folded the knife and handed it back to me. "The M.E. said the knife used to eviscerate the guy is two inches longer and a bit narrower." His expression didn't change, but I thought I saw something warm in his eyes. I could've been mistaken.

I tucked the knife away. "What do you have for me? Get anything from the note?"

"As we both guessed, the newest stain belonged to the dead guy. DNA confirms it was Nesto like I told you. The second stain was interesting, though. Also blood." He stopped.

"And?"

"Kate, the blood was yours."

CHAPTER NINE

My bike was still where I'd parked it. I'd followed the directions I'd left for myself on the key. Somebody had left a note on it—something about motorcycle-riding assholes who take up a space meant for a car. I wadded it up and dropped it, then thought better of it and tucked it in a pocket.

Thoughts raced through my head. How did my blood get on the note? When? Where? Beck had gone back to the station to keep digging, leaving me with no answers, the nagging fear of danger stalking me, and a loose hold on my impulses.

The bike started easily. As I left the parking lot, I didn't look to see if anybody followed me. I didn't care. In fact, I half hoped they would. The time had come to turn and fight. I twisted the throttle hard, leaving rubber as the tires squealed in protest. Head up, body over the handlebars, I let the bike fly down the Southwest Naito Freeway. Running out of real estate, I throttled back and turned into town. Several glances in my mirrors confirmed nobody followed.

Christmas cheer hung from every streetlamp and adorned every shop window. Music and happy chatter rose above the idling thrum of the engine. People filled the sidewalks, ambling, window shopping, wallowing in the warmth of the holiday season. I'd liked Christmas once—the thought hit me with the piercing pain of a bolt from a crossbow. The music. The laughter. The lightness in our house. The joy of family. I felt it in the fluttering in my chest, a longing for something unnamed, intangible.

I felt the flutter of a memory. Christmas. *Another place. Another year. Children laughing. A boy and a girl. Shining faces, open smiles. My brother and I? A tree, its branches bending under the weight of too many ornaments, nestles in the corner, sheltering its packages like a hen with her eggs. The rug is worn but serviceable, one of those braided wool looped ones in a royal blue. Wainscoting marches up the wall, meeting a floral-print wallpaper not quite halfway. Stairs lead upward from the front hall. Bedrooms are up there—two of them with a bathroom between. Through to the front of the house, a couch, book-ended by tables with reading lamps angling over the couch, curves beneath a large bay window overlooking a yard full of decades-old trees. A hammock hanging between two of them catches a light dusting of snow. A still life of an ordinary house for an ordinary family.*

Then the boy, an evil glint in his angelic face, takes the girl's toy and smashes it. Then he cries out, pointing an accusatory finger at the little girl, who sits uncomprehending. Everything is strange, yet familiar, as if I should know.

It vanished as quickly as it had come.

Still caught by the memory, I parked on the sidewalk in front of the Apple store. The memory felt so normal, a part of me, yet sinister. A warning? Some sort of a Freudian manifestation of my worry over my brother? That was the most likely explanation. Although I welcomed the memories, longed for them in fact, I found putting each in its place, giving it the proper context, was almost as difficult as the remembering.

A wide expanse of glass and holiday rush, the Apple store was jammed. A smiling youngster greeted me only half-concentrating as she kept her eyes moving, surveying the crowd behind me. I wondered who she was looking for. Someone in particular or anybody interesting? "What can we do for you today?"

"I need to change my phone number."

"Who's your carrier?"

I concentrated, but the information wouldn't come. "I

don't know."

She looked bored, but eager, a typical Apple employee. "Usually you do that through your carrier."

"It was a gift. My old phone was stolen." Sort of the truth.

Her eyes narrowed. "I see." She didn't say any more; didn't need to. She put my name on the list then whispered into the little mic attached to her collar with a clip.

I had to give them my current name since that's the one Stella would've used, and that was tied to the old number. "A friend ordered the phone for me. Do you need her name?" I prayed I didn't have to say it out loud. Stella had come within an inch of dying because of me. I hadn't a clue how to process that, so I tried to shut it down. Stella would have been able to tell me what to do.

"Really? I mean, sure. That would help." She looked a bit sheepish as color rose in her cheeks.

"I understand the position I'm putting you in. I'm sure folks come in here all the time with stolen phones wanting new numbers."

She clutched her iPad to her chest. "Thankfully not all the time, but it's something we're told to watch out for."

Swallowing hard, I gave her Stella's name.

"Would we be able to contact her to verify all of this?"

"She..." My voice hitched. "She's in the hospital. In a coma."

The girl's face hardened. "Really?"

"Call them. I can wait." I gave her the details.

For a moment, our eyes locked, and we played a game of visual chicken. Her eyes drifted over my shoulder, moving on to the next in line. "We'll find the information we need in the system, if you wouldn't mind waiting."

Taking the hint, I wandered, pretending to be interested in all the tech gear. Really I scanned the shoppers looking for someone out of place. Periodically I'd flick my attention back to the blue-shirted helpers huddled in the back near the Genius Bar, presumably weighing my facts, deciding my fate.

Finally, one clerk peeled from the pack and wove her way

through the crowd toward me. "Ms. Sawyer?"

"Yes."

"What can I help you with?"

"I have this new phone." I pulled it out and handed it to her and eased in closer, dropping my voice to a conspiratorial whisper. "But I have this ex-husband and a restraining order and all, but you know how that goes." She nodded, her eyes dark, intense. "And, I need a new number. He's tracking me on the GPS thing, I don't know much about it. But could you give me a new number without turning the phone on?" I hoped I made sense while trying to remember the details in my notes.

"If you just turn off Location Services, that will turn off the GPS."

"But I'd have to turn the phone back on, right?"

She nodded, at first confused, but then the light went on. "I see." Her expression changed to problem-solving mode. "Has the phone been activated?"

"I'm not sure. It's a gift."

"So I was told." She led me to a nearby computer. "Let's see what information we can pull up."

I didn't hide my nervousness as I watched her, then the crowd, and back again.

"Well, what do you know? Your information checks out." She was too young and too naïve to realize her disbelief hung in every word. "Everything is paid for."

"Can you help me?" Even my voice quavered. Staying out in the open for this long made me nervous. If they came in the front, I had no idea whether I could get out the back.

"It looks like the registration process was started. A new number has been assigned. All you need to do now is set up your account payment info and then sync with the Cloud. I can walk you through it." Her words tumbled over themselves in an embarrassed rush of helpfulness. "We normally don't do this. We would send you to the AT&T store, but you've been waiting a long time and it is Christmas, after all."

Relief hit in a warm rush. Maybe I really would get me back. "That would be great. Are you sure it won't hit the system with my old phone number?"

"Don't worry. I got this covered."

She stepped behind the counter and swiveled the computer screen so I could see it. "All we need is an ID and a credit card, and I can get this done in no time."

"Credit card and ID?" I stalled for time as I tried to think. The ones in my pocket had a different name than the one I'd given her. I pretended to look for the items she asked for. "I must've forgotten them. The holidays! Trying to get all the presents mailed off in time to family back east, then this phone thing."

She acted like she dealt with this sort of thing all the time as she handed me back the phone. "Not a problem. It's really easy. You can do it yourself from home. Just make sure to plug the phone in so you don't burn through the battery. Sometimes restoring from the iCloud can take a while."

"He won't be able to find me?"

"Nope. You're safe. Once you're up and running with the new phone, close the old account and you should be good to go." She stopped as if considering her next words. "There's a shelter. One of my friends went there."

Touched at her concern, I smiled. "I know the place. Thank you."

I pocketed the phone and melted into the crowd.

———————————————

A man, his hands jammed in his coat pockets, his cap pulled low, stared at me from across the street. Wisps of blond hair curled on his forehead. From this distance I couldn't make out his eye color. Slight, with broad shoulders hunched against the chill. I knew him. Not from here.

From before.

My eyes caught his. His smile was weak. With one shoulder, he pushed himself off the wall and started in my direction. Something about the way he walked hit me cold and fast, like a bullet between the eyes.

Hank.

The engine still warm, I straddled the bike.

"No, wait! Kate!" he shouted, but I ignored him. Splitting lanes, low over the handlebars and riding with abandon, I put as much distance between my brother and myself as I could.

He tracked me to Portland. How the hell did he do that? With no answers and no place to go, I wandered, chased by the reality that I was no longer protected, no longer just a face in the crowd, able to blend in, to move at will. By rote, I counted my turns...three to the left, two to the right, staying close to a course I could find and perhaps recognize.

I zig-zagged up through Nob Hill, stopping at a bar tucked in behind some of the new apartments and condos springing up in the area like weeds in a perfect lawn. The Alley, or so said the sign, an asymmetrical piece of hammered metal with faded lettering. I pulled the bike down the alley and around to the back. No one could see it from the street.

What the bar lacked in terms of originality it more than made up for in ambiance. Dark, welcoming, a jukebox playing songs from a more comfortable era, the bar had the weathered comfort of an old leather jacket.

Out of ideas, I straddled a stool at the bar. The bartender, an older guy with kind eyes, a two-day scruff on hollow cheeks, and an easy smile took one look then poured me a double single malt. "Merry Christmas," he said as he recapped the bottle.

My hands shook as I cupped the glass. "That bad, huh?"

"You look like you got a serious case of the down-and-out holiday blues."

"Family," I said as if that explained everything.

"I hear that a lot."

His comment aroused my suspicion. I watched him, looking for any subtext, any subterfuge, but I didn't see any. Guess we all need a hiding place from time to time.

Life.

I pulled a twenty out of my pocket. "Pour one for yourself."

He pocketed the bill. "Don't mind if I do."

The first sip brought tears to my eyes. Only pride kept me from gasping and choking. I pulled Beck Hudson's card out of my pocket and laid it on the counter.

After two drinks, I'd decided what to do. "You got a landline I could use?" I asked the bartender, who had moved away, giving me a bit of space.

"In the back, on the wall by the bathrooms."

After checking both bathrooms, I deposited my quarter.

He answered after the second ring, his voice all business. "Hudson."

"It's Kate. Kate Sawyer."

"This isn't your number."

"Not my phone," I explained as succinctly as I could, given that I'd had no sleep, little food, and more than a bit of the good stuff warming my belly. "My brother, he found me."

"He's here?" Displeasure nipped the words to sharp bites.

"Yeah." I could almost hear him, moving his thoughts like beads on an abacus, calculating possibilities and outcomes.

"You need to come here." He gave me his address and the invitation I'd been looking for.

As he gave me directions, I made meticulous notes. Not trusting my GPS on my bike—they'd tracked me through the GPS on my phone—I had disconnected it and turned it off before firing up my bike. I wished I'd thought of that before. But lost in fear and fragmented memories, I hadn't. As I eased the bike down the alley, I half-expected someone to charge through the entrance, knife drawn, ready to slice me open.

They hadn't had trouble finding me so far.

Slinking in through the side door of a convenience store around the corner, careful to not expose myself to the traffic clustered at a stoplight on the main street in front, I bought a map and marked my starting point and destination. Fighting the urge to race to the relative safety of the detective's house, I deliberately meandered, crossing back and forth over the direct route several times, then looping over the river and back. Watching every car, every face that turned my direction, every casual glance, I rode until I was certain no one followed me.

The Northside Precinct station was a short walk from the detective's home. The parking lot at the station looked to be as good a place as any, and better than most, to stash my bike. I scribbled the directions in my notebook just in case. My shoulders hunched against the deepening chill, I set off with long strides, my body grateful to be unleashed. The lights surrounding the station gave way to darkened neighborhoods, sheltering trees, and the glow of the streetlamps diffused by the gathering fog. The air smelled of damp sidewalks, moldering leaves, pine, and a hint of salt from the not-too-distant ocean. When they'd stashed me in Portland, I'd thought I'd hate it—gloomy and too West Coast. But I was wrong; I loved it—a place so governed by the weather, so bound by the rivers and hills, yet so fresh, so clean. A place filled with possibilities. Funny that. Using the dim glow of streetlamps meant more for ambiance than utility, I'd step into the light to check my map and notes, then eased back into the shelter of the shadows. How the hell had my brother found me? I'd been worrying the knot since he'd surprised me. I still didn't have an answer.

A cute little bungalow with a bright studio in the back was not the kind of place I expected Detective Hudson to call home. The curtains were drawn across the windows on the front of the house—a cop's house. I walked around to the back as he'd told me to do.

Lights spilled through the back windows. A rough-hewn table bracketed by comfortable chairs upholstered with splashes of bright oranges, greens, reds, and blues...even a hint of purple sat in the window. Behind, an oil of two girls painted when neither of them was old enough to fear the future, their faces open and their eyes bright, hung above the blue and white couch.

Music drifted through the open doorway of the studio at the end of the side-drive. He said I'd find him there.

"Detective Hudson, you surprise me."

He stood at an easel, his brush poised over the canvas—a modern piece all splashes of color and light. A pair of well-worn jeans splattered with paint hung low on his hips. His chambray shirt, the sleeves rolled up, also wore slashes and drips of a varied palette. He'd buttoned it wrong, and one tail hung lower in the front than the other, not that he seemed to care. His hair was messy as if he'd been running his hand through it. A tiny streak of yellow paint told me he had. His focus remained on the painting. "It's really funny you called." He sort of half-laughed, prodded by a joke only he got. "So you say your brother is in town? The NYPD cop who you claim is after you?"

I shrugged out of my backpack. Dropping it at my feet, I unzipped the front compartment and pulled out my notebook. Beck's tone, the scowl on his face, the fact he wouldn't look at me, all made me nervous. Distrust and anger permeated the small room as he stabbed at the painting with a brush now empty of paint.

Working my way back in time, I scanned my notes. "I haven't talked with my brother. Dan said he was there when I got hurt, when the bust went bad. Stella told me none of this bad stuff started until they put me in the program at the hospital and told my brother I was alive."

"Hardly indictable." The detective still wouldn't look at me, but his jabs with the paint brush were a bit softer. "How do you think he found you?"

"I would assume through the hospital. Stem cells. My genetic issue. Hank's a cop; deductive reasoning is a big part of his job."

This time, Beck looked at me, immobilizing me with a flat stare, his eyebrows a ledge above angry eyes. "So glad you clarified that."

Anger painted the air around him. "What's going on?" I eased back toward the door, reaching for my backpack.

After smashing the brush into a blob of yellow paint, he went back to jabbing at the painting. "After I left you yesterday, I got a call to a scene at the medical complex. Were you going to tell me about it?"

The faint shadow of a memory shrouded me, blocking the light. "What scene?" I whispered. I knew; yet I didn't.

"Stella Matthews?"

I recoiled as if slapped as the memories flooded back—the bad stuff always did. Two men, blood, lots of blood. Stella. "Is she okay?" Squeezed tight, my voice didn't sound like mine.

His brush paused mid-air. He didn't look at me. Then he made a slashing stroke on the canvas. "Touch and go."

"Dan came." I crossed my arms, holding tight so the memories, the fear wouldn't fracture me. "He took over the scene. The usual drill, he said."

"This is so far from the usual drill."

"No shit."

Suddenly cold, I rubbed my arms. "People dead, hurt. All because of me?" Seeking confirmation, I posed the thought as a question. The concept seemed impossible. Hadn't I been one of the good guys?

I know what you did.

What the fuck did *I do?*

"Evidence supports that." He dropped his head, letting his chin rest on his chest for a moment, then he put down his brush. "Let's talk about the hospital. Your name was on Dr. Mathews' appointment list." His voice sounded like he'd been chewing rocks, each word a pebble gnawed from the rock of distrust.

"Yeah. I got there—the door was locked." The memories played like a movie in my head. "Two guys. Stella." The shivering started again, rattling my teeth. "The rest is a blur. Doesn't get clear again until I'm in the shower at the Marriott. Dan put me there. The rest I've told you. Really, I'm not trying to hide anything. I need your help, so that would be stupid, wouldn't it?"

That logic seemed to work. Beck relaxed a bit, but I could still read the wary in his eyes.

Losing patience. Fear burning through me. "Tell me what you know about Stella," I said, my tone leaving little room to ignore it.

"They tell me Dr. Matthews is going to pull through. Not sure about a full recovery, yet. Marshal Strader told me he'd make you available for questioning if I thought you had anything to add to the investigation." After thinking about it, Beck picked up the brush and stuck it into a jar filled with fluid and swirled it around. The fluid pulled the paint from the bristles, taking on the yellow hue. "I really don't like that guy, but you have to love his irony. You bury a letter opener in a guy's chest and he'll make you available if you have anything to add to the investigation. That guy ought to be on *Laugh-In*."

I had no idea how to place his reference, but it didn't seem important, so I let it go. I'd gotten good at that—trying to pick up on the things I needed and things I didn't. But I was mesmerized by the fluid dissolving the paint and creating a film lacking the vibrancy of the real thing. That was exactly what I feared the disease was doing to me.

The shivers racked my body; I couldn't control them.

"Stella's going to be okay," I repeated that over and over, unable to stop, unable to believe, unable to deal with what had happened, what I had seen. What I had caused.

Dropping my notebook, I pressed my hands to my head, squeezing. Captured in the tangles in my head. I tried to see, to peer into the darkness, only to be blindsided by a random horror. I couldn't make sense of it. The further into the darkness I looked, the more I disappeared. My breathing came fast and hard. Panic tightened my muscles. Stars darted across the darkness in front of my eyes.

As my knees buckled, a kind voice in my ear said, "I got you."

Then I was lost.

———————◆◆◆———————

Sensations registered first. The soft cushions underneath me. A cold, damp rag pressed to my forehead. A feeling of peace and safety.

A deep-timbered voice with a hint of worry. "Kate?"

The police detective. *I remembered.*

"Can you make them stop?" I kept my eyes closed, for a

moment picturing life as I wanted it to be. No more bad. No more running.

"Yes." He sounded so sure.

I eased my eyes open to find myself staring into his. "Promise?"

That actually got a grimace, which I think passed for a smile. "I can promise I will do all I can to keep you safe and to get whoever is after you. Besides, with all these dead bodies piling up, the chief is riding my ass." He lifted the cloth on my forehead. "I'll be right back. Need to make this colder."

I watched him until he disappeared through the cottage door, then I looked around, reorienting myself. He'd put me on the couch in his studio. Canvases, some worked on, some newly stretched, lined the perimeter, leaning against the walls, several deep. A few had been chosen to hang from the walls: two pastel nature scenes; an oil of a girl, the hint of the woman she'd become in her face; small detailed pencil drawings, one of a German Shepherd especially well done. The detective still searched for his style, or maybe he simply bored easily. I missed my art. Somehow, with a brush in my hand, I could frame the composition of a life. Whether it was real or imagined, forgotten or remembered, my life, as it was and as it could be, melded into a reality when I stood in front of a canvas.

One canvas caught my eye—mad slashes of paint, dark colors, angry, blood red dripped, splattered. "Tell me about this one," I asked as he returned, cupping the rag in both hands.

He glanced at the painting, his face closed. "Not a good time." Kneeling by the couch, he laid the rag on my forehead. "Better?"

Afraid to move my head, I resisted nodding. "Yes, thanks." Holding the rag in one hand, I closed my eyes. Everything hurt: my knee, my throat, my face, my head. I thought Beck had moved away. I flinched when he touched me. His fingers traced the bruises on my throat, my cheek.

"Do you know what you did to those men in Stella's office?"

"Yes." My voice was a choked whisper. I swallowed hard. I could feel the warm blood flow over my hand. I could see the man's life ooze away. I shivered. "They tried to kill Stella." I tried to lick my lips, but my mouth had gone dry.

I know what you did.

"I was late to my appointment. I've been beating myself up over that. Just a few minutes earlier..."

Beck went all still. "You know I should arrest you. You killed that guy."

I opened my eyes and risked movement, turning my head so I could watch his emotions change the color of his eyes. Funny, but I remembered the first time I saw that look, those blue eyes touching something deep inside. "Sometimes killing is part of staying alive." I didn't remember the details of the past, but death had touched me, more than once, of that I was sure.

He looked like he wanted to argue, but couldn't find fault with the logic.

With a finger, I pulled my collar away from my neck. The bruises had just been blooming when I'd checked them at the Marriott. They ought to be in full flower now. "It was me or him."

I took the rag off my forehead, then Beck helped me ease to a seated position. The world wobbled a bit, then righted itself.

"You okay?" Beck asked. I raised an eyebrow. "Right." He rocked back on his heels then pushed himself to his feet.

"I was Stella's only chance."

"I know. You just complicate my life beyond measure."

"No doubt." I tried to stand, but when I leaned forward, the world tilted, so I relaxed back into the embrace of the soft cushions. Beck was stuck with me for a bit longer.

"I'm sorry about your friend. And you did leave one guy alive for us to question, although one side of his skull is in bits and pieces, so it may be awhile. Medically induced coma due to swelling issues, they tell me. Had you seen either of them before?"

"No, but I remember one guy's voice sounded familiar." I looked around. "Do you have my notebook?"

Beck picked it up where I must've dropped it and handed it to me. "One thing has me confused." He motioned to the couch beside me. "May I?"

I moved to the side making more room for him. "Only one?"

"Any idea what they hoped to find at Dr. Matthews's office? They knew you were coming, sure, but they were also looking for something."

I tried to remember back. "Stella didn't keep her sensitive files with the others. Mine was in a locked cabinet in her front office. It was unlocked—someone had tossed the keys on top of the cabinet." I eased away, turning to get a good look at him. "My file was gone."

"And it wasn't in her office or on her desk?"

"Hard to say, papers were scattered all over."

"None of this really adds up. They were clearly looking for something. But if they really wanted you, they could just grab you. It's not like you haven't made yourself a target." He didn't look happy as he said that last part.

I wasn't following the dots—too many links in his logic chain. "And?"

"They keep going after people near you, people you care about, but not you. Don't you wonder why?"

I hadn't thought of it that way. "Now that you mention it, yes. Any theories?"

"Not that I can prove, of course, but it seems like they are directing you, forcing you to take action."

My knee zinged me, and I bent a bit to rub it. "So, you think they want me to *do* something?"

"It's a theory."

"What?"

"Haven't a clue." Beck opened the door to a small refrigerator that doubled as an end table, and reached for a beer. He handed me one and took one for himself. "And now your brother shows up."

Fear flashed through me. "He did?"

Beck squeezed my hand. "That's how you ended up here."

I bolted upright. "He knows I'm here?"

"No, no, it's okay."

I relaxed back, but I wasn't as comfortable as I was before. Feeling the scratch of panic, I tried to distract myself. Several canvases leaned against the far wall. They were good. The second one needed some composition work, but the other two were well done. "Did you paint the canvas of the two girls over your couch?"

"My daughters." He held up his can. "Want another?"

"No, thanks." I hadn't touched my first, holding it instead, focusing on the cold.

He gestured toward the second painting with his can. "I can't get that one right. Something's off."

I made a few suggestions. He listened, his head cocked to one side, like a dog trying to understand English. "You just might be right."

"Happened once or twice." My thoughts retreated from the light. "Lately not so much. I'm not sharp. I forget things I used to know, used to do without thinking. I'm playing catch-up, the bad guys one step ahead."

"From what you've said, that's to be expected."

"Doesn't mean I have to like it. And other people are getting hurt."

"It's not your fault."

I know what you did.

"You're wrong."

"Okay." He settled in to listen, his expression open. "Tell me about it. Do you have any idea who these guys are and why they want you?"

Hank. Hank's men. Stella's voice.

"I think it has to do with a bunch of diamonds that went missing. According to Dan, somebody thinks I stole them." I shook my head, trying to get the tumblers of my memory to line up. I filled him in on the details, at least the ones I'd written in the notebook Stella had given me, lining up memory and reality as I read my notes aloud. Beck stopped me once as he pulled out his own pad and started making his own set of notes. I wondered if this would be like one of those parlor games I played as a kid, the story changing in the telling as it was passed down the line. I even gave him Hank, even though I heard a voice from the past telling me you just don't sell out family. I didn't feel good about it, but Hank had forced my hand by showing up here.

"So how'd they get to Dr. Matthews? Did someone follow you?"

I checked my notebook. "No. They had been using my phone. The GPS."

"How do you know they were following you through your phone?"

I scanned my notes for the name I was reaching for. "Sam. Yes. Actually, Sam figured that out. He made me get rid of the phone. To be honest, I didn't know you could do that. My new one was at Stella's office. I told Stella not to turn it on. At least I think I did. I pray I did."

"Even if you didn't, still not your fault."

"I knew, and I didn't warn her."

He took a few long pulls on his beer. His Adam's apple moved up and down. I have no idea why I found that fascinating. He wiped his mouth with the back of his hand. "Your choice to carry that load, but if it were me, I'd let it go."

"Bullshit."

He gave me a self-deprecating half-smile. A blink and it was gone. "Who's Sam?"

"The homeless guy I've been hanging with. I think the gal in the park who fingered me for the murder mentioned him."

"Tall dude. Duster. Plays a mean sax."

I nodded.

"Sam, you say?"

"Yeah."

"He wanted you to ditch your phone?"

"Yeah."

"Interesting." Beck toed open the small refrigerator and

extracted another beer. He removed the first one, now warm, from my grasp, and pressed a new, cold, can into my hand. "You're going to want this."

The undercurrent of his tone flowed strong like a riptide threatening to pull me further out to sea.

He gave me a long look before continuing. "The homeless guy you're talking about? His name isn't Sam."

CHAPTER TEN

My heart lurched. "What?"

Beck looked pained and pissed. "The tall guy, the sax player? The guy you say is your friend? That guy?"

Each word a razor blade slicing a tiny cut. I stared straight ahead. I knew Beck didn't want an answer; he was just making a point.

"The guy who said his name is Sam. Well, he lied."

Something primal and protective had me recoiling from Beck, breaking the connection where our shoulders touched as he sat next to me. After I clasped my beer between my thighs, I crossed my arms, defending myself. Forgotten sins. A treacherous past. The Watchman. Now I wondered if I could even trust the cop.

Who was I kidding? I couldn't even trust myself.

But the cop? Yeah, I could trust him. How I knew that, I couldn't say, but I knew it.

The solid ground on which I stood shifted, turning to quicksand. The spear of doubt plunged into me. Pressing back, I wished the cushions would swallow me.

Beck reached to put his arm around me. "May I?" he asked, before touching me.

I guess he could sense a bit of the rabid dog in me. Avoiding the pity I knew I'd find in his eyes, I nodded once.

He laid his arm across my shoulders and eased me toward him. I let him. The contact felt nice, warm, restorative. His warmth doused the chill inside me, the shivers reduced to a slight tremor.

"Drink some of that beer."

I'd forgotten about the beer. The can was still cold, the beer wet but unable to slake my thirst.

"You want it straight? Or you want me to soft-sell it?"

I stared straight ahead and swigged my beer. Not enough firepower but it was all I had. The Watchman. Just thinking about him, his lie—my life was a Swiss cheese of the half-remembered, held together by the not-true.

"Is he helping the marshal?"

That got a snort out of me. "No. I get the impression he thinks cops just mess everything up."

"Wonder how he came by that?"

I shrugged. I didn't know. There was a whole hell of a lot I didn't know and, the more questions I asked, the longer the list became.

"Why do you trust him?"

"The Watchman? Good question." I tried to remember the details of our first contact, but I couldn't. "He's never hurt me, though he's had multiple opportunities. I never would've seen it coming."

"That cuts both ways."

I thought I followed—earning my trust, sucking me in, that sort of thing. Saying the words would make it at least seem real, so I didn't.

"But it jibes with my theory that whoever these folks are, they want you to do something for them." His blue eyes flashed my direction, too quickly to read his mood.

"Diamonds." I flicked a glance at him. "I'm right about the diamonds, right?"

He nodded.

"That's all I got. My life is like running through the forest. Not only do I never see the bear, sometimes I forget they even exist."

"I really can't imagine." At least Beck didn't offer any platitudes. "Okay. Let's talk about your friend, what do you call him?"

"The Watchman?"

"Right. You know he's got a rap sheet as long as your arm?"

"Most of what I know is in front of me. He's been a friend, or at least I thought he had." Again, I reached for my notebook, flipping pages, but there was nothing about the Watchman. I hiked up my sleeves, then the leg of my jeans. I found a few notations there. "New York, on the streets." As I read, his voice came back to me. I remembered. Yes! I remembered. "I was a cop," I said, my voice riding on a wave of energy and hope.

Beck's face softened as if he understood. "Why risk that? Weren't you undercover then?"

I fought for calm. The Watchman's voice. Yes. I could hear him and see us as we had been. "I don't know."

"You remember that?"

I nodded. "It's a bit fuzzy, but yes." I confirmed that from the few slivers of memory recorded on my leg. I guessed I didn't have my notebook then, but couldn't remember why not.

Beck reached for a pad, but there wasn't a pen or pencil. Cold hit my shoulder where his arm had been. He grabbed a stick of charcoal from his art box and started scratching at the white paper. "Were you in Khoury's organization then?"

"I don't think so. I was on another case, living more or less on the streets."

"Maybe that's how you got hooked in with Khoury."

That sounded right. "Street cred?"

Beck nodded as he made notes. "Tell me what else you remember or you know. Anything that comes to you. Let it flow."

"Okay." Sweat slicked my palms. I wiped one then the other down the legs of my jeans. "He looked out of place on the streets—clean-cut, articulate, educated. Made me curious. And he looked like he could use a friend, so I helped him."

"How?"

"He had some memories and such, but he'd lost his ID and everything else, so I brought in a social worker I knew, and they worked through getting his papers straight."

"Sam, right? He said his name was Sam?" Beck's tone sharpened.

"Yeah. Why?"

"Sam was his brother."

"His brother?" *My brother. He's here.* I shook off the fear. "Was he bad?"

"The brother? No." What he didn't say spoke volumes. "Your buddy the Watchman made me curious. And you trusted him, which made me nervous." He lifted a hand as I started to speak. "Not because of you, but for you. So I lifted a set of prints from a can of soda I gave him, then did some digging. Your buddy—his name is Joe, by the way—started early. Juvenile records are sealed, but he was a regular in the system. Apparently, his younger brother, Sam, was the golden child. Stellar student, even better athlete. He had a couple of scholarship offers. Baseball." Beck shook his head. "Man, every guy's dream. And to top it off, he played shortstop, too."

I could see Beck Hudson playing shortstop in the Bigs. He had the build and, from the way he talked and his eyes glazed, the passion. Tricky things, dreams. His had panned out even worse than mine. I'd wanted to be a cop. And I'd gotten shot—a bite of the fruit, the memory sweet, the absence bitter. Shared disappointments added heft to the rope of friendship, and I felt its tug. With my Sharpie I wrote "Joe" in block letters, then "Watchman." "What happened to the younger brother? What's his name again?"

"Sam."

I made a note of that, too. But the labels and pictures in my head resisted change. I knew the Watchman as Sam, and once rooted, it most likely would stay. "Sam. Right. What's his story?" A red-hot ball of emotion burned in my stomach, dissolving the cold dread. I wasn't sure which was worse, but I had a feeling I wasn't going to like whatever Beck had to tell me.

"They found his body in a dumpster in Brooklyn."

"What?" I swiveled to get a look a better look at Beck. "Brooklyn? A dumpster?"

"Same cut on him as the guy in your bathtub, Nesto."

I blinked, willing the flitting memories to alight, but like moths they circled the candle, hiding the light.

Beck sensed my confusion; perhaps it was written in big block letters across my face. "He was a mule," he said, his voice flat, his eyes probing—for what I didn't know. A chink in my armor? An involuntary twitch of guilt? "Apparently his first and only time. They carved him open and left him like that."

"Like what?" It was there, I knew this, but I couldn't bring it into the light.

Beck explained, in graphic detail.

"Damn. They hid the diamonds inside themselves?"

"Yeah. Orifices are probed, but not surgical incisions."

I resisted making a note of that—somehow, I figured it would stick despite my not wanting it to.

"For whom?" I glanced at my forearm. "Khoury?"

"Not sure." Beck wove his charcoal pencil between his fingers. "But since a bunch of the players in the Khoury case are showing interest in you, my bet would be, yeah, the kid brother muled for Khoury. But a better question would be, how did he cross them? Must've been something big for them to leave him like that. His case is still open. But the Brooklyn P.D. has been looking for his older brother."

"His brother?" Then the synapses closed. "The Watchman."

"Good." Beck managed to say that without sounding condescending like schooling a first grader.

"Why can't people be who you want them to be?"

"Not their job," Beck said.

I hadn't realized I'd asked the question out loud. "Tell me again, how is he involved?"

"Like I said, he has a rap sheet. Goes back a long way. Mostly minor stuff, and most of it old."

When my anxiety settled, my thoughts, like deer at dusk, often wandered out of their dark hiding places. If I just could access all my notes in my phone. Listening to a litany of memories was like a mantra to me, ordering my thoughts, rearranging my emotions. But I was afraid to turn on my phone. The last person to do that damn near died. Stella was hanging on the brink—I remembered that. A very bad thing seared into the gray matter.

Last time I'd called—I couldn't remember when—they'd said she was in ICU struggling to come around. Was that yesterday? Today? Time flowed like a river, but without a leaf carried along, it was impossible to gauge the speed or measure the passage.

"He's sick, I think." I flipped through my notes. He'd told me, I knew he had. I hadn't written it down.

"Schizophrenia. Diagnosed in his late teens."

"Right." The unfamiliar pang of a memory. "And his brother?"

"Clean. Not a black spot anywhere."

"Until he ended up dead in a dumpster in Brooklyn."

"Right. Until then."

Tired, pissed, scared, and feeling played, I sat there, holding the beer can in both hands. The beer, what little remained, was warm. I drank it down anyway. The soft roll of the couch cushioned my head as I lay back and shut my eyes.

Somewhere in the dark an owl called, the reveille of ghosts. At times the weight of a solitary life seemed more than Atlas could carry on his broad shoulders and certainly a far greater burden than my broken frame could bear.

"Is there anything else you want to know?" I asked the detective, as if I had answers.

"A whole bunch of things."

Pressing my hands on my knees, I pushed myself to my feet, favoring my bum leg. "That makes two of us. When I remember, you'll be the first to know. But until then, I've taken up enough of your time. It's getting late. Thanks for the beer." I set the can on a small side table that was covered with paint splatters. "A messy painter, aren't you?"

His eyes followed me. He knew I was leaving, but he made

no move to stop me. "Painting, like life, is to be approached with abandon."

I rested my tired eyes on his face. Creased by life, it was a nice face, a kind face. "Couldn't have said it better myself."

"Look, this is probably a bad idea for both of us, but I've got an extra room. You look beat. Why don't you bunk here? I know you've got no place to go. They'll be looking in the hotels; you know that as well as I do."

"I've got a roll that'll keep me anonymous for a bit."

"A woman alone, paying cash. Most desk clerks would remember."

"I have ID under a different name."

A smile worked the corners of his mouth. It was a sad smile. "Not sure you should be telling a cop that."

"I keep forgetting you're a cop." I needed an ally. I wanted a friend. Head versus heart, at war with myself. Heart won. The last couple of days pressed on my shoulders until I felt like I couldn't stand, couldn't move. "You sure? Not the smartest thing for you to do, especially since I'm a suspect in three homicides. And life's been a bit hard on those closest to me lately."

He stilled. "Am I close?"

"If you are, I'd reassess."

He didn't smile. "We're more alike than you think."

"How could you possibly know that? I can't even remember who I am."

"It's not the who. That you can change. It's the what. That you can't hide. Let me in, Kate. I won't hurt you."

But I'll hurt you.

Truth was, I longed for the connection, his touch, the warmth of a hug. But I couldn't. Not until I knew. "I can't."

He flinched, a boxer dodging a punch, but he didn't retreat. I wanted to take the words back, to see him smile. But people close to me were dying, lying, and maybe killing. I couldn't have that happen to him...or to me.

"I'll lock my bedroom door." He managed a tender smile, one that reached his eyes turning them a smoky blue.

I stepped on the stirring deep inside. A cop. *Be careful.* "You know what I mean." The irony of not trusting cops when I had been one wasn't lost on me. *What the hell happened?*

He touched my arm, stopping me, letting his hand rest there. "Kate, I color outside the lines, just like you. I know what I'm doing. Anything else you need to tell me about?"

Hank. They were Hank's guys. I shook my head as I ignored the spark of doubt in the dusty blue and the warmth of his skin on mine. "I'm not going to leave you hanging out to dry. I will tell you what I know, when I know it. I'm chasing dead ends like you. One of us is bound to find the right thread that will unravel this whole mess."

He seemed to take me at my word, which made me sad. There were things I couldn't tell him, things I couldn't admit and didn't know. Maybe he knew that. Maybe he trusted me. I prayed I wouldn't stagger under the weight of his expectations. "Anybody who'd care I was here?" I asked.

"No." The word was hard, heavy with history.

And my reaction surprised me. I wanted to know. I cared. "A warm bed, a shower, and a bit of safety from people I can't identify chasing me for something I don't remember. Sounds like Heaven. I'd be grateful."

"And don't take this wrong, but you need to give me those clothes."

———————◆———————

The darkness wouldn't let me go. I struggled, thrashed toward the light, but the web of nightmares held me, wrapping tight, choking breath.

Diamonds. A plastic-bound, stamped, and sealed pack of them, names meticulously noted down the side. They weigh heavy in my hand. My heart pounds as I race through the darkness. I have to hide them. No one could find them. My steps splash through water, soaking through the canvas of my shoes. I don't care. My adrenaline spikes. Driven by fear. A desperate need.

No one could know.

We wouldn't be safe.

A sound behind me. I turn my head slightly as I run.

Someone follows. Growing near.

"No!" I shouted.

A banging. I struggled toward the light. Bolt upright in bed, my eyes flew open. Panic. Where was I?

"Kate." A worried voice. The doorknob rattled. "Unlock the door. Are you okay?"

Panting, shaking, I struggled to make sense of what I'd seen, where I was.

The door flew open, banging against the wall.

Pulling the covers high, I pressed back against the headboard.

A man I thought I knew, gun drawn, feet planted in the doorway. His eyes raked the room, taking it in at a glance. I caught sight of my stricken face in the mirror on the dresser next to the door.

My gun? Where was my gun? I didn't see it.

The police detective. His name? I searched the peaks and valleys of my tangled memory. His name on my forearm. Beck. Yes, Beck.

He rushed to me, grabbing me in a tight hug. Warmth. Strength. "You're safe here," he murmured against my hair. He held me until he felt my shaking stop. Easing back, he let go of me slowly, keeping close.

Self-consciously I pushed at the tangle of curls atop the pasty white face with huge haunted eyes I'd seen in the mirror.

"Okay?" He sat next to me on the bed.

My guilt settled deep.

I knew what I'd done.

"Sure. Sure." The same word a second time, a search for reassurance that wouldn't come.

Beck's hair was matted on one side, his face creased with sleep, but his eyes were bright, his expression tense but relaxing. He set his gun on the dresser then stood there awkwardly. "What happened?"

I pushed myself up, plumped the pillows behind me, then leaned back, pulling the sheets to my chest. "Nightmares. I get them a lot."

"Your memories trying to get through?"

If he only knew. "Maybe. They're hard to hang onto." *And hard to deal with.*

He touched my arm, his eyes following his finger as it traced the lettering, the words of my memories. He smiled slightly, a sad smile, when he got to his name. "Why do you write like this? On yourself."

For some reason, I didn't feel self-conscious. When I looked into his eyes, I didn't see judgment, only curiosity. I liked the warmth of his skin on mine. I didn't want to like it. I didn't want to like him. "It's hard to explain and probably doesn't make sense. But no one can take these notes from me. I can lose my phone or a notebook."

He smiled as if he understood. "And when the writing fades?" His finger worked its way up my arm to older, lighter notes, random words, thinning memories.

"I feel like maybe the words are disappearing inside me. Being absorbed so they'll stay." I tried to squelch the joy of the connection, the fascination with his touch, the comfort of his presence. He knew the truth, some of it, and yet he stayed. That was good, right?

"Does it work?"

"Hard to say. But it makes me feel better, as if I can change what is happening to me, control it. Maybe I'm fooling myself. Maybe it doesn't matter."

A smile played with his lips, fascinating me. "You're going to run out of square footage. Maybe you could put a pad and pen by your bed. Write them down when they're fresh. I get some of my best insights into cases in the middle of the night."

I wasn't sure I wanted to write them down, not all of them anyway. As if I could rewrite the past through selective memory.

I knew what I'd done.

I'd stolen the diamonds.

But I didn't know why.

The memory receded; the guilt remained.

I gently moved his hand from my arm. "I don't think this is a good idea. Not now. Not yet."

Reluctantly, he took my hint. "I'll settle for not yet." He stood looking down at me. "Hungry?"

"Famished."

The past had seared through my brain, burning away the muck and muddle, leaving the sharpness of life to cut clear and bright. My thoughts felt free, unburdened by tangled knots and muddied paths. The treatments must be working.

Hope. Then horror.

I knew what I had done.

And I had to fix it. It was the only way I could save myself.

Beck eyed me from the doorway as if he waited for an answer, but I couldn't remember what he had said. "Where'd you go?" he asked.

Should I tell him the truth? Courage failed. "I get lost in the tangles sometimes."

"Me, too." He pushed himself off the doorframe, grabbed his gun, leaving a shell in the chamber—a cop habit I remembered. "When you're ready, I'll have breakfast waiting. Kitchen is down the hall." He closed the door behind him, leaving me alone with the haunting reality of what I had done. And the warm memory of a touch, of kindness, and how it opened my heart. But I couldn't have it; I couldn't have him, not like I wanted. Not until I had me.

This was my fault. Stella. Me. All of it.

Guilt slammed into me, leaving me gasping. Propelled by the sins of the past, I had to move. Now. I needed answers.

A woman's robe hung in the small closet. Rolling up the sleeves, I followed the scent of fresh coffee, my bare toes curling against the cold tile floor. Light, muted like a photographer's soft box, filtered through a half-wall of windows above a farmhouse sink, pulling me forward as if the call of coffee and the prod of the past weren't enough. The narrow hall opened into the warm, bright room, the yellow walls and burnished hardwood floors warming the stark coolness of high-end stainless steel appliances, open cabinets slotted with plates of varying colors. A clatter of pots and pans hung on hooks above the center island and its six-burner Viking range with a grill.

Beck sat at the counter, squinting at the newspaper despite the pair of readers that had slipped precariously close to the end of his nose. He angled his head back to see through them.

"You paint *and* cook. Impressive."

"Not much cooking these days. Not since..." He glanced at me, then paused, his coffee halfway to his mouth. He swallowed hard and looked away. Despite a recent wetting and combing, a cowlick sprouted from the crown of his head,

"What?" I ran my hand through my curls. I'd taken a shower last night, washed my hair even.

"Haven't seen that robe in a while, that's all."

"Oh, I'm sorry. I thought you meant for me to use it."

He folded the paper and pushed himself to his feet. "I did. Sometimes you think you're prepared and you're not, not totally anyway. That's all." He manufactured a smile. "Want some coffee? Your clothes, as clean as I could get them, are on the seat in the bay window at the end of the hall."

"Coffee? Yes." My voice remained steady, even though my body thrummed, anticipating the caffeine hit. My leg ached, but I didn't rub it.

"If I remember correctly, you take it black." He seemed sure of his memory, and with good reason.

I eyed him over the edge of the mug, blowing through the steam rising from the coffee. "Prepared for what? Whose robe was this?"

His back stiffened for a moment. I couldn't see his face, but I felt a jab of his pain. "My youngest daughter's." He cracked a couple of eggs into a sizzling skillet, then pressed the plunger, dropping a couple of pieces of bread into the toaster. "I don't know where she is. Classic story. Got in with the wrong crowd. After her third trip to rehab, I tried the tough-love approach. She left, her mother shortly after. Divorce was quick. It's been a few years now."

"I'm sorry."

"You think you know—" His voice sounded roughed up. Time had closed the wound, but the scab was thin. "I couldn't save her."

I had nothing to say. I knew that kind of pain. Nothing would take it away. It clung to you like a parasite, draining, debilitating. Each of us dealt with it until we arrived at some acceptance, some symbiotic state, or we succumbed to the demons, offering them our souls.

His posture remained rigid. "How do you like your eggs?"

I didn't like eggs, but I didn't say so. "Any way is fine with me."

He relaxed into the familiarity of routine, shifting the eggs to a plate, which he put down in front of me, then cracking two more for himself. He broke the yolks, which made them palatable, although with hunger an animal clawing inside, I probably would've eaten them raw. I shouldn't be famished, but I was. Perhaps one hunger spurred another.

He slapped some butter on the toast and set a piece next to my eggs. "Eat. It'll get cold." After freshening my coffee, he joined me at the table. He swallowed several forkfuls of egg before pausing for a bite of toast and a slurp of coffee. "Have you set up the phone yet?" He focused on his food as he asked.

Had I told him I had it? Did he know I'd taken it from the crime scene in Stella's office? I couldn't remember. If I admitted to having it, would that make me guilty of something? Nothing more than I'd already admitted to most likely. I wished I could remember. "No. I didn't know how or if it would be safe. I was afraid that it wouldn't be as the girl in the Apple store told me," I said, surprised I remembered this much. "She was all of fifteen or something. She wouldn't understand the consequences of not being right."

"And you didn't want anyone following you here. Appreciated, but you don't have to worry about me."

The comfort of his competence wrapped around me, intoxicating in its warmth, dispelling the bleak cold of loneliness.

He reached across the space between us, extending a hand like a peace offering. "Let me see what I can do."

I pulled the phone from the side pocket in the robe. Ever since finding it at Stella's office, I'd kept it close. My lifeline. Even though it wasn't really, not until it had been restocked with all of my memories, simply fisting my hand around it brought a sense of peace I needed if I had any hope of thinking clearly. "I made sure it was off."

He waited while it powered up, glaring through his glasses. "Was this off when you took it from Stella's office, or did you turn it off?"

I worked back in time, but got nothing. "The men. The blood. Stella." I hugged myself. "The blood." I thought I'd said that already but didn't care. "Too much to remember."

"I understand."

"Dan was there." A pang of guilt. Should I call him? He would know maybe. "And he could've turned it off."

"Could've. Sure."

Worried dusty blue eyes caught mine. "Want me to register it?"

"Go ahead. But as a new account, a new phone number."

"Right."

I waited as long as I could. "Is there a phone number showing?" I had him read it twice as I double-checked each numeral with the number written in permanent marker on the inside of my wrist, faint after all this time but still legible. The new number was different, not even close to the old one. The gal at the Apple store had indeed taken care of everything. "Go ahead."

"I'll need your license and a credit card."

I spread the second fake me out on the table, an identity as disposable as a coat in summer. He gave them a glance. "Where'd you get these?"

"Dan. In case my original identity was blown, he said."

Beck gave me a look, but didn't comment. Working through the menu screens like he knew what he was doing,

Beck periodically asked me for information. Several times I had to refer to my notes—passwords and an address off of Stella's notes from her office I had pocketed. Finally, he set the device between us on the table and pushed himself up. "Let it sync with your info in the Cloud. It'll take a bit. It has to download apps and all of that. Your clothes are all folded—"

"—at the end of the hall."

He smiled, this time for real. "Yes."

I'd remembered.

I stared at the black screen with the white Apple logo and the bar underneath ever so slowly turning white, taunting me with its glacial progress. "Can I help with the cleanup?"

"No, thanks. I'm not going to read through your stuff, if that's what you're worried about. We're partners. I trust you to be honest, to have my back as I have yours."

"Okay."

A slight touch on my arm as I passed by. "Trust me, Kate. I won't let you down."

I'd let myself down, but I didn't tell him. "Read what you like. I don't have anything to hide."

There was a time for the truth. This wasn't it. The truth wasn't in my phone; it was trapped in my past.

And now, at this moment, a doorway had opened, wider than normal, the path uncluttered. Was the treatment working? Or would the door slam shut again as before? My back to Beck, I stopped, pulling air into my lungs and searching for courage. Maybe now was indeed the time for truth, for me to come clean. Before the door shut again.

While I remembered.

"I know what I did." My voice surprised me in its strength.

"What?"

Fortified with resolve, I turned. "The note? I know what I did."

Beck set down the dishes he was holding on the drain board. "Okay. Want to talk about it?" He offered me a chair.

Sitting across from him, looking into his eyes, I saw a man who wanted to help, and that made the telling easier. "I took the diamonds."

He cocked his head to one side and gave a quick purse of his lips. "Okay. Can you walk me through what you remember?"

The nightmare unfurled in front of me like a newsreel. I told him everything. He didn't interrupt. He didn't take notes. He simply listened, his face open, his eyes clear.

When I finished, it seemed we both felt better. Beck had more information, and I felt a burden lifting. Oh, the truth weighed heavy still, but the secrets were gone.

Beck leaned back in his chair and grabbed a pen and paper. "Do you mind?"

I shook my head. "No more secrets."

Staring out the window, I sipped my now-cool coffee as he made notes. The window looked out over a small garden. A riot of color, a tangle of vines, the plants looked happy in their untended state, left to grow and thrive as they saw fit. In an odd way, I was jealous. We humans are so sculpted, constrained by our own choices and other's expectations.

"I think I got it all down. I'm pretty good at regurgitation—years of case work." Beck pushed the pad across the table. "Dictate all of that into your phone so you have it." As I rose, he stopped me with a touch. He stood and, listening for any trace of fear, he folded me into his arms.

Stiff at first, I let his warmth melt through me.

Holding me, he leaned back a little. I tilted my head up to look at him.

He brushed his lips across mine. Giving, not taking.

His touch, the connection—700 volts to a silent heart. "What was that for?"

I saw a sadness in his eyes. "You won't remember."

I couldn't argue, and that made me sad, too, and I buried my face against his shoulder. "I'll hurt you."

"My problem. You're not who you think you are, Kate."

"I took the diamonds," I whispered, afraid to hear the words. "This is all my fault."

I know what you did.

Beck dropped me at the substation where I'd left my motorcycle. "Where are you going?" he asked, stopping me as I opened my door.

"I gotta see Stella, but first I've got to see Dan."

Beck's expression turned cold. "What for?"

"I need my file."

He thought that over for a bit. "Hell of a risk. He may tie your hands."

"On what authority? WITSEC is voluntary. After all of this, he'll probably be glad to wash his hands of me and everything."

"Maybe." Beck didn't sound convinced, but I knew Dan—he wouldn't get in my way. "Then you'll be at the hospital to see Stella?"

"Yes."

"You be careful. They may be watching. The chief is barking like a dog over all of this. I've got to bring him up to speed. And I'd like to see if NYPD is in a sharing mood—their file on Khoury would be interesting reading. Then I'll stop by the hospital. They got the guy you left barely conscious. I'd like to see if we can wake him up."

"Okay. I'll see you there, then." I stepped out of the car then leaned back in before shutting the door. "You have my new number?"

"Programmed in." He reached across and grabbed my hand. "Kate..."

"I know."

He left his hand on mine for a moment. It felt warm, reassuring—the connection I craved.

"And the GPS on my phone?"

"Disabled."

I'd asked him so many times to double-check that the tracking feature was turned off I was amazed he hadn't lost his patience. But he hadn't. "Okay." I stood there for a few moments longer than necessary. I knew once I shut the door he'd drive off. Finally, I took a deep breath and let him go. I didn't watch as he pulled into traffic.

He was a good man, better than I deserved. And I didn't want to hurt him. But I had to know. *Why had I taken the diamonds? Who was I?*

Life, an upside to sin. The downside? Having to live with it.

I had to get my hands on the diamonds. And then I needed to use them to get Khoury. Yes, I remembered his name. It was branded on my soul.

What had I done with the stones?

Could my file help me remember?

The sky spit rain. The cold filtered through every gap between clothing and skin as if it too wanted to find a warm place to hide. I turned up my collar as I straddled my ride. Instead of firing it up, I took the time to read through all of my notes from the beginning, and listen to my recordings, even the one I'd dictated this morning from Beck's notes. Everything was there. I was whole again—maybe as whole as I was going to be. The doctors hadn't made any promises.

Scrolling through photos, I stopped on the one of Nesto, sprawled in my tub. Something about him...

CHAPTER ELEVEN

"I want my file," I said without preamble when Dan answered the phone.

"Kate, my God! Are you okay?" His voice hitched, slowing me down.

"Dan, I'm sorry. I really am."

"Why did you leave?"

"I need your help, but I can't let you tie my hands."

"I can't keep you safe, then."

"I don't need you to keep me safe. I need you to help me keep my sanity, what little of it I have. I have to know, Dan. I have to know what I did, who I was...who I am. Do you get that?"

"You won't even see them coming." His worry and anger crackled in the silence. "This one's personal, Kate. You're personal. You know that, don't you?"

I didn't know what to say. Was his concern out of pity? Only after getting myself back would I have the answer. "I need to know. I can't hide forever."

"I don't want anything to happen to you."

"Bad stuff happened a long time ago. Now I'm paying the price. And it's not just me. Innocents are getting hurt."

"I want to get the bottom of this as bad as you do."

I doubted that. "Then help me."

"I really care about you, Kate. You know that, don't you?"

His admission confirmed what I'd been feeling from him, and I didn't like it. His job was to protect me—hard to do when things became too personal. "Dan...I can't deal with this, with you. Not now, not until I have some answers. I need you to help me find some answers."

"I don't care what the answers are."

"I do."

His resignation whispered through the line. "What number is this? You don't have your cell." It wasn't a question.

"I...I lost it. I'm calling from a pay phone. Do you have any idea how hard they are to find? Superman is pretty much SOL."

Silence echoed, a hollow emptiness. I waited. "After all that's happened and you still want to fight. You got balls, Kate Sawyer. You got balls."

I heard grudging respect in his voice, and pain. This was hard for him. I hadn't realized how much he cared, how far out on a limb he'd gone for me with the medical treatments, to give me a long leash that, despite its length still chafed. "Not one of the easier aspects to my personality. Or so you've told me."

"What are you going to do?"

"Memories are coming back, Dan. I'd like to read my file, see if anything in there will jog them further."

"You don't understand." Dan sounded serious, which pissed me off for some reason. "I've done a lot for you, let you run a bit further than you should."

"The program is voluntary."

His sigh blew through the line, carrying his worry and impatience. "I understand, but you haven't formally left the program. Could you just keep me in the loop, let me help where I can?"

"Sure." I knew I was pushing every button he had. Truth was, he'd done a lot for me. The whole stem cell thing was a huge leap for him and his department, so he really was helping me get me back.

"I mean it, Kate."

"I know. Okay. I can do that. Can you bring me my file?"

A long silence. Then, "Where do you want to meet?"

After wandering, following the GPS on the bike, I'd determined no one was following me. This was the first time I'd used the GPS since they'd been tracking me, and I was curious whether it was only my phone, or had they hacked both? Not sure I had an answer, but knowing Dan would be there if trouble found me, I felt better about using it.

I'd picked a nondescript Mexican joint, a hole in the wall on I-5 in Vancouver, Washington. The sign was so faded I didn't even have a name to give Dan, just the exit and a few directions from there. On the north side of the Columbia River fifteen minutes from downtown Portland on a good traffic day, the place was close but light years away from where anyone would be looking for me. I stood when Dan entered, motioning him to the back booth. This time I was prepared for his hug, but not for the emotion there. He held me a bit longer than was comfortable. I let him.

"I've heard the food here is to die for." He settled into the booth across from me, setting his keys on the table—a large gold crucifix key fob, symbols etched vertically down its shaft.

"Let's hope not." Trying to keep the tone light, the hard edge out of my attitude, I angled my head at his keys resting between us. "I didn't know you were the spiritual type."

Self-consciously, he pocketed them. "In this business, a little divine intervention is a blessing." His face sobered. Without another word, he pulled a file from his briefcase. A tattered cover, the papers inside oozing out like an overstuffed sandwich. He pushed it across the table, but kept his hand on top of it. "I'm not supposed to share this."

"In the real world, I'd remember everything that's in there, so you wouldn't have to. Don't see the big deal." I eased the file from his grasp. Thicker than I thought, filled with notes and photos, several of which leaked out onto the table. I raked them together. He caught my hand in his, holding tight, and started to say something. Then he smiled, a tight, weary smile, patting my hand as he let it loose. He finished pushing the photos together and stuffed them in the file. "I hope it helps. I'll need it back."

"A day? That should be enough. Is that okay?" I took his silence as a yes.

A waiter brought chips and salsa. Dan ordered a beer; I decided a margarita would calm the jangled nerves.

Dan hoisted his frosted mug, then took a sip. "Most people would feel a twinge of remorse at drinking so early in the day," he said, his upper lip mustached with foam, which he wiped away.

"Most folks don't have days like yours and mine." With a fingernail, I scraped through the frost on the outside of my glass. A summer joy shared with my brother when we were young. The drugstore on the corner had a soda fountain. Fifty cents for a shake so thick you had to eat it with a spoon from a mug stored in the freezer. Hank had mowed lawns for his two quarters. I'd pulled weeds. "Hank's here, Dan. In Portland."

"That son-of-a-bitch." Dan's voice sliced like a surgical blade across a pulsing vein. "Where?"

"He's my brother, Dan."

Some of the edge dulled. "I'm sorry. Families. Shit."

"Folks you wouldn't invite over for dinner but for the blood thing. Or that's what I've heard, not that I remember."

His eyes glazed for a moment, unfocused, as he stared back in time. "Families are funny. Someone can come into our lives, into your life, and make such a difference. Then some can be born into it only to do damage. But true family is chosen."

That was more emotion, more heart than I'd ever heard from the marshal. "Heart over blood."

"Where did you see him?"

"Outside the Apple store. Last night. He was waiting."

"How'd he find you there?"

"My bike, I'd guess. It was right by the door, and it's pretty distinctive. Nobody else in town has the same model and the same paint scheme, remember?" The bike had been one of a kind, some special anniversary edition or something. I couldn't remember. But I did remember I'd bought it on the spot one day when I'd wandered past the BMW dealership. Cheaper than a car, I'd explained to Dan, but he hadn't been pleased.

"I remember. But the great thing is, so did you."

Hope surged, and I laughed. A strange sound; I hadn't heard it in ages. I remembered!

"Did Hank say anything?"

"I didn't give him the chance."

Dan's breath hissed through his teeth. "How'd he get to you in Portland? It's a lifetime away from New York."

"Tell me about it. But it seems Portland is common knowledge." I drained the rest of my margarita and motioned for another. "He knows a lot about me. I'd sure like to know what you told him when you asked for his help with the stem cells."

"Only that you were alive, obviously." Dan raised his mug, this time drinking deeply.

I watched his Adam's apple bob up and down with each swallow. I have no idea why I found that fascinating. Details lost, a present found.

Dan wiped his mouth with a napkin, then put his empty mug down and motioned for another. "He must've picked you up somewhere. The Apple store wouldn't have been a place he'd wait for you. Where did you come from before you stopped at the Apple store?"

I looked back through my notes—until I had the time to transcribe all my entries, Stella's pad still went everywhere with me. "I'd left my bike in the tram parking lot."

Both palms on the table, Dan pushed himself back in his seat. "That's where he picked you up."

I must've looked like I didn't follow, when in fact, curiously, I did.

"Not too hard to put the stem cells together with trips to the hospital," Dan explained, although I'd gotten there on my own. "That's why you've got to come in," he continued. "I'll keep you safe. That's my job." He didn't try to hide his concern, but he didn't beat me with it either, which I appreciated.

"No."

His face closed, a vault door hissing shut on silent hinges.

I knew the magic words, the combination he looked for, but I couldn't say them. "No more hiding, Dan. I can't live that way. Not anymore. This is my battle. I aim to fight it."

"Kate. People have died. You have to come in."

"I can't."

"Bullshit!" His voice rose on emotion. The restaurant quieted as others turned to look. Dan leaned forward and lowered his voice to a hissed warning. "I need you to come with me."

"No. Stop pushing. It'll be okay or it won't, but nothing that happens will be your fault."

He slumped in defeat. "You know I can't force you to come with me, but stay close. Keep me in the loop, okay? We still have to figure out who's after you and why."

Hank. They were Hank's guys. Stella's blood. "Sure."

We both pretended I meant it.

———————◆———————

Stella had come out of her coma.

Nobody'd called me, of course. I wasn't kin, and I hadn't left my number. But somehow I'd known.

Still in ICU, Stella was easy to find. Nobody stopped me as I parted the curtain and stepped into the tiny space, wedging myself in next to the huge bed. Machines clicked and whirred, a halo of monitors dwarfing my friend. Normally a bigger-than-life presence, she looked small, somehow less. The stark white of the bandage around her head reminded me of the fancy turbans she loved to wear to parties.

"Hell of a party, Stell," I whispered. Anger thrummed under the surface, competing with the steady, comforting beat of her heart. *This was my fault.*

She stirred when I grabbed her hand as I tucked into a

chair next to her bed. Her hand felt smaller, her skin wrinkled as if she'd shrunk inside of it. Bruises, now a dark purple, covered her face, a faint tinted base to her chocolate skin. The circles of the burns had crusted. The gash across her cheek hid under a thick gauze bandage—blood had leaked through and darkened the white. Her lips, parched and dry, the lower one split, moved as she struggled toward my voice. Her eyes fluttered open. One was shot through with bright red, the pupil dilated.

"Kate." Soft, with a hint of steel. "They didn't get you."

"Not yet." I squeezed her hand warm beneath mine. "Who were they, Stell?"

A slow turn as she tried to bring me into focus, followed by a grimace. "Dang, my head is pounding like Leroy on the drums. What did they do?"

This was my fault. Feeling the need to kill somebody, I tried for levity. "Knocked some sense into you."

"Hell, better men than that have tried and failed." The hollow ring of a painful history resonated in her words. "Stell," I patted her hand, trying to focus on what I knew and what I needed to know. "Can you tell me what the men said, what they were after?"

Stella went so still, her eyes closed, if it hadn't been for the strong cadence of her heart rate monitor, I would've summoned the crash cart. "They said Hank sent them. They wanted to know anything you told me about what you remembered. About the diamonds."

"Did they want my WITSEC file?" I'd stuffed the file in my backpack. Holding the weight of my past, and perhaps the key to my future, the shoulder straps cut into my flesh.

"Your file? No. Just session notes." She smiled, but only one side of her mouth lifted.

"But you don't keep session notes. You dictate them to the transcription service that keeps them in the Cloud or somewhere."

"And you thought that was a stupid idea." When her eyes opened, the mischief that was Stella sparked then faded.

"Why were they digging through your files then?"

"They didn't believe me."

"Did you say anything about the cabinet in your front office?"

"The wooden end table one?"

I nodded.

"No, I don't think so." Her smile evaporated. "You saw the men there? You were the one who found me? I thought Dan..."

"What?"

She squeezed my hand. "I shoulda known Dan didn't have the balls to come busting in there like Rambo and take on those two-bit hoods." She pursed her lips. "Dang, everything hurts."

"I'm sorry. This is my fault. The phone."

She waved that away. "They would've found me somehow. You're our poster child. Even though we've kept your identity secret, we all know how those things go. We have one of only two programs in the country to treat your condition. Once someone knew stem cells were involved, they'd figure out where to look."

I didn't know what to think of that.

Stella gave me a look or tried to. "You gonna tell me what you did to those two?"

"No. But I owe you a new letter opener. I'll get you one for Christmas."

She closed her eyes with a sigh, exhaling vigor. Weariness slackened her features. "You lose mine, then gift me one? Cheap bitch."

We shared a chuckle that chased away the torment of the what-ifs.

"I thought I heard your voice." Beck Hudson stuck his head through the doorway, then the rest of him followed. "They told me at the desk that Dr. Matthews had regained consciousness and was strong enough to chat for a bit. I see you've already gotten started."

"And finished," a man in a white coat breezed in past the detective. "She's had enough for today. The nurses were wrong.

I left strict instructions that no one was to bother her."

Beck flashed his badge. "Just a few moments."

"We're not bothering her." I gave him a benign smile.

The doctor angled his head and looked at me from under his heavy brows. "I'm Dr. Swenson, her neurosurgeon. The trauma to her brain...Her skull was like a jigsaw; she's very lucky. But the brain takes time to heal. Please, let her rest. Come back tomorrow." He eased in next to Stella on the opposite side, looking directly at me. "Please." A polite version of "get the fuck out now."

Beck wavered, giving me an appraising stare. Could he see the secrets that hid somewhere in the tangles in my head? He knew what I had done. Did he know why? He held the door.

As I brushed by him, this time I caught the faint hint of breakfast, which made me smile. Would it be so bad if I let him in? If I let myself like him just a little bit?

Even though I would try not to, I would hurt him. And that would make it bad.

I know what you've done.

Could he handle that? Could I?

Holding my elbow, Beck directed me left at the next corner. "I've still got business left to do. Meet me at my house? I'll give you a key." He actually looked like he wanted me to say yes.

Even though I figured it would be a bad idea, I didn't say no. Truth was, I liked him, liked the way he made me feel. I hadn't let myself feel, not like this, not in a long time. He dropped the key into my palm and closed my fingers over it.

"What do you have left to do here?"

He waffled, not wanting to tell me. "I want to talk to the guy whose head you bashed in. Word has it they're bringing him out of the coma. Guess the swelling has gone down."

I pulled my hand out of his and pocketed the key. "You're not cutting me out of that. He's my only real hope right now to lead me back to me. I need some answers."

I could see the word "no" in Beck's eyes.

"I'm still a cop, Beck. And I *have* to know. The keys to a lot of this are locked in my head. If one of these bozos can help me line up a few mental tumblers, we can solve your homicides. Besides, I was there. I heard them talking."

"You're bluffing."

I kept my expression impassive.

It worked. "Suit yourself."

A scream shattered the hushed, reverent silence of the ICU wing. "Stop him!" A nurse raced out of a curtained cubicle down the hall.

A man walking toward us broke into a run at the nurse's shout. A skullcap pulled low, loose jeans and a down jacket. When he glanced up, I caught green eyes, a familiar cut to his jaw.

Not the guy from Stella's, but he'd chased me before. Where? Adrenaline surged, chasing the memories.

I'm down, my left knee broken, shattered, screaming with pain. He'd hit me from behind. His leg swings. A black boot, laced above the ankle. Black pants tucked in. He buries the kick in my stomach. Pain explodes. My breath leaves in one whoosh. My vision swims. The light glances across his face. Mean mouth. Eyes, the flat color of jade. The second kick to my kidneys. I grunt. The pain a vise around my voice.

"No."

Another kick. Another. He pauses. Something rattles. A piece of paper he stuffs in my shirt. Then he kicks some more. I can't fight.

A sharp stick to my stomach. Blood. Warm. Pain.

Until I am lost.

Lowering his shoulder, he hit me at full stride, knocking me into the wall. My bad leg folded. I caught myself. Beck reached out, a firm hand steadying me. I met his eyes. "I've seen him. From before. New York." I started to shake. They were here. And they wanted me.

"Get the son-of-a-bitch," I hissed, as I gritted my teeth against the pain, both real and remembered.

He disappeared. Metal trays clattered. A shout. Another. Then quiet as the chase moved on. I flexed my knee several times, creaky and slow to respond. Nerves tingled. I tried to follow Beck; I *had* to follow him. I loped, a staggering, awkward gait. Pain bolted, freezing muscle. "Damn it!"

A nurse skidded into the nurses' station. "They killed him."

That stopped me. "Who?"

She shot me a look, then ignored me as she barked orders at the other nurses.

I didn't need her to tell me. And I didn't have to ask who did it.

My last witness, my best hope for quick answers, was dead.

And the killer's capture was in Beck's hands.

I sagged against the counter. My body vibrated with unspent rage. The bastards had the jump on me, always one step...or ten...ahead. I needed to fix that. But how?

A strong hand gripped my arm. "I thought I'd find you here." A voice as familiar as my own held the desperate edge of a threat.

Hank.

Like an antelope jumped by a lion, I reacted instinctively. Cocking my arm, I stepped back, pivoting hard, burying my elbow into his soft stomach. Hank's breath escaped in a whoosh. As he folded, I grabbed his gun. With a twist, I broke his hold. Both hands around the grip, I leveled the gun at his chest.

All the commotion, the nurses scurrying, came to an abrupt halt. I felt their eyes on me as they weighed what to do. Someone whispered, "Call security."

"Don't." My voice held a bite. I kept my eyes and the gun riveted on Hank. Years had passed since I'd seen him, or it felt like they had. But I knew him as well as I knew my own reflection. He was a part of me. But he had betrayed that. Anger flared, threatening to consume reason. I worked against it. A losing battle.

My brother had sold me out. Only he knew about the stem cells.

Even though I was wobbly on my wounded leg, my aim was steady, my voice deadly. "Now, what were you saying, *brother*?" I spat that last word.

He'd turned on me, but he was still blood.

I pointed the gun at his heart and something deep inside cried.

CHAPTER TWELVE

The staff, frozen in disbelief, watched open-mouthed. When Hank started to speak, I shut him up with a waggle of the gun. "How did you find me?"

If the photos on the Internet were any indication, my brother was normally well groomed to a GQ spit-and-polish with an entitled white male air. Tonight he looked like something was chasing him, and it was hungry. Dark half-moons under his eyes, a several-day stubble, light blond, roughening his cheeks, lessening the hollows. Younger than me he looked decades older. His eyes...*our father's green*...the memory hit then receded like a rogue wave leaving me emotionally staggered. *Yes, our father's eyes*—they rested on me with indifference, as if he had much larger problems than a pissed off sister with a gun. He smelled of a long journey, cheap pizza, and fear and looked stupid enough to do something we'd both regret.

"Tell me," I growled through clenched teeth. My leg screamed. Despite the damp coolness that lingered even indoors in Portland winters, sweat beaded and rolled down my torso under my shirt. All I could think about were my hands around his throat.

He'd brought the darkness here, the men who killed.

I know what you did.

My pain. My broken body. My shattered life.

Me, my friends, we were fine until they told Hank I was alive and I needed his stem cells.

Rage hit my thin veneer of self-control with the force of a hammer on crystal. I tossed the gun to a startled nurse, who juggled it, then clamped it between both hands with a relieved sigh.

I launched myself at my brother. My body slammed into his, taking us both to the floor. Air rushed out of him as he landed on his back, me on top of him. Straddling him, my legs pinning his arms to his side, I landed an elbow to his face. Cartilage gave way. Blood spurted, then streamed from his nose.

He bucked, working an arm loose. With a grunt, he launched me off of him. I skidded into a metal cart. It rolled on two legs, then toppled, scattering supplies. I heard someone call security.

Hank leapt. I rolled. He grabbed my shoulder and flipped me onto my back. Before he could get his full weight on me, I pulled my knees to my chest, my feet, braced against his chest. I thrust out. He fell back, but caught himself. Pain shot through me as he grabbed my foot and twisted. My bad leg. Something popped in my knee, the touch of an electric shock—sharp then numb. I fell back on my back, gritting my teeth. A wounded animal protecting an injury, I pulled into myself. I bent my other leg, angling for a kick at his head. He twisted harder.

A sneer thinned his lips, his eyes mean and slightly mad. "Enough?"

Two hands gripped his jacket, lifting him like a sack of flour, and flung him to the side. He hit the wall with a meaty thunk, then slid down, crumpling on the floor.

Beck's face swam into view. Keeping a watchful eye on Hank, he knelt over me. Red-faced, he looked pissed and more than a bit concerned. Brushing a lock of hair off my forehead, he asked, "Are you okay?"

"Shouldn't someone call the police?" one of the nurses asked. "And where is security?"

As if on cue, two uniformed guys skidded into the hallway.

Beck flashed his badge. "I am the cops, and I have this under control." He extended his hand. "If you'd quit pulling your gun and killing people..."

Steeled against the pain I knew would come, I bent my knee, easing the angle tighter. Curiously, the pain no longer seared, reduced now to a dull ache. The knee moved more freely than it had in a long time. I let him pull me to my feet. "Can't be anyone other than who I am."

"And you always fight in hospital hallways?"

"Impulse control isn't my best thing."

He lifted his chin toward Hank. "Who's this?"

"My brother." I made the introductions, but left out the details, on both sides.

Surprise registered, along with a cop's curiosity. Beck looked like a bloodhound on the scent as he mopped the sweat beaded on his forehead with a wilted pocket-square.

Hank rolled over, blood smearing his face. He wiped at it with the back of his hand, making it worse. With two fingers, he gently probed the bridge of his nose. Apparently, I'd knocked the stupid out of him. "Why do you always go for the nose? How many times does this make?"

"Half dozen?" I wasn't sure. "This time you're lucky I didn't just shoot you."

"What the fuck for?" His hands, cupped under his nose, caught the blood. "Can you get me a rag or something?"

Molten anger oozed from a dark place. "Hell of a way to get my attention, Hank." My voice a hacksaw, each word slicing until the core of truth lay exposed. "You bury a knife in some guy's chest and leave him in my bathtub. Your goons chase me through town, shooting at me in case I'm not taking their message seriously." My breath came hard, fast, as I struggled for air. "You think nothing of setting a fire in an old warehouse, putting I don't know how many lives at risk, then knifing a poor homeless man because he can't give you the information about me you want. Then, just in case I'm not paying attention, you come after my friend, almost kill her." Emotion smoldered just under the surface. One spark would set me off. I fought it, tamping it down, hoping I had enough control.

Hank pulled into himself, watchful, wary.

I moved to retrieve my gun from the nurse.

Beck stepped in. "Oh, no, you don't. Not until you calm down." He pocketed my piece in his overcoat.

I turned back to my brother. "You knew where I was, Hank. You could've just called."

"They got to you, too." Pain arced through him with the sizzle of an electrical current, contorting muscles, pulling skin drum-tight. Then he sagged, the current spent. "I didn't do any of those things, Katie. You have to believe me."

Trust unfurled like a white flag in a bitter fight. "I want to. Give me a reason."

"I got here yesterday. United from LaGuardia. Have your friend there check the manifest."

"As alibis go, that's a bit weak. You could still have been pulling the strings."

"I'm sure the cops are following up on call logs and all of that. I'll check out."

"You know as well as I do they probably were using those untraceable phones. What do you call them?"

"Burn phones," Beck and Hank said in unison. Neither smiled.

"Yes," Hank went on, "but you can still trace cell towers, and, if you've got the game, you can track their movements using GPS, depending."

That much I knew. "I got a feeling we're dealing with somebody smarter than that." Smarter than I had been, but I had an excuse.

Beck turned and spoke to the nearest nurse, who watched in wide-eyed fascination. "Get them something for the blood."

His order spurred her to action. She searched through the strewn contents of the toppled cart, returning with gauze, surgical tape, cotton balls and hydrogen peroxide.

"Do you have anything for the pain?" I asked her as I gathered the supplies in the crook of one arm, balancing them against my chest.

"Nothing that will take it all away."

"Nothing ever does." I held out my free hand. "Give me what you got."

She shook several aspirins out of a well-marked bottle and dropped them into my hand. I swallowed them dry, easy when you do it often enough.

Hank pushed himself to his knees, then crumpled to a sitting position. Instinctively, the nurses moved to help him.

"No." I kept them back.

Blood pooled on his upper lip before trickling over. Leaning against the wall, his head back, he ignored the blood and shut his eyes. "I just wanted to talk to you, Katie."

I know what you did. Now I did, too. "Yeah, we have a lot to talk about."

With my teeth, I tore open the package of gauze and began tending to his nose. Given my disease and my lack of impulse control, and given his stupidity, this time wouldn't be the last, either.

Beck put a hand on my shoulder. "She doesn't know where they are. And we need to finish this discussion somewhere more private." He jostled my shoulder until I glanced up. "Can you give me the short and dirty on the guy down the hall?"

"He's dead."

Beck's tone flattened as he questioned Hank. "Want to tell me about that?"

"I know how it looks."

"As a cop, you also know that's just what we're going to think until you give us good reason not to."

Hank squinted an eye at me. Before he snapped it closed again, I thought I saw subterfuge or self-preservation, but the glimpse was too quick to tell.

A thought pinged, a random blip in the dark. "What happened to the guy you were chasing?" I asked Beck.

"Lost him. Too many people around to risk a shot. Asshole got away from me in the trees. Put a BOLO out on him. We'll bring him in." Beck turned back to Hank. "Did you kill the guy down the hall?"

"No. I was in the room, trying to get the guy to come to

when I heard a noise in the hall. I hid in the bathroom. I thought the new guy was a friend or something, maybe someone he worked with. I couldn't see what he was doing. When he'd gone, I went back to the guy's bedside. His eyes were open. He was struggling for air. He tried to say something; I couldn't make it out. I'd stepped out of the room and was walking the other way."

"How'd you even know about him?"

Hank's gaze skittered to the side. "I was a cop. I know where to look, how to dig. How do you think I found you?"

"Come to think of it, how did you?" Beck asked.

"Only two programs like this in the country. She wasn't at Stanford. Surprising, really. Kate always struck me as more of a California kind of gal."

I'd love to know exactly what kind of gal he remembered me to be, but, if memory served, trustworthy wasn't an adjective many used to describe my brother.

I was the trustworthy one. And look how that turned out.

"You didn't try to help him, the guy who attacked your sister and her doctor?" Beck asked.

"No."

"Why not?"

Hank squinted one eye as he looked up at Beck. "He wasn't worth it."

I could tell Beck didn't like that answer.

"And the killer, where was he?"

"He'd waited, then followed me. When I made him, he turned the other way, heading back this direction. Then the nurse started shouting, and all hell broke loose."

"Why do you think he was following you?"

"I didn't get a chance to ask."

"Guess," Beck said.

I couldn't tell whether he was buying the story or not. I wasn't sure I was, either. Hank played all the angles, always had.

"I assume he thought I could finger him; that I'd seen what

he'd done."

"Could be." Beck pursed his lips. "Or maybe you two were working together."

"We weren't."

"Maybe he recognized you."

"No doubt." Hank clenched his jaw, the muscle working beneath taut skin.

Beck's tone sharpened. "Have you ever seen him before?"

"Yeah."

My hand paused over his face. "What?" The flash of memory searing hot. I'd seen him, too.

"Where?" Beck asked.

Hank stopped my hand as it dabbed at the blood dripping from his nose. His eyes, dark and serious, caught mine. "Last time I saw the guy he was bleeding out in an alley in New York. The alley where they found you, Kate."

Home.

The air was still, the place quiet. As I clicked on all the lights, I thought I caught the hint of death lingering. Pistol at the ready—Beck had finally relented and had given it back to me—I checked the rest of the condo, leaving my little signs to let me know I'd already been there, done that, and I was alone.

Beck had cut the questioning short, prying ears and all of that. He'd suggested we go to my place. He and Hank had two stops, Hank's hotel and the pizza joint down the block for a pie and a six-pack, so I had some time to compose myself.

The guy sent to kill the one survivor from Stella's office had been involved in the raid. I couldn't stop rolling that thought over and over through my head. And he'd had some connection with one of the injured? Or maybe he was checking on him? Of course, that's assuming Hank could be trusted.

So, assuming Hank was telling the truth, who was the guy?

And why had he surfaced now?

Powerless, guilt gnawing, I felt a frantic need to do something.

But what? Out of options, out of ideas, everybody I had trusted playing some angle, hurting my friends. They wouldn't stop, not until they got what they wanted. I'd give them the fucking diamonds if I could.

Where did I hide them? And why?

The answers refused to come, preferring the obscurity of the dark tangle in my head. I had to stop focusing on that and look for answers elsewhere.

Who was the guy in the alley?

After fingering the safety back on, I pocketed the pistol. Home didn't feel as safe as it used to. I'd come in through the garage, pausing for the door to shut behind me before parking my bike. Although I'd been ready, no one waited for me in the shadows. The guy behind the desk had been glad to see me as he handed me my mail. He didn't comment on the smears of Hank's blood I wore like war paint.

Life was as it had been. Except it wasn't.

I swung my backpack onto the couch and poured myself a hefty dose of single malt. Pausing in front of the window, I drank in my view. The drizzle and fog had moved in, returning the city to the clutches of winter, which I found comforting. The Watchman wasn't on his corner, but it was early yet for him. The weather wouldn't run him off; he was a rain-or-shine kind of guy. Betrayal, like a splinter under the skin, burned as it buried itself deeper. He had helped me, saved me, but he'd also hidden himself in his lies. And now Hank. According to Dan and Stella, he was as dirty as last week's snow. I had nothing solid to go on either way, so I straddled the fence. I'd listen, but I'd be smart. He seemed genuine, but something was hurting him, driving him. It was the *why* that I still questioned.

And the *what-to-do* that gnawed at me.

To gain some focus, I needed to let loose of the pain, the worry, the self-loathing and guilt. I felt defeated. Bone-weary and tired of looking over my shoulder. This had to stop.

My file!

Yes, perhaps it might yield some answers.

The Scotch warming, heating, flowing through my veins as much a life force as blood itself, I settled in. The file was thick, worn, pages stained and photos and notes leaking out the sides. Sitting cross-legged on the couch, I opened it in my lap.

I pushed the photos and the notes, most scribbled on scraps of pink paper, back inside. I'd start at the beginning.

The bust had gone down in a warehouse off of Forty-Seventh Street in Manhattan. I scanned the facts, taking a photo with my phone of each page. Three officers killed, two NYPD one FBI. The names meant nothing to me, didn't trigger any memories. Fazio, Belton, and Reynolds. Two young enough to have left grieving families, fatherless children.

I wondered where the dead guy in the hospital figured into all of this. *Hank.* Could we trust what he told us? With precious little else to go on, it was all we had. That and the dispassionate, untethered recitation in my file. Not enough thread to weave a Brazilian bikini.

Maybe I would find the way to walk away from all of this somewhere in these pages. I knew the facts would present a version of me, a history of what I'd done. While actions outlined a picture, motivations filled in the lines. The file would tell me what I had done, but it probably wouldn't tell me why. At least not the whole why.

And the whole why was what I needed.

In the early stages of the disease, I'd asked myself who would I be when I finally forgot me.

Now I knew.

Bits and pieces of a jigsaw puzzle impossible to fit together without the picture of the whole.

I read on, hoping for enlightenment, but the facts were few—this was my WITSEC file and not the actual police file, so the pages mainly dealt with me. I skipped over the parts about my injuries—the pain was all too real. Flipping through, I found a copy of my lease, signed by Dan, and referrals to Stella and the stem cell program from a doctor in Manhattan. I squinted, trying to read the chicken scratch of his signature. It looked like "Dr. Markham," but I wasn't sure.

A transcript of my memory of the events lit the flame of hope. Maybe there would be more there. Would I find myself in between the lines?

Not daring to hope, I scanned the transcript. I'd infiltrated Khoury's gang, worked my way pretty far in, running the couriers, handling the cash, keeping the inventory records. They'd called me The Accountant.

I leaned back, closing my eyes, consciously relaxing each muscle, working for calm. *Diamonds. A dark alley. A room above a busy shop on Forty-Seventh Street. A picture, fuzzy at first, sharper as I tighten the focus. Yes, diamonds; bags of crystal stones. The room quiet, empty but for me. Fear, tangible, real nips at me, a filthy cur chewing on my resolve.*

I leaned forward, eyes turned to the past. I could see it, smell it. *I pour the stones from small paper envelopes, adding several to each bag. I cut my hand with the knife I used to loosen the tape, leaving it uncut so no one would notice. I suck at the blood that drips down my hand.*

I dribble stones into each pouch, reseal the pouch, then loosen another. Opening it, I add some stones, then repeat the process, periodically holding the free stones up, weighing those that remain with the number of pouches, making sure I have enough for all of them.

Time is running out. Hurry. I have to be careful.

A board creaks behind me. Someone is there. I whirl.

No one.

The buzz of the intercom shattered the past, spiking my blood pressure with a shot of adrenaline as I worked to bring myself back. I spun around. No one behind me.

The memories. Was I learning to summon them? Could sheer will open a conduit to the past?

Easing out from under the file, I almost fell when I pushed to my feet. My leg had gone numb. I rubbed it, knowing the pain would return with the blood flow. Pain. An anchor in a life unmoored. I folded the file and pushed the papers together, then pulled some books on top of it.

Limping, using the wall for support, I reached the button

and pressed it.

"Yes?"

"There's a man here. He won't leave. He needs your help." The desk clerk's voice quavered. "He's in a bad way."

"One man, not two?" My heart staggered. "What does he look like?" My pulse steadied. My thoughts cleared.

"He's bleeding. His face is a mess."

"Does he have blond hair?"

"What?"

"Blond? Is he thirties and blond?"

"No, it's the old dude that plays the sax on the corner. He wants only you."

CHAPTER THIRTEEN

With the Watchman leaning heavily on the young desk clerk, and me propping up the other side, we managed to maneuver him into my place. Every couple of steps he sucked in air sharply. "They busted a couple of my ribs, I wager."

I pressed a towel I'd grabbed on the way down over the cut over his cheekbone. Even small cuts on the face bled like hell. His cut wasn't small. Age didn't help—his thin skin had popped open like ripe fruit.

"That's going to need some stitches."

"I've had worse." The Watchman groaned as we lowered him to the couch. Taking the twenty I offered, the clerk backed away and bolted through the door like the hounds of hell nipped at his heels.

"What happened?" I asked when we were alone.

As I assessed the damage, probing gingerly, the Watchman motioned toward the door. "Lock it." Pain muted his voice, but anger lit his eyes.

I threw the three bolts then pulled out the gun just enough so he saw it and tucked it in the waistband of my pants. Stupid, really. I knew a guy once who shot his pecker off doing the same thing. But, anatomically speaking, I didn't suffer from the same impediment, so I figured the threat was worth the risk. I knelt in front of him, then sat back on my heels, a bit stunned. How did I remember that? Glimpses of the past arrived like flashes of gunfire from an unseen enemy.

"Water," the Watchman wheezed.

"Give me a minute. Let me look at you. We may need to get you to the hospital. That cut needs some stitches. I'm sure you're not up to date on your shots."

"You're making me sound like a stray who wandered in."

"Not a bad analogy, Sam, but that's not your name, is it?" I couldn't remember his real name, the one Beck had told me. He'd always be Sam to me, the name seared into my synapses by a connection I couldn't remember.

His eyes widened then his face settled into resignation paled by pain. "Knew you'd figure it out eventually."

"Why'd you lie to me?"

"I lie to myself. Makes life tolerable." He pressed his ribs one by one, pain contorting his face when he hit a tender spot. "You got secrets like that. I can see them when you're asleep. The truth too painful to bring out into the light."

"Still, you lied." He and I were reading from the same book. That didn't make me feel any better. "You said they got your ribs. Do you hurt anywhere else?"

"Everywhere." He tried to push my hands away as I worked his shirt open, which took some time. Most of the buttons had fallen off, replaced with whatever was at hand: staples, paper clips, an occasional safety pin, or just a straight pin, its point bent. The clothes were clean, carrying a scent of pine. His hands stayed pressed over his stomach. He let me look at his ribs, but kept the rest covered. Breathing in through his nose and out through his mouth, he fought against the pain, the panic in his eyes.

"They almost got me." His skin was white, translucent in spots, a latticework of blue veins visible underneath. Bruising purpled his side.

I barely pressed. "This hurt?"

A sharp inhale. His eyes narrowed with pain.

"A couple of broken ribs, like you said." A long red cut circled under the lowest rib on his left side. "What's this?"

"Tried to stick me," he wheezed, each word carefully

formed, braced against the pain it took to talk. "Like the others, which makes me wonder."

"About what?"

"I got a side door into this game. Benny, the guy in the square with your jacket? He was one of mine. These guys, the ones who left the dead guy in your tub, the ones who killed Benny, they're killing for one reason and scaring for another."

I struggled to put the logic together—I didn't remember the guy with my jacket. I barely remembered the guy in my tub—the details disappearing, a movie fading to black. "What do you know? Why have you been watching me, really?"

Easing back, I rested on my haunches and took a good long look. There was a familiarity in his features. He'd already told me we'd known each other. But he hadn't told me it all. "You were there," I whispered, the truth teasing me, darting into the light, then ducking back into the shadows.

Pain etched the lines in his face deeper. A tic worked in his cheek as he moved, gingerly searching for comfort.

I could tell him he wouldn't find it.

"Where?" he said. Avoiding.

"What do you want from me?" I almost lunged for him, but the pain in his face, the indifference in his eyes, stopped me. But what he said next bolted me to the floor.

"I want to know what you did."

"What?" I whispered, and the past whispered back. "You. You knew the guy in my tub."

"I've never seen the guy in your tub."

I scrolled through the photos in my phone. Finding the one I wanted, I stuck it under his nose. "There. Johnny Nesto was his name."

The Watchman groaned as he fell back against the cushions. He squeezed his eyes tight.

"Diamonds," I whispered. I remembered the diamonds. I pulled the gun out of my waistband. Using two hands, I steadied it and pointed it at his heart. "You're looking for the diamonds, too."

"Nesto and Benny, they worked for me." Undoing the last

few fasteners, he opened his shirt wide. An old scar, purple, thick and wide but flattened by time, zippered his abdomen.

I recoiled as if a snake lay coiled on his stomach. "You were a mule."

His eyes, hard and mean, drifted from mine as he nodded. "Been a while."

"Is that why, all those years ago, you took your brother's identity?" Their names were tangled in my head. "So you could take his place?"

"See, you're better than you think at fitting pieces together." He stuffed a pillow behind the small of his back and let his weight sink into the couch. "You set me up, getting me all those documents in his name. Then you followed me in, although you didn't really know it at the time." His voice steadied. "Kate, you and I worked together. We both worked for Khoury."

"And you knew I was a cop."

"It was part of our deal."

I kept the gun leveled at his chest. "If one went down, both went down?"

"Helps to know who your friends are." The fight left him as the pain took its toll. He was probably bleeding inside, and his breathing was labored. Maybe a rib had punctured a lung.

I knelt in front of him and dabbed at his face with the cloth. For the most part, the bleeding had slowed, but the cut was long and deep. "Let me get you something for that cut." I returned with some butterfly bandages I found under the sink in the bathroom. First time I'd been in there since finding the dead guy. *What was his name?* I shook my head. "Was it you who blew my cover?"

He seemed genuinely offended, which I thought laughable or terrifying, depending. "Man, I'd put everything on the line, same as you. The guys who took out my brother—they thought he was me—I killed them, but I hadn't gotten to the man who ordered the hit. Still haven't."

"That's why you lied to me? You're still in?" My brain refused to wrap around that possibility. So many questions, the answers hidden in the murky past, I kept the gun leveled at his chest, both hands holding it steady.

"Not really, but an organization like that, you never really get out. I'm old. Still sniffing around the edges. They get hold of me when they want something. But like I said, the organization hasn't jelled again after Khoury got taken down. Khoury had a special conduit for the diamonds out of Africa—it takes a while to cultivate those relationships. And the guys who tried to muscle in ended up dead—so have the folks there that night. Khoury's out there and he's cleaning up his mess, working his way back, but he needs the missing stones. The Feds confiscated all his bank accounts, his inventory, when they arrested him. The twenty mil is his buy-in price."

"Honor among thieves and all of that," I said, not finding the humor.

His eyes held mine. "I have to keep their confidence. That's the only way I can find Khoury. He's the one who had my brother killed."

"You were Khoury's boy. What did you do that got your brother killed?"

He winced then shook as he talked, retreating into himself, unconcerned by me, the gun, reliving the horror. "They left him open, his guts hanging out, and they threw him in a dumpster like so much trash. They said he'd been alive for hours. Scratching, trying to get out. His fingernails were torn and bloody—he'd worn them to the bone. Nobody heard him. Nobody helped."

Haunted, his eyes found mine. The skin of his face was pale, the cut like a bit of Halloween gore. "I'm going to kill Khoury. I owe that to my brother. To myself. Then you or anybody else can do what you want with me."

Conviction rang in every word, painted every feature, glinting in his eyes, tightening his mouth, hardening his features. Trusting him went against every bit of logic, except one. He needed me.

"Okay."

He visibly relaxed, taking a deep breath, then wincing as his ribs objected.

"We're both using each other here," I said, maybe more for me than for him. "We need each other to get what we want. I'll help you, but you've got to come clean, tell me what you're not saying." His eyes followed me as I moved closer, closing his cut with another bandage. "You still a mule?"

"I'm not as young as I used to be, so they don't cut on me... haven't in a good while. But Nesto and Benny, they were mine. I got them killed." He gave me a hard stare. "You got them killed."

"How?"

"Khoury thinks you got the diamonds. He's killing everyone, driving us together—you, me, and your brother—hoping we give him the diamonds."

"Could be you doing the killing." My gaze flicked to his.

"A broken man killing people as he looked for justice for his sins." There was no remorse in his words. "An old, tired story. And I'm tired. Tired of living with what I've done. But I have one thing to do before I go."

"You lied before. Why should I believe you now? What's to say you aren't playing me one last time?"

"I haven't killed you."

Curiously indifferent about that, I pulled out my phone. "Just making notes while it's fresh. It's what'll help me remember tomorrow when things aren't so sharp." I dictated the recent conversation into my phone, the Watchman correcting and highlighting where necessary but not adding anything. When I'd finished, I left the record function scrolling. "Tell me about..." I stumbled over his name.

"Sam?" Revenge flattened a wistful note. "He was my brother and everything that I was not."

"Did you resent him?"

"I don't think so. In fact, I worshiped him. None of us can escape the hand we're dealt. You know that firsthand."

"Doesn't mean we have to like it."

"True, but our kind of crazy just is. Can't lay fault. When Sam got that scholarship, man, I was over the moon. We all were."

"What happened?"

The flash of remembered joy evaporated, his voice went hollow as if his heart had been carved out and the words echoed in the hollow cavity. "I happened."

Ignoring my own pain, I pushed myself to my feet, then turned to stare out into the night, my back to his pain. With several broken ribs, if the Watchman intended to kill me, he wouldn't do it tonight.

His voice had lost some of its force, turning breathy, labored, as if he couldn't breathe. "I wanted to be like him, thought I could. The docs had stabilized me. My mom had started to relax, even though my dad had pretty much checked out. I thought I was cured, so I stopped taking my meds. Crashed bad. Nobody knew where I was. Hell, I didn't even know who I was, so I couldn't have found my way home if I'd wanted to, which I didn't. Crazy stuff was going through my head. I fell in with Khoury, started running for him."

"And your brother? How'd he get mixed up in all of this?"

"I didn't know this until later, but he turned down a shot at the majors. Stayed home to hold my mother together, help her look for me." The Watchman eyed me. "You think I could have something to take the edge off? Ribs are squealing worse than a litter of piglets."

I poured him a healthy dose of single malt. He needed both hands to steady the glass to his lips. "Man, that's smooth."

"Did he find you?"

"Yeah. Funny thing, I'd never left New York. He'd been shifting through the trash in the five boroughs—he knew where I hung out. Finally found me strung out and near death in some flophouse in the Bronx on the run, hallucinating, not sure which end was up. Turns out I had been on my way to a mobile surgical site in Brooklyn. The doc was set to open me up. Problem was, I didn't show. Neither did the diamonds. Khoury thought I stole them."

"So why'd he let you back in?"

"He learned I wasn't running; I didn't intend to steal his load."

"That's weak. I don't believe it."

"He killed my brother to make sure I got the message and I'd keep my nose clean. He figured with that hanging over my head, and other family members in the crosshairs, he'd have a motivated employee."

"He was wrong?" I asked.

"No, he was right. He just didn't figure my motivation would be to see him dead."

"This was when?"

"Five years ago or more. I work hard at not keeping track."

"You were a lot older than your brother."

"He was one of those late-in-life blessings, my mother used to say."

Allowing for his brother's time in school, that still put the Watchman at not yet fifty. A hard life had etched fissures into his face. Exposure had tanned his skin like a hide; guilt had done the rest. Seventy had been my guess.

"Some folks stick by family until it kills them," he said.

His veiled warning, a bomb with no detonator, thudded against the emotional wall I'd fortified with justifications. My brother was all I had left of me.

"Did you steal the diamonds?"

His hands still shook, but some color now flushed the deathly pale of his cheeks. "I don't think I intended to steal them. I'm crazy, not stupid. The whole lot of them were tucked in my pants when Sam found me. Trust me, no one was going to look there, nobody but my brother anyway. Apparently, the combination of my schizophrenia, whatever street drugs I was mainlining, and the drugs I needed but wasn't taking, dropped me down one hell of a hole."

His story wound painfully to a conclusion I could reach without his help. To numb the pain, both his and my own, I poured myself a tumbler of the good stuff. "Sam took your place to get you off the hook with Khoury and ended up in a dumpster."

"After he took me to the docs who got me clean. I wish they never had. And I wish like hell I'd never shared my sad story with Sam." He felt gingerly at the bandages closing the wounds on his face. "Funny thing is, I never remember telling him."

"Why didn't you just disappear and your brother could go back to his life?"

"With guys like Khoury, you never disappear. They find you. Seems to me we've had enough evidence of that here recently."

Couldn't argue with him on that. "Can't hide from what you've done." Harsher than I intended, I'd meant that for me. I looked for a reaction. Didn't see one. Either he was numb to it, or he'd made his peace—a place I still sought. "But that doesn't mean the fault is yours. Remember, our kind of crazy just is."

"My dad crawled into a bottle. My mother died of a broken heart. I was a poor substitute for her golden boy. Remembering is my punishment." He said it so simply, and there it was.

I threw back the Scotch, knowing it wouldn't take away the pain. "What happened to you and the others after..." I couldn't bring myself to say it. *After I fucked up.*

"The diamonds were gone. So, like the rest, I had to run. I followed you."

If it was that easy... "Anybody else follow me?"

"A couple. They met a bad end, as they say." He seemed pleased, exposing the cold heart of a killer.

"You know where Khoury is?"

"No." The Watchman's eyes were black holes. I thought I could see where his soul used to be. Or maybe his eyes were a reflection of what they saw as they bored through me. "Another guy stepped in when Khoury got busted. After Khoury got busted out while being transported to trial, the new guy pulled a Jimmy Hoffa."

I raised an eyebrow. "Nobody's seen him?"

"Nope. And nobody's been looking."

I must've looked skeptical.

"Khoury's back in business; I know it."

"How can you be so sure?"

"I've heard whispers. Talked to folks who have seen proof

it's him."

"How long ago did Khoury escape?" I must've seen that in my file but I'd forgotten.

"A few months, maybe a year. Time isn't something I got a good handle on. I'm thinking Khoury can't solidify his spot without the stolen diamonds. Some of the guys are going to be real skeptical—not good for a business that runs on confidence."

"Confidence. Gained or inflicted?"

He gave a shrug. "Both work."

"A nice theory. But I don't know if I trust you. You only tell me when you have to. When you want something." I angled so I could look out the window. Hugging my knees, I caught my reflection. Funny, I still looked like me, but I felt like a pumpkin with a carved smile, my insides raked away, a false light flickering inside. "Who's to say you don't want the diamonds for yourself?" I asked, looking to the horizon, but not seeing.

"Me."

"That's it? Your story could be total bullshit."

"Who told you about me? My background? Somebody did; I can see it in your face. You know I'm telling the truth."

"I knew some of it."

Breathing hard, he pressed a palm against his stomach. "At some point, you've got to choose. Trust somebody. It's your call."

My gut instinct used to be spot-on. Now it seemed to have disappeared down the same rabbit hole as my memory. Or maybe I just wasn't trusting me anymore. "I don't know about your theory, but something's sure up. Things are escalating." I wanted another bellyful of Scotch, but resisted. Wouldn't be good to muddy an already muddled thought process, although it'd sure feel good.

"Folks are dying," the Watchman reminded me, though he didn't have to. Things were sticking, bad things. "Your brother shows up. Interesting coincidences, wouldn't you say?"

Sarcasm. I still got that, or maybe that was a newly

returned skill. Either way, I understood it was both a shield and a sword.

"We're chasing the same devil, you and me," the Watchman said, his voice low, his tone measured.

Was he trying to convince me or himself?

"*You* may be chasing him, but so far he's been chasing me. I aim to change that. You have any idea where Khoury might be?"

"We need to find the guy from the hospital, the one who ran."

"My brother might know. He said he'd seen him."

The Watchman gave me a sideways glance. "Maybe."

"You don't trust him, my brother?"

"I'm pretty sure I just said that."

"If you don't want to go that route, do you know where to look for the guy?"

He shrugged then winced. "I know someone to ask."

"Who?"

"One of my guys. But it's just you and me who are going to find him."

"Two crazies against a whole lot of bad. Hardly seems fair." I didn't like it.

"We don't owe them a fair fight."

At first, I thought he hadn't understood. His smile told me otherwise.

"Why cut me from the herd?"

"Can't trust your brother. Can't take a cop inside. You in?"

"Not sure I have a choice. They've brought the fight to me. Either I run for the rest of my life, or..."

"We fight," the Watchman finished.

Their timing impeccable, Beck and Hank rang downstairs buzzer. I confirmed it was them, then buzzed them up.

"I'm going to think about what you said," I said to the Watchman, as I tried to arrange my features in a less pinched, less accusatory manner. "I'm not sure I can trust you. Hell, I'm not sure I can trust anyone. Not you, not my brother, not even myself."

"The only other player here is a cop. Not exactly welcome where we have to go."

"Tell me where we're going." He had to give me something if he wanted me. I could tell he understood.

"Louie. He plays jazz at the Easy Jazz Club on One-Twenty-Fifth in Harlem. He knew your brother, too."

"Hank?" That I didn't see coming.

"A couple of cops used to hang there."

The Watchman had been watching me. The thought both chilled and calmed me. I wish I knew what the right reaction was. Was he friend or foe?

Beck. He'd crossed the line for me, I was pretty sure. And I couldn't let him go any further. My future rode on a cloudy past—a past that could take us both down if I let it. Until I had some answers, I'd have to go it alone, with the Watchman or without, fighting Hank or learning to trust him. I hated living dogged by the unknown with unforeseeable consequences. "Let's keep this between us for now." I waited for a sign of complicity from the Watchman. I found it in the softening of his features. "We've got pizza coming. You hungry?"

"You never pass up a meal when you don't know where the next one is coming from."

Pizza wouldn't satisfy the kind of hunger that gnawed at him, but it was all I had.

"There's more to tell." He gave me a long stare. "I knew your brother back then. But what I got to tell you is between you and me, right?"

A knock on the door left me with questions but no answers, and a hole where my heart should be. I moved a pot from in front of the door.

"Who is it?"

Beck and Hank spoke in turn. I unlocked the deadbolts and let them in.

Balancing a six-pack on top of two large pizza boxes, Beck pushed past, then paused on his way to the kitchen. "What's he doing here?"

The look on his face told me he couldn't figure what to make of the Watchman and his presence in my living room. "He needed a friend."

"You okay?"

"Better question, is he? Broken ribs and a cut-up face."

"It's you I care about."

I followed him to the kitchen. "You don't know my whole story."

"I know you."

"Not all of me."

He set the pizzas on the counter. When I reached to open a box, he put a hand on the top, demanding my attention. "You're just not going to let me in, are you?"

"You might not like what you find."

"I'm a big boy." He glanced at the Watchman, eyeing Hank's back as he poured himself a drink. "It seems to me *you* could use a friend, one you're sure isn't working an angle that might end up being a knife in your back."

"After this long protecting myself..."

He nodded and removed his hand, as if he'd gotten the answer he wanted. When he opened the box, the smell of pizza roiled my stomach. I hated pizza. Not the taste especially, but something else. A feeling it triggered. The raw tang of terror. Darkness. Answers hid in the 'why' but I hadn't been able to reach them.

Hank had slung his backpack on a chair. Nursing his drink, he moved to stare out my window—I knew the healing power of the view, the way it could tug on all the hurt places inside.

Leaving Beck to parse out the pizza, I moved in, drinking in my view next to Hank. He glanced at me, a fleeting caress of a memory. Blood had oozed, crusting a nostril. His nose still angled off center. It fit him. Less pretty boy, more badass.

"So, who was the guy in the alley? Not the ones who died, the other one? The one who killed the guy at the hospital?" I'd been clinging to that question, repeating it over and over in my mind.

Ignoring my question, he motioned toward the Watchman.

"What's he doing here?"

"He's my friend."

Hank laughed—it wasn't a nice laugh. "You don't remember."

"You'd be surprised what destroying synapses will do to your memory." The warm poison of anger, a beckoning drug. Everybody seemed to be keeping secrets, flinging them at me to keep me perpetually off balance. Hank was playing me. I knew that look on his face. "Be careful, Hank, be very careful. I know you. If you lie," I included the Watchman with a sweep of my arm, "if either of you lies, we all go down and nobody gets what they want."

My fingers itching to fold into a fist, I looked for something else to do with them. Beck looked grim as he handed plates piled with pizza to each of us in turn, then offered the beer, two cans clutched in his hand. No takers. Then he stepped to the side, watching, measuring. I knew that look, too.

"Why don't you tell her?" the Watchman asked, his voice stretched thin. "But tell her all of it."

Hank curled his shoulders, a cobra coiling. "If we have the diamonds, we have leverage," he said, as he sidled over to the bar, keeping an eye on the Watchman as he did so.

"That's all you have to say?" I asked.

"I can't say more. I've got my reasons." He poured a stiff Scotch, then threw it back.

"Fuck it, Hank! People are dying." *I know what you've done.*

"Don't you think I know that?" He slammed the glass down on the bar as he whirled on me, spitting with fury...and something else.

Fear. "What are you afraid of?"

He gave a tight laugh. "Are you kidding me?"

"What do you remember about that night?" Beck interjected, his tone designed to defuse.

Hank recoiled like he'd been slapped, then relaxed and slouched back into a chair. "Acting on your intel, we cornered the diamond couriers in an alley behind Forty-Seventh Street.

Khoury actually showed his face, as you said he would."

"He rarely let himself be seen," the Watchman added. "I had one hell of a time getting into the same room with that man. Was planning on hitting him that night."

Hank nodded once, but didn't look at him, keeping his eyes on me. "I kept looking for you, but you didn't show. After that, everything went to hell. We exchanged fire. The team scattered. We arrested Khoury. Found you in another alley nearby, damn near dead. Fazio had fallen close by. Paramedics cleaned up, and the rest is history."

"And there was an investigation into how the cops ended up dead, and me damn near?"

"Yeah, but you know how those things go. Internal Affairs doesn't share. Either heads roll, or they don't."

"And?"

"Nothing."

"And the diamonds?"

"Gone." He stared at me like he wanted to burn a hole in my skin and see inside. "People think you took them."

"Why do they think that?"

"Nobody came back for the diamonds. Or at least, no one has tried to put them on the market."

"You know that?"

"None of the marked stones have been put into the sales pipeline. And somebody is killing people to find them. The assumption is clear."

No one argued. If the diamonds had been found, no one would still be looking.

"Of everyone involved, you were the only one who couldn't get back," Hank continued after a long pull at his drink. "Because of your injuries. And then your—" he looked away for a moment, "your memory problems."

"There were others who couldn't come back. Unless you believe in ghosts." We needed to remember three cops died that night.

He flinched. I'd hit a soft spot.

Here it was, that moment everyone dreads, the moment

DEBORAH COONTS

that would change everything and it was impossible to say for the better or the worse. Breathing deep, I closed my mind and went with my gut. "I remember holding the diamonds, running with them. But I don't remember taking them." The words landed in the middle of the room like a hand grenade on a ten-second timer.

"What?" Clearly caught off guard, Hank blinked rapidly. His hand sought the arm of the chair, his grip so tight his knuckles whitened. "You?" His voice breathless. "*You* took the diamonds?" He sounded a bit incredulous, which made me happy and a bit defensive.

"The memories are coming back. Bits and pieces from that night. Nothing that makes a lot of cohesive sense, but I distinctly remember carrying a bag of the diamonds, running with them. I had them stashed in my clothing, somewhere. They kept banging me as I ran."

"You took them?"

"Why do you keep asking me that?"

"What did you do with them?"

"I must've hidden them. I can't remember."

"Shit." Hank rubbed his face, grimacing when he hit his nose. "Your memories are coming back? The treatment—it's working, right?"

"Yes, but it's hard to anticipate exactly how it will manifest. Memories, they're like a jigsaw puzzle. I get a few pieces at a time, but not yet enough to see the whole picture. It's hard to tell where they come from and whether they are actual things that happened or more like dreams, based in reality but not entirely accurate."

"Why don't we go through what we do know?" Beck said, the calm voice a beacon in an ocean of emotion. "The guy from the hospital today, you said you saw him bleeding in the alley where they found Kate." He speared Hank with a hard look. He pulled a photo from his pocket, showed it to me, then handed it to my brother. "Had the security guys at the hospital pull it from their video feed."

The guy running through the corridor. Grainy, but a good shot of most of his face as he turned to look over his shoulder.

196

"Tell me about him," he said to Hank. "You act like you saw him before the alley. Where?"

My brother glanced down, swallowed hard. "At the precinct, maybe." He shook his head. "I can't figure what he's doing here offing some goon coming to look for you."

"Was he a cop?"

Hank shrugged. "I don't know."

"The only thing it said in my WITSEC file was three guys got killed."

"It was one hell of a firefight." Hank's interest spiked; I could see it in his eyes. "You got names, the ones who were killed?"

I pulled out my phone. "Fazio, Belton, and Reynolds." I'd watched Hank as I read the names. He flinched on the last one. I put a star next to Reynolds in my notes. That name had hit me, too.

"Nobody else?" Hank asked.

"No. You know any of these three?"

"Sure, you do, too. Fazio was SWAT, been with the force ten years I bet, maybe more. Belton, I didn't know well. Seen him around. He kept to himself but kept his nose clean."

"And Reynolds?"

Hank's face closed, his voice turned hard. "He was my partner."

Of course! Reynolds. "Shifty guy?" I wanted to tell Hank everything would be okay. No matter what had gone down, no matter what he'd done, he was still my brother. But hollow reassurances wouldn't quell the rage that ran just under the surface, the rage I saw in the stiffness of his neck, his clenched jaw, the hardness of his eyes.

"What do you remember about that night?" Beck directed the question to me.

I opened my mind, reaching back through the darkness. "Someone hitting me from behind. Pain. Sounds with no pictures. Fear. It's dark, gunfire in the background. Running, holding the diamonds. Being beaten. All jumbled, out of sequence, the timing off."

Hank leaned back. "Damn." He retreated somewhere I couldn't go. I saw it in his eyes, in the fierce angle of his chin, in the tremor of his hand as his lifted his glass to his lips. Looking anywhere but at me, he spied a slip of pink paper under the coffee table. He picked it up, scanned it, then read it again, his lips moving in concentration.

"What's that?" I asked, but I thought maybe I had been reading my file and maybe I'd seen pink notes in there, but I wasn't sure.

Hank shook his head and pursed his lips. "Don't know. Must be yours." He put it on the table.

"Maybe more will come," the Watchman said. "But even if you don't remember, Khoury doesn't know that. He dropped a guy in your tub; remember that. He's trying to scare you, make you run, make you show your hand. We can get him if we have you."

"We don't need the diamonds for leverage." The Watchman tossed Hank's words back at him. "We just need Khoury and his bunch to think we have the ice." He turned and caught my gaze. "What you believe is more powerful than what is."

That comment was floating on a river of subtext that I had no idea how to navigate.

"So we don't need the diamonds," Hank's voice held a dangerous edge, "because we have Kate."

Hank's eyes, hard and haunted, flicked to the Watchman, emotions playing across his face like scenes across a screen. His words were for me as he stepped into the kitchen, putting his plate with the pizza, now cold, on the counter. "You do know he's the one who damn near got you killed." His eyes never left the Watchman.

The Watchman didn't argue. He angled his head, eyes narrowed. "Why do you think that?"

"Reynolds told me."

The Watchman's only reaction was a raised eyebrow. "Reynolds told you what, exactly?" The tone in his voice carried a warning.

"He told me someone highly placed in the organization was working both sides of the street."

"So he didn't say it was me. You'd just like it to be that way."

Hank rolled in his shoulders, a defensive posture. "Coulda been you."

The Watchman nodded. "Could have. But telling you it wasn't me won't change your mind."

"Reynolds?" I prompted. "Your partner, right?" At his nod I felt hope flare—a tiny light, but it was there...so were some of the memories. "How'd he know?"

"He was a beat cop in the neighborhood and your go-to if anything went bad and a conduit for intel if it didn't," Hank reminded me, finally seeming to catch on that big pieces of my past were missing.

Still, he shouldn't have known my snitch. I wouldn't have given him up, would I? That the Watchman and I were working together made sense—we both had the same goal.

"Why would the Watchman give me up?"

"To save his own ass." Hank was speculating. I could see it in the narrowing of his eyes, the duplicity hidden in his righteous indignation. The same look he used when we were kids and he set me up to take the fall for him time. One of his favorite pastimes. His mantle of perfection irritated like a hair shirt; yet he still donned it.

"Couldn't Reynolds have sold us both out?"

"He didn't."

"Can you prove it?"

A tic pulsed in his cheek as he worried a thread on the arm of the chair. "Don't have to. I just know."

"So the answer is no." I took a deep breath. "Hank, why the hell are you really here? What is it you want? The diamonds? What?"

"I was wondering when you were going to get around to asking him that," Beck said.

"I need you, Katie."

At his tone, I stopped and sat back on my haunches.

"What's going on?"

His eyes flicked to Beck. "No cops. I promised."

"Promised who?"

"I don't know, okay?" Emotion propelled him out of the chair. He raked his fingers through his hair as he stood there immobilized by the need to move, but having nowhere to go. Breathing heavily, he looked at me, and the Hank I knew drained out of him, anger replaced by the quiet of an impending storm. "Katie, they took my son. Leverage, they called it."

A punch to the gut I never saw coming. "What?" All my breath rode out on that one word.

I know what you've done.

He grabbed me and yanked me close. Beck moved to stop him, but I waved him off with a shake of my head. Hank's voice broke as he wrestled with a parent's worst nightmare. "They took him." His eyes wild, amped on hate and helplessness, Hank gestured toward the window. "He's out there somewhere. Just a kid. Scared. Maybe hurt. His mother is crazy with worry and anger. And we're fucking around eating pizza and drinking beer." He pressed his hands to the side of his head as if he could make reality go away. He vibrated like a boiler well past redline.

I know what I did. This is my fault.

"Two years old, not yet, almost. Just a baby. My wife..." I could see him struggling. "I thought you could help. Everything's gone in the crapper ever since..."

"I know." I stepped away from him, my need to think warring with my desperate desire to kill somebody.

Beck stood guard over me as he pulled his notebook from his pocket. "Can you tell us what happened?"

"I told you. No cops," Hank spat the words like an accusation.

"I can help if you'll let me."

Hank waffled, warring with an impossible decision. "Mother's Day Out. Two guys. He was there, then he was gone. Nobody could tell me much."

"Did you file a report?"

Hank gave Beck a look. "Of course not. I *am* a cop. I don't need anybody else around to screw it up."

"But you want Kate to help you."

Hank's eyes shifted to mine, filled with pain. I couldn't bear it.

I knew what I'd done.

"They want the diamonds, Kate."

"But I don't know where they are!" God, what had I done? The cascade of horrors that fell from one moment of greed. And I didn't even know why.

And now a child as a bargaining chip.

I know what you did.

"Doesn't change the fact that whoever put that guy in your tub, Kate, was sending a message to both of you," Beck said. "Your guy," his look took in the Watchman. "In your tub." His gaze flicked by me, pausing, then landed on Hank, settling like a buzzard tearing at carrion. "And they've taken your kid."

"They knew we worked together." I connected his dots.

"And they wanted you two to figure it out."

But they'd wanted to kill the Watchman, if his story could be believed.

Something wasn't adding up.

CHAPTER FOURTEEN

The darkness outside the windows called when the Watchman tried to stir himself from the soft folds of the couch. "I should go."

Beck had taken Hank with him. "Divide and conquer," he'd whispered, as he'd left with my brother unhappily in tow. He hadn't told me to be careful; he'd simply accepted my competence. Unusual and appreciated, coming as it was from the male of the species, hardwired to protect and defend us wilting female flowers. The thought made me smile.

Hank hadn't been as nice. My arm still hurt where he'd grabbed me. He'd bent low, his lips near my ear, the smell of scotch and pizza on his breath. "You watch your back. He's playing you like he plays that damned sax. He's dangerous. And when he gets what he wants..." He left the implication hanging, as if I scared easily. Hard to scare someone who didn't have much to lose.

I motioned the Watchman down. "No, you stay. Take a hot shower. When you do, leave me those clothes; I'll clean them up as best I can. I'll bring you a robe in the meantime." I shut down the argument I saw on his lips. "A soft bed on broken ribs wouldn't hurt now, would it? I think you've suffered enough."

When his eyes met mine, I saw he understood what I meant...all of it.

After making sure he had all he needed and his clothes were in the wash, I broke into my stash, hastily rolling myself a thin stick of pain relief. My leg hurt; hell, all of me hurt after being slammed to the floor. My heart hurt most of all.

Half a joint inhaled, the water in the guest shower flowing, the washer sloshing, I stepped to my favorite wall of windows to try to make sense of the day. As I inhaled, breathing deep and holding it until the pain dulled, I listened to my recordings. To get it all I had to go through the tape twice. These things I knew: Hank was lying about something; the Watchman was playing his cards one at a time. And I needed a fucking Ouija board.

Sitting on the couch, I saw a few slips of paper at my feet. Photos from the file. They'd escaped. I hadn't noticed. I gathered them with the pink paper Hank had picked up.

My cell phone rang, deepening my frown. I checked the caller ID. Dan. "I'm home. I'm being a good girl. No more dead guys," I said without preamble. I wasn't in a preamble kind of mood.

"I know." His voice didn't hold the normal warmth or weariness. Just a bit of Fed seriousness with a hint of pissed off. "Heard you had a ruckus at the hospital."

"Not me. Somebody killed your witness."

"I heard. Not from you, by the way."

I wasn't sure whether I should apologize. I didn't feel the need, so I didn't.

"Hank was there," Dan said. It wasn't a question. "He do it?"

"Hard to tell."

"He's not there with you, is he?" Ah, there was the concern.

"No, Detective Hudson took him with him." I let him leap to the wrong conclusion.

"You get anything out of him?"

His kid's been taken, but I didn't say that. The thought touched me like a live wire on an open current and I worked to keep my voice even. "Nothing useful."

Dan paused, his breath sighing through the line. "You

okay?"

"As good as always."

"So, anything in your file jump out at you?"

"The guys who died. Know anything about them?"

"Not personally, no." I could picture him shrugging his shoulders and rotating his head to stretch his neck—he always did that when uncomfortable, a tell I don't think he was aware of. "As I recall, the investigation didn't turn up anything interesting."

In my experience, investigations turned up what benefited the officers with the most to lose, but I didn't say so. "Then nothing else. I haven't had a chance to dig in, read between the lines. On the surface, the story was straightforward."

"Except for the missing diamonds."

"And who made me."

"That, too."

After pulling every shred of smoke into my lungs, I tamped the tiny butt in an ashtray. "Dan, do I have any children?" The thought had been eating at my insides since I'd had the dreams, the visions—the two kids, bucolic home. Whatever they were, they felt real, as real as any emotion I had now.

"Why would you ask that?" He laughed as if he found the question funny.

"Do I?"

"Of course not."

"Why would you say it that way?"

"Kate, trust me, kids weren't your thing. Not the way you were wired."

I didn't know whether to be relieved or sad.

"Kate, I need to know anything, anything at all, that hits you when you go through that file. I've got folks dying, being assaulted, a hurricane of bad shit whirling around you. We need to stop it."

I didn't promise anything. Didn't have to. After a few awkward pleasantries, we signed off and I settled in with my file. I worked through it again, from front to back.

The day drained away, taking with it the adrenaline I lived on. My eyes refused to focus; my thoughts wandered. Sleep fuzzed the edges. I didn't resist.

The daylight softens the melancholy of the neighborhood, its pink glow chasing away the graffiti-laden despair marking the steel shutters on the storefronts that locked inside what little bit of hope remained, its soft light diffusing the background. The rumble of traffic thrums, not close. The day hadn't awakened here. The street quiet, a time of day when only sinners stir. A lone tree thrust upward through a tiny square of soil in the concrete, its thin branches bare. Leafless, brittle, the tree had died. A bum sleeps in the meager shelter of a doorway. The smell of ripe garbage perfumes the streets. A couple of kids, hoodies protecting them, hands jammed in pockets, hurry away from me. My pockets empty, fear a vulture pecking at the carrion of my rotting soul. I'd never felt this empty, this alone...this afraid.

"Your friend, he owes the man," a voice growls behind me. I don't turn to look.

"He can't pay."

"He will, or you maybe. One way or another."

The Watchman was gone when I awakened. Curled on the couch, lost to the dreams, I hadn't heard him leave and he hadn't bothered me. Instead, he'd tucked a blanket around me. The note on the table said he'd find me. He also said he'd taken the picture Beck had left, the one of the killer at the hospital.

The Watchman had gone hunting. I didn't feel good about that.

I ran fingers through my hair, sucked down two mugs of coffee as quickly as I could without taking too much skin off, then chased that with my meds. I grabbed my keys and bolted a piece of cold pizza as I headed out the door.

Hank was waiting, not a surprise. This time, the weather, a steady cold rain, had driven him into the lobby. "Where are you going?"

I shrugged into my rain gear, zipping my jacket as I checked my box for mail. "I've got an appointment at the hospital. After my treatments they like to make sure my brain hasn't turned to mush."

"Look," he stopped with a hand on my arm.

I didn't look at him; guilt didn't allow it.

"Here's a picture of my kids. Don't know if you remember or not, but you haven't met them. When Sara was born, you were deep undercover, then the shit hit the fan, you went down and disappeared." He raked his hands through his hair making it stand up in spikes. "Hell, I didn't even know if you were alive. Thank God Mom and Dad didn't live to go through this."

"If you're trying to lay blame, this isn't the time and there's enough to go around. We both made choices."

Hank shrugged off my point as he pointed to the picture. "His name is Jaime. My wife...Well, you can imagine how she feels. Sara can't understand where her little brother is. Ten months between them, they act as one."

The reference wasn't lost on me. We'd been that way when we were young. "What happened, Hank?" I whispered, still unable to look at him.

"You changed."

Stuffing the photo in my pocket, I pulled my arm from his grasp and leapt into the open maw of the elevator.

I needed air.

The hospital no longer held happy, hopeful, warm vibes for me. Death had visited a friend of mine here, thankfully leaving without taking her. But Death was a normal visitor to this place. I don't know why I'd never noticed the dark presence lingering in the shadows, waiting for the call.

Logan sat behind his desk, head bent over some papers, unaware of my presence. Yellowing papers and journals were stacked from floor to ceiling, darker at the top of the stacks where the paper caught the sunlight filtering through the paper canyon from the window hidden behind, dust dancing in the columns of light spearing daylight into the otherwise gloomy interior. Various plaques and awards gathered dust and weighted the tops of the piles, as effective as paperweights in a gale. Framed documents, only partially visible, hung on the walls. Presumably diplomas and certifications, but impossible to tell.

When I tapped on the doorframe, Logan's head snapped up. A lost look of reentry into the present, then recognition flared, a warmth infusing his smile. "Hey. Come on in."

"Is it safe?" I nodded toward the piles, which tilted precariously, threatening to bury us both. Careful not to jostle anything, I eased into the lone chair opposite him.

"Scientifically balanced, you have my word." He lowered his head and gave me an appraising stare.

I squirmed. "You trying to read my mind?"

"You know, there's scientific substrate to that possibility. Nothing empirical, but still, you wouldn't believe the inroads we're making. The brain is simply a complex tangle of electrical impulses, so in theory, it would be possible to first identify the impulses associated with various thoughts then capture them externally."

"That's terrifying."

My lack of appreciation deflated him. "Yes, in the wrong hands, all science is terrifying. But, the flip side, as with everything in the Universe, is brilliant. If we can capture memories, thoughts, we can replace them if they are lost."

"Like a reboot from an external hard drive."

"Exactly."

"But the great thing is, new research is showing the memories aren't lost—not in cases like yours. Access is lost. But the memories remain. Makes the job a bit simpler, in theory anyway. Isn't that awesome?" He hit the desk in emphasis, launching a cloud of dust, which he waved away. "I don't let the cleaning crew in here."

"Yeah, the Workman's Comp exposure would be

disincentive enough."

"Oh, I like the you coming through."

I was coming back; he was right. The reality flooded through me, quickly suffocated by my newfound cynicism, hard earned. "I'll stay the me I used to be, won't I?"

"This is all new territory, so I can't make any promises. But I don't see any clinical reason why not. You're still in there. Of course, the disease could progress through other native tissue, but we've got the solution. At least it seems we do. We can find you. I know it."

I thought about bringing up the rejection issues and all of that, but he knew the pitfalls and hadn't any answers. Hollow reassurances would be none at all.

His business face fell into place. "I would have Dr. Matthews here as well, as per our normal practice, but she had a terrible accident."

I know. I was there. I clamped down on the thoughts before they could turn into words. "I heard. I'm going to visit her after this."

"She'll like that. She has a soft spot for you; we all do." His cheeks pinkened.

"Are you flirting with me?" I adopted a teasing tone.

"Of course not. That would be unprofessional." The twinkle in his eyes told me he was lying.

"I'm a rule breaker myself."

"I know." His knowing look made me wonder how much he actually did know, but I thought it best not to probe too deeply. "Tell me how you've been feeling. Any new symptoms after the treatment? We amped it up pretty good."

"That a technical term?"

"Absolutely." He scratched notes in the open file, the one he'd been reading when I showed up. My file. "Your humor is definitely improved—" He looked up. "At least in understanding if not quality."

"Cute."

"My point exactly."

"I'd like to look at my notes just to make sure I get it all right." I reached into my pocket for my phone. When I pilled it out, a piece of paper came with it, then fluttered to the floor.

"Let's not do that. You tell me what you remember. I'll write down what you say, and we can compare notes, mine and yours, when you're done," he said, as I bent to retrieve the paper.

A photo. I didn't recognize it immediately, then remembered Hank had given me one. His children, he'd said. I rotated the photo for a better look, prepared to face what I had done.

I bolted upright. My hand shook.

The faces from my dreams.

I must've gasped or looked like I'd seen a ghost or something, Which I had. Two of them. Not ghosts exactly, but ephemeral faces from my past. My memory.

"What?" Logan frowned, concern puckering the skin between his eyebrows.

I put the photo down in front of me, carefully turning it so the children's visages faced him. With a finger, I pushed it across so he could get a good look.

"Do you know these children?" he asked.

"Yes and no. I see them in my dreams, in flashbacks, but I've never met them."

Curiosity replaced concern. "Have you seen pictures of them?"

"No. I've been in Witness Protection, cut off from my family. These are my brother's kids. One born right before I entered the program, one just after. I hadn't seen or heard from anyone until my brother showed up yesterday." I waved away the questions I saw forming. "Dan's got a handle on it," I lied.

"What about online?"

"Nope. My brother's a cop; they keep personal stuff very tight."

"Where'd you get the photo?"

"My brother gave it to me this morning." I could see the wheels turning as Logan chewed on all the possibilities. At least he had some.

How could I see what I didn't know? "Any ideas?"

Logan held up a finger as he reached around behind him, pulled a journal out of one of the stacks and opened it. After reading a bit, he turned the pages so I could see them.

"Just explain it to me."

"You know about the anecdotal evidence of memory transference with the transplantation of higher-level organs?" He paused for my 'no', then continued. "After transplantation, the donee remembers things or has appetites, tastes, aptitudes, etcetera they didn't have prior. The newly acquired manifestations all traced back to the donor."

"Creepy."

"No, interesting. And far better than being dead."

"Or gone." I wasn't sure I believed it even though I said it. If I didn't have me anymore, would I be happy with someone else in my head? The idea creeped me out.

"Exactly. We have no empirical studies to confirm this with unassailable scientific proof, but recently a study proved that traumatic events actually change our DNA. Memories can be stored, actually are stored, in our cells. A scientific explanation for déjà vu, in a way. Although, mystery always remains."

"Our cells." I touched my head, thinking of my brother's cells growing there. "Some of him has become part of me?"

"All our cells—well, except for red blood cells and a few others that aren't important—contain DNA. That's the only theory I can think of that would explain a memory of a past event that you didn't experience." He leaned back, lacing his fingers behind his head as he stared at the ceiling. "Kate, this is huge! Amazing really. God, the stuff we don't know."

"I have somebody else in my head and you think it's great?"

That little bit of reality didn't even slow him down. "We have to prove it, of course. We have to think how we can harness his memories versus yours. This will be a bombshell. Think of the possibilities."

"I'm a bit dark on that at the moment. I regain me only to

also find another voice in my head."

"You're hearing voices?"

"Metaphorically schizophrenic."

Finally, he seemed to notice a person sat where he saw a lab rat. "Wow," was all he could think of to say.

"Can we separate me from my brother? I'd really like to keep a handle on what's me and what's not."

"Okay, okay." He nodded as he thought. "Is there anything different about the memories you know aren't yours and the ones that are?"

"I'd have to think back. Not that I know right now."

"Pay more attention. When you have a memory or flashback, write it down, record the details. We'll see if anything jumps out at us. Other than the new memory issue, has anything changed?"

I stared at him, my focus lost. Voices, memories competed, flashing by—visceral danger, like standing too close to the train track as the Express blew through.

A face I don't know, yet I do. The background blurred. Fear radiates off him like heat off a furnace, waves disturbing the air. "Help me, man." He nervously shakes out a cigarette, the butt of an old unfiltered. Cupping his hands, he pulls the flame taking a few deep draws before expelling the smoke as if he resents the need to smoke. "You gotta help me, man. I'm in deep."

"I talked to them," I say. "No dice. We gotta figure a way to pay."

"They know where I live, the kids. They said they were gonna kill my family." I flinch, moving to wipe away his hand as he grabs for me.

My hand found only air.

"Kate, Kate."

The worried face of Logan filtered through the blur. The guy disappeared, leaving only the sharp tang of his fear.

I fell back in the chair, spent, and more than a little bit shaken. "Holy shit."

"Where'd you go?"

"A man, desperate. Needs my help. He said they were going to kill his kids; he was in deep."

Logan scribbled as I talked. "Keep going. Give me all the details while they're fresh. Did you know the guy?"

"It was weird. Yes and no. Something inside me." I pressed my hand over my heart. "Something here told me I knew him. But he didn't spark any rational recognition."

"What else?"

"He was the only thing I saw clearly. Everything behind him, around him was blurry."

His head lifted slightly, his eyes dark and intense, focused. "Okay. Any other details?"

"He smoked." I let my focus blur as I reached back for the memory. "The butt of a half-smoked unfiltered stick."

"Like he'd picked it up somewhere?"

"No, not living on the streets. Clean-cut, shaved, pressed cotton shirt. More like money was tight. Nothing went to waste."

Logan finished his last note, then set his pen down, carefully aligning it with the edge of his journal. He wrote in tracks of tiny block letters, meticulous in their precision as they marched across the page.

"Can you remember any of the other episodes with as much clarity?"

"Not right now." I grabbed the arms of the chair, needing the world to stop spinning. "Perhaps in a calmer moment I can pull something. I will try. There are answers there."

"To what?"

"No. To why."

———

Damn. I'm not even me anymore.

What comes after me?

Still reeling and more than half-creeped out at having my brother in my head, I couldn't shake the thoughts.

Unsure of where to go, what to do next, I was idling next to the curb in front of Voodoo Donuts. Hunger had most likely led me there, my inner nutritionist clearly not part of the decision. I couldn't remember what day it was, but it must be a weekday; because the line was only halfway down the block.

Distracted, I was only half watching for the guys who were after me, half hoping they'd find me. Apparently I wasn't paying as much attention as I thought—the Watchman scared the shit out of me.

He grabbed my arm before I saw him. Numb, I didn't jump, although my heart gave a weak lurch. The guys who had been after me had been curiously absent, as if their job was done, or they held all the cards. I didn't like it.

I dismounted and secured the bike, pocketing the keys after making a note of where I'd left it. "You're lucky I didn't shoot you."

His edges looked frayed. His hand shook as he let go. Sweat sheened his brow despite the chill.

"You okay?" Stupid question. I knew what a crash looked like.

"Ran low on meds. I'm falling into crazy." He rubbed his arms, swiping off something crawling on him only he could see. "It's coming. They're coming." Wild eyes skimmed past me, alighting like the touch of a butterfly, then fluttering on.

"Where have you been?" I asked, trying to focus him.

"Flashing that photo around."

I didn't dare hope. We'd run up against enough dead ends already. "Anything?"

"The guy from New York, the guy your brother saw in the alley—he's got a badge, or had one."

"What?" Narrowing my eyes, I tried to tell if that was the crazy talking. "He was a cop?"

"Couldn't say. But I know who to ask." He grabbed my shoulders, hanging on before the demons came. He needed help, and he needed it now. He looked around, wild-eyed. "You see your friend?"

I didn't know who he meant, which friend, but his question

triggered thoughts of Stella. Man, I forgot Stella! Some friend. "On my way, in a roundabout sort of way." I fudged. "Let's get you safe. Then you wait for me. Can you do that?"

"They're coming."

"Not if they can't find you."

He put his hands over his ears. And shook his head.

I circled him with an arm, pulling him next to me. "Stay with me. Find the voice that's real. Listen to that. You can do this. I can help you, but I need you safe first. You need a doctor."

"No!" His eyes wild, his voice the growl of a cornered animal. "No doctors." He pressed a hand to his stomach.

"You need meds." He shivered as I held him. "I don't know where else to take you."

"No doctors. Bad. They hurt me."

His body rigid with determination, I couldn't fight him, couldn't force him. Maybe Logan could help, or Stella if she was still alive.

Without a better idea, I took him back to the place he'd called home.

Gutted by the fire, the red brick was blackened with soot where flames had thrust through the windows and turned toward the sky. Still holding him, using my presence to ground him, I felt his posture relax as we stepped over the yellow tape and through the darkened doorway. The wood was pockmarked, yet the doorframe still held. Amazingly, the wooden beams also bore their burden. On the first floor, in the far back corner, I found a few familiar faces huddled around what looked to be the Watchman's hibachi, warming their hands.

One man rushed to help. "Needs his meds," he said as he grabbed the Watchman, looping one of his arms across his shoulders to carry the weight. The Watchman relaxed into him.

"Keep him here. Keep him safe. There are people looking for him." I could see in his glance he got my drift. "I need him. I can help him."

As I turned to go, two men forced their way into our space.

Big, ugly, they had trouble etched in their scowls.

I reached for my gun. The lack of a killer instinct made me a nanosecond slow. The larger of the two men shook his head as I stared down the cold black eye of his pistol. With his eyes and slight nod, he motioned for me to place my gun on the floor. "Kick it over."

The people gathered behind me scattered like rats, leaving the Watchman slumped on the floor, wringing his hands, talking to someone who wasn't there. So much for keeping him safe.

I palmed my pistol, showing it to him, then did as he asked. It skittered and bumped on the rough wood as I kicked it across to him.

With the languid arrogance of one who thinks he has the upper hand, the second guy stepped toward me. I darted to my right, putting him between me and the shooter, who shouted a warning. This time, *he* was too slow. I grabbed the guy nearest to me, one hand on his wrist, wrenching his arm straight, the point of the elbow on top.

As I cocked my other arm and coiled my weight, the other guy got a shot off. A sting across the meaty part of my upper arm. I flinched my head to the side. His second shot whizzed by my ear. Using every bit of leverage I could muster, I brought my arm down on the elbow. Tendons popped. The man screamed and doubled over, clutching his arm. I dove over him, rolling as I landed.

Finding my feet, I crouched, my hand finding the Watchman's knife in my pocket. I thumbed the switch, popping the blade open, then backhanded it into the shooter's stomach.

As he fell, he got a third shot off.

This time I wasn't so lucky.

CHAPTER FIFTEEN

Movement stopped as I staggered into the emergency room with the Watchman clutching me, shouting at invisible foes. Blood soaked my jeans. Pain seared every nerve ending; the ones I had left anyway, to the point I felt nothing other than cold. I was so very cold.

His fear tangible, I fought to control the Watchman as his panic redlined. "No doctors. No. No. No!" His arms crossed across his belly; he curled against his fear. Twisting and turning, he tried to break free.

He was strong, his fear like a wild animal.

Blood ran warm down my leg taking my strength with it. "Can somebody fucking help me?"

That galvanized the nurses to frantic activity and the onlookers to buzzing like bees with no queen. Two men in scrubs worked to offload the Watchman, who grabbed me with a vise-like grip. His voice cleared, the panic left his eyes as he looked into mine. "Don't let them hurt me." The he was gone, his eyes turning back to the two men.

It took both of them, and my cajoling, to calm him a bit so he could focus. "I'll be right here." I touched his face, turning his head until his eyes met mine. "They'll keep you where you can see me. I won't let them hurt you."

The scrub-clad men ignored me as they wrenched the Watchman's arms from around me with a cool indifference.

The Watchman groped, struggling to hang on, his eyes wide in panic.

"Nooooo!" A curdling scream, a primal wail arousing every protective instinct I had.

My knee pulsed with pain. My vision tunneled. I clung to him with one hand as the orderly tugged, trying to separate us. "Let him go. You're making it worse."

The orderly ignored me.

I pulled my gun and leveled it at the orderly's chest. The loss of blood had my good knee shaking with effort to hold me upright. Somehow I summoned the strength to hold the gun steady. "You'll do as I say."

One of the nurses gasped. "Call 911."

"Just help him," I said. "I'm not going to hurt anyone—just needed to get your attention."

The man gripping the Watchman stopped, frozen, as he stared at my gun.

The second man, the one who had been watching, put his hands up. "Let me help. We'll do what you want." Waving the orderly away, he took hold of the Watchman.

I reversed the gun in my hand and handed it to him, butt first.

As if he could sense the man's calm, the Watchman stilled, allowing the man to lead him back close to me.

"I'm Dr. Galt, the attending doctor in the emergency room tonight. You have my word; he can stay with you. You calm him. Any idea what he's got going on?"

Carrying a lifetime of guilt, I wanted to say, but an emergency room guy wasn't going to help the Watchman shrug off that load. "Schizophrenic and crashing off his meds. He ran out. Hard to find on the streets."

The doctor handed my gun back to me. "Just don't shoot anybody, okay?"

I put my pistol back in my pocket. I could almost hear a collective sigh of relief. "He's my friend." My words conveyed my warning.

"Got it. We can help him. Does he have a doctor?"

"VA."

"So, no." He called to one of the nurses behind the desk. Presumably a drug and dosage I didn't know or understand. He eyed the trail of blood I had left. "You're next. We need to stop that bleeding. What'd they do to you?"

"Shot me in my fucking bad knee."

Beck found me in a cubicle in the emergency room awaiting my sentence.

"Can't leave you alone for a minute." His glib tone didn't mesh with the worry in his eyes. "Do you think one of these times you could leave somebody alive so I can question them?"

"I left one before. You lost him, as I recall." I fought through the haze of Demerol, my thoughts diffuse, the pain a distant dull ache.

"You remember."

"Like I said, the traumatic stuff tends to stick. With you, that's all there is."

"No, that's all you remember. And it doesn't have to be that way."

I didn't know what to say, how I felt about that, but I thought I knew what he was implying.

As if he knew what I needed, he rested his hand on my arm, his skin warm, his touch comforting. "I'm glad you called me. You okay?"

"Waiting on my surgeon. The emergency folks took one look at my knee and wouldn't touch it. Apparently it's held together with duct tape and baling wire."

"Could be worse."

I didn't know how, but I was finding it hard to see the positive side of things.

The Watchman stirred in the corner. He'd tucked in behind the curtain when Beck walked in.

"You don't look so hot, Joe," Beck said. "Need something?"

"No, thanks. Kate got me what I needed." The Watchman swiped at his face, gently probing the bandage over the cut in his cheek. The crazy was gone. "She saved me again."

"She's good at that." Beck's comment carried a subtext I couldn't read. "I'm glad you texted me from the taxi," he said, turning back to me. "I still can't believe you called a cab. And even more incredible, he let you two in the back seat."

"One of life's minor miracles. We needed help. He had a Good Samaritan streak a mile wide. Did you work the scene at the warehouse?" He didn't mention the gun, so I didn't either. I'm sure the cabbie would file a report. Time eluded my grasp. I'd lost the day, the intervening hours or minutes.

"No, I came right here. Preliminary is they got one guy—found him dead behind a dumpster about twenty feet away. Blood trail. He'd bled out. The knife nicked his aorta, so he was a dead man when you stuck him. Once they run his prints, we ought to have a name, not that that will help us much. Haven't found the other guy, but we're checking the hospitals and clinics. You said you broke his arm?"

Stymied for a moment. I thought I did, but I wasn't sure.

"She did. His elbow," the Watchman answered, filling in my gap. "Didn't really register at the time, but I heard it. Still hear it."

"How'd you know it was his elbow?"

"Not a sound you forget." Spoken like a man long on experience and enemies.

Beck had the same thought; I saw it in his eyes, in the quick raise of his eyebrows.

"Stella!" I gasped as reality hit home. Galvanized, I sat up, then crumpled back in pain. "You need to protect Stella. I don't think they got what they wanted from her." The beeping of my heart rate monitor accelerated.

"Pretty sure they didn't; you saw to that," Beck said, a smile warming his voice. "But don't worry, already done. Since yesterday. Sure wish we had a line on these guys."

"You and me both." I eased back, holding my thigh, and trying to keep my knee still.

"I think I can help with that," the Watchman said, his voice gaining a solid timbre. "I still have my fingers in their pie, but hanging with all you cops isn't doing a lot for my employer's confidence. They may already have decided to cut their losses."

Beck squeezed my shoulder as he watched the Watchman through narrowed eyes. "You playing both sides? You hurt Kate..." The threat hung there, icicles overhead on a warming winter day.

"Had I wanted to hurt her, kill her, take her, it would be done." The words held a cold certainty.

"It's okay, Beck. I already know." That got his attention. "He told me. Before you and Hank came to the house." Memories were sticking. I could hear his words. Of course, the bad stuff, the betrayals, those were easiest to remember.

Beck weighed the words for a moment, then turned back to the Watchman. "On the inside, you say. The man in the park." Beck put the puzzle pieces together easier than I did.

"Bennie. One of mine." The Watchman stayed in the corner, out of sight if anyone passing by got interested. "I'm barely pecking at the edges of Khoury's food chain. Trying to find the man. But it's like he's a ghost or something. Got everybody spooked. He's looking, and he's leaving a trail of dead bodies."

"Khoury himself." Beck nodded as if it made sense. "Any leads?"

I listened as the Watchman filled him in. Although I knew he'd told me before, some of it sounded new, but I had held onto bits and pieces, which renewed my hope. I was getting better. As he wound down, the Watchman said, "I need to find one of my local guys. Then I'll have a better idea of our next step."

Beck's eyes landed back on me. "M.E. is processing the dead guy. You wouldn't have the knife, would you?"

"In my pocket. I pulled it out of the guy before we left." I might have killed him when I'd done that. The thought didn't bother me.

"You the one who called the cops?"

"From a burn phone the Watchman had." I pressed a hand over my eyes. My world spun, a kaleidoscope of memories clashing with reality and uncertainty. "Dan. You need to call him. With me involved, he'll need to know." I was fading, the light blinking out. Too much pain. Too little everything else.

"You didn't call him?" Beck's voice was guarded.

"I called you."

Darkness.

I run. Fear a predator nipping at my heels. I'd heard Hank. "Stop!" he'd shouted. The words weren't for me. Then he runs. I follow.

How had the takedown gone so bad? A setup for sure. One I hadn't seen coming.

Who had sold us out?

The fight behind us, darkness in front, I lose Hank—he's faster than I am. I stop just outside the glow of a streetlamp. The nigh is cold, the air heavy with moisture, haloing the streetlamps. Ominous. A time for ghosts, my mother had called it. I shiver as I scan the street for movement. I catch him, a dark shadow drifting through the light. Two blocks ahead. He pivots and bolts into an alley. I know that alley.

A dead end.

Out of breath, knowing he isn't going anywhere, I take off at a lope but don't push it. As I close on the alley, I slow. Fear still nips. My brother. But he can handle himself. I'm backup, nothing more. So I need to know what I'm walking into. I pause at the corner, my back to the wall, my gun at the ready.

I start to ease around the corner.

Gunfire! One shot.

I wait, my heart in my throat. I want to rush in. Make sure my brother is okay. Training had taught me to wait. I take a few deep breaths as I listen, trying to transform sound into an image. Who? Where? What are they doing? I whisper a call for backup into my radio.

Another shot. The echo pounds through me.

"Hank?" The scream boils up from a deep, holy place.

No reply.

Holding my gun at the ready, taking a deep breath, I step from behind the wall. A neon sign in an office window above paints the alley—a freak-show kaleidoscope of alternating green and red.

Two men down. Reynolds, Hank's partner, a bloody red spot in his forehead, the back of his head missing.

Hank. His vest had taken the hit, but he is moving, but stunned. His gun lies a few feet away to his left as if he'd dropped it.

He still holds a package of diamonds clutched in his hand.

"Hank! Hank!" I shouted.

He stirred. "I'm okay." He squints at me. "Katie?"

Something moved in the darkness.

I grabbed the diamonds and ran.

I blinked against the bright light. Someone held my hand. "Someone shot Reynolds. Hank was down. The diamonds. I ran." I couldn't remember the details of what happened next, but I could remember the pain. The white-hot searing pain. And that visceral cold reaction of my body when it knew it had been gravely injured.

Then nothing.

Except a voice. Panicked. Elevated, yet not loud. Normally far away, but now closer. *"Kate? Kate? Where are you?"*

Something about the voice.

"Kate. Kate. It's okay, honey. Come back to us."

Stella.

I blinked several times until my vision focused, my world came back to me—the dream let me go. "Oh, dear God, Stell. You're okay." That thought, that reality, rushed through me with the fire of a healing elixir.

"Of course I am." From her wheelchair, she stroked my hand and looked at me with serious eyes, her face pinched with worry, the confidence in her words not reflected in her eyes.

The bandage around her head looked smaller than the one I'd seen before...when had that been? Along with my memories, the days were jumbled

"It's okay now, honey." Stella said. "You were screaming. It's all gone. You're safe here."

"Beck?"

Stella let the hint of a smile peek through as she nodded toward the other side of the room.

His long legs in front of him, his arms crossed across his chest, his head drifting to the side, Beck sprawled in a chair, his eyes closed, his breathing heavy.

I lowered my voice to a whisper. "How long has he been here?"

"All night." Stella didn't need to say more—I could read it on her face. Beck had impressed the heck out of her. Me, too, and the thought made my stomach jump. What would he ask of me? I wasn't used to trusting people. Hell, I wasn't even sure I could anymore.

"Hank?" I asked, keeping my voice low. The memory that had awakened me still held me in its grasp.

"Haven't seen him. Not sure I'd know him, really, but no one has come around. At least not while I've been here."

"Not while I've been here either," Beck said, his voice husky with sleep. Still sprawled in the chair, he hadn't moved.

When he looked at me, I remembered the first time I'd stared into those deep blue eyes. I'd been afraid of him then. I still was, but for very different reasons. "You didn't have to stay."

"A thank you would suffice."

"Oh, yeah, there's a man who can take your shit and sling it right back." Stella started to laugh, then gingerly clutched her head. "Man, now I know what Humpty Dumpty felt like."

"Well, when they put you back together, they could've left out the wise-ass."

"Honey, that's the glue that makes me, me." Stella stopped stroking my hand and leaned back.

Beck stood and brushed himself down. "Let me get you

back to your room," he said to Stella. "You've defied the doctors long enough."

She didn't argue.

He wheeled her around the corner and was back in an instant. "I handed her off to a nurse." Beck pulled a chair into the spot Stella had vacated.

"Is she going to be okay?"

"Yes, but it will take some time. The doctor said she still has some swelling on her brain that they are watching closely." He took my hand in his—warmth covering my cold. "If she followed rules better...but then you two wouldn't be friends, would you?"

"Rhetorical, right?" I relaxed back, taking a deep breath. "Thank you."

"None required. I was joking."

"I know. And that scares me."

"Give me time, Kate." Perhaps afraid of my response, he didn't wait for one. "Where's your phone?"

"Considering I'm hard pressed to know exactly where I am and how I got here, I think you might be overestimating my powers of recall. What time is it anyway?"

"Dinnertime. Are you hungry?"

"Not unless you're offering a very thick chocolate shake."

"That does sound good." Pawing through a plastic bag with my name misspelled on the side, he pulled out one item after another, apparently looking for my phone. Finally, he found it at the bottom of the bag.

"What do you want with my phone?"

After shaking open a pair of reading glasses and donning them, he pulled his notebook from his shirt pocket. A quick consult, then he powered up my phone.

"Would you mind telling me what you're doing?"

"Downloading an app." He began tapping the screen.

"You have my password?"

"You gave it to me at the house, remember?"

He glanced at me over the pair of cheaters he balanced on

the end of his nose.

"Yeah," I said with a smile. "Yeah, I remember. I've been remembering a lot more."

"You're coming back."

"God help you."

That got a chuckle. He finished what he was doing with my phone then pulled out his own, working between them for a bit.

Pain jangled up my leg. The anesthesia was wearing off. I knew the worst was yet to come—that point where your whole body rises up to fight the indignity that has been done to it. That point where it even hurts to breathe.

"Here." Beck set my phone within reach on the articulated table next to my bed.

"What did you do?"

"You now are my friend on Find My Friends."

"I'm not going to like this, am I?"

"Doubtful, but humor me, just until you get a bit more mobile, okay?" When I didn't respond, he continued. "This app allows me to find you wherever you are, as long as your phone has a signal."

"You're right; I don't like it. It's not like I have anything to hide; it's just invasive."

"Agreed."

He looked determined and I was too tired to argue. "Okay, I'll let you win if you'll find me that milkshake." I tried to smile, but it was probably stretched into a grimace by the pain that pulsed in time with my heartbeat. "Please." I wanted to press on my knee, to move the pain, but I didn't dare.

He pursed his lips as he thought. "Okay," he finally said. "You can't heal without sustenance, or so they say." He reached around to the small of his back and pulled out his backup gun, a small Beretta. "Nine millimeter, sub-compact, six plus one. Keep it close until I get back."

"What happened to the gun I came in with?"

"I seized it as evidence. You got it off the dead guy you and I met over, didn't you? The one in your tub."

"I remember." I wasn't going to confirm or deny. The tiny gun felt surprisingly heavy in my hand. "Make my shake super thick."

"It's going to take me awhile. I've got to stop in at the station, then maybe go home for a quick shower and change. I'm pretty ripe." He didn't look happy.

From the look on his face, it wasn't hard to tell what he was thinking. "I'll be okay. I can take care of myself."

"You've proven that." Still, he lingered a bit, self-consciously brushing his lips against my forehead.

After he left, I put the gun on the bed next to my right hip. Someone, probably Stella, had laid a set of neatly folded purple scrubs on the foot of my bed. Pushing myself up higher, I gritted my teeth against the pain. I skinned the hospital gown over my head—snaking the IV through it, bag and all, took some doing. Tossing the gown aside, I reached for the scrubs. The shirt was easier, even with the IV—the pants not so much. Drenched in sweat by the time I'd shimmied myself into them, I fell back. The bandage on my knee gave me a bit of a problem—a tight fit and any pressure making me almost scream with pain—but managed. The last thing I did was tuck Beck's gun in the waistband, drawing the string tight to hold it, then pulled the shirt down over it. As an afterthought, I slipped my phone into the deep pocket of my pants.

Okay, now I felt more like me—armed and somewhat presentable.

I'd fought the pain down to a sharp ache when the doctor breezed into the room without knocking, head bent, eyes scanning an iPad he held in one hand. Stopping at the edge of the bed, he didn't look up, his lips moving, forming silent words as he read. "Good. Good." He nodded as he finished and looked up, catching me looking at him. "How's the pain?"

"It only hurts when my heart beats."

"Want something for that?"

"No."

He gave me a steady stare. "Next time you pull a Superwoman, could you remember you don't have that whole bulletproof thing going on?"

I blinked at him, unable to make a quick transition from dead serious to light-hearted banter. "There wasn't much time to think."

He seemed to accept that. "Luckily, this time you escaped. I had to do a quick graft on a tendon the bullet grazed, but really, you should be fine."

"How fine?"

"A little bit of therapy, then you'll be as good as you were before you got shot."

I told him about the pop in the knee, then less pain, more range of motion.

"That's a good thing. Scar tissue. Adhesions breaking loose. Don't be alarmed." He gave me a stare he probably reserved for his residents. "But don't go getting shot again. No guarantees next time."

I didn't make any promises. "How long are you going to keep me?"

"Tomorrow you can go home, but you'll need someone to drive you."

"Curiously, that much I could figure out on my own."

With a grin and a few hastily scribbled notes on his iPad, he was gone.

Silence enveloped me. They'd found me a private room, and I lay there, vibrating with unspent energy, yet too exhausted to move and relishing a moment of peaceful alone time.

I'd managed a few calls when Logan blew in like the downdraft before a storm, cool but carrying a hint of darkness. "Getting shot is a bit excessive, don't you think? If you wanted some hospital TLC, all you had to do was ask."

"You know me; I tend to overcompensate."

He pulled a chair next to my bed. "Seriously, Katie. What the hell?"

"Worried about your lab rat?"

He had the decency to color just a bit. "You hold the keys to a lot of things."

If he only knew.

He moved his chair closer. "Look, I've been thinking about your memories and the fact that you seem to be manifesting memories that belong to your brother and not to you. Are you up to telling me everything, going over it again? I'd like to help you find a way to differentiate between yours and his. I can see how that would be unnerving to you."

This time, when he looked at me, I felt he saw me and not a Nobel Prize. "Okay." I didn't have to ask him for my phone. I still clutched it with a death grip, my lifeline, now not only to me, but also to the truth. I rewound my verbal notes, pausing to listen to snippets until I found the beginning of the section where I dictated Beck's notes about my dreams. We both listened.

Logan had me run through it again as he took notes, then he reread what he had written. "It seems like memories you identify as your own are much clearer, the background details sharper. Would you agree?"

"It's hard to say. The memories of them fade so quickly."

"Okay." He scanned his notes. "Let's find a memory you know is yours."

I told him about the one at Christmas. The house. Hank taking my toy and blaming me. The one with the dead cop and the diamonds I kept to myself, even though I knew it was mine. Hank was in it, and he was out cold. It couldn't have been his memory.

Logan looked for that one and didn't find it. "Tell me about it."

I did, remembering the details of the house, the rooms, the smells, the sounds.

"Good. Now one that was your brother's."

The children. A woman at the stove. But I couldn't see anything else. I couldn't place the kitchen.

Filled with wonder, I looked at Logan. "You just might have hit on something."

I saw my pinched face in Logan's eyes. "What?"

I rewound my notes, listening for the dream where I held the diamonds, where I ran with them. The details were sketchy, not enough to differentiate.

Was it my dream? Hank's? Or a bit of reality winding its way through my subconscious?

What had I been doing? Where did I go?

I had the diamonds. I'd run. And then what? What had I done with them?

Why couldn't I remember?

I'd just started wondering where Beck was when Hank stepped into the room. His hands jammed in his pockets, his face grim, dark circles underscoring his eyes, he'd aged a decade in the last twenty-four hours. "I'm glad you're awake."

"Good to see you, too." With Hank, it was hard for me to keep the sarcasm out of my voice...and the disappointment.

Logan caught the undercurrent. "You want me to stay?"

"It's okay. This is my brother, Hank."

Logan looked at him with new eyes, then he shot me a questioning glance.

I shook my head.

"I'll let you two visit, then." With his hands on his knees, he pushed himself up. "You sure you're going to be okay?"

"Fine. Thanks."

Hank stepped to the side to let Logan out. When we were alone, he nudged the door shut with a foot.

I could tell he was at war with himself. "What's going on? Any news about your son?"

Rubbing his arms, he shifted from foot to foot, but didn't move any farther into the room. "I hate to do this, Katie."

"What?"

He pulled a pistol out of his pocket. Aiming at my chest, he said, "You need to come with me."

CHAPTER SIXTEEN

"They've got me, Katie. They've got both of us."

I had a different opinion, but Hank didn't look like he wanted an argument. The gun shook, his knuckles white as he gripped the butt—an accident waiting to happen. I'd already been shot once; I didn't want a repeat performance. Wincing with pain, I eased my leg over the side of the bed. The other leg followed, and then I pushed myself to a stiff-legged stance. Beck's gun stayed lodged at my waist, hidden under my shirt.

Hank rambled, his words riding on a tide of nervous energy. "It's a trade—you for my son. You understand, don't you? I don't have a choice."

"You've convinced yourself, so I don't see how what I think matters."

He grabbed me, his hand a vise on my arm. I could take him...maybe. I could certainly work this situation to my advantage—I didn't have to go with him. But he was going to take me to the bad guys...to Khoury, I guessed. And I was more than ready to face that bastard down.

Gritting my teeth against the pain, wondering whether I'd ever walk without pain again, I let Hank lead me through the hospital—nobody paused in their hurrying to give us even a cursory glance. Out front, Hank had a cab waiting. He helped me stretch my leg across the back seat, then took the passenger seat in front for himself.

"Westside. Drop us near the gate to Chinatown."

Nobody said anything as the cab snaked through the Christmas cheer of downtown. Hank had tucked his gun out of sight and didn't seem concerned that I might try to make a run for it whenever the cab stopped at a red light. Sweating with the pain, my teeth clenched tight, it was obvious I wasn't going anywhere, at least not quickly.

Once he'd gotten me out of the cab and paid the driver, I watched with a sinking feeling as the red taillights disappeared back toward the heart of town. Dizzy, my energy flat-lining, I realized I had once again overplayed my hand.

"We have to go the rest of the way on foot," Hank said as he grabbed my elbow.

Rain pelted us. Fog filtered through the tops of the buildings, blocking out the world. I flipped up the hood on my jacket, but cold water still found its way down my neck. As discomforts went, it was way down on my list. My stomach clenched and roiled against the pain in my leg. My body hummed with shock.

Night was falling, but I didn't know on which day.

On emotional and physical overload, I played my last ace. "You took the diamonds, Hank."

I felt him flinch. I'd hit a nerve.

"You let me believe..." I swallowed hard. My body shook. "You let me think I'd..." I couldn't say it. Hell, I could hardly believe it.

"It's not what you think."

I could tell even Hank thought his words sounded lame.

"You took the diamonds, Hank. You."

He didn't deny it. "Then you showed up, and the diamonds disappeared."

"Why'd you take them?"

"It's not what you think."

"You keep saying that. I wish I could believe you."

Pain in his eyes as he absorbed the blow. "Me, too." He stepped back into the shadows, reestablishing the moat of distrust between us. "There's more you remember, isn't there?"

The memory, the knowledge of what my brother had done wallowed out a hole inside me big enough to swallow all of me. "I saw you running. I followed you."

"I didn't see you."

"I came in...after. Reynolds was dead, his brain sprayed all over the alley. Funny how a small entry made such a mess." I struggled with the memories drifting away, the puffs of smoke drifting on the wind after a mortar attack.

Hank paled. "What else?"

"You were down, but breathing," I continued as I forced my focus back to the fresh nightmare. "Your vest saved you."

"Not my ribs, though." Hank rubbed his chest where the bullet had hit. "What else?" His eyes refocused, finding mine. "I need it all, Katie. *We* need it. Somewhere in that head of yours is the answer, the solution we need."

I closed my eyes, wishing all of this was a bad dream. But sometimes the truth hides in what we know but choose not to remember. "Your gun. It was off to the side. A few feet away, like maybe you had dropped it when you fell." I squinted my eyes tighter, the memory dimming.

"Where?" His focus pinpointed. "Where was my gun?"

"Between you and the building with the green door."

"What did you hear?"

"Hear?" I worked to remember, to put myself back in that alley. "Two shots."

"Together?"

"No. Time in between."

He snapped upright, a dead man stretching to relieve the pressure of a noose around his neck. "How long?"

"Long enough for me to wait then call for backup."

Something he'd heard, something I said, had lifted a bit of the weight Hank had been shouldering. "I didn't shoot him, Katie. Even though it looks like I did."

"What did ballistics show?"

"The bullet that killed Reynolds was fired from my gun. I didn't pull the trigger. I swear it."

"Then who did? All I saw was you and Reynolds. Only one way out of that alley and I was blocking it."

"How come you're not in jail?" I asked.

Hank rubbed his chest. "Reynolds shot first."

If he hadn't been wearing his vest...

"If what you say is true," I said, "then someone else must've been there."

"Don't think I haven't been looking. Man, that's all I've been doing in my free time. The guy, whoever he was, is a fucking ghost." Hank leaned into me. "Don't you remember anything else, Katie?"

"I heard a sound to my left, but..."

"But what?"

"I didn't see anyone. And that's all I remember. The dream ended there."

"What kind of sound?" Hank's eyes glinted in the half-light, boring into me, mining for a nugget to hold up to the light.

I closed my eyes, summoning calm. Breathing deep, I consciously relaxed each muscle, banished the worries darting through my head, bats circling a cave.

A sound. Metal on metal. A scrape. Then a click.

I told Hank.

"Someone was there, Katie." The thought bolted him forward. "Come on."

"Where are we going?" I asked, even though I knew. Somehow, I sensed the game had changed for Hank. Something I'd said maybe.

"We're going to meet that fucking ghost."

The neighborhood crumbled around us. The sidewalks uneven, the storefronts open, nothing left to guard. Lights spotty and weak, hiding those who worked in the shadows.

"Where?"

"Tunnels."

I lunged, grabbing a handful of cloth and tugged him to a stop. Leaning over, I placed my hands on my thighs, drawing breath, searching for relief. "Where?" Afraid to touch my knee, I squeezed my leg above it, hard.

Hank kept his eyes moving, looking past me as he indulged my need to know. "They gave me a meeting place—down the alley up ahead, through a grate in the wall. That's all I know." His hand gripped my arm like a vise. "We'll get our answers, Katie. I know we will."

"If they don't kill us first."

"They want the diamonds."

"And they think I can help them." We both knew that wasn't going to happen—I couldn't remember. But Hank was beyond listening to logic. He shut down. He knew what they would do to try to make me remember.

The gun Beck gave me nestled warm against my hip. I'd shoot my brother if I had to, but not yet. I needed answers as badly as he did. Finding the man who Hank had said he'd seen in the alley, the man who'd killed our only witness, he was the key to opening the lock to my past. I knew it in my soul.

Sounds behind us scratched at my consciousness. I angled my head, cocking an ear.

"What?" Hank asked as I slowed our pace.

"Someone is back there."

The footfalls stopped.

He listened, his breathing shallow and fast. "I don't hear anything."

"It stopped." We moved on, this time faster, driven by urgency, sharper now.

At the entrance to a side street, narrow enough to allow only one car, Hank stopped. We listened. A sound to the right. His eyes darted to mine.

He lifted his chin down the main street. "Keep going, slower," he whispered.

We started off as before with him leading and me wincing along right behind.

I heard the man before he hit me chest-high. A moment to brace myself and make a half-turn. He buried his head in my chest, driving us backward. One hand grabbed the back of my neck as he swept Hank's legs, then rode me to the ground. Hank staggered, one hand to the ground.

The press of a blade against my side.

Twisting away from it, I worked the point of my shoulder underneath, absorbing my fall and the attacker's extra weight. His knife clattered into the darkness.

My head glanced off the concrete. The air whooshed out of me. My eyesight pinpointed as my brain searched for oxygen. But it wasn't the knockout blow he hoped it would be. Pushing off my foot, I screamed in pain, my knee on fire, tearing, grinding. But I pushed past the pain, pushed with all the strength I had left, rolling us over.

The attacker loosened his grip slightly—he was using only one arm. I threw myself to the side, grabbed the hand he wasn't using on a hunch and wrenched. He rewarded me with a scream. The man with the broken elbow.

I thought I recognized his stink.

Fear, its stench potent, almost tangible.

I flipped him over, straddling, holding his arm steady, but ready to twist anew if he fought.

He didn't. "Be careful," he gasped, his words riding on the faint current of defeat. "He's watching. He knows."

"Khoury?" I eased closer to hear.

He opened his mouth. His eyes cleared. "That's what they think, but there is..."

With a growl, Hank raised his arm. A glint in the weak light. The knife. "Where is my son, you son of a bitch?"

"No." The edge in my voice a knife point, drawing blood. Hank held the guy down with a foot to his chest and the threat of the knife as I rolled off of him.

I thought I caught the glow of the man's eyes, the feral yellow of a predator.

I reached for the gun at my waist, but the man on the ground was faster. Using both hands, he grunted in pain as he grabbed Hank's leg and twisted hard. Hank fell and the man was on him before I could raise my gun.

The two men locked together, rolling, fighting. I squinted

against the darkness looking for my shot.

A grunt. A body went slack.

A man pushed off, then staggered to his feet.

I fired. One shot. Center mass.

He dropped like a stone.

I rushed to my brother lying on his back, and crouched down next to him. My knee screamed as I forced it to bend. Unable to find enough light to see, I patted him down. My hand found the warm rush of blood. A gash in his neck, the blood pulsing.

His hand fisted in the front of my shirt. "Get my son, Katie. Take him home."

"Come on, Hank." I lightly tapped his cheek. "Stay with me." My hand closed over the phone in my pocket.

"I need you to show me where." I wanted to shake him. "I need you, Hank!"

But it was too late.

Hank's body went limp. His hand falling. The blood stopped pulsing.

"No! Hank!" I slapped his face harder, willing him to respond, his eyes to focus.

I knew it was hopeless; yet I pumped on his chest, frantic to press life back into a lifeless body.

My brother had left.

I couldn't bring him back.

I fell back. Sitting with my arms curled around one leg and under the other, I tried to fight the anger that boiled up. Rage. Fear. Revenge. A tsunami that carried me away.

The rain had slowed, leaving a cold discomfort.

I checked the gun. A full magazine; a round in the chamber.

A cold resolve replaced the anger.

I knew what I had to do.

The grate in the wall would have been easy to miss if I hadn't been looking for it. Halfway down the alley, just as Hank said. Grabbing the bars, I lifted the cover, exposing a hole large enough to crawl through but hardly enticing. A musty smell drifted up from the bowels along with whiffs of excrement, rotting food, and derailed lives.

I tried flexing my knee, biting down on a scream.

Bending through the opening, I looked down into darkness. But I thought I caught a faint hint of light off to the left. A pipe climbed the wall to the opening. If it would hold my weight, I could get out.

An exit plan. Always know how to get away.

I worked my bad leg over the edge then eased to a straddle on the lip. My good leg followed. Pausing on the lip, my feet dangling into darkness, I took a few deep breaths. This was stupid—I knew that. It also was inevitable. If I waited, if I called for backup, the bad guy would be gone and my nephew with him. And, with Hank dead, my nephew would no longer be needed.

Galvanized, I slid into the dark void, feeling for the floor, something solid. I landed, favoring my injured leg, letting the semi-good one absorb my weight. Thankfully, it held as I stabilized myself against the wall. I turned toward the hint of light at the far end of the tunnel to the right.

The ceiling pressing down slowed me down. The surface under my feet was uneven, water standing in the low spots, the smell of death and hopelessness hanging in the air. Every now and then my foot slipped or I stepped wrong, leaving too much weight for my injured knee. I gasped even as I welcomed the pain, embracing it, using it to stay present.

What air there was hung stagnant, unmoving, occasionally ruffled by a wheezing sigh from an intersecting passageway. Muffled sounds of traffic vibrated through the walls, the life I knew close but as distant as another galaxy. I inched my way along, my gun...Beck's gun...held at the ready. He would be apoplectic with worry. I hoped he'd understand.

The tunnel widened, and the light grew stronger. Pressing my back against the wall, I held the gun at my chest with both hands as I listened. The crackle of a fire, I thought. And some stirring. The whines of a child, weak but there.

Taking a deep breath, I eased my head around.

The tunnel widened into a rounded brick alcove with a higher ceiling. A man, holding a child on his lap, sat on a crate in front of an open fire, the smoke filtering straight up. My eyes traced its path higher, then through a small metal grate.

I'd seen random plumes of smoke and steam, but I had no idea where they came from—a life underground, a parallel universe.

The man fed the child pieces of a banana with one hand. The other hand held a knife at the child's throat.

With blond curls and bright eyes, the child accepted each piece like a baby bird taking food from its mother, mouth open, eager in his hunger. He had a smudge of black on his right cheek.

The boy from the fire. My nephew! Had the Watchman known?

I pressed back against the wall. *Could anyone be trusted? Could I?*

"You can come out." The voice held a hint of evil. "I've been waiting for you."

I blinked back my fear.

Raising my gun, I stepped into the light.

The man stood, balancing my nephew on his hip. He pressed the knife into the boy's neck. "Put the gun down." The man stared me down.

The man from the hospital.

The one Hank had seen bleeding in the alley after the diamond bust.

"You were there." I stepped around to the right.

He followed me, clutching the boy tight. "I wouldn't."

I stopped. Taking a deep breath, I worked for calm as I looked for an opening.

"I wouldn't do that, either," he said, reading my mind. He pressed the knifepoint against tender skin. The boy yowled as a drop of blood inched down his neck.

"You're a cop." I took a stab at the truth.

A slight widening of his eyes.

I had my answer. "You set the whole thing up."

"No, I just took advantage. Then you had to come along." He regripped the knife, his knuckles turning white.

"Why did you have your goon kill my brother?"

"I no longer needed him. I thought perhaps he could help you remember. Maybe that the two of you were in on it. He convinced me otherwise. He told me you were the one."

I didn't believe him—I didn't want to believe him. Hank would never...would he? The answer remained hidden. "You didn't have to kill him."

"He knew too much."

"You mean he knew about you." And now I shared that knowledge with my dead brother.

"I need those diamonds, Kate. What's it going to be? You decide how this goes down, who dies, and who lives to walk out of here."

After a moment, I relaxed my posture, letting the gun lower a bit. Taking a hand off the grip, I moved to put the gun on the ground. "You're right."

Watching him, I waited for it.

A hint of relaxation. The boy slipped a little on his hip.

In one move, I raised the gun and squeezed.

CHAPTER SEVENTEEN

The gun bucked in my hand. The report echoed around the chamber, thunder crashing, then dying into the echo. The man had fallen back. With his feet toward me, I couldn't get a look at where I hit him. He didn't move.

That didn't mean he was dead.

Working my way around the room, I kept the man in my sight, my gun trained at his inert form, as I checked for any possible hiding places—any other men waiting, watching, ready to strike. A tunnel stretched into darkness off to the left and slightly behind where the man had been standing. Nothing moved, at least not that I could see.

I completed a pass around the room. We were alone.

The boy, still clutched in the hook of the man's arm, didn't move. He didn't make a sound.

What had I done? My nephew. My thoughts raced, my vision swam. I'd had one chance and I took it.

Then I heard it.

A weak cry.

The man still didn't move. Shifting the gun to one hand from two, I kept it at the ready as I moved closer. Circling, I stayed out of reach.

The child wriggled.

The man's arm still circled his waist.

Ready, my finger tightening, I moved closer, working my way around to the man's head. His knife had dropped when he'd fallen. I pocketed it. He didn't move. I didn't dare get too close, but I couldn't see any rise or fall of his chest.

The shot had creased his left temple, an ugly red gash. Blood filtered through his hair then dropped, coloring the sand on the ground.

The boy, butt in the air, his feet under him, backed out from under the man's arm, which fell to the ground. Rooted to the spot, I didn't move. The boy cast large blue eyes my direction.

Maybe he recognized me?

I stuck the gun back in the waist of my pants. I bent down until the pain from my knee stopped me. Holding my arms wide, I waited. The boy hesitated.

I didn't move, didn't breathe.

Then he rushed to me and threw himself into my embrace. Falling back, I braced myself as the sand absorbed the worst of it. Then I buried my face in his curls, breathing him in. His small hands gripped my hair.

"It's okay. I've got you." I kept saying it, over and over, until I'd convinced myself we both were safe. And we both were alive.

Finally, the world steadied. I looked around, then remembered the pipe leading up to the opening I came through. "We have to get out of here," I whispered as I loosened my hold on the boy so I could get a look at his face. He let go of my hair, grabbing my shirt instead. "You've been so very brave. Can you be brave just a bit longer?"

He nodded. "Mama?" His voice was surprisingly strong, almost demanding.

"I will make sure you get home to your mother." I swallowed hard, so thankful he didn't ask about his father. If he had, I wasn't sure I could've held it together.

"Now."

He had Hank in him for sure. "Yes, sir." Somehow, despite the boy's added weight, I struggled to my feet—I wasn't about to put him down, I couldn't.

The man still hadn't moved.

I limped back the way I'd come, the gun back in my hand just in case.

When I found it, I traced the pipe up to the opening. The distance was farther than I thought. With the boy, and a knee that now was numb and almost unresponsive, I had no idea how to get us out. We were stuck there, me at a loss, the boy wanting to go home. My phone showed no service.

The boy started to whimper as I leaned against the wall, gathering strength and trying to think.

Hank was dead.

That's all that ran through my head. Over and over. My brother. Dead.

The boy quieted as if he sensed my pain. My knee throbbed anew as I tried to figure a way to get us both out. As I stared up at the opening, I thought I heard a voice shouting my name. Cocking my head, I stilled as I reached for the sound.

"Kate? Kate, where are you?" Faint, getting closer. "Kate?"

Beck!

I shouted up toward the hole. "Down here! We're down here!"

"Where?"

"The grate on the wall."

"Keep talking, I'll follow your voice."

I blabbered, mostly nonsensical stuff about how sorry I was to have run off, and how I hoped he could forgive me, and how much my knee hurt.

His head appeared through the opening. "Are you okay?"

"Yes."

"Back up. I'm coming down." I did as he said, my back finding the wall on the far side of the tunnel.

He landed in front of me.

I reached out and touched his face. "You're really here." I could see in his eyes he understood. "How?"

"Let me get you out of here, then we'll talk. Here," he

grasped my nephew under the arms, "let me take him."

The boy leaned into him as I loosened my hold. "The ghost is dead." I glanced back down the tunnel. "He's down there." I returned my gaze to his. "And Hank? Did you see Hank?"

"Yes," he said, his voice soft with hurt. He shook his head at my silent question. "I'm sorry."

My brother really was dead. And still no diamonds, no answers, no closer to me, to knowing what I did.

"Why can't I remember? The killing would stop if I could remember." My world swam. My knees trembled.

A strong arm encircled my waist.

"I've got you," he whispered as my world went black.

My own heartbeat pounds in my ears, my breath coming in ragged gasps as I peer into the Stygian darkness. Hank! Oh, dear God! I kneel beside him and feel his chest, searching for blood I can't see. There is none. He flinches, then moans, sucking in a tentative breath. I relax. He is alive. I rise and look toward Reynolds. One step. I don't need to check him. Fighting the bile rising in my throat, I turn. My foot touches something. A bag of diamonds still in Hanks hand. I bend to pick them up. Confused. Had Hank taken them? What had gone down here? I can't be sure, can't wait to find out. Have to protect Hank. Frozen in indecision. A scuffling sound. I look up, peering into the darkness. The doorway to my left.

Someone is there.

He whispers my name.

Something glints, catching the weak light. A shield.

I run.

Footsteps behind me. Closing. My throat raw, my chest heaving, my lungs screaming. I can't run anymore. I have nowhere to go, no one to turn to.

I have to stop and fight.

There. Another alley. No one will see.

The voice in my ear. "Kate, where are you?"

I came to with a start, pulling in a deep gasp as I tried to sit up. Feeling cornered, bound, I struggled.

"Easy, Katie. It's okay." Beck's voice, soothing and calm.

"Where am I?" I pulled at my constraints as panic clawed inside me.

"Ambulance." Beck hunched in next to me holding my hand. He released the straps holding me down.

Peace dampened the panic. "Where's my nephew?" I reached for a memory. "Jaime. His name is Jaime."

"My partner, Carla, took him to the hospital for assessment. After that, we'll find a safe spot for him until his mother can get here."

I thought of the sister-in-law I had yet to meet. Today she had regained a son and lost a husband. Knowing she would never be the same, I wondered what she was like. "Don't bring them around me, not yet. Too dangerous."

"Agreed." Kindness infused the harsh word.

"Where are we going?"

"Home."

"I'm racking up the dead bodies. I'm sure your boss wants me off the streets." So many had died, yet we were still in danger. "This whole thing feels like fighting a hydra—chop one head off and three more appear. I've lost my brother. My family. Myself." I pinched the bridge of my nose as I squeezed my eyes tight. "Is any of it worth it? Are we any closer to solving this, getting the assholes off the street?"

"The chief wants to play it out. He okayed taking you home—I told him it would be easier to protect you at your place than the hospital." He rubbed his face, the stubble on his cheeks making a sandpaper sound.

Hadn't he said something about a shower? "You haven't been home?"

"No. I'll need to get a statement from you when you feel up to it. The doctor said he'd come by to check your knee and give you something for the pain if you want it."

"No." I was so cold. My concentration came and went,

drifting on the pain. But the pain told me I was alive.

"That's what I told him you'd say." He touched the spots on my face that I guessed were bruised. "Jesus, Katie."

"I must look pretty bad."

He gave me a short laugh. "When I lost your signal, I thought I'd lost you. I about died myself. So, no, you look terrific actually."

"Beck, I'm nothing but a bad dream."

"Not from where I'm sitting."

The look on his face shut down any argument. "How did you find me?"

He held up his phone.

"That app? What was it?"

"Find My Friends. I'd just made it to my desk when I saw you moving, leaving the hospital. I made it as fast as I could, lights and siren, but the traffic through town was a mess with Christmas coming and all." He squeezed my hand. "I'm sorry about Hank."

Emotion welled, and the tears trickled out of my eyes. I didn't care. Too defeated, I didn't wipe them away. I couldn't stop the shaking. I gave up on that, too.

"What was his role in all of this?" Beck asked, the detective in him overriding the friend.

"I don't know." I thought about my brother, how our lives had both been blown apart by the same event but had taken different paths. And I realized I didn't want to know what Hank had done; I didn't care anymore. I needed to remember him as he was.

"When you're ready, I need to know how that went down."

"Not much to tell. Hank came and got me. A trade, he said. Me for his son. He had no choice, really. The guy hit us...well, you know where better than I do. The guy jumped me, but went after Hank." I leaned back, squeezing my eyes shut, fighting tears...a futile battle. "I had a gun. I should have..."

Beck didn't offer a platitude.

Wrestling with my composure took awhile, then I continued, a bit stronger. "I couldn't get a clear shot. When I did, it was too late. He killed Hank; I killed him."

"I'm sorry."

I could tell he was. "Yeah. Me, too."

We rode the rest of the way in silence. When the ambulance stopped under the *porte-cochère* at my building, I let them pull me out on the gurney, but then insisted on walking the rest of the way.

For once no, one argued. The desk clerk nodded and smiled. I made it to the elevator before I caved and leaned on Beck's arm. I had a moment of panic when I realized I didn't have my keys—life had swallowed them at some point and I couldn't remember where. Turned out not to be a problem...I hadn't locked the door.

Beck scowled at me and I shrugged. "Danger has a habit of finding me regardless."

"No use inviting it in," he said as he pushed open the door and helped me inside. The EMTs who had followed us filtered back down the hallway and disappeared into the elevator.

Home. I kept coming back here, but my feelings kept changing. Maybe that was more a reflection of me. Today my apartment felt good, not safe, but strong. I stepped to the windows and drank in my favorite view, imagining most of it as darkness hid my mountains from view.

"I can see the end from here," I said, surprising myself that I gave voice to that thought.

Beck busied himself in the kitchen. Ice in a glass, a promising sound. "We're getting closer," he said as he stepped in next to me, then handed me a glass. One ice cube, three fingers of amber liquid. "Medicinal."

I relished the burn of the first sip as it slid down my throat. Three fingers would be enough to dull the sharp edges of pain but not enough to dull the pain in my heart.

Beck was a little more cautious with his bourbon than I was with mine. "I talked to one of the cops in charge at NYPD when your bust went bad."

If he was waiting for a big surge of emotion from me, he was in for a disappointment—I couldn't have mustered that if my life depended on it.

And it might.

The thought left me strangely unaffected. "Any blinding insights?"

"Just one." He turned to look at me. "Khoury's dead."

"What?" I stared at the darkness outside, imagining my mountains, immutable when compared to the fragility of human life. Yet with enough time, even a tiny trickle of water could erode a huge fissure.

"They found him a few days ago. A shallow grave not far from where he busted out while being transported to trial."

I tried to process this new twist. "But if it isn't Khoury coming after me, then who?"

"Good question."

"The ghost?" Could Hank's ghost have been the mastermind?

"Mind explaining?" Beck's eyes caught mine, both reflected in the glass.

"The guy in the tunnel," I said, trying not to remember.

"What guy in the tunnel?"

I whirled toward him. "The dead guy. In the tunnel."

"We looked, Katie. There was no one there."

I almost took the sedative the doctor offered. He'd breezed in with a police escort just after Beck had dropped his little bombshell. As he fussed over my knee, I tried to rein in my irritation. Sitting on the couch, leaning back into its comfortable embrace, I snagged a pillow and held it over my stomach. "Are you done?"

He didn't look up. "You're welcome."

"Sorry." But I wasn't, not really. Life had thrown a number of sucker punches lately, the last hitting me when I was down.

He pushed himself to his feet. "I'm as good as I thought," he said through a grin. "Knee held. So, apparently, did your luck." He shook his head, looking like he wanted to say more. Wisely, he didn't.

Beck saw him out after I made a few hollow promises about taking it easy and all of that. After he saw the doctor down the hall, Beck left the door open. Shrugging into his overcoat, which he'd hung on a hook by the door, he looked unhappy. "I have to go. The chief is probably pacing a track through the carpet in his office waiting for my report."

"And you need that shower."

He shot me a quick glance and could see I was joking. "Right. You still have my Beretta?"

I patted my hip. "Right here."

"I've got teams placed all around the building. You should be fine."

"I will be."

Looking caught in a web of indecision, he shifted in place for a moment before closing the distance between us. He bent down and brushed his lips across mine.

I pulled him back for a longer kiss. "I remember."

A smile lit his eyes making them go all smoky blue. "Shoot first."

"Ask questions later. Got it."

After he left, the room's emptiness closed around me, the air cooler, heavier, harder to draw into my lungs. Pain was the only tether as my thoughts drifted.

Hank was gone. And just when I'd found him again.

I couldn't shake the visual...the man and Hank struggling, rolling, thrashing in the dark. A hand raised. A knife catching the light. Fear paralyzing me. Unsure, I couldn't pull the trigger. In the end, Hank died anyway. Why hadn't I taken the shot, any shot? Tortured, I felt my resolve weakening and found myself powerless to fight it.

Frankly, I wasn't sure I didn't prefer the fog of the forgotten to the harsh light of reality. Unable to move, I stayed rooted to the couch, the weight of loss an anchor buried deep. I wasn't sure I could keep going, keep fighting.

Lost. Alone. Pissed as hell. I didn't know where to go or

what to do. I burrowed back into the embrace of defeat.

Dan found me that way.

Keys in hand, he pushed through the front door, the crucifix key fob banging against the wood. His face pinched and gaunt, his eyes sunken in deep hollows, his hair disheveled, his suit wrinkled, he seemed at a loss when he saw me.

"Oh!" he said as he paused, then regained his composure and rushed to me. Easing in next to me, he gathered me in his arms. "I expected you to be at the hospital. I thought maybe you could use some clothes and such, so I decided to swing by and grab some things for you."

I let him hold me. His nearness felt good—not the way Beck felt good, but more in the way that human connection could breathe life into a dead soul, that kind of good.

"I've got your back, Katie." He whispered against my hair as he held me.

A memory stirred, barely discernible like the faint flutter of a tiny heart. I cocked my head, listening. "Say that again."

Releasing me, he pulled back. The expression on his face closed. "What?"

I went all cold inside. "What you just said."

He propelled himself to his feet. "You've had a really shitty day. I'm sorry about Hank—well, sorry that his loss obviously hurts you. He wasn't a nice man, Katie."

An undercurrent of something tugged at him—I could see his struggle. "What is it, Dan? What aren't you telling me?"

He spied the bar and made a beeline, as if grateful for a reason to move, to not look at me.

"You have a brother?" The words escaped before I could corral the thought, the memory rushing to be heard.

Glass pinged on glass as his hand jumped in the middle of the act of pouring. "What?"

"A brother. Didn't you tell me you had a brother?"

"A stepbrother."

"Are you close?"

"Sometimes." He turned and looked at me over his

shoulder. "Why?"

"Since I just lost mine, perhaps I'm trying to grapple with the emotions." I worried with the piping on the edge of the pillow I clutched to my stomach like a shield. The edges had started to fray, the thread weakening, no longer able to hold everything together.

Dan appeared in front of me, extending a glass. Another lone ice cube floating in three fingers of amber liquid. I took it, but didn't drink. Something about the past. Something about his voice. The words.

I've got your back, Katie.

The answer slipped into my consciousness with the ease of a sharp blade between my ribs. "It was you."

Ice clinked against his glass. "What? Me? Where?"

"In my ear. You were the FBI guy who ran me in the takedown. The voice in my ear. That's what you used to say: 'I've got your back, Katie.'" My hand shook as I raised the glass to my lips. I didn't know whether to be afraid or simply angry. This time I took a long sip of my bourbon.

He raked a hand through his hair as he turned and stepped to my window. "Yeah, it was me. You were my responsibility." When he looked at me, he looked like a different man. "I didn't have your back, did I?"

"I don't know. What did you do?"

"Do?" He tried for a laugh but no sound came out. "Hell, it's what I didn't do. I let them take you down. You damn near died. Then the Alzheimer's thing flared up. All because of me." He pulled a chair around to face me off to the side. "That night has tortured me ever since. I'm not sleeping. I can't get the noises out of my head—you running, then being taken down. I heard it all through your mic."

"It was part of the job."

"Not for me." He leaned forward, his elbows on his knees, his glass cupped in both hands. "You must know how I feel about you. Letting that..." he lifted his chin in my direction. "...this happened to you. My worst nightmare. I'm so sorry, Katie."

"No need to be. It was just bad business." No longer able to face his torment, I shifted my gaze over his shoulder. "Is that why I'm here?"

"I've moved Heaven and Earth trying to get you the best care. To make you whole again." He leaned back, his shoulders slumping. "I feel so guilty."

I knew I should reach out to him, to comfort him, but I couldn't. Something stopped me. "You've done all you could and way more. I appreciate it. I really feel me coming back." I gave him a weak smile. "I'm not sure that's going to be an altogether good thing."

He shrugged as if he understood.

"No need to torture yourself anymore, Dan. None at all. Life—we don't control it, although we'd like to think we do."

The pain left his face, although I could still see hints of it in his eyes—the legacy of a cop's life. We all carried it. There was always something more we could've done.

Hank. I gasped at the memory. He was gone.

"I'm glad the treatments are working, that you're getting you back, as you say."

"Yeah." I took another sip, relishing the warmth, the dulling of the sharp edges. "I'd forgotten that memories carry pain."

"A counterweight to all this unbridled joy," Dan deadpanned.

This time I laughed. It felt good. I'd been afraid I'd forgotten how. "Yeah, things are racing back, memories all jumbled and tumbled. It's hard to make sense out of them." I eyed him over the lip of my glass as I took another sip. "Or to trust them."

"I guess that makes sense." He looked as at sea as I felt.

"But one thing is really bothering me." I found his gaze and held it. "If I'm remembering so much, why can't I remember where I hid the diamonds? I remember having them, but that's it. Why can't I remember? If I could, I could make this whole nightmare end."

Overcome with a sense of hopelessness, I fell silent. I

didn't know if I could keep fighting. How many more would have to die before I remembered?

Why can't I remember?

I know what you did.

"What the fuck was it I did?" I hurled the words like stones. "Would somebody tell me?"

Dan drained the last bit of his drink then set the crystal tumbler on the coffee table. The thoughts racing through his mind rippled across the surface of his face, changing his expression.

"What is it?" I asked. "Do you know what I did?"

When he looked at me, there was a strange light in his eyes, a renewed energy surging underneath his calm exterior. "Maybe you didn't do anything at all."

I snorted. "Right. That's why everyone is after me."

Leaving his empty glass where he put it down, he rose. Something was bothering him—he had that look.

"What is it?"

"Hmm?" He patted his pockets, then pulled out his keys, the gold crucifix fob glinting in the light. "Maybe we've been looking at this all wrong."

I shifted, hoping to move my leg from its resting place on the coffee table, but the pain, so sharp it almost took my breath, shut down that idea. The price for Hank's desperation and my complicity, and now I was sorry I didn't take the doctor up on his offer of some serious painkillers. Defeated, I leaned back, breathing heavily against the pain. "Care to share?"

"Later. When I'm sure."

"No. Now."

With a dismissive wave, he strode to the door. It slammed after him.

I was helpless to stop him. "Damn!" With no goal in sight and my mind whirring like a wheel with broken sprockets, I reached for my file that Dan had shared with me, which was still where I'd left it on the coffee table, hidden under a couple of books. I pushed them aside. Idly flipping through it, hoping for a bolt of enlightenment, I'd made it about halfway when my phone dinged.

A message from Beck. Three photos—different angles of Khoury taken at different times. He looked as I was beginning to remember him. Thin, feral, mean.

But it was the second photo that stopped my heart.

Khoury. Holding a set of keys.

I leaned back and closed my eyes. Images from that night.

The office. The diamonds. I'd made sure the marked ones were in each bag, then resealed everything just as it had been. They'd never know. The shipment is ready.

A body filled the doorway, jump-starting my heart. Khoury. A small man with a lifetime of scars on his soul. "Everything ready?"

I nod and step back. "Just making sure."

"Good." Prideful and vain, every day he wears a three-piece suit. Today's is black. A gold chain loops across his flat belly. "Twenty-nine-inch waist," he always tells me, as if that makes up for everything else he lacks. Tugging on the chain, he pulls out his pocket watch and snaps it open. "Right on time." Today, unlike other days, he pulls the rest of the chain, circling it with the watch and the gold fob in the shape of a crucifix, then pushes them deep into his front pocket. Maybe he has a feeling, I don't know, but the look in his eye leaves a cold place in my gut.

"Let's go." He rakes up the three packages, cradling sixty million in his arms. I wonder what that feels like. Of course, it isn't really his. He's already taken out his cut.

A black sedan waits in the alley. Three men, two I recognize, wait by the door. I look into eyes I know.

The Watchman.

Like tumblers in a lock, everything fell into place, and I knew.

Pawing through my file, I pulled out the pink scraps of paper—notes in Stella's hand.

Dan had taken them from her office.

Why? He had access to the full file.

Following a dread curling in the pit of my stomach, I used

my phone to find the website for the U.S. Marshals Office. I called the number. When an agent answered, identifying herself, I did the same and gave a brief summation of who I was. She patched me through to someone higher. Another quick briefing.

"Who did you say you are?" the agent asked.

"Kate Hansford."

"Kate Hansford died over a year ago."

I could hear the clicks as he started a trace. I disconnected.

Dan. The idea so preposterous, so hurtful...so horrible...I rebelled against it. The one man who had helped me, who had gone out of a limb for me.

His betrayal left me breathless. He'd planned all of this. I was powerless with no one to protect me. He'd moved me across the country, told me I was in WITSEC. He'd fooled everybody.

To get me to remember.

A laugh escaped, as I was set free. The joke was on him.

I didn't remember.

Dan hadn't come here tonight to get me anything. Once he found me here, by myself, he never asked if I needed anything. And he'd been surprised I was here. Hadn't he seen the cops Beck had stationed downstairs?

Or did he have a different way into the building? The thought stopped me cold. What if he could come and go as he pleased? He had a set of keys. He'd arranged for the apartment. He could've put a dead guy in my bathtub.

My phone dinged another text. I hastily texted Beck back. "What's the name of Dan's stepfather, the one in the NYPD?"

The answer took a few minutes. "Fazio. Why?"

Fazio. I flipped through my file, looking for the report of that night. The fallen men. What were their names? Another couple of minutes lost, then I found it. With a finger, I worked quickly down the page. There it was.

Fazio. I ignored the beep of another text from Beck.

Revenge. And Dan had a brother...a stepbrother, if I remembered correctly. For once I didn't doubt that I did.

The ghost.

What had Dan come back here for tonight? Not the file—he left without it. Me? Maybe. But he acted surprised I'd been there. A ruse to put me off guard? Maybe.

But he left without me as well.

Why?

He no longer needed me.

If so, why didn't he kill me?

Too many cops around. Someone had seen him.

Okay, so he didn't need me.

Why not?

Maybe he had his answer or knew where to look for it. That night, that horrible night that had brought us all to this place and this time, his voice had been in my ear. And was listening. He heard everything.

And now he knew what I couldn't remember.

I took a deep breath and mentally pushed everything aside until I found the calm in the hurricane of my thoughts. Other than Dan and his stepbrother, the man Hank referred to as a ghost, there was one other person there the night the diamonds disappeared. One other who might know what happened to the twenty mil. And who was responsible for Dan's stepfather's death that night.

And I knew where Dan had gone and why.

Pushing the pain aside, I hobbled to the front door, grabbed my jacket—I couldn't find my keys—Beck's gun a heavy comfort in the jacket pocket. I shot off a quick text to Beck. "Meet me at the warehouse." I heard the ding of a reply, but didn't stop to read it. I knew he'd come.

The Watchman.

And Dan had a head start.

CHAPTER EIGHTEEN

My F800 GS thrummed to life—I'd never been so happy to see that bike. I couldn't remember where I'd left it last—maybe the Watchman's warehouse? But someone had brought it home and left the keys in the ignition. I figured I had Beck to thank for that. The growl of the engine drowned out my scream as I bent my knee to get my foot on the peg. Twisting the throttle, I roared up the ramp to the street, then wheeled down Burnside. A glance to the left as I passed my building.

The Watchman's corner was empty.

Dan didn't know him like I did, but he knew where to find him.

The Watchman's warehouse wasn't far. Stopping a block away, I hid the bike behind a dumpster. Approaching on foot, I needed to find a side entrance. Mid-block I stopped, gazing up at the red brick—sooted by fire, yet it still stood.

I ducked into a sandwich shop on the ground floor of a three-story building showing signs of recent renovation, unlike its neighbor—the burned shell of the Watchman's abode. Ignoring the startled stares of the two bored counter clerks, I strode through, then out the back. The back entrance deposited me in a narrow alleyway that dead-ended before the warehouse in a high wall separating respectability from something less. Funny how money and effort could change one to the other like magic.

Above me, the fire escape accordioned out of reach for someone my height. The thought of jumping froze my muscles—so I pushed it aside. Two tries. Two muffled cries as I landed, trying to let my good leg absorb my weight. On the third try, I caught the chain and tugged. The fire escape unfolded on new hinges that only creaked and groaned a little. I took the stairs as fast as I could. At the first landing, I shimmied over the railing and dropped on top of the wall, letting my good leg hold me. I sat, easing my legs over. Anticipating the pain, I dropped down between the wall and the warehouse. White heat seared through me as my leg absorbed part of my body weight, paralyzing me for a second.

I palmed the Beretta, double-checking that a round was chambered.

Bent low, I hobbled around to the back of the building. I leaned in a doorway, summoning energy.

With no real plan, I tested the door. The lock long rusted out, the door swung inward when I pushed, just enough for me to slip through. Piles of pallets, abandoned boxes, and shelving hid me as I worked my way deeper into the warehouse. The fire hadn't reached this far.

Taking a deep breath, I checked the shells in the magazine. Six plus one, Beck had said. I'd used two. The four left would be enough to handle both of the Fazio brothers. I knew what his brother was capable of, but Dan was a wildcard. How far would he go?

I hoped like hell Beck was taking his own advice and finding this friend on his phone so he'd know exactly where I was. Without him, the odds were not in my favor. Using pallets and old barrels to shield me, I zigzagged deeper into the warehouse, pausing to look for movement. They had to be here.

Finally, I found the metal stairs up to the Watchman's floor. With a foot on the first rung, I tested the metal. It squealed in protest. A shot whizzed in from the right, pinging off the metal and sending me diving for cover.

On my butt behind a large metal drum, I whirled in time to see Fazio, crouched low, moving to another position. My shot was late, hitting behind him. But at least I knew where he was. In the middle of the warehouse floor behind a forklift, he couldn't run without risking being shot. My guess was he was counting on his brother to bring the cavalry.

Keeping my eye on Fazio's position, I waited. So focused on the scene in front of me, I didn't sense the man sneaking up behind me until he was almost on top of me.

I spun around, the gun raised, my finger tight on the trigger.

"Katie, don't shoot. It's me."

Beck. "Shit!" My heart rate redlined, and I saw stars.

"Sorry," he said as he crouched down next to me. "Fazio?"

"Behind the forklift. Did you happen to bring reinforcements?"

"SWAT is setting up a perimeter." Beck chewed on his lip as his eyes darted around the warehouse, measuring, assessing. "Any ideas?"

"I'm guessing Fazio is waiting on the Watchman." The pain in my knee clipped the words. "If he was here, we wouldn't be having this stand-off."

"Let's hope he doesn't show up. Between the two of us, we can handle Fazio."

I hadn't seen Dan. "There's something else." As I started to explain, the side door to our left burst open.

The Watchman skidded into the center of the warehouse.

A glint of light as Fazio moved.

I didn't think. I just reacted. Rising, I placed my gun on the ground, then bolted from behind the drum. "Get down."

The Watchman turned. Surprised. But stayed rooted.

Two strides and I crashed into him as a shot rang out. We hit the floor, me on top.

Beck returned Fazio's fire, giving us cover.

I rolled off, grabbing him. "Hurry."

But I was too late. Beck's firing stopped. He rose slowly from behind the drum. A young kid with the look of a hood and the badge of a Fed stood next to him holding a gun to his temple. "I got him, Sergeant."

Fazio kept his weapon pointed at me. "Good work, Marshal." He gestured to me with his gun. "Move away from the old man".

"Do as he says," the Watchman whispered. "This is not your fight."

"Not my fight?"

He shook his head.

I eased away, but not far.

"I'm a cop," Beck said to the kid holding the gun on him.

As he started to reach for his pocket, the kid said, "Hands where I can see them." The kid was young, red-faced, and scared. An accident waiting to happen.

Beck seemed to see it the same way. He didn't argue.

Fazio stepped into the open, a twisted grin slashing across his face. "Give me what I want, old man."

"You?" I asked the Watchman, stunned.

"Jesus, Hansford," Fazio started. "Don't you remember? You took the diamonds off your brother and ran with them. I chased you. I lost you. I didn't know where you'd gone. I'd just found you, was going to make you give the ice, tell me everything. Then this guy," he flicked his gun indicating the Watchman, "he damn near killed me. Left me bleeding in that alley. When I came to, you both were gone."

The pieces started falling into place. I had them all, or most of them, just not in Fazio's order. "You shot Reynolds."

"Your brother shot Reynolds." He laughed, tried to act casual, but I could hear the nervous in his voice.

"No, my brother's gun was used to shoot his partner, but that doesn't mean he was the one to pull the trigger. I think you did that, then I rushed into the alley before you could get away with the diamonds."

"You took the diamonds. You were taking evidence. I followed you."

"Neat and tidy." I looked into the Watchman's eyes as he stared at me. "Except for him." I nodded to the Watchman. "You followed me, didn't you? You had a chance to get Khoury, but you followed me."

He didn't say anything; he didn't need to.

"And you pulled Fazio there off of me."

"Darn near killed me, too. Although at the time I didn't know it was him. Didn't know it until just now. Killed all the others. He was all that's left. Never would've figured an old guy like that..." Fazio growled. "I'll return the favor, but complete the job when you give me the diamonds, old man."

"Why did you follow me?" I whispered, the world falling away as if the Watchman and I were the only two people in the warehouse.

"They would've killed you."

"And you've been protecting me ever since. Why?"

"Maybe my way of balancing the scales. I've done some bad things."

"But you missed your chance to get Khoury."

"I took a better shot."

"The diamonds, old man." Fazio raised his voice as he stepped closer, regripping his gun in his right hand.

Keeping his hands raised, the Watchman lowered his head as he slowly turned toward Fazio. "You give me Khoury."

Fazio laughed. "Khoury? You stupid shit. Khoury's rotting in some shallow grave not far from where we sprung him."

The words hit the Watchman like hollow-point bullets, each one tearing flesh.

"It's true," I said. "I saw the photos."

The Watchman stilled. A peace fell over him, relaxing the ever-present torment in his face. He gave me a wink.

Too late, I figured out what he planned.

He launched himself at Fazio.

Fazio got off two shots. One got the Watchman in the leg, staggering him, but he didn't slow. The second hit his shoulder. I thought I heard him laugh as he grabbed Fazio's gun, twisting it out of his hand, then hurling it into the darkness.

Then he was on him like a starving wolf, gnashing and

growling from years of pain. They fought, tumbling to the ground, rolling, punching, blood flying.

I glanced at Beck. With a resigned shrug, he grabbed the young Fed's gun, wrenched it away with one quick twist, then tossed it to me. "You're closer. Take a shot."

The two men clung to each other, pounding, beating.

"I can't get a clear shot." Sweat beaded. Thoughts of my brother flashed through my brain.

Fazio flipped himself on top. Raised his hand. A blade glinted. He brought his arm down as I pointed.

A shot reverberated.

But the gun in my hand didn't recoil. I hadn't fired.

Fazio turned. Looking behind me, his eyes widened. He opened his mouth. Another shot. His head flew back. His body tumbled backwards out of sight.

I ran to the Watchman, glancing over my shoulder, anticipating a bullet. It didn't come.

A man stepped into the light as I eased down, next to the Watchman.

"Kate? Kate? Where are you?"

That voice.

Dan.

He nodded toward me. "I got your back."

"I've got your back."

My world tumbled; my life shattered. And I knew I'd been right.

He spoke into his mic as he lowered his gun. "Stand down."

I didn't have time to think, the past, the present, the horror of blood in front of me. The Watchman's stoic face watching me. Pain lighting his eyes, but something else, too. Peace. Finality.

"You will not die on me." I clawed at his shirt, saturated with blood. A gash down his stomach, like the others. He tried to hold it closed as his eyes held mine. "They were looking for these." He pulled his hand away.

Diamonds.

Bits of crystal carried on a river of blood. Hundreds of them.

Where he'd always carried them.

I heard Dan talking behind me, moving the troops. Beck knelt beside me. "I called an ambulance. They were already on the way. At first shots, someone called them."

My mind whirled. Snippets of time, recent and past, connections firing. My eyes narrowed. Hank gone. The Watchman? I didn't know. Me broken. Life shattered.

I grabbed my gun. In one smooth movement I turned, aimed, and fired.

The bullet caught Dan in the chest, center but slightly left.

A heart shot.

His arm fell. His gun slipped from his fingers and surprise registered, his eyes on mine. Then the light went out and he dropped.

CHAPTER NINETEEN

For a moment no one moved. The past collided with the present, and I knew exactly how everything had gone down.

"Dan," I whispered. I squeezed the Watchman's hand. "Did you know?"

"No."

"Fazio was the one who took out my leg and beat me that night. He was waiting. He killed Reynolds with Hank's gun, probably would've killed Hank too."

"Except you showed up." The Watchman wheezed, a tinge of frothy blood at his lips.

"Don't you die on me. I can't lose you." He had watched me—afraid they'd come after me. And he was there when they had, trying to piece it all together just like me.

And Dan. He'd been running the show from the start. Waiting for me to remember. So he could get the diamonds and step into the void left by Khoury after he had killed him.

Dan had been the voice in my ear. He'd run me that night.

With his hands on my shoulders, Beck eased me back. "The paramedics can take over now."

I pushed myself backward with my good leg until my back found something solid.

Beck sat down next to me. His hand sought mine as we both watched the EMTs work. "Jesus, Katie, you shot a Federal officer."

"Yeah." I actually felt pretty good about it, too. The bastard. Playing me. Planting things in my head. All the while looking for the diamonds so he could fully assume Khoury's position.

All he needed were the diamonds.

And he didn't get them.

"He was supposed to protect me. He had my back. I knew there was something about his voice. He was FBI. Went Fed, as he said. His brother stayed with the local cops."

Beck's eyes registered the hit. "Fazio was his brother?"

"And his second in command. His guy on the inside at NYPD and in Khoury's ring. And I doubt Dan is still with the Marshals Service."

"Can you prove it?"

"Now there's the rub. All I have is circumstantial." I laid it out for him. "The file Dan gave me, it was the one from Stella's office. He took it."

"How do you know it came from Stella's office?"

"The notes written on pink paper." I pulled the note out of my pocket. "This is a piece from Stella's sticky note pad." I handed it to him. "You can check it out."

"That's all?"

"No, but it might as well be as far as the law is concerned." I started ticking things off on my fingers. "He called me on my new cell. I never gave him the number. He told me he knew where I'd been. I didn't take him literally at the time. He kept his guys away at the Marriott, let me get away. His name is on my lease. He arranged all of it. I'm sure we'll find a key to my place on his key ring—he let himself in after you left tonight. My being there surprised the hell out of him. And he had Khoury's gold cross. He had that thing with him everywhere he went. How'd Dan end up flashing it around? And that leads me to Khoury. The Marshals Service is charged with transporting prisoners. Khoury escaped from a transport." I glanced at Beck. I didn't have to connect the dots. "And why would an FBI guy take a demotion to the Marshals Service?"

"That's all you got?"

I shrugged. It was enough for me. "Well, there's the note. The one with my blood on it. Still not sure how he got ahold of that."

"Jesus, Kate. A hell of a risk."

CHAPTER TWENTY

I didn't like New York—well, not anymore. The cab ride from LaGuardia did nothing to change my opinion. Dirty buildings, ramshackle warehouses, weary neighborhoods sagging under unrealized dreams, giving way to the concrete jungles of Manhattan where people scurried like rats, protecting their space if not keeping their distance. Metal doors scrolled down covering storefronts, and graffiti slashed across brick and concrete facing, angry cries against a cruel life.

Hope lived above the streets in the high-rise offices of Midtown, the cloistered apartments lining the park on both sides, the cold, unfeeling marble of the financial district cloistered from the huge wash of humanity below.

Car horns, the incessant cries of frustration against an uncaring world, provided the background music to the clutter of voices and languages hurled on the streets.

New York was a hard city. Evil lurked in the dark corners. This is where the bad had begun. Even the holiday dressing couldn't put a gloss on it.

I had slept on the flight. I'd fallen asleep listening to the melancholy notes of *Autumn Wind*, one of the Watchman's favorite tunes I recorded on my phone. An imperfect recording, but one that grounded me in the present.

Curiously, the nightmares had left me in peace. Dreams, memories, the demons driven out by reality? Or had I traveled so far I couldn't hear them anymore?

I had come to New York in search of answers, answers about me but mostly answers about Hank. I had him in my head, but in pieces. I needed help putting together the puzzle. I knew what I had done, but what had he done? And why? My brother. It was important. Were his memories that still slipped through my dreams real?

The neighborhoods slid by as the cab inched uptown then across town. I half-listened as the driver gave me the fifty-cent tour. The neighborhoods changed as he talked. The bustle of Midtown, then the quiet opulence of the Upper East Side tailing away as we moved north. The overwhelming ostentation of a Midtown Christmas, giving way to the odd string of lights and an occasional plastic Santa.

Time hadn't been kind to Harlem. The Great Depression, despair, racial conflict, each had torn off a chunk of flesh until only the bones remained. But as the streets rolled past the windows of the cab, I saw hope here—a fresh coat of paint, a new playground where kids climbed and slid and laughed under the watchful eyes of their mothers.

The driver told me that back in the '20s, Harlem had been Mecca to the jazz players. In the shadow of the Apollo Theater, clubs sprouted along One-Twenty-Fifth. The well-heeled mixed with those less fortunate, bound by their love of this new thing called jazz. Slightly naughty, wonderfully enlivening, despite the admonitions of the morality police, jazz was here to stay. And Harlem was its beating heart.

Finally, we eased to a stop in front of the Easy Jazz Club. A red door, smoky windows, and faded neon sign that sputtered and flickered. "Live Jazz Nightly" it read, although the "J" was burned out.

Hank's memories had brought me here.

"Good thing to know jazz isn't dead," the driver said as I peeled off three twenties. He started to make change.

"Keep it."

He rewarded me with a smile.

Louie Silver still played at the Easy Jazz Club, at least that's what the sign on the door said. Louie. Louie would have some answers.

I caught him at the bar.

As I shook his bony hand and stared into eyes yellow with age, I figured he not only played here, he probably lived here, too. Like crumpled parchment pressed flat, his skin bore the lines and folds of time. His hair had fled, leaving a bald dome that shone in the thin light. Tall and thin, wearing the years like a comfortable coat, Louie embodied the elegance of a bygone era and the casual acceptance of the life he'd chosen.

The dark interior, hiding decades of secrets and hundreds of musicians' hopes and dreams, suited him. He followed the handshake with a hug and bright eyes, not at all what I was expecting.

"I understand you're a friend of Joe's."

The Watchman—the memories were clearer now. My trust in them had been building. "Yeah."

He smiled as if the thought that a friend of Joe's might turn up after all this time was impossible. "Dang. A friend of Joe's. It's been too long since I clapped eyes on him. He played some smooth jazz for a white man."

"Still does. Don't think he gets much appreciation for it anymore, but that's not why he plays."

Louie gave me that smile again, stained teeth, a few missing. "To some, music is the rhythm of life. Without it, life's song stops. Joe's like that. Music kept him here. Know what I'm talking about?"

"Yeah. Calmed his demons. I get that." I tugged on the sleeves of my jacket, but not before Louie's eyes flicked to the chain of lettering, words and numbers, memories...me. "He plays for me," I said. I guess Louie could read all he needed about me, or maybe the Watchman had given him a heads-up; didn't really matter.

Louie relaxed back, an elbow on the bar. "He still got Nellie?"

"Nellie?" I asked.

He gave me a lead, but not the answer. "B.B. King had Lucille."

"His sax." I nodded. There was a story there, but it wasn't what I came for. "I need your help."

Louie seemed to know why I'd come. I don't know how I knew that. Maybe in the way he cocked his head and looked at me. Maybe he knew something was up the minute I stepped through the door.

"You talk to Joe?" I asked. They wouldn't even tell me if he was alive.

"Sure."

"When?"

"Been a bit," he hedged as if he was used to it.

"What has the Watchman told you?" At his quizzical look, I glanced at my left wrist. "Joe. What has Joe told you?"

"Only that you needed some answers, and he asked me to give them to you. Well, he also said you don't remember too good—something medical." He flashed me that lopsided smile; there was kindness there. "I don't remember too good, either."

"That's why I write stuff down." I tugged my notebook from my backpack. "Mind?"

"No." He gave me a look that seemed to pull the truth from my soul. "From the looks of you, you be comin' about Hank."

"How do you know him?"

"Back in the day, he worked this beat. We got along." A whole lifetime lingered between his words.

"I'm his sister."

Louie nodded like he already knew that. "I seen it in your eyes. He used to talk about you."

That surprised me a bit and piqued my curiosity. "Really? Care to share?"

He motioned me to follow. Louie moved through the cramped interior, with its worn club chairs, and high-top tables ringed by stools, casually resting a hand on a chair, lightly touching a table top, a caress, a mark, an old lion claiming his territory. A table in the back suited him. He pulled out a chair for me. "Sit. Let me get you a drink, then you can ask me what you came to ask."

Nervous energy made it hard to sit still, hard to wait, while

Louie insisted on providing the niceties before we got down to business. Finally, we were settled at a club table, Louie stretching his legs in front of him, settling in. He set a soda in front of me. I ignored it.

He took a pull on a thin cigar, a shaman with his pipe. "I heard Hank didn't make it. I'm sorry."

Still not settled with the truth, I shrugged, not knowing what to say.

"You want some pieces to that story. Hank's story. The one what got him there."

I didn't hear a question, so I waited, shifting, moving away from the pain that still burned like fire in my knee.

"How much do you know about his partner?"

I flipped through my notes. "Reynolds?"

Louie nodded, and his eyes turned hard. "That's the one."

"He and Hank went back a long time. Kids together. Hank was always pulling his friend out of trouble." Thoughts washed over me. My parents had tolerated Reynolds but never liked him. He had a hard home life, they'd said, but they didn't elaborated.

"Reynolds is the one who first brought your brother in here." Louie rubbed a hand across his chin. "That kid had a nose for trouble." He stared over my shoulder as if looking into the past. "Your brother always was pulling Reynolds's ass out of the fire." His eyes found mine. "But some people can't be saved. Eventually, they're going to pull you down with them."

"That's how this went down? Reynolds was up to his ass in trouble?"

"Yeah. A debt he could never hope to repay."

I rubbed my knee. It didn't help. "You know about the diamonds?"

"Sure. He told me what happened. Hank wouldn't let him go through with it."

When he said it, I knew it was true. I could see it, hear the words between them. That memory I had, and it was real.

I tugged at my sleeve and read.

Hank's memories.

Oh, dear God. Hank. Doing a noble thing. Trying to stop a friend from ruining his life. Then me, trying to save his ass by taking the diamonds, hiding the evidence, only to have it all implode. "I thought I was protecting my brother."

"You were, child. You were." There was wisdom in Louie's eyes, and a profound sadness. "Reynolds was dead; the diamonds were gone. Hank didn't know where they went. At that point he didn't care. He kept his mouth shut. Reynolds had shot him—that alone got him off. After that, Hank really bottomed out. Don't know if you knew that. Quit the force. He was working security, mainly small-time stuff."

One night. One friggin' night and life goes to hell. "I didn't know."

"I know you and your brother weren't always shoulder-to-shoulder, but he did a good thing, not turning on Reynolds. Maybe the guy didn't deserve that kind of loyalty, but he had a couple of kids, one in a real bad way, needed a lot of care."

I sat back, sadness creeping over me. Sad for Hank, mainly. Loyalty to the wrong person...one simple mistake with disastrous consequences. "Reynolds."

"His family didn't deserve to take the fall," I said, processing the past out loud. "If Hank had ratted, then Reynolds's wife would lose all her benefits, if it came out her husband stole the diamonds."

"Nice thing your brother did."

I wasn't sure I'd go that far. But what a mess we made. Hank was covering for Reynolds, and I had covered, or thought I had, for Hank.

"What was the debt Reynolds owed?"

"Had a bad gambling problem. Got into Khoury real deep."

"The guy was a money launderer *and* a bookie?" I scoffed. "Stellar bit of human waste. So Hank kept quiet; nobody looked under the rug at the Reynolds house. He was buried with honors as a fallen soldier."

Louie nodded.

I wondered if Hank would make the choice he made knowing the consequences.

"I wouldn't have put it past Reynolds to sell out your brother and you along with him."

"It wasn't Reynolds." I didn't say more.

Turns out I'd been right about Dan, about everything. Not that it could bring my brother back or make me whole, or save the Watchman's soul.

But it was something.

I stayed with Louie for a while, even though I'd gotten the confirmation I needed. There was something comforting in sitting with a man who knew my brother and the kind of man he was. This bit of Hank was all I had left. That and the memories of his still filtering through my brain. Well, okay, that and his wife and family.

Shelly. Shelly and the kids.

They lived in the Bronx.

The 6 Train clattered and clamored, old rails, old train, as I headed north under the Harlem River into the Bronx. Manhattan was a hard place to live—the outer boroughs even more so. In Brooklyn where I grew up, as protection against the anonymity of the crowded streets, everyone got to know their neighbors—the guy cooking an egg on a roll for them each morning at the diner, the postal carrier, the couple who ran the laundry, the grocer—each connection making a cold city a warm community. Survival skills.

But I wasn't so sure that was the way of life in the Bronx.

As we rolled farther away from the new growth in Harlem, the imposing structures gave way to smaller buildings, honed to the bare essence, hope carved away as the years slid by and the promises of youth remained undelivered. I knew this neighborhood. Hank and I had grown up in one similar in Brooklyn, where my mother could be close to her Italian roots. I pushed past twenty before I realized what she meant by that. Her people with memories of the old country had lived all around us. I didn't see any of the joy, any ethnic pride on display in the Bronx. Reed-thin boys lingered on the corners, their shoulders hunched, hands jammed in their pockets, black voids for eyes staring out of the shadow of their hoodies. Anonymous in their shared posturing against a world they didn't understand and had no skills to conquer.

The swaying of the train had a hypnotic effect. My eyelids grew heavy as I fought sleep, fought the dreams, but they pulled me under.

I run toward the light. Reynolds. Outlined in sharp relief, everything else a blur. You son of a bitch! My gun drawn, I pound after him. He'd get all of us killed or, worse, a lifetime ticket to Rikers. He rounds the corner then dives into an alley. Slowing as I enter the alley behind him, watching, listening, my gun at the ready. I don't think he has seen me, but he could've. The footfalls in front of me disappear. I know this alley; it is part of my beat, his, too I think. And it is a dead end. No way out.

I'd made it halfway down when he steps out of the shadows, his gun pointed at my chest. "Don't, man. You gotta leave."

"We're being stupid. We can't do this. You think they aren't going to miss that?" I nod at the package he holds in his hand. We'd taken it. A moment of opportunity. Stupid, really. Suicidal. "We've got to put them back."

Reynolds shakes his head and backs away. "I'm taking them. We've gone this far."

I step toward him. "I can't let you do this."

He shakes his gun at me. "Don't." The look in his eyes a warning. He isn't bluffing. "You have no idea what I've gotten myself into, how deep I'm in."

"I do. We can fix it." Of the emotions coursing through me, guilt hits me the hardest. I'd let Reynolds set this up. Use my sister. Use everybody to save himself. Turns out he doesn't want saving. He wants an out.

"My kids, my wife. Shit." His voice turns hard. "I'll kill you if you try to stop me. Hell, I'm dead already. This is my only shot for my family. You said you'd help. You'd score these." He held out the package. "You did it. We are so close. This can fix

everything."

I move a step closer. I can smell his fear now. See his eyes, the glow of a wild animal in the darkness. My finger tightens on the trigger. "No. I was wrong. It'll fix one thing but create an even bigger problem."

His eyes go dead. "Like I said, won't be my problem."

"You really want to leave it for the rest of us?"

"My family or you? No choice, man. Sorry."

"You do what you're thinking about doing, you take those rocks, and the Man will hunt us down one at a time."

"You know the Man?"

"Yeah."

He lifts his gun. "Then you know why I have to do this."

A shot. A punch to my chest that knocks me off my feet, the wind rushes out of my chest as I land on my back. My head hitting the concrete.

The lights blink out.

I don't know how long I'd been out. Not too long, I don't think. The distant popping of gunfire, whispered commands over the radio on my shoulder. The fight is still going down. Stars swim as I pull a lungful of air, gasping, wheezing. Kevlar caught the bullet, but flesh absorbed the blow.

Reynolds!

Flat on my back, I struggle for breath, my ribs on fire. How long have I been out? I squirm for a view as my world swims, slowly coming back into focus.

Reynolds is down.

A bullet to his head.

The diamonds are gone.

A high squeal jolted me back with a start. The train. Slowing. My eyes scanning, looking for trouble, or familiarity, to the extent those weren't the same.

The last vestiges of the dream, smoke from a distant fire, swirled around me. Hank's dream. Fuzzy, lacking the sharp focus of my own. Yes, Hank's dream.

Could I trust it? Or was my brain making associations I

wanted?

That's what I was here for. Louie had given some confidence, confirming what I remembered and filling in the holes where I didn't.

I grind the heels of my hands into my temples, squeezing my eyes shut as I pressed...hard. The memories were there, burbling like water just before it boils. The trick was to trap them, hold them until I could make sense out of what I saw, what I remembered.

I felt eyes on me as I stepped off the train into a world that wasn't mine, but one I knew. Pretending not to care, I jammed my hands in my pockets and headed west, following Louie's directions. Head down, ears open, I kept walking.

Hank's wife, my sister-in-law, I glanced at my forearm again, Shelly...her name was Shelly. She lived in a neighborhood past the point of caring. If anyone razed the homes, the fact that no one would build anything in their places was the only excuse keeping the structures intact. Mailboxes once lining the streets had been reduced to poles sticking out of the ground like the remnants of a dock after a hurricane. The mailboxes, like the old docks, had been smashed too many times to replace. The concrete sidewalks buckled and heaved as if sighing from the heaviness that remained when the lightness of hope vanished. The houses, with only light hints of the colors they used to be, now squatted, bending under the pressure of time and neglect, their boards gray, their shutters hanging from rusted and broken hinges. Bars protected the windows and doors, drawing a telling line: although no one had much, the people inside were worth protecting. But like all the other neighborhoods like this one, those who called this place home, needed Christmas. So each house, no matter how sad or ramshackle, sported a jaunty string of bright lights, electric candles in the windows. Something, anything, to remember that life could be kind, that it still held hope.

Shelly's house was in the middle of the block. *Hank's home.* Several strands of lights roped from the roof. A plastic Santa waved from the front stoop. This house held more hope than the rest.

With a bright blue door, white trim, and fresh gray paint, it stood out like a beacon in a storm. Hank had made sure, I'd be willing to bet. The small gate in the low chain-link fence squeaked when I opened it. A voice called through a window. "Close that. Don't want the kids getting out. Street's no place for them."

The front door opened before I'd trudged up the few steps and wiped my feet on the mat. A young woman, easily a decade younger than me, with straight blonde hair and bright blue eyes, gave me a smile as she beckoned me inside. "You must be Kate." Red-rimmed eyes. A shy smile. She hadn't even begun to process her loss...our loss. She gave me a fleeting hug. Awkward, yet a start.

But, even though Shelly and I were family, a death lurked between us—I felt its cold presence. Shelly's piercing scrutiny had me ducking my head. The last years had been spent trying to be invisible; I wasn't used to standing in the harsh light.

A television blared from the back of the house. Cartoons, maybe. The smell of pizza lingered, the box still open on a coffee table in front of a threadbare couch. A single slice remained. A girl, three, maybe four I guessed, curled into the corner of the couch. She ripped off a bit from the slice in her hand as she watched me, curiosity flickering in her eyes.

A tiny Christmas tree stood on a small table in the corner. Lights and a star, but no presents underneath.

"Take that to the kitchen, honey," her mother said. "I need to talk with Kate."

The girl unfolded herself, her long legs snaking from under a tiny body like a spider. She was going to be tall, and a looker—perhaps the best of both her parents. The girl looked at the bits of writing she could see extending down my wrists. My sleeves covered the rest. "Teacher says we don't write on our skin."

"Honey, we don't say those things," her mother admonished. With a hand to the child's back, she encouraged her toward the kitchen. "I'm sorry."

"Not a problem." I looked at the child and was amazed I

remembered her from the photo Hank hand showed me. Yes, my memory, sharp and clear. "Your teacher is right. Sometimes I can't remember things. This helps."

"You write on both arms?"

"Yes. Only in block letters, but I can write with both hands."

The girl took that in, then wandered into the kitchen.

Shelly flipped off the TV. The same program fired up in the next room.

She kept her back to me for a moment—a moment to breathe, I suspected.

"Hank. I couldn't save him. I'm so sorry," I said, unable to wade through any more preliminaries. Even though I knew I did my best, the fact remained I *didn't* save him, and because of that, I wasn't certain I'd done my best. Guilt kept me awake nights; the memories haunted me. I was going to have to find a way to live with the remembering. Ironic.

Shelly swiped at a tear as she motioned me to sit.

I took her daughter's place, still warm. "He was a good man. A good brother. I feel like part of me has been carved out and thrown away."

Shelly, her eyes bright, her dress a thin faded cotton, grabbed the rib-backed chair across the room, pulling it closer before seating herself on a cushion that had torn a bit, exposing a pucker of foam. "I know." Her gaze flicked toward the kitchen. "I haven't told the children. I don't know what to say." Shelly worried with the frayed hem of her dress. She crossed her ankles like a schoolgirl in church as she turned and looked out the window. The view held a sad tree and the flaking siding of the house next door. "He loved you. He talked about you a lot. When they found your disease, it's like everything was washed away and he knew where you'd gone."

The tears I'd been fighting welled and trickled down my cheek. No use swiping at them, there were more to come. I figured I'd cry until I was cried out. And to think he died not knowing how much I loved him back, and how I never really doubted him—my heart never let me.

Why hadn't I told him?

Another memory I'd have to live with. "This remembering stuff totally sucks."

Shelly's quizzical look told me, once again, I'd said something out loud that was meant for me. "Sorry."

"Hank told me about the memory issues." She glanced at my skin, the letters extended past my sleeve already fading. "How are they?"

"Much better, thanks to Hank's stem cells." No way in hell was I going to tell her I had him in my head—she'd never see me for me, and Hank would always be between us. "He didn't have to give me his cells. You know, the hard part of all of this is I never told him I loved him. Never took the time to tell him…" my voice broke and I took a steadying breath, "…everything." Even though he was taking me to trade me for his son, I still didn't hold that against him. A child. My child. I would've done the same. But, mad or not, that didn't change the fact that I loved him.

Shelly bridged the gap between us, reaching for my hand. I clasped her cold one in my warm one, and we both hung on. Somewhere, I felt my brother smiling. *I'll take care of them, Hank. I got this.*

"You're all the family I have left," I said, feeling profoundly sad and hopeful at the same time. Hank had left, but he left a piece of himself behind. Maybe not enough, but it would have to do.

"And you are ours." Shelly released my hand with a pat and leaned back. "I miss him. The kids more so. I can see it in their eyes, in their scared expressions. They sense something wrong, but they don't ask."

"It's not real until someone says it out loud." A game Hank and I used to play when we were kids. I could hear his voice, taunting me to tell whatever it was he wanted to know.

"Hank used to smile just like that at those words. He used them often. I think he was always thinking of you."

The tears still flowed. I tried to blink them away so I could see, but each blink smeared my vision like a bad set of windshield wipers.

"He took good care of us," Shelly said. And I could hear the words she didn't say: "What are we going to do now?"

I rooted in my pocket and pulled out a crumpled check that had been burning a hole in my pocket. Pulling it over the edge of the table, I smoothed the creases. "How much do you know?"

"A little bit. Hank said it was best that I didn't know too much."

"Do you know about any diamonds?"

"Hank's looking for them...was looking for them." Her face crumpled.

"I found them."

That sparked a hint of interest. "All of them?"

I thought about the Watchman, his open gut, the stones spilling out in a rush of blood. "I think so. Hank helped me. He did the right thing, Shelly. All the way down the line, he did the right thing. You should be proud of him."

Her hand shook as she pressed fingers to a quivering lip. "It wasn't his fault?"

"Not any of it." I was glad she didn't ask whose fault it was. I didn't have an answer. I'd keep Hank's secret. Reynolds's widow would keep his pension.

And I'd take care of my own.

I put the check on the table and pushed it across to Shelley. "Those diamonds? Turns out there was a finder's fee of sorts. Half of it is Hank's. Now it's yours."

With a shaking hand, she leaned forward to look at the check, then gasped. "This is for a million dollars! This is half?"

"Yes." Apparently, I could still lie.

"I can't take this." Looking afraid to touch it, she crossed her arms, tucking her hands in next to her ribs.

"Hank earned that with his life. So you can take it. And you will." I guess she heard the no-argument in my voice.

She turned inward, her shoulders bowing. Burying her face in her hands, she sobbed.

I stepped in next to her. My knee wouldn't let me bend too far, but I held her as best I could. She cried for a good long while, and I cried with her. Finally, we were both reduced to hacking sobs. Unsure of what to say or what came next, I went back to my spot on the couch.

Shelly dabbed at her eyes with the hem of a sleeve. I used the heel of my hand to wipe away the evidence of my own tears.

As if on cue, my nephew wandered in from the hallway to the right, rubbing his eyes. Catching me sitting there, he stopped, angling his head as he looked at me. A moment, then a big smile, before he launched himself at me. I caught him to my chest and hugged him tight, burying my face in the crook of his neck. Breathing him in, I thought I could sense all the goodness in the world.

And I felt my brother's joy.

CHAPTER TWENTY-ONE

The Portland airport was jammed with holiday travelers and family waiting to greet them with hugs and smiles. A few steps outside the secure area, I stopped and leaned against a pole to watch. Joy radiated off the small clusters of folks grabbing their loved ones in bear hugs, peppering them with kisses. The kids were the best, bright-eyed, filled with joy and wonder. And love.

The stirring of a hope, a joy I hadn't dared let myself feel fluttered to life in my chest. I wasn't the person I'd feared I was, the one Dan had told me I was. No, I was at the core the me I'd always been, and that was a great place to start.

Maybe life had family and friends, maybe even love, in it for me.

Wrapping that thought around me like a warm blanket, I pushed off the pole. No need to stop at baggage claim; the backpack was all I had. The thought of home tugged at me, urging me faster.

Without any real expectation, I scanned the faces streaming past me. Beck wouldn't be among them; I knew that. Although, as I stepped out into a rare, bright winter day, I was sort of sad not to see his face.

I tossed my meager possessions into the back seat of the first cab in the queue and climbed in.

"Where to?" The cabbie eyed me in the rearview, a Santa's

cap pulled low.

Stella had been moved to rehab, and I was dying to see her. But they'd told me she'd had enough Christmas today, that tomorrow would be better. I couldn't wait to give her the new letter opener I'd gotten for her. It had a malachite handle...and not a drop of blood on it. But I'd have to wait until tomorrow.

"Home," I sighed. "Take me home." The demons were gone, and Portland was mine.

"Could you give me a hint?" the cabbie said with a smile.

"Oh, right." I pulled up my left pants leg and read from high on my calf. The ink had faded and I had trouble making out the numbers and letters but I knew what they were. I held that inside.

The cabbie nodded, and I settled in for the ride, watching the scenery roll by with new eyes and a fresh perspective. Over the Columbia, follow the Willamette, then over it as well. I loved the rivers. Something so peaceful about them. Time and harsh conditions had altered their course, changed them; yet they flowed on.

The cabbie found my building without any trouble. I handed him a hundred. "Keep the change."

"Wow!" His smile threatened the edges of his face. "Merry Christmas."

"You, too."

The lobby looked the same, as if nothing had changed. But everything had. The desk clerk nodded and smiled as I walked in. "Welcome home."

"Yes," I smiled. "Home."

Christmas music played in the elevator, and I wondered what day it was. I'd lost track. I turned the key in the lock and pushed my front door open.

Home.

I paused in the doorway, drinking in the unfolding view as the door opened wider.

Home.

Stepping through, I didn't bother to lock the door behind me. Nobody would be bothering me anymore.

After tossing my backpack on the couch, I headed straight to my windows, drinking in the view. The sun, just setting, bathed everything in a pink glow, snow off Mount St. Helen's and Mount Rainier glowing in reflected light. Yes, from here I could see all the way to Heaven.

Down below, people streamed past. The holiday rush.

As I had done every day before I left, I looked at the Watchman's corner.

It was always empty. But I looked each day just the same.

I gasped.

He was there.

Playing his sax. Nodding as folks tossed coins into his hat on the sidewalk.

As if he knew I was watching, he looked up, and raised a hand.

I smiled and lifted a hand in return. Life returning to normal.

All that time, he'd been watching over me.

My focus shifted. A painting reflected back at me in the glass. Not one of mine.

The painting Beck had been working on the night I showed up at his place. Colorful and light, happy. He'd gotten it right. It hung in a small space on the far wall next to the kitchen.

A note dangled from the corner, my name scrawled in a masculine hand across the front. It read: Welcome home. Merry Christmas. Champagne in the fridge. Call me if you feel like sharing. Beck. P.S. I can hear you ask; how did I know you were coming home today? I'm a detective. And cops can't keep secrets.

I pulled my phone from my pocket and dialed his number.

He answered on the first ring.

THE END

Thank you for checking out After Me. For more fun reads, please visit www.deborahcoonts.com or drop me a line at debcoonts@aol.com and let me know what you think. And, please leave a review at the outlet of your choice.

Other Books by Deborah Coonts

The Lucky Series

"Evanovich....with a dose of CSI"
—*Publisher's Weekly* on *Wanna Get Lucky?* A Double
RITA(tm) finalist and NYT Notable crime Novel

WANNA GET LUCKY?
(Book 1)

LUCKY STIFF
(Book 2)

SO DAMN LUCKY
(Book 3)

LUCKY BASTARD
(Book 4)

LUCKY CATCH
(Book 5)

LUCKY BREAK
(Book 6)

LUCKY THE HARD WAY
(Book 7)

Lucky Novellas

LUCKY IN LOVE

LUCKY BANG

LUCKY NOW AND THEN
(PARTS 1 AND 2)

LUCKY FLASH

CPSIA information can be obtained
at www.ICGtesting.com
Printed in the USA
LVOW04s1257030117
519562LV00020B/478/P